BLOOD
RULES

JOHN TRENHAILE

BLOOD RULES

HarperCollins*Publishers*Ltd

First Edition

Designed by Alma Hochhauser Orenstein

Canadian Cataloguing in Publication Data

Trenhaile, John
   Blood rules

ISBN 0-00-223896-9

I. Title.

PR6070.R36B56   1992   823'.914   C92-094619-4

---

92 93 94 95 96 97 98 99 ❖/RRD 10 9 8 7 6 5 4 3 2 1

For Teri Lin Mao Long
With silence and tears. And with love.

A woman I know told me she had married her husband
because what he said was always unexpected—
a good adventurous reason for matrimony, I thought.

FREYA STARK
The Southern Gates of Arabia

AUTHOR'S NOTE

One of the most important characters in this novel is not a person but a TriStar jet: the aircraft that services flight number NQ 033. Without her, no story; and without my friend, Flight Engineer Bob Osborne, no NQ 033 either. So it gives me great pleasure to take this opportunity of thanking him for his expert advice, and when Bob chuckles over such technical errors as remain, I hope he will be good enough to remember that they are mine, not his.

The same applies to Dr. Hamish Aitken, who enthusiastically applied himself to the problems facing my diabetic passenger and provided me with the necessary solutions—I'm most grateful.

"Memuneh" is what Israelis call the head of the Mossad, their external espionage organization roughly corresponding to Britain's MI6 or the American CIA. By convention, the Memuneh is also head of the entire intelligence hierarchy. He is responsible to the Prime Minister and can be dismissed by the Knesset.

The two Yemens, North and South, have now joined to become a single country. In 1984, however, they were separate.

Finally, I want to pay tribute to three people, each a special individual "character" (nonfiction!) in his or her own right, each a major contributor to the novel: Ed Breslin, whose masterly touch guided this from the first; Charlie McDade, whose perceptive comments and illuminating editorial *aperçus* went hand in hand with charm, good humor, and friendship; and Jessica Kovar, who mediated, commented, harmonized, and helped until the job was done. When in doubt, say the editors, keep it short. So I will: Thank you all, very, very much.

DAY
ONE

Colin Raleigh looked at the big hand with awe: brown, hair-covered, adult, this was the hand of love. His father's hand. The boy's own white fingers lay tucked inside it, serene and trusting.

They were flying. Light filled the cabin. Asia lay somewhere below, to the left. He turned so that he could see out through the Skymaster's porthole. He knew it was a Skymaster, but Rose, the stewardess, told him that the plane was called "How Easy Uncle," after its registration letters, HEU. When you were seven years old and still timid about flying, that was a nice thing to know.

Another plane was flying alongside. Not a Skymaster, not How Easy Uncle. Cream-colored, with a big red star painted on its side and a red nose. Colin smiled, waved with his free hand.

But the other plane had gone.

Colin wanted to say something to the owner of the big brown hand. Before he could speak, however, the flower appeared. It grew in the side of the hull, by his feet. First a black circle, then the petals opening outward from its heart. *Boom!* went the flower. Next to it, a little higher, another flower sprouted. *Boom, boom!*

The noise in the cabin suddenly grew louder. Voices. One voice, shouting: "Mayday! Mayday! Losing altitude, engine on fire!" Crying now. He was suddenly, violently, tilted forward, as if on a swing gone out of control. More flowers, flowers everywhere, in the ceiling above him, beside his seat, huge leering flowers that filled the plane with an acrid scent.

Something dark and heavy rose up before Colin and he opened his mouth to scream, but this dreadful thing smothered his breath—*Mayday! Mayday!*; out of the corner of his eye, before the light finally died, streaks of flame were snatching at the wing, almost vertical now—*Ditching! Ditching! Ditching!*

As the black shape crushed him, Colin screamed out his soul.

20 July 1984: 0010: Oxford, England

Thirty years later, Colin Raleigh sat bolt upright in bed. Three great thumps of the heart, bile in his mouth: bathroom, quick!

He rested his weight on the basin while he tried to vomit and failed. Water, lots of it, on the face, in the mouth. Cold seawater? *No, no, no!*

He groped for the string that operated the light above his shaving mirror. Oh, God: eyes shot through with red, with terror. Haggard, sunken cheeks. Jesus, help me, *someone help me!*

Slowly, so slowly, the dream faded. He took deep breaths, swallowed more water, cleaned himself up. Harsh light boosted by gleaming tiles did him no kindness, but at least it told him where he was. Not on a plane, high over Asia. Not seven years old. Colin Raleigh, law lecturer, stared at his own reflection, watching it steady into something recognizable.

He went back to the bedroom and threw open the curtains to look out at a fine, moonlit July night. Somewhere in the middle distance a motorbike hammered away to silence, leaving Iffley Road silent as a cemetery.

Colin tiptoed along the corridor to the second bedroom. At first he could see nothing; then, as his eyes accustomed themselves to the gloom, a hunched, shadowy shape came out of the darkness to meet him with its familiar old warmth of welcome.

Colin crept to the side of the bed and brushed Robbie's forehead with a little finger that trembled slightly. The boy's skin was moist, his breathing scarcely audible. Colin felt as if he were looking down into a deep narcotic pool, at the bottom of which his son lay asleep, at peace.

Soon, now, the world must break in on that peace and dismantle what he, Colin, had humbly sought to build. Last week, washing the sheets, he had noticed the irregularly shaped stain, pale in the center, darkened at the edges, and for an instant he'd stared at it unbelievingly ... then he'd laughed out loud. Fourteen, yes, of course: probably a late developer. Fourteen. Already.

A sigh forced its way through Colin's lips and he shook his head, amused as ever by the futile search for a fresh start through another's soul. A search made by every parent since Adam first bit fruit.

He had meant to go back to bed once he'd reassured himself that all was well with his son, but somehow here he was sitting on the floor, unaware of how he'd got there, his little finger still stroking Robbie's brow. Clicks in the boy's throat heralded a cough; he arched his back, coughed again, and allowed his limbs to seek their natural place on the bed, all in the same deep slumber.

Colin suddenly found himself at the mercy of uncomfortable memories. This tall, gangly adolescent had been a baby, once. A certain evening, Colin's turn to bathe him. Robbie would not stop crying; his face red and ugly, he responded neither to caresses nor the bottle. Colin, ragged tired, tried everything he could think of to quiet his child. Nothing worked. Until at last he began to shake this ugly red doll, shouting, "Stop it! *Stop it, d'you hear!*" And the doll, surprised, had stopped in mid-cry....

The memory shafted its way into Colin's guts, as well as his mind; he bit the back of his hand, hard, wanting to cause himself pain as blood payment, which is what every father did when drawing back from the brink of violence perpetrated against a beloved child. What every father ought to do....

That day, the day he'd shaken the poor doll, Leila had come in, seen everything at a glance, and had comforted not Robbie but

Colin, who needed comfort more. That was when Robbie had a mother. And in those days Colin still had a wife, instead of unquiet affairs to tide him over.

He stood up from Robbie's bed, making more noise than he'd intended but somehow anxious to be away, by himself, beyond the reach of the tangled emotions given off by this adolescent boy who stained his bed sheets: his son, whom he loved.

Should he make that telephone call now? No. Still too early....

As he lay down on his own bed he reflected that soon they would be airborne, on the first leg of their odyssey to Australia. Soon he would have to make himself go along the jetway, strap himself in, and wait for the terror to start. He could do that. He could do it for Robbie. Just for him.

About an hour after Colin had drifted back to sleep, a Green Line coach drew up at some traffic lights on the outskirts of Staines. It contained a single passenger who sat in an aisle seat halfway down the bus on the left-hand side. Next to him lay a gray canvas bag, on which had been stenciled the words CHILD'S LIFE RAFT.

The Green Line ran a service between Gatwick and Heathrow airports. It operated on a twenty-four-hour basis, but during the night the number of buses was reduced to one an hour, on the hour. Because the passenger, Halib Hanif, had been watching this service for over a month, he knew that of the one o'clock, two o'clock, three o'clock, and four o'clock buses, two were guaranteed to be empty. Always. But they ran them nonetheless, presumably because they needed the empty coach at the other end if they weren't to foul up their schedules.

The route they chose was interesting.

Rather than drive three-quarters of the way around Heathrow's perimeter, these coaches were allowed to cut across the airport's secure area, entering by the cargo bays and leaving alongside Terminal One. When the projected M25 motorway was in place all that would change, but for now the bus had to traverse taxiways, duck through a tunnel beneath one of the two principal runways, and finally weave a path among aircraft parked on the apron outside Terminal One. Depending on the driver, this took five to five and a half minutes: the period of time between one red-and-white security gate at the entrance lifting and another closing as the bus once more accelerated into the airport's public sector.

No one ever checked these coaches or their passengers. A wave from the driver, up went the barrier, through they went. Just like that.

So the only thing left was to find the right driver. Which was not difficult, because these men weren't paid much. And when Halib had chosen his man and taken him to one of the clubs in the Edgeware Road where, for a thousand pounds, you could buy a bottle of scotch and rent a table by the stage and a couple of whores thrown in for laughs, at that point life became easy. Boringly so.

Halib had long been wrestling with this boredom thing. He was forty-two now, but when he was younger and resident in Beirut he would sometimes sell his Lebanese pounds in exchange for U.S. dollars; then arrange a little incident, a car bomb, perhaps, just enough to flush the world's press out of the Hotel Commodore's bar for a taste of their much-loved "bang-bang," as they liked to call it; then, next day, when the Lebanese pound had gone through the floor in response to the bang-bang, he'd sell his dollars and buy back those pounds; and he did all this because there was nothing else to do and he was bored out of his mind.

Greed, other men's greed anyway, got so tiresome after a while. There were no nuances in greed.

He had one more problem to overcome: it was necessary to ensure that "his" driver operated an empty service; Halib must be the only passenger. But experience taught that once the driver had taken the bait he would find a way around any awkwardness of that kind.

"Easy," the driver had said. "I'll see I'm rostered for the one o'clock. If another passenger turns up, I'll fiddle me wiring and kill all me interior lights. Police won't let me operate without interior lighting, see? But the dispatcher'll still send me to Heathrow, to get the repairs done and make sure I'm in the right place to take out the four-thirty back to Gatwick. I'll pick you up a mile down the road. Easy as pie, squire!"

But there had been no other passengers. From his seat Halib could watch the driver hunched over the wheel as he waited for the traffic lights to change. He studied the man's shadowy reflection for signs of conscience, reluctance, fear. Nothing. Of course it was possible that he'd tipped off the police, but Halib didn't think it likely.

The lights changed. Another mile, and Halib could see the red-and-white airport perimeter gate. Ah, already opening, even before the driver could wave.... He stared out the window through vacant, tired eyes, a very early passenger or a late one, depending on your point of view, but in either case no one so weary, so evidently depressed, could pose a threat.

An orange ribbon of light burned on the far horizon, but here all was darkness. The driver turned, following a sign to the tunnel beneath the runway. Halib looked back. They were out of sight of the security checkpoint now. A glance forward showed the road curving away to the left where the tunnel mouth yawned.

He stood up and made his way along the bus, lugging the canvas bag.

They had almost reached the tunnel.

Halib placed a hand on the driver's shoulder and squeezed gently. "Now," he murmured.

The driver pressed a switch and the passenger door slid open. The brakes went on. When they were traveling at a bare ten miles an hour, Halib heaved the gray canvas bag into space. Standing on the step, he caught a glimpse of a figure emerge into the sodium glare, saw it stoop; then the coach was swallowed up in the descent to the tunnel, cutting off his vision, and he knew that things were, literally as well as metaphorically, out of his hands.

"You did well." He spoke softly to the front, not looking at the driver. "Keep going."

His hand dipped into an inside pocket and emerged holding a fat envelope, along with something else. He put the envelope on the ledge where more conventional passengers deposited their fares. The driver glanced sideways, avarice alight in his squinting eyes; then the coach swerved dangerously, for he had seen the other thing Halib held.

"We have a contract." Halib continued to speak to the windshield, his voice carrying no farther than the driver's ear. "A contract confers rights." The muzzle of his Makarov PM pistol waved in a gentle arc. "It also imposes obligations."

The driver was breathing in short gasps. He nodded.

A second red-and-white gate materialized ahead of them. By the time they reached it, Halib was once again sitting halfway down the bus, staring out of the window through vacant eyes.

The maintenance engineers would be changing shift soon. One of them, a Muslim Brother, which is shorthand for someone who can be made to believe in a cause and then die for it, would have the gray canvas bag marked CHILD'S LIFE RAFT in his holdall as he walked out to the apron. But not for long.

Halib looked at his watch, calculating times. In London, just before two, so in Bahrain, four.... Leila would already be awake. It was early, but he knew his sister's habits as well as his own. She never slept well before an assignment. And today she would be taking a plane that contained her only son, a son she had not seen for more than two years. So Leila would be awake.

20 July: 0145: London

Rafael Sharett muttered encouragement into the phone, endlessly repeating the message that he knew his caller longed to hear: It will be all right, it's going to work, it is. Really. Trust me.

Finding the right words was hard, however, because he didn't want the other occupant of the room to pay too much attention to this phone call. It came as a relief when at last he was able to replace the receiver and take his seat opposite Yigal.

The two of them sat in a simply furnished hotel room that smelled of ancient cooking and furniture polish. This establishment—cheap, clean, and in a quiet Bloomsbury thoroughfare—was much patronized by visiting academics, but it did not naturally lend itself to business meetings, and in any case Rafael (or Raful, as he was mostly known) liked to spread himself.

He opened a small tin and popped a white tablet into his

mouth, letting it dissolve under his tongue. "Gas," he said, as he patted his stomach.

The word was accompanied by a quick uplift of the right shoulder and the ghost of a wink: Raful Sharett's trademark. Honestly, he didn't need to know the daily code words to identify himself; no one "did a Raful" like Raful himself. That's what they called it, the Mossad seniors who knew and the puppies who wanted to impress, "doing a Raful": "Memuneh was in a rage; never did you see such a temper." "How did Benny handle him?" "Oh, he just did a Raful."

The tablet dissolved slowly; it tasted vile, but after years of living with an ulcer Raful scarcely noticed any more. Taking medication served to distract Yigal from the recent telephone call, and anyway, the taste was better than the pain, that much he knew. He was fifty-eight, this clear London summer's night, and just as he cared about fewer things than when he was in his twenties, so he worried about even less. The stomach he patted was at long last starting to bulge out of his shirt and it wasn't as hard as it used to be; the mustache he absentmindedly stroked was white, rather than gray; his face had become a map of broken veins and wrinkles: and much he cared about any of it. Much he gave one good goddamn.

But he cared very much that the man sitting opposite, who was half his age, should not know about the ulcer. Raful Sharett was director of the Mossad's Operational Planning Division, and he still had something to do before they put him out to pasture. So he schooled himself to keep pain off his face, he ate lightly and exercised daily, and because he was an emotional man he made an effort to hold himself in check, to kill the gut feelings and the heartburns that were nothing at all to do with his ulcer; because revenge is a dish best enjoyed cold, and that was the thing he had to do before they found out he was past it, and sick, and they retired him: he had to take revenge.

"So," he said lightly. "Stepmother. You be a good boy, Yigal, you tell me all about her."

The younger man opened a cardboard file but did not look at it. "Leila Hanif, code name Stepmother, most recent alias Susannah Duclerc, last known whereabouts Bahrain. Highly successful female terrorist, having rare combination of controlled methodical planning coupled with daredevil execution. Fearless and courageous. I like this woman, Raful."

"I *love* this woman, Yigal, so you get in line."

"Currently number two on our 'B' list, after Ilich Ramirez Sanchez: eliminate on sight without reference to higher authority. Aman report that she's planning to hijack an aircraft somewhere over the Gulf on behalf of Iran, in a bid to free nationals of that state now held in Baghdad."

"Flight NQ oh-double-three." Raful's voice was dreamy. "From London to Manila, via Bahrain and Kuala Lumpur."

Now the man called Yigal pushed the file across to Raful.

"I've seen it." Raful waved away the proffered file. "I *drafted* it, yes, I did."

"Okay, and here is something you didn't draft." Yigal resorted not to the file but to an inside pocket of his coat. Raful allowed his eyes to widen, affecting surprise, but he knew what this was, what it had to be, and he wouldn't sign it, not even to please Avshalom Gazit's (God bless him, keep him safe) son opposite.

"What is this, Yigal? Mm?"

"A receipt for the thing you asked for."

"And what did I ask for?"

Yigal did not answer in so many words. Instead, he took an object from his pocket, held it cupped in his right palm for a moment while he squinted down at it, and finally pushed it across the table to his companion.

The cigarette lighter was gold and bore the logo of a well-known brand. While Raful was examining it Yigal said sharply, "Be careful." And then immediately, as if to cover up his nervousness, "Why do you want this?"

Raful smiled, said nothing.

"Sometimes," Yigal said, "a man gets funny ideas into his head. Desk men feel bored. 'Oh, it's sunny outside,' they say, 'I'll take a turn around the block.' Which is fine, in its way. Sign this, please, Raful. For me."

But Sharett steadfastly ignored the paper.

"Raful ..."

Sharett stood up. He went across to the bedside table and once more picked up the telephone, transporting it back to their makeshift desk while he prayed that the lead would be long enough not to spoil the effect by bringing him up with a jerk and making him look like one, too.

"In Jerusalem," he said, as he resumed his seat, "it's not so early, not really. Phone him. Phone your father." He lifted the receiver and handed it to the other man. "Phone Avshalom."

"Oh, Raful." Yigal rolled his eyes ceilingward and heaved a sharp sigh.

"Call him."

"I know how it was when you were all in the Shai—or was it the Haganah; I can't remember—and you were running around blowing up the King David and getting hanged next day by the British—"

"Just one call. For my sake."

They were talking across each other, not caring, indifferent to what each had to say.

"But in this world, you know, this is—I mean, Raful, this is 1984 for God's—"

"For his sake. For your father's sake, don't destroy your career, Yigal. Just one sweet phone call."

"These days we have rules: mavericks are out, I mean *out*."

"And you'll be telling me next, I know what you're telling me—"

They were standing now, their faces hissing and spitting across the inch or so of space that separated them, but making very little noise.

"Memuneh Hofi has you in his sights, Raful, *squarely* in his—"

"—telling me that since we'll be talking to Yasser Arafat eventually we might as well talk to him *now!*"

Raful's fist came down on the desk, his face contorted in what he hoped his opponent would take as rage, though really it was pain, and there was silence. For a moment longer the two of them continued to gaze at each other. Slowly, slowly, the anger drained out of their faces.

Yigal said, "Nobody knows you're here?"

Raful shook his head.

"Which means nobody knows you're leaving, either."

"That would seem to follow."

Yigal nodded, a patient accepting the diagnosis of cancer. "And so nice," he said, "if you never came back."

Raful's gaze dropped away. In saying that, the young man was demanding too high a price, aware that Sharett had no option but to pay it. The knowledge soured Raful. It flew contrary to his old-fashioned notion of how you bargained.

"Look," he said. "Look. Stepmother's taken out in midair, the plane lands in Malaysia, I disembark and disappear, and I'm back in Tel Aviv before anyone realizes I'm missing."

"And if someone does realize?"

Raful half winked, jerked his right shoulder, but Yigal did not laugh. By "doing a Raful" Sharett meant to convey, Well, that's tough, I'm getting on now, not much time left and no life plans worth the name; let them cut my pension if they want to be that petty. But Yigal, he knew, didn't read it that way. Yigal merely thought him irresponsible.

"I'm going now," Raful said at last. "Stay well, don't worry." And loosen up, he added mentally as he rose; they won't be sending you to Tripoli for talks with the PLO just yet.

He collected his overnight bag, cast a final glance around the room, and then paused on the threshold.

He wanted to say, You're one of the best of the best, Yigal. Educated. Aware. Tolerant and civilized, you are a better Jew, a better Israeli Jew, than I can ever hope to be. You believe absolutely in the things we hold dear, and your generation will do more to hold the line we drew than we ever could. I salute you, Yigal, and I love you.

But: "Kacha, ma laasot?" he murmured to the young man's hunched shoulders. That's the way things are, what can we do?

He did not take the obvious route to Heathrow. Partly that was out of a sense of caution inbred over the years, but mostly it was because he knew this would be his last visit to London and he wanted to make a little pilgrimage.

He turned down Charing Cross Road and parked opposite the churchlike facade of St. Martin's School of Art, which he contemplated silently for a moment or two. There were no cars, no people. After a while he delved into an inside pocket of his houndstooth jacket and took out a leather wallet. From this in turn he extracted a photograph.

He'd had the snapshot heat-sealed in plastic, because he wanted this humble pictorial record to outlive him. He studied the photo briefly—a needless exercise for one who knew its lineaments by heart—before again raising his eyes to the college opposite. At this time of morning, no students milled around, no one sat on the steps Sara'd been sitting on when the photograph had been taken all those years ago: her right leg tucked up, the left fully outstretched, both hands raised to extend long black hair to either side of a narrow, smiling face. Sara, Raful's only child.

He could still remember the day of her graduation, summa cum laude, in Hebrew studies. Raful had stood side by side with her mother, tears streaming down both their faces, while the strains of "Hatikva" floated beautifully, gravely, above the throng; dinner afterward; the stunning blow she had delivered over nightcaps in the Baka apartment: no government service, not one hour on a kibbutz; no boyfriends, no life in Israel ... but to London! She would go to London, there to study fashion design and spend the rest of her life making clothes for rich goyim.

The war between them had been long, one of the few Raful ever lost.

He smoothed the plastic a couple of times before putting away the photo. These were mortal memories: the fight, while his wife, Esther, stood miserably on the sidelines; the reconciliation; the slow coming to terms with a grown-up daughter's assertion of independence. All those things had led, like the long straight road linking Jerusalem and the West Bank, to death.

Sharett had been forced to accommodate death too often. In the old days, yes, as Yigal said: running around and blowing people up and getting hanged by the British ... though that had been different because it was *other* people who were blown up, *other* people who got hanged. But then the cast had changed. Then family and friends started to vanish, permanently, from Raful's landscape. A certain friend called Ehud Chafets—oh, yes, he was dead, his brains shot out of his skull on the road to Beirut airport. Esther—she had died of barbiturate poisoning, they said, but that was only because doctors shied away from certifying "broken heart" under CAUSE OF DEATH; doctors tend to ignore what they cannot cure.

Sara's certificate was even less informative. "Massive terminal trauma" had always struck him as an odd way to describe the effects of being blown apart by a bomb.

20 July: 0200: Oxford

"Voilà!" said Robbie. *"Le* breakfast *en lit, pour un."*

Colin pretended to struggle out of sleep, rubbing his eyes. "Whass' time?"

"Deux heures. De bonne heure, encore."

Colin sat up. His son stood beside the bed with a tray in his hands, grinning broadly.

"Le café de Nes, from a jar purchased, in a single lot, from one of our most exclusive *supermarchés,* and opened, personally, *par moi. Les oeufs, frits. Et le* ... I dunno what bacon is, Dad."

He lowered the tray onto Colin's lap. Toast, juice, eggs and bacon, coffee. "What's all this, then?" Colin asked suspiciously. "What are you after?"

"As if I would ask the aged P for anything! Who, *moi?"* Robbie laid a hand across his breast, looking pained.

Colin sniffed. "Wallet's on the dresser," he growled. And then, "Thanks, son. You eaten?"

"Yes. Couldn't sleep. You talking on the phone woke me up; who called?"

Colin stirred his coffee. "No one called. You must have been dreaming. You say you couldn't sleep, but you were doing all right when I looked in on you. Anyway, what's with the *français* all of a sudden?"

Robbie shook his head, that same cheeky grin, the grin of

innocence, splitting his face in two. "Just excited, that's all. Silly."

He flushed crimson, embarrassed, and Colin, who knew better than to take his hand, which was what he wanted to do, said, "So am I. Butterflies."

"Me too." Robbie perched on the bed and took a fingerful of bacon.

"Hey!" Colin stabbed with his fork. "That's mine!"

"I'm a growing boy." Robbie's tone was unctuous. "I need building up. Besides, it doesn't go to fat on me, like on *some*one I know."

"Ouch! Leave off." Colin sipped coffee. "Hey, this is good. Thanks."

The boy flushed again and looked down. "What's K.L. like?" he asked suddenly.

"Oh ... noisy, a bit dirty. Hot and humid. But some lovely buildings, and lovelier people. You'll like it. Anyway, *I* should be asking *you*; you've done nothing all month but read guidebooks."

"Yes, but I've been looking at the Australian ones, mostly. I can't wait for Melbourne, Dad."

Robbie meant: for Celestine. For the mother of the mother of *my* mother, who went away and never came back. For my roots, my past, my self. As Colin formulated this to himself, he wondered what the boy would say about Leila to his great-grandmother, when they met again. He must have prepared something: a spell to exorcise the anger he felt toward his father, his mother, the unrighteous world that allowed such things to happen.

Colin did not know how his son had dealt with Leila's desertion. He'd never found a way of asking.

"Wish we didn't have to hang around in K.L.," Robbie said.

Colin had been invited to lecture in Sydney. Oxford had granted his request for a sabbatical without demur. Academic friends in Malaysia, eager to repay some hospitality, had invited him to stop over with them. When the ticket arrived and he saw the university had treated him to business class, it seemed like an omen. Colin cashed the ticket in for two economy seats and decided to take his son on the holiday of a lifetime.

They needed a holiday. They had not taken one for over two years, not since Leila went out of their lives forever.

"I'll get up now," Colin said, his sharp tone causing Robbie to start. "Can you take the tray? Thanks."

He watched his son carry the tray out of the bedroom. The boy's hands and feet were too big for the rest of him, and he needed fleshing out a little; nature, having given him her all for so many years, had paused for breath just short of completion, leaving him out of sync and lanky. At fourteen, though, he showed no signs yet of reaching the moody phase that must come: emotional development proceeded like its physical counterpart, in fits and starts. Maturity came at its own pace; over the past two years, Colin had learned when not to push.

As he swung his legs off the bed his meticulous lawyer's brain reminded him that he had not lied to his son about the phone. No one had called.

Robbie sat next to his father and map-read. "Exit Four. Two more to go. Then you leave the M-four, take the third exit, and you're on a slip road."

When Colin said nothing, Robbie realized he'd been superfluous. For a moment he knew that hard, angry feeling like the start of a tension headache, but it passed. Today was too great to spoil with shit like that.

He wanted to ask the questions he'd composed in his mind, but they spiked out like missile warheads. If he fired them, somewhere in the air between his tongue and Colin's eardrums they would automatically become armed, possessed of unimaginable destructive force. This might be a good time, though. Dad seemed relaxed; he'd really appreciated the breakfast. And compared to most other fathers he was just *so* incredible. Like, human, you know? In touch, pretty well the whole time, really. Trouble was, they were flying today, and for some reason Dad hated that.

If Robbie wanted to ask about Leila he had to pick his moment very, very carefully.

"Dad."

"What? Did you say two more exits, or—"

"Two. Dad, I never really thanked you properly for this trip."

Colin smiled. "No need. And you did thank me."

"I mean, you might just have shunted me off to Muriel."

Muriel was Colin's mother, and a right royal pain in the ass.

"Cruel and unnatural punishment, old boy, outlawed by the Constitution."

Robbie laughed. "Mothers," he said, "can be tough." Pause. "Can't they?"

Silence.

"Dad, I—"

"Exit five, great; next one's ours. Still got plenty of time." Colin was staring into his mirror with peculiar intensity, as if the lorry behind had suddenly transformed itself into a dinosaur.

Robbie gazed at the map book spread out across his thighs, looking for a route of a different sort and finding none. He wanted to talk about his mother. About Leila. When she left, he'd hated her at first; what kind of monster abandoned her family? He'd cried a lot, too. Now he no longer hated her, but there were things he needed to *know*. Like: why had Mum and Dad divorced? Was it his fault his parents couldn't get along?

Whenever he thought of his mother he knew sorrow, rather than anger. But it was a sorrow that sapped his strength and gnawed his guts, and he was sick of it.

"Dad." The word came out quietly; there was a definite tremor to it. Colin was pulling off the motorway, heading for the slip road. Robbie didn't want to wreck his father's concentration, really he didn't ... "Dad, it's about Mum. I'd like—"

"Sorry, Robbie, just a mo: which exit do we need?" Colin sounded panicky. "Which way do we need to go here?"

"I—"

"*Quickly!* I've got to make up my mind."

"But I don't—"

"Well, look at the tickets, for Christ's sake! Oh, damn, I've missed it!"

He drove on, hugging the inside lane, while Robbie wrestled with the briefcase's clasps.

"Oh, come on!"

"I've got it, I've got it, wait ..." Robbie flicked open the cardboard wallet in which the travel agent had sent them their tickets. "Terminal Three!"

Suddenly, Colin laughed. Not out loud, just a little puff of air through the lips. He turned his head slightly, enough to look at Robbie's miserable expression and wink. Robbie pumped out the same half laugh.

"Ladies and gentlemen," Colin cried, "this is our third circuit of the Heathrow slip-road roundabout. And now, by popular request, let's go round one more time."

So they did. They could hardly see for laughing, and it healed the breach that had threatened to spoil a wonderful first day of the holiday, but it made them late. So late, in fact, that by the time they came to check in the flight was overbooked and Robbie no longer had a seat, because he'd been bumped.

20 July: Dawn: Bahrain

The passport was French, the name on its front SUSANNAH DUCLERC, and both were false. The document lay aligned with the lip of the plain wooden dressing table. To judge by the way its owner had placed it, just touching the rim of the qibla disk that indicated the direction of Mecca, it belonged to a neat, methodical person possessed of a tidy mind. Beside it were a first class air ticket, Bahrain–Kuala Lumpur, two thousand dollars' worth of traveler's checks, and a black Étienne Aigner purse. Apart from these things, the dressing table was bare.

She sat squarely, facing the point where dawn would begin to define her reflection in the mirror. First a line of whiteness picked out the side of her nose and left cheekbone ... forehead ... chin. Slowly, slowly, she blended out of the night—the Arabic word for which was *lailah*, her real name.

She watched without flinching, hands clasped over the arms of her chair. Once enough light had insinuated its way through the half-drawn curtains, she rose to switch off the twin bulbs flanking the mirror before settling back into her former position. She had this gift of absolute stillness, so that if you had come upon her in a waxworks you could have been forgiven for taking her to be an exhibit. She'd once found herself locked in the Uffizi gallery because the curators simply hadn't noticed her sitting there, lost in contemplation. She was not quite of this world, not all of the time.

She had an excellent figure, this woman of thirty-six. The first thing you noticed about her was the athletic body, the stream-lining that had survived both marriage and pregnancy. She was particular about the cut of her clothes, preferring to have the material beneath and around the breasts drawn a little tight so as to hint that her bust was a large one kept in check, whereas really it was smaller than she would have liked. She carried her head high, chin up, like the nannies taught, and when she looked someone in the eye—her lifelong habit—their brilliant whites contrasted so starkly with the mahogany of her irises that the person observed would sometimes blink, feeling pierced. Perfectly matched, finely plucked eyebrows hooded those sparkling eyes; they and the mouth, suggestive of iron will, gave the face what character it had. But on the whole it was an unremarkable countenance: one that passed unremarked, and often, before the watchful gaze of those whose duty it was to hunt her down. She had been lovely once; in those days she had yearned, as young girls do, to be noticed. Now she asked nothing more than to go, as the diverse languages of her many passports had it, "without let or hindrance," fading from the mind like a portrait executed in disappearing ink.

When she rose and moved across to the window of her suite set high in Bahrain's Intercontinental Hotel, the creamy light of a Persian Gulf dawn greeted her without kindness. She was Lebanese by birth, her skin palest olive, allowing her to pass as European in Beirut or Arabian in Paris, whichever might prove expedient; but this morning it was greasy with the fatigue of long vigil. From her aerie she could just discern the beginnings of the sea. Ahead of her, beyond the desolate void of the largest parking lot she had ever seen, and one entirely empty of vehicles, lay the business and financial district, its glass skyscrapers unmarred by the dense mists of dawn that surrounded the island without encroaching on it. A spit of sand, its northern end smothered with concrete, the whole veiled in fog. If Bahrain had not already existed, God would surely have felt no need to fill the gap.

She let the gauze curtain slip from her beringed hand, her mouth curling in contempt at the thought of the rowdy Europeans she had observed spilling out from the bar the night before. Yes, and there had been *ghutras* as well, red and white headdresses, Saudi accents, so many tomcats swarming down the causeway in search of outlets for their unsanctioned thirsts and lusts. Scum ... but profitable scum, oh, very, with their never-ending willingness to pay for the death and destruction Leila dispensed, for a Saudi contract would always hold up.

The Arabs in the bar were not the real ones, any more than the pseudo-princesses who had haunted the Hamra shopping district of her Beiruti childhood represented the European aristocracy they so pitifully aped.

The silver coffeepot felt cold beneath her hand. She dialed room service, making her request with the minimum of words. Because she had not spoken for over a day, her voice sounded alien to her.

Those people were not the real Arabs. They were not even real people.

There once had been a certain house, where real people lived and loved.

Yarze, overlooking the whole coastal swath of Beirut, with its stunted skyscrapers, red-tiled roofs, and white walls amid the concrete. It was an L-shaped, three-story house called "Kharif," Arabic for autumn, not far from the American ambassador's official residence; you turned off the road, through high wrought-iron gates that were always left open, and climbed a steep drive that curved tightly round upon itself to reach the oak front door. Inside, coolness and peace. An expanse of exquisite mosaic flooring, leading you seductively onward, past doors, all open, ever open, to the French windows at the back and the garden.

Leila, coming home from school, would run through the house, blind to all else, until she burst out into the sunshine again. But this was her own personal source of sun: Grandfather, sitting under the jacaranda tree in his wicker throne beside the marble pool, dozing, oblivious to the leaves as they shifted their shadowy lattice patterns this way and that across his pale face. "Grandpa!" she would shriek, and he would jump awake as if electric current had been passed through him, allowing the book (there was always a book) to slide from his lap, often as not colliding with his thick ebony silver-tipped cane; and he would reach forward to pick these things up, but Leila was there ahead of him, sweeping everything aside in her need to clamber onto the old man's lap, put her arms around his neck, and nibble at his gray beard that smelled of latakia and Eau de Portugal.

Then Azizza would come out, hands clasped in front of her as usual, Azizza the servant; perhaps there was a piece of paper some-where—in a registry, say, or some ministry—that described her occupation as "servant," because you couldn't write down LOVED as a job. Maybe not. Leila hoped not. She knew that Grandpa would have had the tact to enter her as "aunty," because that was his way. Azizza would come out, scolding across Grandpa's pleas for a bowl of strawberries, or a piece of that wonderful Nestlé's Devon Milk chocolate that only he knew where to buy.

"I hear she was terrible at school today," Azizza would bark. "Three out of ten in English, *mais, c'est affreux!*"

Then Grandpa would tilt his patrician head on one side, just five degrees, so, and look as if he wanted to burst into tears, and Azizza would unclasp her hands for long enough to throw them high above her head in a gesture of despair before retreating to fetch whatever treat the old man had requested.

While they ate together—the three of them, naturally all three, Azizza as well—Halib might come back, and for a moment Leila could bring herself to abandon Grandpa while she rushed to be picked up by her brother and swung around. Afterward he would throw himself down at Grandpa's feet, resting his head on the old man's knee, while Grandpa told them one of his stories. About his youth, as a pirate in Malacca. Or when he was a mer-chant prince in Africa and the black men wanted to eat him, but he escaped, with the help of a beautiful slave, "Not as beautiful as Grandmother, but close, close!" And then sometimes they would hear the chimes of the front door and know they had a guest. "Stay there," Azizza would say, "I'll get it!" The old woman would trot through the house, eager to know who had come. And she would open the door. Yes. Azizza opened it, because that was the rule.

A buzzer sounded; not in the house at Yarze, overlooking the blue Mediterranean and its Phoenician city of gold, but here in Bahrain, on a morning of damp mist and memory.

Leila, caught between two worlds, remained immobile for an instant; then she walked over to the dressing table and picked up her handbag. She opened it to check that the P7 pistol was in its proper place before advancing, slowly, to the door.

She hated opening doors, admitting people into her life. Even when—a peek through the viewer confirmed the fact—it was room service, bearing hot coffee: the only drug she permitted herself to take as antidote against a poisoned past.

20 July: 0430: Heathrow Airport

The check-in clerk saw father and son as two entries on a bar graph: side by side, one shorter than the other but wearing similar clothes (white top, dark trousers), connected and somehow absolutely relevant to each other.

"I'm very sorry," she said, "but we do sometimes get this overbooking problem. It does say on your ticket to arrive at the airport early, at least two hours before flight time."

She wondered what they would do next. She'd been trained to deal with all eventualities short of a homicidal attack with malice aforethought, and she liked to think she knew how individual passengers were going to react to the news that, thanks to her employer's greed and indifference, they had been bumped. So it surprised her when Colin Raleigh said, "I'm afraid we got caught up in traffic, miss. I wonder, is there anything you can do to help us?"

For he, too, knew a lot about people. He understood that the satisfactions of letters to the chairman, perhaps even a county court action, lay far in the future. What mattered now was getting them both seats.

"You see," he went on, "I'm a law tutor and I've been invited to

Kuala Lumpur by some of their senior academics to give a talk. Look."

He produced a letter from his friends in K.L., putting his hand over the lower half and keeping up the patter while the clerk's eyes flickered between him and the paper.

"This is my son; he's fourteen and he's never flown before; they're meeting the flight, bit of a delegation, actually"—winsome smile, self-deprecating gesture—"so it would be rather embarrassing if the British Council bod and the Dean of the Law School and so on all piled up at K.L. airport and I didn't."

"But you're on the flight, Mr. Raleigh."

"Ah, but I could hardly travel without my son. The house is locked up, we've nowhere to go and stay; I mean, what's he supposed to do, check into a hotel for the next eight weeks?"

"There might be a seat for him at the weekend—"

"No, I'm sorry. Both or neither."

She gnawed her lip. Colin continued to smile at her in a way she appreciated. *She* knew that *he* knew none of this was her fault. "Let me have a quick word with my supervisor," she said, slipping off her stool.

Colin looked at his son. *Colin* knew that *Robbie* knew he was to blame for everything.

"Don't worry," he said, laying a hand on Robbie's shoulder. "They'll sort something out." Robbie shook off the hand, going to lean against an adjacent unmanned check-in desk so Colin couldn't see his face.

"Mr. Raleigh"—the clerk had come back and was leaning forward to invite confidential discussion—"I'd be awfully grateful if you'd keep this under your hat," she said, "but we're going to give one of you a seat in business class."

Colin nodded gravely, wondering if this girl knew of the irony whereby he'd cashed in his own business class ticket just so Robbie could fly. "Thank you, miss. You've been so helpful. Do you think I could have a note of your name?"

"Patsy." But by now she was in a hurry; it took her less than a minute to check their bags through to Kuala Lumpur before sliding two boarding passes face down across the counter as if they were dirty photographs and she wanted to be rid of them.

Once in the duty-free shop Colin dithered over what brand of malt to buy for the Fadillahs, their hosts in Malaysia.

"Honestly, what is it about you and these big decisions, Dad? First the roundabout, now the scotch."

"Yes, terrible. Deciding to have you was much easier—though that wasn't so important, I suppose."

"Oh, you!" Robbie raised his fist shoulder high and brought it down on Colin's forearm. Then he realized what he was being offered and quickly said, "Did you and Mother really decide to have me, or was it, just ... you know?"

"I think ... the Glenlivet. Just a quick poke on a dark night?"

"Dad!"

"Whoops, sorry, I forgot." They had nearly reached the cashier and Colin was fumbling for his boarding pass. "Never did get around to telling you about the birds and the bees, did I?"

Then it happened. Two Arabs thrust their way past them, causing Colin to stagger. His heel slipped on the polished floor and he fell awkwardly. The bottle of malt fell from his hands, and although protected by a cardboard case he could tell from the sound that it had smashed.

"Sorry," one of the Arabs disdainfully offered, over his shoulder. "Plane to catch."

"And you think I haven't?" Colin shouted as he hauled himself vertical again. "My God, you people should be lynched!" The Arabs, tossing large denomination banknotes at the cashier, paid no heed; until, that is, Colin raised the soggy cardboard case and said, "To the health of General Ariel Sharon."

The Arab who had pushed him swung around at that, and Colin read the murder in his eyes, but his companion clasped his arm and muttered in his ear, until the first Arab turned away, relegating Colin to a realm beneath contempt.

Colin went to collect a replacement bottle. "That wasn't like you," Robbie said as he returned. "A bit ... over the top, wasn't it?"

"A bit." Colin heaved a deep sigh. "That's how I met your mother," he said. "In a roughhouse with Arabs."

Robbie, seeing the valley suddenly materialize before him, took one deep breath, spread his wings, and soared. "Tell me!"

July 1969: Oxford

Foregone conclusion," Mark Stamford observed gloomily. "Don't know why they bothered to viva you. You'll stay on to do the BCL, of course?"

"Haven't decided."

Two young men were walking by the river near Oxford, up Marston way, on a weekday afternoon of sun and puffball cloud. There was no one else about. The bank became difficult here, overgrown with high reeds and prone to sink into bog where the ground looked firmest, but Colin Raleigh knew the path. A loner by nature, he'd often sought out this tranquil stretch of river. Mark was the nearest he had to a friend at Oxford, but even so, it was unusual for him to invite anyone on these solitary tramps. Today, however, he wanted advice.

"I don't know about staying on for a BCL," Colin went on. "I buggered up the trusts paper in finals, you see. Completely misread one whole question."

"Oh, come on! You got a *first!* As everyone knew you would."

Colin shrugged irritably. He hadn't dragged Mark up here to discuss what everybody knew.

"Anyway," he said, "I scraped through, and I'm fucked if I know what to do next." He plucked a long reed and threw it on one side, as if it had offended him and he were obeying some hitherto unpublicized biblical injunction about it. "What do you think I should do?"

"Oh, the higher degree, without question. Even if you opt for the bar later, it can only stand you in good stead. But you won't, will you—you'll teach."

"Christ. 'Those who can, do; those who can't—'"

"Sit up half the night drinking vintage port, having no thought for the morrow. Let's not be *too* quick to reject that, shall we?"

"Yes, but imagine it," Colin exploded. "Spending the next forty years stuck in the Bodleian Library, churning out textbooks."

"What do your parents think? Oh, your father's dead, didn't you once tell me?"

Colin nodded. He'd scarcely talked about his parents to anyone since arriving in Oxford. "Do you know Andrew Smythe?" he asked.

"History bod, isn't he?"

"That's him. He was on my staircase for two years. About once a year he'd mutter something about going off to visit relatives in Winchester for the weekend; then one day I found out he meant his parents. Which about sums it up in my case too."

"Mother difficult, is she?"

Colin just grunted. "At least she can't stop me living my own life now," he said after a while, as they continued to force a path through the weeds. "There's a bit of cash, thanks to Father's will and so on. Nothing much." He glanced sideways at his companion. "No rich wife in the offing."

Mark laughed. He'd just become engaged to the girl he'd fallen in love with during his first week at Magdalen; her father owned casinos, a ceramics factory, and much else; soon, Colin thought privately, he would own Mark Stamford.

"You're priceless," Mark said, still laughing. "You'd find life easier if you'd only stop fooling around and find the right person."

"I'll take your word for it. There's a place near here where we can get some tea...."

When Colin deviated left, plunging into the meadow, Mark followed blindly, trusting his friend even though here the grass was chest high. On the other side of the copse that fringed the field lay an overgrown space, half public and half private, by the look of it;

two overflowing litter bins suggested that Oxford City Council had a not very effective say in what happened here, but the single narrow outlet to the highway was blocked by a couple of oil drums and two logs laid to form an elongated X.

"No girl's good enough for you, that's the problem," Mark was saying as they entered the copse.

"One might be," Colin said. He stopped, causing Mark to cannon into him and half turned, laying a hand on the other man's chest. "Don't move."

For a moment, Mark could not make out what Colin had seen. They were standing about five yards back from the clearing, invisible to anyone in the open space. Then a girl crossed Mark's field of vision. A turn of the head showed him a white Ford parked back from the road; evidently the girl must have driven in and then rearranged the barrier, for there was no other entrance.

"Gosh." The word escaped from Mark's mouth in a dying fall. "Do you know her?"

Colin pulled Mark back into the copse. "No," he whispered. "But I'd like to."

The object of their attention showed no sign of having seen either of them. She was wearing a pair of clinging white pants and a dark blue tank top, not tucked in at the waist. As she walked up and down she kept her hands thrust deep into her pockets, stretching the material tightly over her bottom in such a way as to remind Colin of a peach. When she turned he caught a glimpse of her face, already familiar to him after many a surreptitious scan in the past; she was fair-skinned, but he would have known she wasn't English even if he hadn't managed to discover her name, through one of her fellow students at St. Anne's. The girl with peach buttocks was called Hanif. Leila Hanif.

Leila meant darkness, in Arabic, and *hanif* meant true believer. Or so the acquaintance said, claiming to have received this information from the mare's mouth. Colin could believe it. This girl, glimpsed on the other side of smoky bars, at the next counter in Blackwell's bookshop, in a punt going in the opposite direction, had started to come between him and his sleep.

She was beautiful, not least because she so obviously cared

about herself. She wore her wavy hair, black with the glossiness of a newly developed monochrome photograph, at shoulder length, with a hairband, or sometimes just white-framed sunglasses pushed back to keep the tresses from falling over her eyes: so unlike your typical female undergrad, with unkempt rats' tails drooping to the waist. She wore clothes that amounted to a proper wardrobe too, discarding the uniform of faded jeans and baggy sweaters in favor of designer pants, like the ones she was wearing now, and tailored shirts; even the tank top she wore this summer's afternoon was by Mary Quant.

Leila's cheekbones were high and ever so slightly concave, bringing out a sexy contrast with lips that tended to pout. Colin did not know about her eyes; he'd never got close enough to find out what color they were. All he knew was that when she laughed—she had an amazingly sexy laugh—her eyes squeezed shut, radiating a skein of premature laughter lines around their corners. A happy woman, then.

"She's Lebanese," Colin muttered.

"East of Suez, eh? Lucky coincidence, us running into her like this. Why are we lurking in the undergrowth, incidentally?"

When Colin made no reply Mark looked at his friend in time to see him blushing furiously. "Ah. Not a coincidence."

"She comes here sometimes." Colin's tone was sulky. "This is the tearoom car park."

"Perfect opportunity: no one about, just barge right up to her and—"

"*Some* people can do that," Colin hissed. "It's all right for them." He clicked his teeth and sighed. "Besides, she comes here with friends."

"You've been watching her, haven't you?"

Colin made as if to hurl Mark a defiant look but narrowly failed to follow through.

"Well, well, *well.* Anyway, Uncle Mark will ride to the rescue. Watch."

Before Colin could stop him he had marched forward, almost to the edge of the copse, when suddenly he came to a dead halt. "Oh, shit."

For another car, a black Mercedes-Benz, had silently driven up to the X-shaped barrier and someone was getting out to clear it aside: an Arab-looking man in his thirties, with a square head and thick black wavy hair and something about the hang of his suit to suggest he wasn't comfortable in it. He pushed the logs away and waved the driver through before replacing them. As he straightened up, his right hand went to the waistband of his trousers, and for an instant the two young men watching from the cover of the trees shared a perception that each was unwilling to articulate for fear of being thought stupid: This Arab packed a gun.

Without taking his eyes off the scene unfolding in front of them, Colin laid a hand on Mark's chest and pushed him farther into the protective shadow of the copse. From the instinctive way in which Mark followed his lead, Colin guessed that he, too, was frightened.

The driver of the Mercedes got out, straightening the jacket of a suit that looked identical to his companion's, seam for seam, tint for tint. He, however, was an altogether leaner specimen; perhaps richer also, for gold glittered across the insteps of his black leather shoes, on several fingers, even in the smile he flashed at Leila Hanif as he went to kiss her on both cheeks, holding her at arm's length like a long-lost prodigal daughter.

The second Arab did not greet the girl. Instead, he donned a pair of dark glasses and began a survey of the rustic parking area. Colin and Mark retreated a few steps farther, although they knew that from the glade they must already be invisible. The second man kept adjusting the lapels of his suit while he wiggled his shoulders. Nervous, uncomfortable, armed: the composite impression forced itself on Colin like a physical assault, lashing his heartbeat up off the scale.

The driver and the girl talked in low voices. At first the man continued to hold Leila as if she were a close friend. But then he began to draw her in to himself, and she resisted; not powerfully, not with violence, but with a tension that found expression in the rigidity of her shoulders. Suddenly her hands flew up, destroying his grip. The man stepped backward and surveyed her for a moment without ever dropping his golden smile. He spoke a few words; to judge from the look on his face, words of great tenderness and affection.

He struck her on the side of the face, once.

She staggered, recovered; for a moment she merely held a hand to the site of the blow, as if in stunned disbelief. Then she raised her own hand to retaliate. But the man was quicker, moving to one side and capturing both her hands in his own. He shouted some words while holding his face very close to hers. Then he transferred both her wrists to his left hand, and Colin knew he did that because he meant to hit her again.

"I thought I'd come to blows with the senior examiner," he said loudly. When Mark Stamford looked at him in petrified astonishment, he grabbed his friend's arm and marched him forward, almost shouting. "I said I couldn't see what—Leila! For heaven's sake. Leila Hanif, my God."

Now everybody was looking at him, each coping with his or her own brand of fear: Leila, dreading the next blow; the two Arabs, aware only that they had been caught out in a crime, not yet realizing the weakness of the forces ranged against them; and Mark, who knew in his heart what Colin also knew: that the object they both had seen at the second man's waist was in truth a gun. Colin had the initiative. It was for him to decide how the scene played.

"Leila, we were talking about you only this morning."

As if through a fog Colin recognized Mark's voice speaking those words, he knew his friend was recovering faster than the opposition, and his heart lifted.

"Hi, youse guys." Leila's smile, unforced and serene, would have launched more ships than Helen's. "Long time no see. Thought you must have gone down, or something."

Her contralto voice wrung something deep in Colin's guts, but he could not concentrate on that, for pace and timing would dictate the outcome of this scene. He was director, star, and scriptwriter rolled into one. He called the shots, and if he called them wrong....

"No, no," he said confidently. "I'm staying up for the vac. Mark's going home next week. Friends of yours? Hi ... I'm Colin Raleigh."

He turned to the Arab who had struck Leila, offering his hand. The man stared at it, then his eyes flickered toward his companion. After what seemed an interminable pause, he said something like "ha."

"And this is my friend, Mark Stamford. He's been to your part of the world, haven't you, Mark?"

The Arab's hand briefly touched Colin's before leaping away as if stung.

"Oh, yes, absolutely," Mark said. "Tabriz. Know it, do you? Persia, actually."

"Leila, can you do us a huge favor?" Colin smiled into her eyes, giving his co-star direction in the only way he knew how. "Mark and I've got an appointment with the Dean and we're going to be hideously late...."

"Of course, I can drive you back into town." She shot a furious look at the two Arabs, whose livid faces were more than a match for hers. "The keys are in the ignition, Colin, why don't you drive?"

"Mark?" Colin nodded in the direction of the barrier blocking their exit to the main road and Mark hurried off to dismantle it. Colin took Leila's arm—it was surprisingly muscular, for a woman's—and escorted her to the car. He did not know what the two Arabs were doing behind his back.

It seemed a long walk, the longest he'd ever taken. *Don't throw yourself on the door and wrench it open,* he told himself; *don't look weak.* But still his fingers crushed the handle hard enough to leave a bruise.

The engine started first time; Colin heaved a short, jerky sigh of relief. Leila was in the front seat next to him. Ahead, he could see Mark standing beside the logs, their exit clear. Colin put the car into gear.

He knew at once that they weren't going to make it.

The Arabs' Mercedes was parked just inside the clearing, perhaps a quarter of its length still blocking the short driveway. Colin stared through the windshield at Mark, who raised both hands from his sides in a forlorn gesture of helplessness. Strain on Mark's face.... *Oh God, on mine too; relax!*

His brain wouldn't work. He had a first in law and he couldn't have told you his own name to save his life. Leila was staring at him. She expected him to come up with the solution. There was no solution.

His hands tightened on the wheel. They were shaking. He banged the wheel in sheer frustration, then, very slowly, wound down the window.

"Excuse me." He forced himself to look at the Arab with all the gold. It amazed him to hear how confidently his clipped, assumed upper-class accent cut through the warm July air. "But would you mind awfully shifting your car? Just a few feet should do it."

He wound up the window at once. Don't wait for an answer. Expect to be obeyed as a matter of course. Glubb Pasha, he thought savagely, that's me; Lawrence of Arabia.... He put the car back into neutral and prayed.

For a moment, neither Arab stirred. Then the driver, the golden one, spoke a few words out of the side of his mouth. The other wanted to argue, but the first man cut him short with a chopping gesture. They got into the Mercedes. The driver started the engine.

The Mercedes sat there, immobile and threatening. Seconds ticked by. Why the hell didn't they move? The answer came to him along with a sick feeling in the base of his stomach. *The Arabs were going to ram Leila's car.*

A choky little moan forced its way through his lips. He heard Leila swallow; then she laid a hand over the nearer one of his, giving it a squeeze, and Colin, overloaded with inconsistent emotions, nearly fainted. He stared at her hand. Suddenly he heard a crunch of gravel, stones flew up to strike the paintwork of Leila's Ford, and the lot was empty.

Colin slumped back in his seat. "Thank God," he was saying, over and over again. "Thank God, thank God...."

He saw Mark stagger to his feet, dusting himself down. Why was he doing that? For a moment Colin refused to see it; then the truth burst in on him: The driver of the Mercedes had charged straight at Mark, heedless of whether he got out of the way in time.

Colin turned to Leila. "Care to tell me what that was all about?"

Mark came over to join them, sliding into the back seat. His face was the color of raw pastry.

"They were ... they claimed to be friends of my father." Her voice, in contrast, was quite even. She had long ago removed her hand from his; the intimacy of that shared moment might never have been. "And it's true I'd seen one of them about the house in Beirut, sometimes."

Colin waited for her to continue. When she did not, he prompted her. "We were standing in the trees, watching you. He hit you. We saw."

"They ..." She tailed off, staring at the dashboard, and he sensed she was thinking up some story that would satisfy them. The perception angered him. "They wanted me to go with them," she said finally.

"Why?"

"They wouldn't say. So of course I refused. That's when he hit me."

"I see." There clearly wasn't going to be any further explanation, so Colin put the car in gear and drove off.

For the first part of the journey back into Oxford he concentrated on keeping the car headed straight while he tried to master an irritation he knew to be pointless. If Leila chose not to confide, no appeal lay against her decision, even though he'd saved her life. Oh, childish, *childish!* he berated himself. Saved her life, what crap!

After a while, however, the anger faded, to be replaced by a much more interesting set of feelings.

It dawned on him that here he was, in the presence of someone he'd wanted to be close to for months now. As soon as he dared take his eyes off the road he began to glance in her direction. The white pants she was wearing stretched across the tops of her thighs in a way that made him long to reach over and stroke them. Her skin, what he could see of it, was moist with perspiration, and he thought how nice it would be to lick that, slowly, relishing each fricative stroke. But what got to him most was her smell.

She was wearing a fragrance of some kind, but she also had an utterly distinctive body scent, rising above the artificial perfume while somehow combining with it to produce this magnificent aroma. He struggled to find words to describe it and failed. Citrus tartness was there, something herbal as well, musk.... Colin didn't know what musk smelled like, but he knew this had to be musk from the way he kept taking deep breaths in an effort to absorb Leila through her scent. And from the way his jeans had grown tight at the crotch....

She was looking at him too; not directly, not even often, but enough to let him see she was interested. Colin should have felt happy. He didn't. He never knew what to do in these situations, which in any case had been few and far between for him. Did she want him to make a move? But how, with Mark in the back seat?

Say something.

What?

Anything.

"Where can I drop you?" he faltered. "I mean ... oh, God, it sounds so silly, driving your car."

She laughed, a laugh with no shadows or reservations, and he shivered.

"I want to go to the Randolph."

"The hotel?"

"Yes. My brother's arriving today; he's got to know about what happened this afternoon."

"You'll tell the police, of course?"

"My brother will decide everything."

He felt disappointed in her. To let a man make up her mind for her, so ... so ... well, yes, *nice*—as long as you could be that man.

Conversation languished. He glanced at his watch. At this rate, it would take no more than fifteen minutes to reach the Randolph Hotel. Then goodbye.

He felt very strange. All his limbs seemed light. His vision was amazingly clear; he could hear every rustle of her clothes as she shifted position. She was wearing her severe look now, an expression suggestive of self-containment, hard work, proper self-esteem. It grew upon him with frightening intensity that this girl was *right*. The person he'd been waiting for all his life. The one.

The cleanness of the perception was what astonished him most. There were no fuzzy edges to it. Not a single "but" marred the smooth surface of what he suddenly knew to be his rapturous love for Leila Hanif.

Later he would tell people, "As the lights changed and I turned out of Cornmarket, I fell in love for the first time."

As the lights changed and he turned out of Cornmarket, he burst into peals of laughter, but when Leila asked what was funny he shook his head and replied, "Nothing."

It was because he'd fallen in love with a smell that he laughed.

Mark Stamford left them at the hotel, muttering something about a stiff drink. But then Mark did not have the restorative power of love to help him. Colin and Leila stood beside the car in silence. He found himself smiling; that was because she had smiled first.

She reached for his hand and shook it. "I haven't thanked you properly," she said. But her grave tone contrasted with the manner of her handshake; she was flicking his own hand up and down as if they were children at play. He read her eyes. They were brown, he discovered: dark, but shining as if with newly coated varnish, and now those premature laughter lines cut deeply into her face.

"You should thank Mark too," he said, remembering that Mark was no longer there.

"No," she replied. "I shouldn't." Before Colin could question that, she went on. "Come and meet my brother. You'll like him."

Colin and Leila were shown up to a suite. The door opened to reveal the back view of a tall man wearing a dark coffee-hued jacket over pale slacks. He had the phone receiver to his ear and was carrying the other half of the instrument in his left hand. Hearing them enter, he swung around. He clapped eyes on Leila first and his face lit up; then he saw she was not alone and the expression of malice he turned on Colin was enough to make the young man shiver.

"My brother, Halib."

Halib snapped a few final words of Arabic and reconnected

the two parts of the telephone, dropping it onto a nearby table from a height.

"Halib, I want you to be friends with Colin Raleigh. He helped me this afternoon. I mean, *really* helped me."

For a moment, Halib's expression did not soften. Then, quite suddenly, his face broke into a beam and he came forward to embrace Colin, kissing him on both cheeks.

"My very, very dear friend, it is impossible for me to know what to say to you. If you helped my sister, you helped me; if you helped me, you helped the Hanif family, which is in your debt for evermore. Sit down, tell me everything."

"There's not much to tell." Colin felt ill at ease. Halib spoke lightly accented English in a voice that, for all its softness, its almost poetical rhythms, troubled him. Perhaps it was too soft, too sibilant: the voice of a snake wrapped around a tree.

"I was walking with a friend of mine, when—"

Halib threw himself down on a sofa next to Leila, crossed his legs, and began a rapid speech in Arabic. Colin stopped speaking, his mouth open while he waited for the interruption to cease. But it looked as though his contribution to this party was over, for by now brother and sister were locked in an animated conversation he could not hope to follow.

Colin looked around the suite's living room. Halib was, it seemed, a rich man. His clothes, the leather valise just visible through the half-open door to the bedroom, and, beyond that, the matching two-suiter stretched open on the bed—all these things spoke in muted tones of wealth. But the object that really caught his eye was Halib Hanif's briefcase.

It lay on an occasional table by the window: black calf edged with maroon, gilt reinforcements on all eight corners. A gold American Express tag hung from its handle. Colin could almost smell it. One day he would own a briefcase like that, he promised himself. What was inside? Papers, millions of dollars in treasury bills, drugs?

Why did Halib make him think of illicit gains? Ridiculous! The briefcase was the perfectly normal accoutrement of a successful businessman.

"My dear Colin."

He came to himself with a guilty start, realizing that Halib must have seen the direction his eyes had taken.

"My dear Colin, now that Leila has told me everything, I can say, sincerely, that we are more than ever in your debt."

He rose from the sofa and came over to clasp Colin's hand. He shook it several times before resuming his seat. Something about this curiously formal ritual touched Colin. He began to feel rather better about Halib.

"I cannot offer you a full explanation of what happened, because I do not know myself. But you are entitled to share in our ... our theorizing."

He emphasized that last word with a show of good humor, and Colin found himself softening further. Halib had his sister's deep-set eyes, hooded by fleshy brows; when they were wide open, as now, and his lips widened in a smile, he took on something of her physical attractiveness. There was a definite family resemblance, though his skin was a deep brown, much darker than Leila's.

"Our family is very mixed, Colin. European and Arab blood. We settled in Beirut three generations ago. Our grandfather was a banker, like our father, like me. Leila is studying for her PPE, here in Oxford; when she goes home, it will be to join the family business. The situation in our country is complicated. We are prominent in business and in politics. We think the men you saw may have wanted to kidnap Leila."

"*Kidnap* her?"

"And hold her for ransom. Something not unheard of in Lebanon."

"Will you tell the police?"

"No." Halib sat forward. "Now, Colin. I know you will find that strange. But the ramifications could be horrifying." Seeing Colin about to protest, he held up a hand. "Please! This is England, yes, I know. But you see, Leila will one day come home to Beirut, marry her beloved fiancé Yusif, and believe me, life will be simpler for her there if we just forget all about today. Under the carpet, eh? Will you promise not to go to the police? Will you?"

His mouth was full of almost blindingly white teeth. The smile on the face of the tiger? Colin didn't know. All he knew was that Leila had a fiancé called Yusif, she was engaged, she'd been toying with him. Well, why not? Every queen needed a jester. He hated her—no, he didn't. He hated himself.

He glanced at Leila. She smiled at him and nodded briefly, puckering up her mouth, showing her laughter lines. She wanted it kept away from the police too. Right, then.

"Um.... No harm was done, I supp—"

"Good. Fine, wonderful, great."

Halib bounded up; Colin instinctively rose also. Now he was being shepherded to the door by an ebullient Halib. Leila came to his rescue, taking him by the arm, her fingers tight around his flesh.

"Don't mind him," she whispered. "He's adorable once you get to know him."

He looked at her, trying to instill contempt into his gaze and consciously failing. Just get out, he told himself wearily. Cut it short. *Go!* He was almost halfway down the corridor before something prompted him to throw over his shoulder, "Leila, I live on the High—Number sixty-two, first floor."

Then he was being thanked yet one more time; the door was closing; he caught a final glimpse of Halib standing with arm raised to wave farewell; he was dismissed.

It felt like that, he mused, as he wandered along Turl Street. I'm a servant, I did a good deed, I've been thanked by the master, and now here I am, belowstairs again, in my place.

He returned to his room on the High, with its view of the garden at the back, now at the very height of summery charm, and put on an LP: Puccini, *Madame Butterfly*. After a while—it was stupid but he couldn't help himself—he felt water on his cheeks. He swore, dashing away the tears. He began to knit all the bad words into oaths of great intricacy, attempting to weave a spell, a curse, on the woman who'd reduced him to such weakness. To such a pile of puke.

A few minutes into Act Two, there came a light knock on the

door. Colin ignored it. But then the visitor knocked again, and spoke. A woman's voice. "Colin?" One word, just that.

But what a word. What a voice.

Colin, his heart beating fast, ran over to lift the needle. His hand was shaking so much that he scratched the LP—his favorite, too, and he didn't care. He switched off the machine. He took a deep breath.

"Come in, Leila," he called.

20 July 1984: 0500: London

Halib had taken no chances over the reservation. He'd telexed the Penta Hotel as long ago as May, specifying the room number he required and charging it to a Diner's Club card. From his vantage point by the soundproofed window he had a panoramic view of Heathrow Airport's Terminal Three. In the early light, with the aid of binoculars, he could even make out the tail insignia of a certain Lockheed TriStar that was parked on stand Juliet Fourteen.

Halib lowered his glasses long enough to consult his watch: less than an hour to go. They would be loading the fuel, the food and drink, checking individual suitcases against the list of issued boarding passes. The cleaners would have finished by now, leaving the cabin crew to set up the galleys ready for service after climb-out. The co-pilot would be walking around the plane, completing his visual check for oil leaks before testing whether there was sufficient nitrogen in the tires to support a fully laden landing in case of emergency. Early passengers would already be assembling in the holding lounge. Duty-free liquor and cigarettes would be coming across from the bonded warehouse, ready for stowage. The captain was reading his weather reports, calculating weights and speeds, updating his list of radio frequencies, studying today's Notices to Airmen. And maybe, just maybe, some bright member of the cabin staff had thought to check the life rafts in case they had to ditch....

Halib raised the thumb and middle finger of his left hand to the bridge of his nose, massaging it gently. He took another look at his watch before once more lifting his binoculars. Thirty-six minutes to push-back.

The overhead lockers were all still open when Senior Steward Alex Perkins began his routine check of the passenger cabin. He started at the back, giving each cavity more than a cursory glance before slamming shut the door. One of his responsibilities was to examine potential hiding places for weapons and explosives; despite the fact that he'd never found anything, he took the job seriously. A friend of his had been killed in 1982 when Abu Ibrahim and the Organization of 15 May blew up a Pan Am jet as it landed at Honolulu.

He worked his way forward, out of economy and into club, until at last he reached the first class cabin. He crossed the forward galley and set off down the port side. In the very last locker, right at the back of the plane, was the familiar gray canvas bag marked CHILD'S LIFE RAFT. He reached up and pushed it to the end of the locker, where it would not slip during takeoff. It seemed heavy for a life raft. He was about to lift it down for inspection when a nearby phone buzzed. Cockpit. Alex picked up the receiver.

"Perkins."

"Three coffees, if you've got a moment."

Alex had nothing against Captain Thorneycroft, a morose little man who always looked as if he were on the point of losing his temper, though he'd never yet done so, at least not in Alex's presence. But for all his punctiliousness, he commanded the kind of instant obedience every captain longs for, few merit, and a tiny minority obtain.

"Three coffees," Alex murmured. "Coming up."

Before returning to the forward galley he remembered to slam the overhead locker shut.

Colin and Robbie sat in one corner of the departure lounge. After his father had finished telling him the story of how he'd met Leila, Robbie spent a long time staring out of the window. To one side he could see their waiting aircraft; beyond that, an expanse of grass and concrete, distant houses, a pale, early morning sky. Somewhere beyond all those things, his mother roamed the surface of the earth. He did not know where she was or why she had gone, and he missed her hands around him when his face ached with the strain of keeping back tears, missed the stories she used to read before kissing him good night, missed her like a sick man craves the sense of well-being he took for granted before illness struck him down.

For the last two years he'd known it was his fault that his mother had taken off like that. Must have been. Something he'd said, something he'd done. But what? She'd not stayed around to tell him. No second chance....

"*You* miss her," he said suddenly. "Don't you?"

He turned to his father, willing him to answer honestly. For a moment Colin's face remained set in marble, with eyes to match. Then he opened his mouth to speak, but before he could do so another voice interrupted.

"No one's sitting here."

Not a question but a statement; had there actually been someone occupying the seat next to Colin's it would perhaps have amounted to an order to vacate. Colin looked up to see a middle-aged, middle-height, bespectacled man glowering over him in challenging contempt.

"Not as far as I know," he replied shortly.

"Be so kind as to watch my bag."

Colin was about to refuse to accept responsibility for someone else's hand luggage when the man stalked away without a backward glance, leaving his briefcase on the next seat where Colin could not help but read its label, written in angry red capitals: JAN VAN TONDER.

"What a cunt."

"Robbie!"

"Well ... talking to you like that."

"You just watch your language, son. They won't appreciate words like that in K.L., and Celestine'd kill you."

Robbie's expression turned sulky for a moment. He muttered

something, keeping his voice low enough to prevent his father from hearing, but Colin knew it would be along the lines of "All the other guys say it all the time." Being a sensible father, he ignored that.

"Funny accent," Robbie said, emerging from his mood as quickly, and as unpredictably, as he'd entered it.

"Seth Efrican." Colin grinned. "Not that there aren't a few English schoolboys who could show him the door where rudeness is concerned."

"Oh, p—ish. Pish off."

They laughed. "Look out," Colin said, "he's coming back."

Van Tonder strode up to take possession of his seat, carrying a copy of the *Herald Tribune*. He sat down without a word of thanks to Colin for minding his case and opened the paper. After a few seconds he began to snuffle and snort. He hurled the paper onto his lap and reached into his jacket pocket for an inhaler, which he proceeded to ram up each nostril in turn. The Raleighs watched in guilty fascination. Suddenly the man's beady eyes swung around to glare at them.

"Yes? Can I help you?"

"Sorry," Colin muttered.

"Perhaps you are one of those people who find illness in others amusing. If so, I am sorry for you. After spending ten days here I have to tell you that I am sorry for your pathetic little country, and I am sorry for you also."

He replaced the inhaler in his pocket, picked up the paper, and was soon lost in its foreign pages, with only an occasional catarrhal grunt to punctuate the silence.

Colin shrugged. He took a coin from his pocket. "Which of us is going business class to Bahrain? Toss you for it."

"Okay."

"You call."

"Heads."

Colin spun. "Tails."

"Shit."

"It's not so bad, actually. Between Bahrain and Kuala Lumpur it'll mostly be night; you'll sleep much better up front."

"Suppose so."

Passengers had started to board the aircraft. There was the usual holdup on the jetway; then the two of them were turning right at the door, heading through the galley and the small first class cabin into club, where they parted company for the time being.

Colin had been allocated a window seat on the starboard side of the plane. The mere act of settling into it filled him with child-like excitement. There was plenty of leg room and he only had one other person next to him, not two, as in the rear cabin. Somebody was offering him a hot towel. Somebody else was carrying a tray on which stood tall glasses of orange juice, beer, and something straw-colored that fizzed; surely not …

"Champagne, sir? Or would you rather have—"

"Champagne will be quite simply wonderful."

Everything, in fact, was wonderful—the stereo headphones, the leg rest, the bag filled with Crabtree & Evelyn cosmetics for men—right up to the moment when the altercation began.

"I have to get past. Excuse *me!*"

Impossible to mistake Van Tonder's obstreperous tones. Colin's lips twitched, but he did not allow the South African to distract him from his magazine. Only when he heard the response did his head jolt up and *Time* fall from his hands.

"Look," another voice was saying. "My friend. We all have to get past. Now would you mind—"

The second speaker seemed to become conscious of Colin's eyes upon him, for he suddenly broke off and looked along the aisle. The South African seized the moment, pushing past his opponent with an angry flurry of his squared shoulders, until he could drop into the seat next to Colin's.

"What are you doing here?" Colin's voice came out in a light, hollow monotone. His throat hurt. Tension, fueled by champagne, had wrapped a multilayered bandage around his forehead and was busy twisting the tourniquet.

"This is my seat," Van Tonder replied huffily.

"No, my friend, it is not." The other man, the one who'd quarreled with Van Tonder, was standing over him. "It is mine.

First you shove me aside; then you steal my seat. Move, please."

Colin spoke again. "What are you doing here?" he asked Van Tonder, in the same vacant monotone.

"I'm flying to Malaysia," Van Tonder replied with vigor. "So is that suddenly a crime?"

"This seat," said the man in the aisle, "has been assigned to me. Here is my boarding pass. Look."

There was a long silence while Van Tonder looked between his own pass and the one that had been thrust under his nose. At last he gave a nasal grunt and stood up, but with no hint of apology.

Sharett lowered himself into the seat next to Colin's with a shrug that did not quite amount to doing a Raful. He was irritated by his spat with Van Tonder.

"So," Colin said. "A long time. New York, I seem to remember?"

"As I recall." Raful smiled. "Thanks for defending my seat. You look well."

Colin grunted. "Sorry if I woke you this morning," he said after a pause, and his voice was low. "I was feeling—"

"I know."

Raful's mouth wrinkled into a smile; he held up both forefingers to pursed lips. Both men lapsed into silence. Colin picked up his magazine again. Raful settled himself low in his seat and tried to clear his head, but disturbing images had been aroused there and he could not concentrate. He kept remembering how Colin had twice asked Van Tonder, "What are you doing here?"

The same question had been put to him years ago in a similarly challenging tone, and the unwanted memory grated in his brain, much as the airline's salted peanuts were going to scrape his ulcer raw.

1974: Jerusalem

The year 1973 had been a bad one for Mossad Bitachon Leumi, Israel's Institute of State Security, better known simply as "the Mossad": first there was the Norwegian business at Lillehammer when they killed the wrong Arab, then came the series of high-level intelligence reports—lofty in more ways than one—that new Syrian troop concentrations were merely routine. Unfortunately, however, far from being routine, they turned out to be the first stages of the Yom Kippur War.

Once the dust had settled, there was time for the big men to sit down and decide who to break, who to make. Eliahu Zeira, head of Aman, Israel's military intelligence, had to go, of course; Memuneh Zamir was also for the chop. As new intelligence supremo they appointed Major General Yitzhak Hofi, commander of the northern front during the 1973 war, and a national hero. So the game of musical chairs began. Raful Sharett, trailing in the wake of half a dozen bigger players, moved rapidly from Political Action and Liaison to the Collection Department, himself collecting a promotion to the rank of *aluf mishne,* or colonel, on the way. When in the summer of 1974 the music finally stopped—and after the various debacles of 1973 the band played on for a long time—he found himself Director of the Operational Planning Division, which was exactly where he'd wanted to be ever since they'd blown up his daughter in London, five years before.

Avshalom Gazit, young Yigal's father, had seen through him. He was the only man who ever could. "Why are you here?" he'd asked, that famous day in the summer of 1974. *"What are you doing here?"*

"We moved office in 1967," Raful had answered disingenuously. *"That* year in Jerusalem; down the highway from Tel Aviv, you make a left at—"

Avshalom lowered himself into the chair opposite and tapped gently on the desk, calling for silence. Raful complied, in itself a telling measure of his companion's authority.

"You could have stayed in Tel Aviv."

This was true. The Ministry of Defense had remained in Hakirya, avoiding the general migration to Jerusalem, and Aman was under the jurisdiction of the Ministry of Defense. When Avshalom became number two in Aman he'd invited Raful to join his staff, with better pay immediately and the prospect of promotion in a few years' time, but although Raful would have relished becoming a major general he had declined the offer.

"You *should* have stayed in Tel Aviv," Avshalom added.

This was not so much true as debatable. Aman lacked an executive arm operating outside Israel. Raful now required certain facilities—good neutral word, "facilities"—beyond those supplied by military intelligence, facilities such as kidnapping, torture, every kind of sudden and unwelcome death; these were to be the tools of his trade. So on balance he was glad he had not stayed in Tel Aviv.

"Yet you are here. Still." Avshalom's long, significant pause was followed by a question larded with irony: "I wonder why?"

Raful knew his oldest friend had not given up half a Shabbat to come down the road to Jerusalem and shoot the breeze. Avshalom was one of those rare men who might have modeled for a biblical patriarch, if only he hadn't kept his white beard so short and tidy. The chin was prominent, and because he always held his head upright it jutted out like a physical challenge. His eyes were huge and blue, better lie detectors even than the microwave respiration monitors they kept at the Allenby Bridge. But that weary, lined face was incapable of concealment: a bad trait for a professional spy, which is perhaps one reason why Avshalom Gazit never aspired to be other than somebody else's deputy.

"I wanted to be where the action is," Raful replied. "The biggest game in town has moved here: You know it, I know it."

Avshalom nodded slowly, his whole torso moving, not just his head. "And yet," he said, "I think that is only half the truth."

By looking a fraction to one side Raful could glimpse the Western Wall out of his window. It shimmered in that very special kind of debilitating heat that only September Saturday afternoons seemed to generate. Sweat soaked his open-necked shirt. He felt tired, a little ill maybe, but there was nothing to go home to and here, in the Mossad's headquarters, he could at least derive a crumb of comfort from the physical proximity of stenographers, communications staff, duty officers. He was stuck in this temple of truth, listening to his old friend speculate about half-truths, and for a moment Raful wanted to die because he couldn't think of a single thing worth living for.

Then Avshalom picked up his briefcase, put it on the desk,

and opened it in such a way that Raful couldn't see its contents.

"I think," Avshalom murmured from behind the lid of the briefcase, "that you are telling me only half the truth, and maybe this is the other half."

He handed over a buff envelope, sealed in three places with blobs of wax connected by a thread. A few seconds of silence intervened, void moments when the old city and everything in it ceased to exist. Then slowly, very slowly, so as not to disturb the flicker of hope that had sparked inside his guts, Raful leaned forward to take it.

On the front someone had written the single word *goel*. This Hebrew word meant "the avenger of the blood," one who, according to ancient Jewish custom, had the right of taking vengeance on the murderer of a kinsman, before retreating to the city of refuge appointed for his safety. Raful saw the word and trembled.

"What is this?" he asked softly, knowing already.

"What you asked me for. I am sorry things took so long. Coordinating classified material is a job fit for the devil."

In the week after Sara's funeral, Raful had asked Avshalom to do what he, Raful, had not the power to do: he had asked him, *begged* would be a more honest word, to use his friendships with the politicians, to play the Haganah card, as he'd called it, and demolish all interdepartmental barriers in the attempt to find Sara Sharett's killers.

This was not a pointless request. The Mossad had its own files on terrorism, of course, but there were other intelligence records its officers could never hope to see: those held by Aman, by Reshud, by Shin Bet, and Shabak, murky organizations one and all. Avshalom Gazit, scourge of the British occupying force, war hero: he could see everything, and if "they" tried to tell him that certain of those records did not exist, he would also be able to see that they were lying.

"Show me the room, Raful. The shrine."

Sharett's hands shook. Instead of breaking the thread, tearing off the wax seals, they laid the *goel* envelope on the desk and clasped themselves together as if for mutual comfort.

"Shrine?"

But Avshalom rose, towering over Raful until the other man actually felt himself to be in shadow. He, too, stood up. He tucked the envelope under his arm. The fingers of his right hand traced their way down a chain leading from his waistband into his trouser pocket, and there they sought keys. He led the way out of his office and set off down the north corridor. At the far end was a door with a number on it. When he inserted a key and opened it, the hinges creaked. Evidently this place was not often used, for the two men left traces in the dust on the floor as they entered.

Raful watched his friend's face, seeking a reaction. Any reaction would have done: reproof, contempt, sorrow, pity. But nothing scratched Avshalom's slatelike visage. He looked around slowly, like the good intelligence officer he was, taking in the white-washed walls, the desk and table, the man-high safe.

There was scarcely room for both of them in this cupboard, with its single tiny window. Avshalom approached the table, perhaps noting how neatly arranged were the teddy bear, the brush-and-comb set, school yearbook, and graduation certificate. And the photograph.

Neither man spoke for perhaps five minutes. It sounds so little; when we want to indicate a brief, barely noticeable interval of time we say, "Oh, five minutes," but three hundred seconds from now can be a long, long time.

"Some people believe ..." Avshalom had picked up the photo of Sara, taken on her graduation day, and was examining it. Now he turned to face Raful, as if he too needed to record a reaction, any reaction. "Some people believe that you keep a woman in here, Raful." His attempt at good-humored laughter was a dreadful failure. "Some say, We need the office space, the Director has no right to keep it locked up, him having the only key."

"Some say this is where I make my nightly broadcasts to Baghdad and Damascus."

"But we checked. And you don't."

It hit Raful to know they had actually checked. Hit and hurt him. Such an unprofessional reaction. But then, preserving this room in the heart of the Mossad's nerve center was in itself so unprofessional that perhaps the implications it carried for others had passed him by.

"Why not keep it all at home, Raful?"

Because he had tried that, and it hurt too much to have her paraphernalia around him while he ate, when he slept or tried to sleep, and he couldn't bring himself to throw it away. Perhaps Avshalom guessed at least part of this answer from Raful's haggard expression, for he said, "You can't go on living it forever. There must come a time ..."

"Never."

"A time for letting go, Raful. Not for forgiveness, but—"

"She was blown apart, Avshalom." Raful swallowed. He could feel moisture on his own cheeks and he hated himself for that weakness, but the other man's austerity, his coldness, somehow drove him on. "Nothing left. Nothing you could identify." His voice rose to a wail, fell silent. He tried again. "She was twenty-two, she was lovely." He took the photograph from Avshalom and stared at it, shaking his head from side to side, as if by doing that he could somehow stem the tears that by now were flooding down his cheeks. "And they drove metal splinters through her face, her stomach, her legs...." He raised his eyes to Avshalom, a child pleading to be let off the rest. "They butchered her. She went to a party, a friend's engagement party, and they cut her up. She'd had no life to speak of. It was all starting for her. Avshalom, Avshalom ... *what if they'd done it to your Yigal?*"

Avshalom Gazit turned away, saying nothing for a while. At last he expelled a heavy sigh and said, "Open the envelope. Open it."

Sharett sat down at the small school desk. He had to wipe his eyes several times. At last he broke the red seals.

The envelope contained some fifty sheets of paper, typewritten, single-spaced. He skimmed through, finding the report to be in two parts. The envelope also contained some black-and-white photographs, but these he put aside, knowing instinctively that by doing this he was leaving the best for later.

He began to read. The first and longest section detailed the measures taken to establish the identity of the terrorists who had killed his daughter. With some of this material he was already familiar, some was new to him; some enraged him because he realized it must have been known to others, supposedly on the same side, for a long time, yet they had never shared it with him or recognized his need to know.

At an indeterminate point, while the shadows of afternoon softened and dissolved into one another, bringing down the short dusk, Avshalom Gazit left. Raful did not notice.

Only when he had finished reading the first section of the report did he turn to the photographs. Each was identified at the bottom by means of an adhesive-backed color-coded label. He spent longest on a full-face shot of a woman, and by the time the last of the light had gone, Leila Hanif's features were impressed on his brain as clearly, as indelibly, as his own daughter's.

Raful went to switch on the single light bulb that dangled from the ceiling by a few inches of flex before turning up the second section of the report.

Someone—the report did not state who, but Raful knew it must have been Avshalom Gazit—was proposing that a Wrath of God team be sent to kill Leila Hanif. The reason he knew that this proposal must have originated with Gazit was that normally Director Sharett would have had to be informed about any Wrath of God activities, but he had learned nothing of this and only Gazit could have kept it from him. Why would he do that? His way of neutralizing the poison that was eating its way through Sharett's soul like the acid that ate through his stomach wall? Gazit had guessed that Raful would have insisted on accompanying the Wrath of God; guessed rightly, too. Raful would have died for very shame if anyone else had succeeded in killing Leila Hanif.

Gazit's proposal had been rejected, for unspecified "operational" reasons. Strange, Raful thought, how in his mind this old friend had suddenly become Gazit. No longer Avshalom. Gazit.

He would get that rejection overturned. He would.

There were more photographs. A husband, Colin. And a son, Robbie. Raful sat in the pale yellow light for a long time while he committed to memory the features of the other two members of the Raleigh family, now all legitimate targets for him and the awesome forces at his command.

"What are you doing here?" Gazit had asked. At last Raful knew.

20 July: 0600: Heathrow

"ASI bugs and pitch index?"

"Checked."

Captain Simon Thorneycroft made a tick on his checklist.

"Clock, engine, and TLA bugs?"

"Checked."

Thorneycroft lifted the internal phone and dialed Alex Perkins. "All set," he said. "You?"

"Everyone's boarded, Captain. Ready for safety demonstration."

Thorneycroft nodded to his second officer. "Start clearance."

The copilot reached for the radio. "London Ground, November Quebec zero-three-three on stand Juliet Fourteen, for start-up?"

The hiss changed. Then—"November Quebec zero-three-three, clear to start. Call on one-two-one decimal nine for pushback."

At first Halib wasn't sure if the plane's rudder had really moved or if it was his imagination. He jammed the sight rings of his binoculars against his eyes until they smarted. A few seconds later, there could be no doubt: NQ 033 was heading for the taxiway.

He fetched the phone, placing it on a table in front of the window, and began to dial while keeping the glasses to his eyes, not looking at the digits, not needing to.

There were thirty more checks to perform during taxi. Then the aircraft held on the threshold of the runway, awaiting its turn for the sky. So early in the morning, traffic was light, and before long the passengers heard a murmur over the speakers: "Cabin crew take your seats for takeoff."

In the cockpit, Thorneycroft raised an eyebrow at his second officer, who nodded.

"Right, gentlemen, let's go to Bahrain. Three, two, one, *now*."

He pushed the throttles forward.

"Twenty knots ... fifty knots ... eighty knots ... airspeed building."

The plane already felt lighter in Thorneycroft's hands; he could sense its skittish desire to be airborne.

"One hundred knots."

"Power checked."

"V-one ... rotate."

As Thorneycroft used his palms to nudge the stick back, a frisky gust of wind celebrated the aircraft's return home to where it belonged and he compensated gently; then they were up.

When Halib was connected to Susannah Duclerc's suite he waited to hear his sister's voice before he spoke.

"This is just to let you know," he said, sounding almost brusque, "that your cargo got away safely."

NQ 033 was still a speck in his binoculars. While he waited for her to reply, his hand never trembled, keeping the plane in the dead center of his focal image.

"Thank you."

He replaced the receiver with a slight frown, not even sure if he had really heard those whispered words. Halib justly prided himself on his command of English nuance: it occurred to him that Leila's voice had sounded not so much distant as altogether absent.

20 July: Noon: Bahrain

The light had changed now. It was stronger, even less kind than before. Leila sat in front of the mirror, with this new, hostile light coming from her left. She looked strangely pallid. The eyes reflected in the glass were never quite still, not even when she stared directly into them. She could not control the flickering of her own eyes, and that failure, petty in itself, disturbed her.

She did not know how many hours had passed since Halib's last call, informing her that NQ 033 was airborne. She had eaten nothing today, nor was she hungry. The coffeepot had been replenished twice, that she did know, because the waiter's arrival necessitated action on her part, and she remembered action, always.

Her right foot had gone to sleep. She wriggled the toes, wincing slightly as life flowed back into them. Soon it would be time to go. Soon she would look at her watch, but not yet. Her inner self would tell her, to the minute, when to consult her watch, knowing in advance what the watch would say. She had been programmed, as a child, by reference to a particular moment, and ever since then she had revolved around that moment, gyroscopically, without fault or flaw. So many years, months, days, hours, since *then*.

Leila stared into the mirror but did not see herself. She saw a man without a face, just a black oval above the shoulders where a face would normally be. This was her old friend. Lover, almost. She could not live without this man. He gave her existence whatever meaning it had managed to retain since *then*.

The glorious old house called Kharif in the hills overlooking Beirut. For some reason she had a memory of blue sea and white waves that day, she did not know why: the angle was wrong for a view of the beach; from the upstairs rooms you could only see the Mediterranean far out, beyond the harbor, where sunlight made it almost colorless. But azure sea and white-streaked waves were part of the memory. Part of *then*.

Grandpa had been telling her a story about Babar the elephant king. At nine she was really too old for Babar, but she did love him so! And even more his queen, Celeste, because that name reminded her of Grandmother Celestine; Leila felt she would never, never outgrow those stories. Grandpa had the book on his lap, she could see it now across the years, oh, so clearly. Beside him, on a cane table, the bowl of strawberries mixed with raspberries, still wet from their shower at the hands of Azizza. Leila was frolicsome that day; the math test had made her top of the class; she let everybody know.

Grandpa had pretended to be incredulous. If only he'd taken her word for it, not teased her.... She'd half-realized he was joking;

then, as he carried the jest too far her confidence had slipped; she turned first indignant, then sulky, then cheeky by turns, until at last she had floated indoors aboard a fit of the giggles, intending to collect her workbook from her bedroom. Her proof.

But she'd gone no farther than the hall when the doorbell sounded once, twice. Not aggressively, not suggestive of tragedy, no; two rings, merely. Visitors! "I'll answer it," she had cried, happy that there were visitors, happy to be of service, of use. She forgot the rule of the household: Only Azizza may answer the door. Looking back, she could remember voices raised in protest, and here came the first of the mysterious blanks: in her brain, she *knew* that the voices were warning her not to answer the door, it was only the words that escaped her memory, she had never been able to recapture the words.

She flung open the door to see him there, her lover, her need. He was wearing a cream shirt open at the neck, and the triangle of visible chest was fiery red with sunburn; he wore cheap blue serge trousers and black lace-up shoes. Yes. Did you ever forget your first time? Any detail?

He wore a jacket. Strange, for such a hot day. A dark blue jacket that did not match the trousers underneath, and in one of the pockets something heavy made a bulge. Ah, no: be precise. The right-hand jacket pocket was the one dragged out of shape.

Only the face was another blank: void, a black oval.

He knelt down and said, "Hello, little girl." He spoke in French, a language she adored, though his accent sounded rough. A workman. "Is your grandfather around?" he said.

"Oh, yes. Go through." She pointed. "Down there, in the garden."

And having dispatched him on his way, Leila was wafted by a magic carpet woven from pride and laughter and a self-important conceit up the stairs to her bedroom, where she would find the red exercise book with a panel picked out in black on the front cover, space for her name, school, and form. She was pulling it out of her satchel when she heard two bangs, very close together. She felt nothing. Well, surprise, maybe. Because her room was at the back of the house, three steps took her to a window giving onto the garden. Grandpa's head had fallen into the berries, that was her first thought: all red, covered in scarlet berry juice, how funny! And she had laughed. She remembered that well, because she had not laughed again for over a year.

The screaming began. Azizza, hands held to her face. Halib, racing from nowhere, skidding to a halt, making of himself a statue in stone. No sign of her beloved, the one she needed, craved above all others—the man in blue with the bulging pocket; fickle, cruel, he had abandoned her.

Her heart thumped. Something was wrong. She knew exactly what was wrong.

She crept down. Her father, Feisal, had appeared. He was bending over Grandpa, who still lay half in and half out of his chair. Leila could see the bowl of berries on the table by his side. Untouched. By now her heart was racing like a little motor. Her head felt full, as though it would burst with the density of knowledge lurking there.

Feisal looked up, looked across Grandpa at Halib. He said, "Who let him in?" His voice was as she had never heard it before: appalled as if by some blasphemy that could not be forgiven.

Halib said nothing. He put an arm around Leila's shoulders. She was trembling. He pulled her close, letting her feel his solidarity, one and indivisible; just for a second, but a lifetime of solidarity he promised her. Then he was leading her inside, up to her bedroom. They sat down together on the bed, holding hands, and he continued to hug her to him. After a bit he began to rock her to and fro, silently, gently, while she quivered like a child in the last reaches of a mortal fever, and slowly, slowly, the light of Lebanon went out....

The light was changing again. In Bahrain, noon had brought suffocating wet heat and hazy horizons. The sea was transparent; dhows floated on nothing. Diamonds flashed in the windows of the buildings on the other side of the parking lot. Leila at last looked at her watch. Twelve-fifteen. Time to pack and go.

The car, a white Mercedes 500 SEL, was already on the forecourt as she left the hotel. She waited until they were traveling along the Corniche before reaching into her handbag and passing the driver her pistol. Her mind was not on the journey to al-Muharraq and the airport, however; she drifted, as always, in the amniotic fluid of memory, its prisoner and its child.

She had not seen Robbie for two years. Or Colin.

White-walled houses slid past on her left. Expatriate homes, for people like Colin Raleigh, who every Friday would get drunk in the bar of the Intercontinental, or the Ramada, or the Delmon. Houses with video machines, in a country boasting two cinemas, both of which showed only Arab-language films. Houses with empty bedrooms kept clean and aired, for when the children came out at the start of the school holidays.

He would be fourteen now. Manly, in his own mind, but still her boy. Everything was for him. She had not a thought in her body for anyone but Robbie, unless it was Halib, and him only sometimes. She loved Halib because he was her brother and he had saved her from destruction more than once, but Robbie she had fashioned from inside herself and he was hers.

She had been scheming to get him back ever since New York, but Halib restrained her. Halib would not authorize a kidnap in England, because he believed that Robbie was well guarded there. We must wait for a chance to lure him out of the country, he'd told her. So she had waited. Then six months ago Halib negotiated a contract with Iran for the release of some prisoners being held in Iraq. A political hijack, that was what the Iranians wanted, and Halib had agreed to provide one. Leila would carry it out. She had no scruples about that. She was good at her job and she liked working for her brother, because she could trust him not to let her down afterward, when the assignment was over. A lot of employers used terrorists and then disposed of them; not dear Halib. Not the beloved brother who had allowed her to target the plane on which her own son would be traveling, as a means of getting him back.

What would Robbie be wearing? she wondered. How would he have changed? Would he recognize her? Yes. He would know her, when their moment came. And soon she would discover all that had happened to him, over these past two empty, wasted years. She would hold him close, and they would talk, sharing secrets. "I love you," she would say. "I love you more than I've ever loved anyone, more than my own life. More than my soul—Allah forgive me!—more than my hope of paradise. My son, my son...."

She did not pause to consider how he might reply. Instead, her mind restlessly darted to the new flight crew, in whose professional hands she intended to place her own life and that of her son. She should pray for them.

The car glided to a halt beside the passenger terminal and a host of porters rushed forward. As Leila stepped onto the pavement she steeled herself to obey the will of Allah, the Compassionate, the Merciful, who would not deprive her of her child after such a desert of time spent without him. The flight crew would be wonderful. They would be perfect: *elect.*

Silently she repeated the *basmallah* to herself as she followed her suitcase inside: Allah, al rahman, al rahim.

Give me back my son.

20 July: Lunchtime: Airborne

Robbie examined his companion's tray with interest. "That looks good. Better than mine, anyway."

"I'm diabetic, that's why. I think it's every bit as pukey as yours."

Robbie, in the window seat, had found himself sitting next to a pale, freckled boy of about his own age called Tim Campbell. Tim's father worked for a bank in Kuala Lumpur and he was on his way out to join his folks for the holidays. At first the boys had played Dungeons and Dragons. Then came lunch, and the discovery that Tim was diabetic.

"You mean, you have to give yourself injections?"

"Yes."

"What would happen if you forgot?"

"I'd go into a coma and die. Don't even think about it; I should have stocked up before I left, and forgot. God, this stuff's revolting! What *is* it?"

"Broccoli, I think." Robbie jabbed two fingers toward some green substance lying on the side of Tim's flameproof tray and said, *"By all the powers of fire, be thou burned, be scorched, be charred—disruption!"*

The boys stared at the green stuff. "Those fire spells never work," Robbie observed gloomily. "I fancy a beer. You?"

Tim shook his head. "No, I mustn't."

"Bad luck. Hey, miss ... why do they never look your way when you want them?"

"Because they're busy chatting up rich studs, that's why." Tim pushed his specs back up his nose. "I do this trip twice a year. You have to be dying before they serve you. Mind you, that girl doesn't look so bad."

"She's stunning. Hey, your turn as Dungeon Master; I want to be a Cleric, this time. *Miss!* Yoo-hoo! ..."

Van Tonder had a window seat at the back of club class, on the starboard side. As Captain Thorneycroft pushed through the curtain that divided club from first, the South African was in full flood, abusing a flight attendant. Seeing Thorneycroft he stopped, glared, then turned back to the girl.

"You're a lucky young woman," he said witheringly. "I have the organ grinder now. *Thank* you."

"What seems to be the trouble?" Thorneycroft addressed his question to the girl, not the passenger.

"This gentleman, Mr. Van Tonder, was allocated the wrong seat in London and—"

"*And*, captain, when we land I shall be making a formal complaint concerning this airline's attitude to safety. Do you know what I found underneath my seat?" He paused for maximum effect, before holding up a half-burned cigarette. "This! Alight, let me say. *Alight!*"

Thorneycroft's face gave nothing away, but inside he was cursing. The audience, that was his real problem. Van Tonder's immediate neighbor had his head buried in a newspaper, and the rest of the cabin was silent as a communal grave. Complaints about amenities were one thing. Safety was another.

"Excuse me, but you are mistaken."

Thorneycroft diverted his gaze a fraction to discover that the passenger sitting by the window directly in front of Van Tonder had turned around; evidently it was he who had spoken, for now he went on. "I'd gone aft to check on my son, and as I came back this gentleman was in the act of picking up the cigarette. It was as you see it. Not alight."

"How dare you interfere?" spluttered Van Tonder. He half rose in his seat. "Are you accusing me of being a liar?"

"I'm saying that you are mistaken." Colin glanced up at the captain. "My name is Colin Raleigh, I witnessed the incident, and I'd be more than happy to give you my address in case this goes further. I'd just like to add, Captain, that your crew have dealt impeccably with this quite intolerable person, and they deserve medals. God knows, so do the rest of us."

Thorneycroft smiled and nodded his thanks. "Right," he said, turning back to the South African. "I'm sorry about the cigarette end you found, but we don't have total control over the cleaning contractors. If you want to persist in your allegation that it was alight, by all means do so. But there'll have to be an inquiry, and my company, it seems, has a witness on its side."

"You have no right—"

"Under international law, Mr. Van Tonder, I have the right to order you to be handcuffed to the floor for the duration of this flight, and if you continue to antagonize the other passengers that is what I shall do."

In the silence that followed, Colin became aware of engine noise for the first time and wondered how he could have failed to notice it earlier.

Thorneycroft winked at Colin and nodded renewed thanks before returning to the cockpit. His intervention seemed to have silenced Van Tonder, at least for the moment, for when Colin rose to visit the toilet he saw the South African fast asleep, a frown crumpling his face. His spectacles had slipped from his nose and were lying in his lap. He was snoring, offensive to his neighbors even in repose; but Colin, looking down at him, felt a sudden stab of irrational sympathy. Something had made Van Tonder the way he was: not the kind of something the man would have chosen for himself.

The rest of the flight to Bahrain passed uneventfully. Afternoon sunlight cast shadows across a hilly, maroon-colored landscape, which stretched as far as the eye could see. Then the engine pitch changed, Colin's ears told him of the pressure change as they descended, and he could make out distant gas flares over the sands, where Arabs in truth had money to burn. He watched, fascinated, until the sight of those scattered torches from the rigs eventually inspired him to think of his son. Robbie was fourteen now. Soon there would be girls. In love as in life, Robbie must navigate the desert between flares, somehow avoiding the Leila Hanifs of this world on the way.

At first the thought amused him; after a while it became unsettling and he went aft to find out how the object of his musings was getting on.

"There you are." The flight attendant gave Robbie a plastic cup and a miniature bottle of Johnny Walker. "Are you *really* eighteen?"

"Cross my heart and hope to die."

When Tim Campbell choked out a smothered laugh Robbie dug him in the ribs. "You must excuse my friend, he's not accustomed to the high life. Joke, geddit?"

The girl smiled. He *might* have been eighteen....

"Are you going all the way?" she asked.

"I will if you will."

More suppressed grunting from Tim Campbell, but Robbie's gaze was disturbingly direct.

"To Manila, silly!" Eighteen—twenty-eight, more like!

"K.L.," Robbie said. "Then on to Australia. Dad's teaching there. I'm going to meet my great-grandmother. She's, like, grossly antique. Seventy-something." He began to count off on his fingers. "There's Celestine, that's my great-grandmother; then there's her son, Feisal, he's fifty-six; then"—he colored; his fingering faltered for a second "—then there's my mum, she's thirty-six; then me. I forget how old everyone is exactly, but I know if you add all of us together it comes to a hundred and eighty-two."

"Are your mum and dad traveling with you?"

Robbie's cheeks boasted two high points of color that pulsated in time with his heart. "No," he said to the seat in front of him. "Dad's traveling business class; Mum, she's, they're ... they're divorced."

"Mine too," the flight attendant said after a pause. "It's rotten at first, isn't it."

Robbie nodded.

"How long ago did they split?"

"Two years."

"Same as mine."

He looked up at her, and now there was nothing cheeky about his expression. "How was it for you?" he asked, in a small voice, and it never even crossed the girl's mind that this could be more of the sexual tease he'd tried earlier.

She made a face. "Not so bad, really. At least we got some peace in the house. You?"

Robbie lowered his gaze. How to answer that question rationally? Tell her about the day he'd slit up the sofa cushions with a carving knife? No. The tears? She'd know about all that. Anger, then; should he tell her how much it enraged him that his mother had buggered off without a word?

"It was okay," he said firmly. "You get used to it pretty quick. Actually."

He cast around for some witty remark with which to smother the hissing tangle of emotions inside him. He composed his face and looked up at her, wanting her to know he thought her pretty, but instead his eyes first crossed, then locked onto those of his father, standing a few yards away up the aisle with an unreadable expression on his face.

"Oh-oh," he muttered. Then, "Is the captain of this plane called Spock?"

"No."

Robbie heaved a sigh. "Then am I in deep shit."

Long before Colin reached Robbie's seat he realized that he had no reason to worry and yet he ought to be worried to death.

A flight attendant stood in the aisle; something about her posture let Colin know that she'd been there a long time and was happy to stay. This puzzled him. Then, as he approached and the angle of his vision expanded, just for a moment he saw the boy through her eyes. In that second, before paternal mechanisms of self-preservation swung into play, what he saw was a stocky adolescent well past puberty, looking far older than his fourteen years, with all his equipment in full working order. Your son will go away soon, he seemed to hear a voice say. He'll find your ideas stale and you boring and he'll have better things to do. Like her, for example.

In the final instant before they became aware of him he saw the plastic tumbler on the tray and knew that orange juice wasn't that color. Robbie had persuaded the girl to give him a scotch.

Because he envied his son at that moment, and suffered the pain of knowing all he had lost, Colin would inevitably have said the wrong thing. So it was as well that the landing announcement came over the intercom just seconds after Robbie raised his eyes to catch sight of his father and blush. Colin raised a hand, smiled, and beat a retreat before the unsettling mixture of pain and pride inside him could show on his face.

He regained his seat just in time for final approach to Bahrain. Looking out, he caught a glimpse of ubiquitous whiteness ribboned by black roads, drifts of sand partly obscuring their tarmac. Then the plane was floating over the airport perimeter, for a breathless moment they seemed to hover, the back wheels touched down, and they had landed.

Leila Hanif did not go to the Dilmun lounge, although her first class ticket entitled her to do so. Instead she took the stairs to the coffeeshop on the terminal's mezzanine floor, whence she could look down on the crowded concourse milling with shoppers in search of duty-free bargains. She rested against the rail and kept her eyes fixed on gate number five.

She was, she thought, inured to tension. But when the TriStar nosed in to dock and came to a shuddering halt her heart shuddered with it, filling her with wonder. He was there, mere feet away from her. Robbie. Her son.

Leila wore a striking deep-purple ensemble: long skirt, jacket buttoned almost to the neck, and a silk scarf of like hue wrapped around her face in a compelling version of Islamic "lawful dress." Not only did this protect her from the importunate lusts of men, it provided a wholly effective disguise, so when passengers began to stream through the gate she did not withdraw.

Robbie was almost the last to come through the gate. He took a green transit card, smiling at the girl who gave it to him, and were it not for that smile Leila would have failed to recognize him, he'd changed so much. Forcing each breath into her lungs became a battle. Her mouth was dry; her tongue seemed to have swollen to twice its normal size.

He was so grown up—that was her first conscious thought. Already half a man; and she had not been able to imprint herself upon that man, how terrifying! How mortifying....

Colin had not left the plane, it seemed. He trusted Robbie alone. Leila's lips formed the faintest of smiles. If only he knew....

She came to herself to find that she had unconsciously begun to descend the stairway to the concourse, and froze. For the first time that day she knew a moment of uncertainty. What did she think she was doing? But then she continued down, rationalizing it as a sensible thing to do, much less likely to attract attention than turning back. Especially since Fouad had noticed her.

A young Arab wearing a smart gray suit, red tie, and matching handkerchief leaned against the transit desk, alternately trying to catch the eye of the harassed agent and surveying the concourse. His face did not change by so much as a millimeter, but Leila knew Fouad had registered her on the stairs, that probably he'd detected her hesitation as well. Essential not to worry him. Fouad was Halib's favorite, but Leila had never seen him tested to the limit.

Selim also would be around somewhere. Selim was the most invisible human being Leila had ever met, if "met" was the right word to describe contact with someone of such small signature. No one could ever give a half-good description of Selim. He'd once murdered an ambassador in a way that inspired even Leila's awe.

That day he'd been standing a little back from the fringe of the crowd, holding a child on his shoulders as if to give the lad a better view. Policemen, seeing the child, assuming that Selim was his father, actually helped him move to the front. When the ambassador's cavalcade was only a few feet away, Selim had dropped the child, drawn his revolver, and put four shells into the target's heart. Everybody was too busy trying to comfort the screaming little boy to recall the face of the man who'd abandoned him. No one, not even the police who had forced a passage for the doting father, could remember a single thing about Selim, then or later.

The other three hijackers under Leila's command were already aboard, having joined the plane in London. They had orders not to disembark while in transit.

She had reached the foot of the curving stairway. Deliberately turning in the opposite direction to the one Robbie had taken—a simple action requiring more of an effort of will than she'd expected—Leila made for the ladies' room. It was time to swallow the first of the amphetamines that would keep her going for however long it took. Also, there would be few opportunities to urinate after takeoff.

Raful, knowing it would not be clever of him to disembark at a Gulf airport, waited for the cleaners to finish before stretching his legs. He sauntered back into economy, exchanging nods and smiles with certain passengers, chatting to them as if they were strangers who happened to find themselves on the same flight. Not all of these passengers were strangers, however.

Raful was glad to note that Dannie Neeman had managed to grab seat 24H, halfway down the main economy cabin. They'd agreed beforehand that it would give the best advantage, the cleanest field of "fire"—although none of the Israeli team were armed in the conventional sense. Seat 24H meant pole position, as far as Raful was concerned, and Dannie, a favorite since New York days, was the man to occupy it.

He glanced at his watch: fifty minutes since touchdown. Refueling would be complete by now; they'd be boarding passengers shortly. He ought to take his seat; once back in business class Leila Hanif would be unable to see him. But instead Raful dealt with temptation in the time-honored way: by yielding to it. He lounged to the front of the plane and took up position beside a bulkhead, where he could get a clear view of the door without obstructing the aisle.

"You didn't get off?"

Colin Raleigh had come to stand next to him, hands in pockets. Damn!

"No, just taking a look at my fellow passengers," Raful answered good-humoredly. "Where are they going and why?—that kind of thing."

He swung around to lean against the bulkhead, easing Colin into a new position with his back to the door.

"Where are *you* going and why, I wonder?" said Colin.

But Raful made no reply, because at the far end of the jetway, where it made a turn, a figure had appeared. Someone he was expecting but couldn't be sure would come, however carefully he'd scattered bait in her path: a woman. For a moment he was so engrossed with this newcomer that he failed to notice Robbie coming through the aircraft door ahead of her.

Colin half turned when the boy touched his arm, and for a moment Raful tensed: *How could he fail to notice Leila?* "Your new traveling companion," Colin told him. "This is my son, Robbie."

Raful nodded, though his eyes remained fixed on the woman who was slowly advancing along the bridge. He withdrew slightly, not wanting her to see him. There was a chance, the merest chance, that Leila would recognize Raful Sharett, although she had only seen him once before, and then briefly.

He was aware of Colin explaining to his son that he had met him, Sharett, in New York, and wasn't that an amazing coincidence. *Idiot! Take the boy away before he sees her.*

He made small talk with Robbie, wanting to distract him from Leila, but when she was twenty feet or so short of the plane he sensed a fresh source of hot desert air entering the cabin and couldn't stop from looking over Robbie's shoulder. Yes! Someone had climbed up the exterior ladder from the apron and entered the jetway through a door beside the control panel: a workman, wearing the gray overalls and ID badge of a Bahrain Airport employee. He nodded at the soldier on guard, who evidently recognized him, for he smiled. Then this newcomer began to walk back along the jetway, toward the terminal. Toward Leila Hanif....

Raful forgot all about Robbie. His face set into a mask of concentration. Other boarding passengers partially obscured his view, but he knew what was going to happen. He saw the airport worker reach inside his overalls, saw Leila slip open her carry-on bag, already unzipped and ready to receive what the man dropped into it, noticed how skillfully she slid the zipper shut.

Earlier in the day, before coming to the airport, she would have handed her gun to someone with access to the airport apron, enabling herself to pass through all the security checks without hindrance. Now she had her weapon back again.

"How did you two meet?" he heard Robbie ask, and knew that the question was meant for him. "Where in New York ...?"

"Oh." Raful made an almighty effort, knowing how much depended on this. "Where was it, Colin? ... Look, I think they want us to go back to our seats, it's late."

He should have taken her out *here.* A civilized place, Bahrain: full of English influences, not wholly indifferent to certain aspects of the Israeli position ... he might have managed to spirit her away. He should have done it. Raful suddenly knew, with fearsome conviction, that he should. He was about to risk the lives of some two hundred innocent people on a revenge that was almost entirely personal. He might be a *goel,* an avenger of his daughter's blood, but he was not an animal, not on a par with the woman he'd hunted for so long. He felt the skin tighten along his brow and was conscious of sweat seeping down from his hairline.

A quick glance showed that, to his immense relief, Colin and Robbie had gone back to their seats, Robbie was now in business class. He withdrew still farther into the shadowy toilet recess, far enough to guarantee that she would not see him as she daintily stepped aboard, presenting her boarding pass as if it were a royal invitation, with a smile that showed in a creasing of the scarcely visible eyes. Exquisitely dressed, dignified of bearing, she diminished everyone around her. But within the hour, this woman would be as dead as the cohorts of corpses she had left to lie in the wake of her regal progress. As dead as Sara his daughter was dead; dead as Esther his wife and Ehud his friend were dead. Raful wiped the sweat from his forehead, drawing savage comfort from the reminder.

An attendant was closing the door, sealing it, ready for flight.

As Raful went back to business class he could not resist a last, long look at the woman sitting in first class, row 2.

She had taken a copy of *Gulf News*, the English-language newspaper, from her carry-on bag and appeared to be deep in its back pages. What did you think about, he wondered, as you counted down to a hijack? Did you put the finishing touches to your design, behind that placid mask of a face? Or were you so calm, so detached from the horror of it all, that you could study the small ads for real?

Leila kept her expression under control, but deep inside herself she was aware of disquiet. As she had taken the gun from her driver, transformed for the necessary few minutes into an airport baggage handler, she'd raised her eyes, expecting to see Robbie, and instead found herself looking straight at Colin Raleigh's back. He plainly hadn't noticed her, which was all that mattered, but she was angered by the way that one brief sight of him unsettled her. Leila stared at the advertisements for Filipina maids with no sense of what she was reading.

She must concentrate! She'd sworn to Halib she would complete the business of the hijack before giving any thought to the rescue of her son. As far as she was concerned she'd embarked upon a kidnapping pure and simple; but to Halib, who had made all things possible, it could only be a politically motivated hijack. First she must deliver the Iranian prisoners, and only then would she be free to continue with the real purpose of the exercise. So— the hijack....

Her ex-husband looked less tortured than she remembered him.
Think about the hijack!

Colin had shed a few years, to the point where he again reminded her of the man she'd met at Oxford, long ago. Slowly the newspaper descended into her lap. Colin had utterly ceased to exist for her. Utterly!

1969: Oxford

Halib waited until Colin Raleigh had reached the lift before closing the door of his suite and rounding on Leila.

"You are crass," he said. "To involve him, bring him here ... how could you be so stupid?"

"I was supposed to die quietly?" She flounced to the nearest sofa and threw herself down on it, gazing at her brother through sulky eyes. "How could *you* be so stupid as to send the boys after me? Eh?"

"Father sent them. And have a little respect—the boys are family too."

"Is that why they slapped me around? My own cousins! Great God, are you and Father both mad? In daylight, in a car park? Respect!"

"Father felt that when someone you love stops listening to the voice of reason, you take steps."

"Not in England, you don't. And anyway, is this how we deal with each other now—through intermediaries?"

"I wasn't consulted. Father needed me in Paris. I hadn't the least idea he'd asked Rafic to move in on you. Of course, if I'd known, I'd have stopped him." He came to sit down on the sofa next to Leila, putting an arm around her shoulders. "Seriously, angel, if you don't answer Father's letters ..."

"Is he angry?" Leila, so defiant a moment ago, sounded more like a cowed schoolgirl.

Halib nodded, gave her shoulder a squeeze. "Don't worry, he loves you; we all love you. Look, I'll have to make peace back home. Rafic was blaspheming his way to hell on the phone, he's terrified of Feisal. You and your friends screwed everything up. Tell me what's troubling you."

"Well." Leila shrugged in a deliberately theatrical way, bringing a smile to Halib's lips. He had this very special, lovely smile, which cracked his face into concentric circles; she'd only seen that particular pattern of lines on a few young faces, always Arab, and she found it irresistible. If Halib had not been her brother, he would have made such a perfect husband....

"Father's started to nag," she went on, not meeting his eyes. "In his letters he keeps on about how he wants me to promise to come home and stay there."

"So? You've finished your finals now; what's keeping you?"

"I could stay on. Perhaps do a doctorate."

"And what would Yusif have to say about that? Your fiancé is keen to become your husband. Anyway, how can you do a doctorate when you only got a second-class degree?"

"Not here. Bristol. Or maybe Edinburgh."

He stared at her blankly. "What's wrong with St. Joseph? Or the American University in Beirut?"

"They're in Beirut; gracious, isn't that enough?"

"Oh, come, poppet." He laughed, gave her another hug. "You make it sound like hell."

"Well, it is," she flared. "Father wants me in the business. And don't call me poppet!"

"Banking's an excellent business to be in."

"Oh, come on, Halib! You know as well as I do what our business is. Rafic spelled it out: we're Shia Muslims, we're one of thirty families controlling the entire hash crop, in Beirut we're fighting for our very survival, and we're in up to here with the PLO. We're zaim—leaders! Mafia!"

He released her and shifted away, partly to look at her better and partly, she felt, to distance himself from the possibility of contamination. But Leila, carried away by a message she had waited too long to deliver, could not be stopped.

"I love Europe, England. Here I don't need a bodyguard, or an armored car. I want to live a normal life, Halib! An ordinary person, with a nice husband and a baby or two."

"Raleigh, for instance?"

"Of course not! He just happened—" Something clogged her throat, and she blushed; the flow of blood was not so much hot as painful. "Will you shut up about Colin and listen to what I'm saying?"

"But it's a dream, Leila."

"It is *not!*"

"An unattainable dream. What you're saying is that you want to go through life in neutral. And where we come from, there are no neutrals. There are Maronites; there are Muslims, F'listins, and Israelis."

He did something vile to that last word, giving it unwonted, sinister sibilance: "Ish-*r'eye*-lees."

"You can't make me fight against my will."

He stood up and went across to the dresser, where he picked up a pack of Black Russians and lit one, deliberately exhaling a lungful of smoke in her direction as if it were a curse.

"I can make you do anything, Leila. All I have to do is remind you of a certain day, when you admitted to our house a certain Ish-*r'eye*-lee agent."

She stared at him, unable to credit that he could use so foul a weapon against her. Then, seeing him about to continue, she raised both hands to cover her ears, violently shaking her head from side to side.

"An agent of the Mossad. Now a general. He came in with a gun and he shot dear old Grandfather Ibrahim, shot him dead, bang-bang, all because a little girl with no more brain than a centipede—"

"Stop it!"

"—thought it would be fun to open the door to anyone who knocked."

"You're so unfair! I was just a child. No one had told me; if you wanted me to be more careful, you should—" But she was shouting through tears now, the words came out distorted, and Halib wasn't listening anyway.

"'Who let him in?' That's what Feisal wanted to know. But I took you away and I fought for you, Leila, fought for a day and a night, until Father no longer wanted to hang you up by your pretty ... little ... thumbs."

He shook the black cigarette at his sister as if aiming to dislodge the ash on her lap.

"You ... let him in. The Ish-*r'eye*-lee. The killer. You."

Leila keeled over on the sofa and lay there sobbing. They were dry sobs. Her whole body shook, but no sound came out.

"So we swore a holy oath, to be revenged. And every year, on the anniversary of sheikh Ibrahim's death, we have renewed it."

"Not Celestine." Leila sat up, straightening her hair with rough sweeps of the hand. Guilt was giving way to anger. "Grandmother never swore. She said it was an oath against the spirit of the Holy Koran."

"She was weak. But *you* swore."

"I was *nine*. A child is only a child."

"And an oath is only an oath? No, Leila." He paused, looking around the room as if in search of inspiration. "See here...."

He went across to the hide briefcase that Colin Raleigh had so admired, half an hour before, and carried it over to where she was sitting.

"This stuff isn't real, of course." He opened the lid. "But it's how it will look on the day."

She gazed down at the arrangement of wires, the gray putty-like substance, at the slide switch, at all the mundane apparatus of indiscriminate death, and suddenly she felt exhausted. She wanted to go away and find a hole in the ground, crawl into it, and never come out.

"You can't be serious." The words were wrung out of her in such a flat, toneless way that she felt them inadequate and tried again. "You can't be serious."

"If Father wants you to go home," Halib said, "you'd better go. That's all."

"I won't."

"We are at war, Leila."

"Our clients are at war!"

"It comes to the same thing. Their cause is our cause, for the moment."

She stared up at her brother, aware of something new in him. "You enjoy this," she said slowly, "don't you?"

He nodded. "To have important, interesting work; yes, it's good. I don't have to preach to you about the F'listin catastrophe."

"Palestine. The English word is not F'listin, it's Palestine."

"So? You're losing your roots, know that? Our enemies stole a country from a gentle, decent, farming people and made it into a fortress against all Arabia, against all the world. And they killed our grandfather in cold blood, because he bankrolled F'listin resistance."

"They *said* he did. That was a lie."

Halib laughed. "Of course it wasn't a lie."

She caught her breath. "How dare you say such a thing?"

"Because it is *true!* Ibrahim believed, passionately, that Palestine was Islamic 'from the river to the sea.' So he lent the PLO millions of *liraat.*"

Leila's face had turned white, except for two unhealthy blotches in her cheeks. She was breathing heavily. Halib, seeing the state she was in, relented.

"Poppet, angel: listen, I love you, eh? 'My brother and I are against my cousin; cousin, brother, and I are against the stranger.' That's how it is."

"Not the whole of it." She stood up. "If you're going to quote, quote the first bit, too: 'I am against my brother.' That's how it starts. 'I am against my brother; my brother and I are against—'"

"I see." Halib's voice was tight. "You say that to your *own* brother."

"If you accuse Grandfather of collaborating with those ... those Palestinian butchers, then you are not my brother. I don't know what you've become, but you're not my brother."

"He only supported them because he was naïve! *Y'Allah!* Can't you see the tip of your own nose? *He* didn't realize that every cent went on Mercedes-Benzes and Katyusha rockets!"

"He never did that. Never, never, *never!*"

Halib's fists clenched, matching her own; related and riven by blood and a legacy of hatred, they teetered on the brink of saying unforgivable things. In the silence, Leila's brain caught up with words she'd uttered unthinkingly: "You're not my brother." They'd spewed out because she would have said anything to fight him. But now she realized that truly this man, whom she'd loved to distraction all her life, was a false deity.

If Leila thought about it for a second longer she would come face-to-face with the reality. So she did the only thing possible in the circumstances. She ran away.

Later she had no recollection of how she got down to Beaumont Street. She came to herself on the corner of the High and Cornmarket, hearing bells chime five o'clock. She looked around her, saw the comfortingly strong-looking wall of a bank, and went to lean against it. After a while her legs failed her; she had to slide down the wall and sit on the pavement, where people cast glances varying from sympathetic to censorious before hurrying on.

Time passed. More bells. Leila raised her head. She could not stay here on the pavement outside Nat West forever. She stood up, aware now, painfully aware, of the stares of others. She began to drift down the High. There was no one she could turn to, nowhere she could go. This, then, was desolation. The outer darkness. Hell.

Numbers jostled for attention inside her head. After she had walked a long way, they coalesced into recent memory: sixty-two. And there was a one also, to be fitted in. Number 62 on the High, first floor. Colin's place.

Perhaps she could talk to Colin about the way her life had just ended.

For a long time she stood on the pavement by the junction with Longwall Street, gazing up at the frontages opposite. The house, one of a pinched terrace, did not look like much. Its windows obviously hadn't been cleaned for ages. Did she really want to go in there?

At home the old women used to shake their heads in token wisdom and mutter, "Do not trust a man and a woman alone together for any longer than it takes for water to run out of a jar...."

Well. She was climbing the stairs. She was knocking on some-one's door. Nobody in. But when she tried another one it opened to reveal Colin standing there, so tall and straight. His face looked honest. It concealed nothing.

She was going in. Accepting tea. Listening to music that brought a kind of solace.

She was lying across his knees on a sofa while he stroked her hair, and the soft mauve light of an Oxford evening leached away to silence and peace.

20 July: 1530: Bahrain

During the one-hour refueling stop, Simon Thorneycroft yielded command of NQ 033 to his replacement, Roger Morgan. The new captain ordered eighty tons of fuel for the flight to Kuala Lumpur, giving him a global takeoff weight of approximately two hundred and fifteen tons all told: a heavy mass to bring to takeoff speed in the gulf heat. He set his flaps to 10 degrees and elected to use the full length of runway thirty. He was two thirds of the way along it before they reached the critical V-one speed beyond which the takeoff could not be aborted. As Second Officer Adrian Ross called "Rotate" and Morgan palmed the yoke backward, a huge flock of gulls rose out of nowhere, circled, and flew straight toward the plane at an angle of 20 degrees.

Morgan swore. The copilot and flight engineer held their breaths. Black shapes thudded against the windshield, and the crew ducked, cowering in the face of a potential disaster they were powerless to prevent. Just when they thought they were out of it, the port engine, engine number one, coughed and surged.

"Airspeed?"

"One-ninety, building.... Jesus!"

Suddenly power drained away from engine one and the plane lurched sideways. Morgan wrestled with the yoke, pulling her up and out of trouble, desperate to do only one thing: increase his speed to the point where the loss of his port engine would not cause them to crash.

"Peter, what have we got?"

Flight Engineer Peter Hudson cast a swift eye down the bank of dials in front of him. "Power on one rising through seventy percent, increasing; two and three both at one hundred percent."

"Radio tower and report; we'll climb while we work out a course of action. Get permission to stack."

While copilot Adrian Ross obeyed this order, Morgan allowed the TriStar to talk to him through the yoke in his hands. He knew the hideous devastation a bird strike could cause. A single animal, sucked into the front of one of the big jets, could break any number of fan blades before being minced into a porridge of blood, feather, and bone. Not all the damage occurred at once, not always. There was a real danger that they might climb to cruising altitude before a critical number of damaged fan blades finally gave way, causing the engine to fail. Then he would be forced either to continue on two-thirds power or seek an emergency landing. But if he turned back to Bahrain, only to find that damage was minimal and the plane was passed fit to fly, he would have cost his employers thousands of pounds in lost fuel, time, and passenger goodwill. It boiled down to a commercial decision, one that only the captain could take.

"What readings?" he asked.

"All three engines now producing one hundred percent power."

"We go on. Notify Bahrain and request resumption of filed flight plan."

Back in the passenger cabin, there had been a few white faces as the plane made its sudden lurch while still only a few hundred feet above the runway, but when nothing else happened the incident was soon forgotten. Leila unfastened her lap strap the moment the NO SMOKING sign was extinguished. As the seat-belt sign went off she was already on her feet, moving down the aisle toward the port-side first class toilet. She clicked the bolt shut, placed her bag on the seat, and drew out the pistol her driver had handed over on the jetway: a Heckler & Koch P7 which she'd chosen for its easy squeeze-cocking grip.

As she silently pulled back the door bolt her heartbeat was normal. She felt buoyant, alert. The only physiological change showed in her hands: they were tingling slightly, as if recently dipped in ice water.

She came out of the toilet, keeping the pistol concealed in her palm, before turning right, into the galley area, and immediately left again. Now she was by the cockpit door. Two flight attendants, furiously loading trays, paid her scant attention. She picked up the handset lodged above the crew seat and punched in 31, the flight-deck extension.

Second Officer Ross answered. "Yes?"

"Coffee coming in." She turned a dial on the handset's rest to ANN, for Announcement, and spoke the single word "Medina." It could be heard throughout the plane.

She replaced the handset and turned swiftly to find the two flight attendants staring at her. One of them started to speak, saw the gun, and fell silent. At the same moment, the door to the flight deck swung open, unlocked from inside by the flight engineer.

As soon as the seat-belt sign went off Raful moved forward, through the curtain separating business from first class. He kept to the starboard side of the plane. Stepmother's seat was empty; she must have gone to the toilet, probably to collect weapons. He took up position in such a way that he could cover the galley area and cockpit. He was fingering the cigarette lighter that Yigal had given him, but for the moment he kept it concealed in his pocket.

A flight attendant looked up impatiently. "Can I help you, sir?"

"No, thanks. Waiting for the toilet."

She glanced at the warning light. The words TOILETS OCCUPIED remained unilluminated. "There shouldn't be a holdup," she said pointedly, but Sharett merely did a Raful, like the old rascal he was, and the girl could not but grin.

Raful heard the lavatory door being unlocked and started across the galley. Before he reached the midway point Leila had spoken to the flight deck and issued her men the order to engage:

"Medina." Now she was turning, gun in hand. Raful had waited a long time for this moment. He was smiling for Esther and Sara, and for Ehud Chafets, too; but mostly he was smiling for Sara.

By now the aircraft was well out over the Gulf. It had reached 3500 feet and was climbing at an angle of seven degrees, speed up to 280 knots and increasing. Captain Roger Morgan flicked the stabilizer to retrim, noticing the reassuringly familiar feeling of sloppiness in his controls, and told himself that number one engine would hold. Five minutes after starting his roll, Bahrain Departure handed him over to Dubai ATC on the horn of Oman.

"November Quebec zero three three, you are cleared for fifteen thousand feet. Await my word to leave zero nine-two degrees for a right turn onto vector one-one-eight degrees."

"November Quebec zero three three, awaiting your direction."

The handset beeped. Second Officer Ross picked it up. "Yes? … Ah, great, wait a second."

He replaced the receiver. "Coffee up, chaps. Let her in, would you, Peter?"

The flight engineer reached back to unlock the cockpit door. As he turned the handle, something exploded in Roger Morgan's left ear. His eyes shot to the red light flashing on his panel.

"Compressor surge! Massive compressor surge."

The plane yawed violently to port and dropped straight through a hole in the sky.

"Engine one out!"

Ross tightened his grip on the yoke, fighting for control, while Morgan tersely reported the loss of his port engine to Dubai ATC. The aircraft went into a steep curve, turning on its left wing tip.

The flight engineer, glued to his instruments as he tried to work out what had gone wrong, was vaguely aware of a commotion outside the cockpit: shouts, glass breaking, a scream. Panic, he thought. *Damn!*

Morgan's fingers went automatically to the engine start switches at the base of the central panel. He heard the APU force compressed air through the dead jet and knew a second of relief. Ross was getting ahead of the turn now; the left wing tip was coming up as he reduced power to the starboard engine and stabilized the aircraft on a new course heading.

The dead port engine whined, failed, and fired. "Ten percent and climbing," Hudson said. "Fifteen percent power and climbing steadily."

Then a new voice said, "I have the aircraft, Captain. Do not touch the radio. Prepare to adopt a new course."

A woman had spoken. As Morgan turned he registered, in a confused way, that her voice was not quite English and not quite foreign either, but it was a hard voice, accustomed to command and be obeyed. He saw the gun held to his flight engineer's neck, saw the face above the gun, knew at once he had a problem beyond the reach of the psychologists and their textbook solutions.

His left hand strayed beneath the arm of his seat, where a black button was set flush with the panel. He pressed it quickly, knowing that the slightest delay could prove fatal. The button activated an emergency transponder. From now on it would send a "77" signal to the ground, causing NQ 033's image to blink on the radar screens. The world already knew that this plane had been hijacked.

"I have the aircraft," she repeated. She was looking at his left hand and had a secret smile on her face; Morgan realized that she knew about the transponder. She'd wanted him to activate it.

A man appeared on the threshold of the cockpit. He was holding what looked at first like a grease gun; in fact, an American M3A1 submachine gun. Morgan's gaze shied away from the woman to the weapon. He'd always secretly believed this could never happen to him, never on any aircraft he commanded.

Now he was facing Adrian Ross across the central console. "Maintain present course, altitude, and speed. Engineer, continue to call engine performances."

"Acknowledged."

The other two members of the flight crew spoke simultaneously in the flat, unemotional tones that hijack manuals demanded, deliberately ignoring the terrorists at their backs.

Leila Hanif advanced to the front of the flight deck. From there, she had an unimpeded view of the Gulf through the windshield, while being able to cover both pilot and copilot.

"You lost an engine," she said matter-of-factly. "What happened?"

Morgan told her, making no concessions to the layman. She appeared to understand his technical jargon, however, for when he had finished she asked him a question about the RB211 engine's static thrust. That shook Morgan. Flight Engineer Hudson had to supply the answer.

Leila listened carefully to his explanation, then said, "Reverse thrust will be unaffected?"

"An engine is an engine. If it works in forward, it'll work in reverse."

"Very well. Bring me your high and low altitude topographical charts. You! Copilot! Move slowly; make sure I can see your hands all the time. Any tricks and he"—A nod at Selim, guarding the doorway—"has orders to shoot out your windshield. We will all be sucked out to our deaths; the plane will crash; you can choose to murder two hundred passengers or you can obey me. This order stands until we are on the ground."

She spoke carefully, without passion or discernible fear. The three members of the flight crew looked at one another, searching for encouragement, finding none. Ross lifted his hands and slowly rose. He edged past Leila, forced so close to Selim that he could smell the man's pungent sweat diluted by a sickly sweet cologne, and took the charts from the locker.

"Which ones?"

"Tactical pilotage chart, sheet TPC J-seven-D. South Yemen."

Captain Morgan knew then that his aircraft was in the hands of an expert, and all thought of staging a recovery left his mind.

"Your target reference is XU three-one-one-zero."

She thrust the map at Morgan, who quickly folded it so that only the lowest sectors were visible. "You want me to put her down *there?*"

"Yes."

He tried to make sense of the terrain. The point she had designated was to the north of Al Ghaydah, on Qamar Bay. "Flat rock," said the map; "sea level."

"What's there?" he asked sharply.

"Nothing is there."

"What kind of surface?"

"Volcanic rock: flat, but with some loose gravel. Let us see if you are a genuine pilot or merely a computer clerk."

"And the engines?" Morgan spoke quietly, trying by his manner to instill reason into her, knowing it was hopeless. "Do you realize what will happen to the jets if anything bigger than a pebble gets into them?"

"The blades will buckle and break; the engine will fail. That is not a problem. Your 'runway' is over three miles long, and you will not be leaving Yemen under your own motive power. Contact Dubai ATC; tell them the new course that I read to you. I will be listening, Captain Morgan. Do not make requests; *tell* them your demands."

Morgan's face was white. Sweat trickled down his forehead, stinging the corners of his eyes.

"Listen to me," he said. "Please listen to me."

Leila motioned angrily at Selim. He marched forward, raising his submachine gun level with the windshield, and snapped back the bolt.

"*Stop!*" Morgan squeezed the yoke, fretfully trying to think of a way to stall, to save his passengers and crew. "I'll ... I'll do it. Just ... calm down."

"It is I who am calm, Captain Morgan. Now. The radio."

Behind them, the passenger cabin was almost totally silent. Almost: a baby cried ceaselessly, and every so often a teenage girl at the back of the economy cabin would utter a whimper before biting the back of her hand. Nobody else uttered a sound.

They were watching the new officialdom.

Like most people, the one hundred and eighty-four passengers aboard NQ 033 unconsciously recognized that their lives were ordered by others. Civil servants, policemen, judges, politicians, those who ran the big industrial conglomerates: they were the powers who conspired at one and the same time to deprive others of their freedom of action, while convincing them that they had never been more free. Free will, free choice: these were largely illusions, but they were cherished illusions. Now the passengers had come face-to-face with a very different reality.

On hearing the single word "Medina" spoken over the loud-speaker, five men had risen simultaneously from their seats. Four others had followed suit so quickly that they seemed to be part of the same team, rather than the opposition. Despite their numerical inferiority the odds were on the Israeli side, because they knew what to expect and their enemies didn't. If the port engine hadn't failed, the odds would have favored an Israeli victory. But when the plane lurched, dropping several hundred feet, those odds evened themselves out on the floor of the plane, along with the nine men in whose hands the fate of the passengers now depended. The Arabs were milliseconds quicker, that's all.

The first class passengers were sent back to the economy cabin, along with the cabin crew. One gunman kept business class covered; two others stood by the toilets at the back of the plane, from where they could survey the whole of the economy cabin. Fouad was dealing with the four Israelis who had identified themselves by standing up in an attempt to frustrate the hijack. He found no firearms, just a selection of oddities: aerosols that didn't seem to work, penknives with strangely tinted blades, cigarette lighters that refused to open. All these he pocketed, before forcing the Israelis to lie on the floor, hands clasped to their necks, until Selim came back down the aisle to help bind them fast.

All except Dannie Neeman, in seat 24H. Dannie had not risen with his colleagues; he had obeyed orders and remained seated, for it had always been Raful's intention to keep him in reserve. Now he sat staring stonily to the front, wondering if his false Kuwaiti passport would stand up, mentally practicing his Arabic, and praying with all the considerable passion at his command that Raful might yet be alive.

Robbie, too, wished that Sharett would live.

The hijackers had overpowered the Israeli and dumped him in the vacant seat next to the boy's, where he lay like a shapeless sack of flour and of the same color. Blood ran down his cheeks, enhancing their pallor. Robbie wanted somebody to talk to, wanted comfort from his father, but all he had was this unconscious stranger whose blood-soaked head lolled on his chest with the pathetic helplessness of a broken doll's.

Robbie's bag lay on the floor between his feet. He waited until the hijacker guarding their cabin was looking the other way, then rummaged around inside it until he found notepaper and a pen.

Dear Celestine, he wrote. *We're not going to make it. Maybe someone will find this.* He swallowed. He could not think what to write. All he knew was that he should leave some testament to what was happening, draw a line under his short life. His pen hovered over the paper. *I know I'm going to die.*

He was not alone: other passengers begged total strangers in nearby seats to pass on last words to loved ones, if they succeeded in getting out. As the minutes ticked away into eternity, the people on that plane discovered things they had not previously known about themselves. They learned how extreme fear sends adrenaline coursing through the system in overdrive, producing unendurable back pain. Their bladders distended to limits they'd never been meant to bear. Cold descended over them like an invisible blanket of snow, chilling their feet to the point where they could no longer feel them. Prayers, long forgotten, elbowed their way back into minds suddenly grown receptive. God revealed himself to many, collecting promises of better conduct hereafter, if only they could be given another chance. But once the initial shock diminished, for the most part the passengers simply focused on how best to ingratiate themselves with the ones who mattered.

The light had started to go by the time NQ 033 arrived over South Yemen. Morgan was surprised that no fighters had come to intercept him.

"What do I do if I'm attacked?" he asked.

"You will not be attacked."

He believed her. He could smell sweat and gun oil, but these scents did not originate with the woman. She smelled as she looked: like something out of the Arabian Nights. She had planned this down to the last detail, and if she did not fear aerial attack then neither did he.

He had plenty of other things to worry about.

"There?"

Morgan looked down through the windshield and his voice was hushed. Ross whistled softly through his teeth.

"There," the woman confirmed. "You can have contact with my men on the ground, if you wish. The frequency is eighty-nine decimal two. They will give you details of wind and visibility."

From his seat on the port side, Morgan saw an indigo sea lying almost dull in the late afternoon sunlight. Beyond that, a coast of white sand, with mountainous black cliffs to the west. He was steering magnetic north; far ahead the red Jabal Al Fatk stretched across his flight path like a ridged palate. The land below was flat, utterly featureless. What looked like a vast forked estuary narrowed into deep wadis at the foot of the mountain range, and by craning his neck he could see the small conurbation of Al Ghaydah. According to his charts, there was a minor airfield there, with a soft landing surface only, but nothing rose up out of the mauve twilight to intercept him, and his radio remained silent. Since communicating his new circumstances and course to Dubai ATC, no one had tried to contact him at all.

The absence of military interference both reassured and worried him. He knew of times when fighters had flown slowly in front of commercial aircraft under hijack, forcing them to lose speed and consequently height. Sometimes the fighter pilot got it wrong, causing the civilian plane to crash. But why was nobody apparently interested in their fate?

As if reading his thoughts, Leila said, "South Yemen is a communist country, one of the poorest in the world. You are entering its easternmost province, the Sixth Governorate, Al Mahra. There are almost no roads, the scattered tribes cannot speak Arabic, the government itself does not claim to control its hinterland. It is desolate beyond belief, lonely beyond description; there is nowhere like it in this quadrant of the globe, which is why I chose it."

"Any fire-fighting equipment on the ground?"

"None."

Morgan gripped the yoke harder. "I'll need a fly-past at a thousand feet," he said at last. "And I'll need to ditch fuel. Right down to the stack pipes."

"As you wish. You are as aware as I am that without fuel the aircraft's air-conditioning units will rapidly fail. The weather is hot and humid; I cannot tell you when your ordeal will end."

"I can't risk landing with all this fuel aboard."

"It is your choice. If you jettison down to the stack pipes, you will still be left with ten or eleven tons. Call the ground now, please."

She had not used the word "please" before. Morgan chalked that up as a minor victory. He did not register that it was merely the first of her steps along the path toward subverting him.

Ross made contact on the frequency she had given him, recording visibility, wind speed, and direction. The man on the ground spoke clear English, though it plainly was not his first language.

"What is your QNH?" Ross asked. The voice answered with sea-level air pressure, and the copilot automatically reset his altimeter without noticing that whoever was on the ground must have done this before. But Morgan understood, and once again he experienced the by now familiar crawling sensation along the nape of his neck. When the voice added a vector for final approach, the impression hardened. These people were technically perfect.

He circled counterclockwise, because that way the port wing tilted down and he had a better view of the ground, reducing height all the while. The surface looked flat as an ice rink. At three thousand feet, he couldn't see the gravel, but his mind had insidiously come to accept whatever the woman told him, and he knew the gravel was there.

He called for the log, not content to rely on memory. His plane was hardly new, but it had only flown thirteen hours since its last B check, when every system would have been examined and either passed or replaced. Short of a full month-long overhaul, it was the toughest inspection an aircraft could undergo. In theory she was as capable as the day she received her airworthiness certificate. And by God, thought Morgan, she'd better be.

He put away the log and looked down. Somebody had lit a fire. No, more than one ... four pillars of dense black smoke billowed into the air, seemed to hover, then began slowly to drift from left to right, toward the sea. They pinpointed the four corners of an elongated rectangle. The runway.

Morgan glanced at Ross. "What do you think?"

Ross compressed his lips and drummed twice on the side of the yoke. Morgan understood. His second officer was saying, If it's flat enough, and broad daylight, you can put her down anywhere. Which was true, as far as it went.

Morgan glanced up at Leila. "I'm going to fly due east, out to sea, very low. If it's *yes*, I'll come around and start my approach. If *no* ..."

"It will be *yes*."

"And if I judge we can't make it, what then?"

Leila replied with a shrug, "Then we shall go our separate ways, we to heaven and you to hell."

Morgan looked into the glossy darkness of her eyes, saw the charcoal glowing there, and told himself, She means it. He took the TriStar down to a thousand feet and let Ross fly her while he stood to peer through the left-hand windshield panel. Smoke clouded his vision for a second; then they were through and climbing again to a safe height.

Ross looked at him questioningly. Morgan felt the wetness on his back and tried to ignore it, tried to clear his mind. "All right," he said at last. "It's a go."

Leila did not relax by so much as one iota. Indeed, her concentration seemed to wind itself up in tune with Captain Morgan's, while he dictated flap settings, altitudes, vectors. All the while the two pilots were conscious of her listening, monitoring their discussion more closely than any of the company's test captains, astute to detect the first hint of trickery.

"I will do the landing," Morgan announced. "No one else is to have any responsibility at all. Is that understood?"

Ross said yes.

"Peter?"

A momentary hesitation; then the flight engineer nodded.

"All right. I have the yoke. Speed brakes ... three, two, one, *now*."

The plane shuddered and perceptibly slowed. They were coming around, into the wind, still far out over the Arabian Sea, and the sun was in Morgan's eyes. He nudged the nose down, keeping his speed constant, and began a standard series of landing checks, as if they were making a daylight approach to Heathrow: fuel reserve, altimeters, flaps.

Ross picked up his mood. His hands no longer grasped the control column as if it were the only thing between him and the abyss. This was his world, the one he knew best, the one he'd been trained for, and as long as he could take refuge inside it, working from second to second, he feared nothing and no one.

They calculated throttle settings in case they had to abort, although both of them knew they were only going to get one shot at this. Through the windshield they could see the four great bonfires gliding up toward them, inexorably as on the simulators, only this was real and the rock was real and if they misjudged the approach there would be no friendly voice over the intercom saying, "Ouch! Why not run it through again, Rog?"

"Speed: two hundred thirty knots."

"Flaps eighteen."

The flaps extended, the aircraft shuddered again and sank. The bonfires were billowing up now, in vast towers that seemed to fill their vision.

"Two twenty knots."

"Gear down."

A distant rumble. "Gear down and three green lights."

"Anti-skid five releases."

Speed dropped dramatically. Morgan edged the plane onto its final approach path, boosting the throttles to overcome the danger of a stall on the turn.

"One ninety knots."

"Flaps twenty."

"One eighty ... full flaps, forty-two."

At five hundred feet, the runway was one and a half miles away. Just in time, Ross remembered to turn on the seat-belt sign, make a hurried announcement. In the passenger cabin, people braced themselves. They were noisier now. Many were crying or praying aloud. "Mary," one man kept shouting. "Mary, Mary, Mary...."

The hijackers strapped themselves into rear-facing crew seats, keeping their weapons trained on the cabins.

Raful Sharett lay slumped in his seat. Leila had chopped him when the engine failed. Blood streaked his face; a strip of skin had been torn back from his skull, revealing white bone. With every jolt of the plane his body shook, a helpless doll. He moaned, licked his lips, opened his eyes. Where was he?

Robbie folded up his letter and stuffed it into the seat flap in front of him. He gripped his knees and tried hard not to think about what would happen next. *Dad,* said a small voice inside his head. *I love you.* And then, he wasn't sure why: *I'm so sorry I wasn't a better son ... I'm so sorry, Dad ... Mum.* At the word *Mum* a tear trickled down his cheek and he dashed it away, but he could not still that small voice, not even when it suddenly burst out, *Why, why, why did you have to go away?*

In the cockpit Leila slid onto the observer's seat and shouldered the belt.

"Four hundred feet," Ross said. "A hundred to go ... three hundred, *decision height!*"

And Morgan answered him, as smoothly as if calling a bridge hand, "Continuing. Touchdown at one hundred and fifty knots."

"That's too high!" Ross's voice came out almost in a scream.

"I'll need the control on that surface. Now *be quiet and fly!*

One hijacker had been left to cover the Club Class cabin. Raful's eyes focused painfully on him, sitting upright and alert in the crew seat. Sometimes he looked down the port side of the plane, sometimes the starboard. Raful's right hand strayed to his pocket, made contact with a hard object....

Meanwhile, Morgan was planing between the first pair of bonfires and he was too high; Ross's shout had thrown him, *damn,* nose down, left rudder, just a touch, *just a touch....*

He throttled back.

The plane shuddered; Raful Sharett saw the hijacker's watchful eyes squint in apprehension. Now or never. He leaned forward, bringing his head as close as he could to the seatback in front of him, and gagged loudly.

"You! Sit back, or I'll shoot!"

Raful heard the click of a safety belt being undone, but the lethal cigarette lighter containing cyanide gas was no longer in his pocket; it lay deep in the elastic pouch sewn onto the forward seat. He slumped backward, exhausted but triumphant. The hijacker lowered himself into the crew seat, keeping his eyes fixed on Raful. By now the plane was quaking like an animal in its death throes.

"One hundred feet above ground," Ross called. "Fifty ... forty ... thirty ..."

Morgan's right hand descended to the throttles. A sudden vision of his wife sitting in a deck chair on the lawn of their house in Weybridge flashed through his mind and was gone.

"... twenty ... *fifteen*."

Morgan shut down the throttles. Flare out, nose up, angle her into the crosswind ... nudge the stick forward to get the nose wheel down, then back a touch....

The main wheels scraped the surface. Morgan squeezed the yoke forward, half a second, less, then back again. He felt the gear take the plane's weight.

All hell broke loose.

It sounded like the end of the world: a hundred machine guns opening up at once, raking the underside of his hull. Gravel! Abort! Too late, too late, get her down, *just get her down in one bloody piece!*

He yanked the throttles through the gate, into reverse thrust. The surface wasn't flat at all, it was ridged every which way, and it was covered with loose stones. He could hear the screams in the cabin behind him but it meant nothing, because he was hauling on the throttles with all his might, the plane was shaking and shuddering itself apart, seams would be bursting soon, there'd be stones in the engines, explosion, *Christ, don't think about that....*

The spoilers came up, killing the lift on the wings. He got the nose down somehow; God knew how, Morgan didn't. He was still traveling at one hundred and thirty miles an hour. Ahead of him he could see nothing at all, just whiteness. The plane was juddering so much that Morgan thought his brains must shake out of his skull. He braked. Nothing. Again: this time, some drag communicated itself through the soles of his feet, but the banging went on like the worst artillery barrage in the world; he could feel drumming come up through his shoes, into his legs, his torso, his neck ... *tire burst!* The plane lurched to one side; the left wing went down. He tried the rudder, tried too hard, overcompensated, somehow got her out of the deadly slew.

One hundred miles an hour. Ninety. It was like being in a metal foundry, or a super-sophisticated studio where the engineers were determined to demonstrate every noise in the canon: tiny taps, shells exploding, panel beating, bang, *bang*, BANG! Eighty miles an hour.

More rudder, keep that ruddy wing tip *up!*

Sixty miles an hour.

The starboard engine went out with a snap and a whine, and Morgan jabbed down on the rudder with his left foot. He braked again.

He could hear himself think.

Forty miles an hour. He reached for the nose-wheel rudder and it responded.

"Flaps in."

Ross watched a fish-white hand stretch out to the switches, only later realizing that it was his own.

Slowly, slowly, the inhuman, unbearable noise died away. The plane lurched around to the left, sank a little, and settled into a deathlike silence.

Morgan had finished with engines. He switched them off. As he did so, he allowed himself to acknowledge, for the first time, that they were down. They were alive.

He became aware of a strange noise. For a long time he couldn't identify it. Then it came to him. Clapping. The rear cabin was racked with thunderous applause, in which tears and laughter mingled.

Ross was saying something incoherent, had grabbed both his hands between his own, and was shaking him as if he wanted to tear them off. When another hand descended onto Morgan's shoulder, he turned, startled, to see that the woman terrorist had risen to stand behind him. He stared and stared, unable to comprehend what he saw. Her face was wet with tears.

"Yes," she said, and as she spoke the word she shook her head, squeezing his shoulder. "Yes, you are a pilot."

Selim lifted the handset from its bracket by the first class galley, the one Leila had used to initiate the hijack.

"Ladies and gentlemen," he said, "you have landed in South Yemen, where you will be held as hostages for the release of certain Iranian war heroes now in prison in Iraq. We have no wish to hurt any of you, and we will not do so unless one of two things happens. First, if our demands are rejected; second, if you try to escape. If either event *should* happen, then things will change." He paused for emphasis. "Things will definitely change."

Like all the other passengers, Colin listened as if his life depended on catching every word. After Selim had finished his announcement, the cabin was quiet. No one moved or spoke. The euphoria generated by their safe landing had dissipated. Colin heard someone being sick a few rows behind him. Apart from that, the silence that descended on the cabin with the final click of the intercom stayed perfect.

"My God, my God," he heard a soft voice say beside him, and he turned, quickly, aware of another person whose need outweighed his own. He was sitting next to a boy about the same age as Robbie. His face was distemper-white, splashed with ugly, unformed splotches of crimson. His hands lay in his lap, twisting something back and forth. They were shaking. Every so often they would jump in spasm.

There was an empty seat between the two of them. Colin raised the armrest and slid along to sit next to the boy. He laid a hand on his forearm. "It's going to be all right," he said firmly. "Hold on."

"Can't ... can't."

Colin gripped the forearm more tightly. "You can make it."

"I'm diabetic," the teenager muttered. "I'd only got one shot left."

Colin looked at the object in Tim's hand, saw it was a small bag made of clear plastic and that the ampoule inside had smashed.

"It broke," Tim said. "In the crash, it broke."

"You."

Something hard nudged at Colin's shoulder. Not a blow, not aggressive, just a hard tap. He swung around to find that one of the hijackers had come to stand in the aisle opposite his seat. The muzzle of his submachine gun rested a few inches from Colin's face.

"Don't change seats again."

Colin looked into the man's eyes. They were intelligent. To judge from the lines around them, they were capable of expressing humor. He was wearing an expensive gray pinstripe suit, his hair was neatly combed, and he did not look the least bit like a killer. This man might have been the ambassador to one of the gulf states. But for the gun.

Colin swallowed. "No. I won't." He cursed himself for capitulating so readily and so early on in the crisis, but being able to speak at all represented some small victory.

The man slowly walked away down the aisle. Colin closed his eyes. He wanted to think, without distraction.

He should never have boarded this flight with Robbie. *Never!* Celestine had warned him, but he'd chosen to put his son at risk regardless. Don't think about that, he told himself, it's futile. Think about the future.

Someone, soon, would come to rescue the passengers. He must be ready for that. He must prepare. Because he was going to get out of this alive and in one piece. Robbie too.

The only thing standing between him and survival was conscience.

He might have to kill in order to survive. Or to save his son. Most of these passengers wouldn't see it that way. They'd think they could do whatever was necessary to escape, but when the time came they wouldn't be able to shrug off the decent, basic humanity their parents had instilled in them.

Colin had already committed the features of one hijacker to memory. When the moment came, there must be no mistakes. Kill or be killed. He could do whatever was necessary, to save Robbie. He knew that.

He'd done it before.

20 July: 1600: Sussex, England

Celestine Hanif lay on her back with her legs raised at an angle of 45 degrees and wondered who had masterminded the transformation of Gravetye Manor into a hotel.

"... ninety-seven, ninety-eight, ninety-nine ..."

She would have painted the ceiling a different color. But the four-poster bed was exquisite.

"... one hundred and twelve, one hundred and thirteen ..."

You got to be quite an expert on ceilings if you were seventy-six and determined to keep fit. If you were twenty-six and attractive you knew your ceilings too (and your four-posters, come to think of it), but that was different.

"... one hundred and forty-five, one hundred and forty-six ..."

Her cheeks were puffed out and red, everything ached, the arthritis she refused to acknowledge was hell-bent on revenge. The heart, also, was not wonderful. Nevertheless, she expected obedience from her lean old body, and her lean old body complained but complied.

Celestine let her legs crash to the carpet with a bump. You were supposed to lower them in ladylike fashion, but "*Merde!*" she cried.

She had flown in from New York a few hours ago, arriving earlier than scheduled but still too late to make a surprise call on

Robbie and Colin before they left Oxford. No matter; she would catch up with them in Melbourne, as originally planned. Flying did not worry her: seven hours from the East Coast, another twenty-five to look forward to; it was all in the game. But she relished this break in her favorite manor-house hotel, and a good workout was just what the doctor ordered.

Hearing a knock on the outer door she got up. This took time, certainly more time than it had taken when she was in her twenties and used to inconvenient postcoital knocks on doors, but things were less urgent now, the consequences of not springing into the nearest wardrobe less severe. As she passed out of the bedroom she caught sight of her reflection and was not displeased: the hair somewhat disorganized, perhaps, and the turkey neck, well ... but pink leotards continued to do interesting things for Celestine, those thighs still shot all the way up to *la derrière*; oh, how she longed to be *taller.*...

"Come in, my dear." She stood to one side with an eighteenth-century court gesture of welcome that was still going on when Marjorie put the tray down on a table by the mullioned window, with its view of that wonderful garden. Celestine was very fond of Marjorie, one of her surrogate granddaughters. She had honorary families all over the world, but here in England she only had Marjorie. For some reason the country was like that—one hotel, one restaurant, one friend, one "granddaughter."

Marjorie was an under-manageress, and she knew what Celestine liked. She liked honey, wheat-meal toast, and ginger spice cake served with Earl Grey at four o'clock. Celestine expected to see two of everything on the tray, because she required Marjorie to stay, eat a good tea, and, above all, chat. The hotel could spare Marjorie for this purpose. Hotels frequently did things for Celestine and then had to spend hours with the auditors trying to think why on earth they'd done them. She'd devoted an entire career to suborning other people; she could have made a modest success of some little sideline, like a division of General Motors or one of the lesser Soviet republics perhaps, but had preferred to have fun instead.

"Pour," she commanded. "I'm drier than a menopausal kangaroo's pussy."

Marjorie spilled tea. "Oh, *please* don't start," she begged, suppressing a giggle.

"But it's in my phrase book!" Celestine protested. "If it's good enough for the Government Tourist Office"—she rapped on the sideboard—"it's good enough for me. I adore to speak Australian. It's so"—she paused, searching for the right word—"*Gentile.*"

Celestine disappeared into the bedroom, to emerge a moment later carrying her perfume sprayer. It was made of cut glass and trailed a long tube connected to a rubber ball. Tube and ball were clad in silk, with the bulb additionally boasting a gold tassel. The reservoir contained Elizabeth Arden's Blue Grass. None of her intimate circle could believe this. They would press her to admit that the wonderful breath of fresh air which heralded her entrances was inspired by Calèche, or Chanel No. 5, or this, or that; but to Celestine these were just ridiculously overpriced scents. Blue Grass was a personality all by itself, a lover to whom she had stayed faithful for years.

"Have a squirt," she suggested matily, before proceeding to go at Marjorie as if she were a hapless fly and the spray contained Flit.

"I love that perfume," Marjorie said. "Your signature. You spray Blue Grass on our curtains, don't you."

"Of course," Celestine said, with a broad wink. "It's my way of checking how often you dry-clean them. And of reminding you that it's *my* room. Anyway, what's happening in your world? That delectable Austrian chef you were seeing?"

"Went to visit his mother in Innsbruck and hasn't been heard of since."

"What a fool. But then mothers ... ah, well."

Marjorie shrugged. "Life goes on. I got a rise, the government upped taxes; that's it, really. Quiet, you could say. Everyone's on about the hijack, right now."

Celestine spread butter on a slice of toast, topping it off with a rich drizzle of honey. "Hijack?"

"It's just been on the telly, the Bahrain hijack. Some Arabs pinched a TriStar today and downed it in South Yemen."

Celestine hurriedly put down her toast. "Bahrain ... where was this plane going?"

"Malaysia. K.L."

She mentioned the airline and Celestine jumped up. "My God, what flight number? NQ oh-three-three—was it NQ oh-three-three?"

"I can check for you. Why, Mrs. Hanif, you look ill, can I get you—"

"Just tell me one thing." Celestine's voice was hoarse. "Were there any casualties?"

"They don't know, but the plane landed safely."

Celestine dropped into her chair. "When did this happen?"

"Just an hour ago. I'll put the radio on; there should be a news bulletin any minute."

"Yes. Do that, will you?"

Her breaths came in fast, short gasps. She was fond of Colin, but Robbie she adored. If anything had happened to her great-grandson....

While Celestine waited for the news to begin she smoked a menthol cigarette. She allowed herself five a day at specific times, and this one did not fit into her schedule, but since some instinct warned her that she would be smoking a lot from now on, that did not worry her.

"I warned him," she said unexpectedly. "I told him not to advertise it."

"Sorry?"

"My grandson-in-law, Colin. I told him there was too much publicity about his trip to Australia. Lecturers going away to teach aren't news. Yet I read about him going, twice. I warned him. I—"

The time signal put a stop to her recriminations. The BBC led with the hijack. Details of the flight were given, along with a rough breakdown of the passengers by nationality. The pilot was congratulated on a remarkable feat of flying. No one knew who the hijackers were, although they had asked for an Iranian television crew to be sent by helicopter to monitor the hijack and this, coupled with a demand for the release of some Iranian prisoners of war, was taken as a clue to the identity of the perpetrators. There were no reports of any injuries, let alone fatalities. At home, the prime minister said in the Commons today—

Celestine switched off the set and turned to Marjorie. "I have to make a call," she said in a clipped, businesslike fashion. "You stay there, dear, I may need your help in a moment."

She picked up the phone and dialed a very long number from memory. The other party answered at once.

"Feisal. Mother." She spoke in Arabic.

A pause. The pause alone told her much.

"How wonderful to hear your voice, Mother."

"This hijack."

Pause number two, even more informative than the first. "So you've heard."

"Who's responsible?"

"Oh ... who ever knows these days, Mother?"

"Who?"

"Hezbollah." The voice at the other end had turned sulky. "Who the devil cares?"

Hezbollah, the Party of God, acting on behalf of Iran ... Abu Nidal? No.

"It's her," she snapped. *"Leila."*

For a long moment the line echoed with hollow resonance, a little like the sea heard from the depths of a cave. Then came a series of clicks ... and the hum of disconnection.

Celestine slammed down the phone, lifted her shoulders until they were almost touching her earlobes, and allowed them to fall again.

"I must go," she said. "My grandson-in-law and his son were on that flight. Marjorie, be a dear; get me on a plane to Larnaca. I'm not fussy which airline, as long as it leaves today."

"I'll fix it. And Mrs. Hanif, I'm so very sorry."

"So am I, dear, so am I."

Sorry I was born: the words echoed in her mind as Marjorie closed the outer door to the suite. Sorry I spawned this hell breed. No, don't think about any of that. Pack. Do it quickly, do it *now*.

As Celestine folded her clothes she worked out the odds. Everything depended on Colin, that good man. Robbie wouldn't understand, but Colin would. He was vulnerable. He was defenseless.

The phone rang. "BA to Larnaca," Marjorie said. "Eight-fifty, gets in at three-ten tomorrow morning, local time. It's the best I could do."

"It's the best. Marjorie, one more thing: phone Qantas and cancel tomorrow's reservation for Melbourne."

As Celestine locked the last case she would have given all she owned, not excepting her life, cheerfully, thoughtlessly, in exchange for the comfortable knowledge that Colin still had the gun she'd given him.

June 1974: Beirut

It was all of ten years ago, in June of 1974, that she'd handed her gun over to Colin.

After lunch the weather turned cool with a belligerent breath of wind off the Mediterranean threatening rain in a sulky, unpredictable kind of way. Celestine walked up and down the garden of Kharif, her house at Yarze, incessantly smoking menthol cigarettes, in that era not yet self-rationed, and wondering if the man would bring her great-grandson to see her.

The porticoed villa was a magnificent example of its kind: an old Levantine house, with lead tracery windows and narrow stone columns adorning its balconies. Ever since she'd been exiled to the hills by a son not prepared to set aside part of each day to receive her salutary advice, it had felt empty. Not lonely—Celestine did not know what it meant to be lonely—but it cried out for parties, as in the good old days: skiing on Mount Sannin in the morning, followed by a bouillabaisse lunch at Lucullus on the Avenue des Français, with a sparkling sea visible through the restaurant's great glass windows framed by palm fronds, then swimming at the Hamman Normandie until it was time to change for the Casino Liban, or listening to Farouz in some nightclub off Hamra ... that was Beirut. The real dream, as she liked to call it: *le vrai rêve*. Then the house had been alive, humming like a well-oiled, much-loved machine, a Rolls-Royce engine perhaps, twenty-four hours a day. Now, it slumbered. It needed shrill young voices raised in play to rouse it again.

Celestine paused to finger a small orange, almost ripe on the bough, then decided against picking it. This used to be such a naughty house, once. Young girls would come for the weekend and go away again minus a vital part of their childhood. Adulteries flowered alongside the garden's purple anchusas, altering lives forever; young people discovered surprising truths about their sexual preferences; people fell in love. She tapped the orange, suddenly whacked it with her fist, smiled not altogether happily. Yes, those days were gone.

A peculiarity of this house was its acoustics. Sometimes the noise of a car by the quarry would arise without warning, sounding very close, only to fade away to silence. This happened now. Celestine raised her head. The Citroën's distinctive rattle: Azizza must be almost home.

Celestine entered the house, pausing on her way through the study to put out her cigarette in a sturdy confection of Arabian brass, already stuffed with half a day's intake. She opened the front door in time to see a sky-blue Citroën Dyane ease to a halt in the driveway and stall, violently, when Azizza forgot to let out the clutch. Behind it came a green Fiat compact. For a moment Celestine was aware of nothing except the smell of warm petrol and the sound of metal as it yawned and stretched. Then the Fiat's offside rear door opened. Oddly enough, no one appeared. Instead, the door closed again. Seconds afterward, a small figure appeared around the back of the car. Seeing Celestine, it stopped. Then, evidently reassured, it started forward again. Celestine heard other doors opening and slamming, was conscious of two adults, but ignored them. Very slowly she lowered herself into a crouch.

A boy, dressed in white shorts with a black belt and gold buckle and a faded red T-shirt. His sandy hair, sun-bleached but still streaked with darker shades, was cropped short on top and left long at the back, in wisps that overrode his collar; absurdly, her first thought on seeing her great-grandson was that this style must be making him hot, how careless of Leila....

"Hello," she said softly. "Hello, Robbie."

He came up to her, a fearful frown sullying his face, and raised a clenched fist to his brow. He used his knuckles to wipe beads of sweat away, revealing a plump little arm not yet filled with muscle, its white-and-red skin flecked with tiny spots. His face was rounded like the arm, as if that, too, required a filling; the sun evidently troubled him, for his eyes were two chips narrowed against its light. What scarlet lips he has, she said wonderingly to herself. What perfect little hands....

"'Lo." He unclenched the fist but not the frown. Then, as if the information processed via invisible antenna proved satisfactory, he held out his hand to be shaken. It felt warm, a little moist, and it was tiny, so tiny, he was only four years old, but something about the spontaneous gesture breathed trust into Celestine like a bubble of oxygen.

"Are you my great-grandmother?" he inquired, in a pleasantly musical voice, low-pitched, much lower than she'd expected.

"Yes."

"Really?"

She placed her hands on his miniature shoulders. "Why so astonished, little chum?"

"My mother's ... father's ... mother?"

"Yes."

His mouth formed a great O, revealing diminutive, absolutely white teeth, sharp and ridged. Without trying to free himself from her gentle embrace, he leaned backward, as if to give himself a better view. "You must be very, very old," he said slowly, delivering the result of some inner debate.

"Very. I am a dinosaur."

For a long moment they surveyed each other in silence and immobility, smiles prepared behind the scenes but not quite ready to play. Then she swept him up into her arms with laughter in which other voices joined.

"You are Colin Raleigh," she said to the man who had come around the front of the car and was standing a few feet away.

"Yes. So pleased to meet you at last, after hearing so much about you."

Celestine laughed. "I'll bet."

She liked his tousled look, for his thick hair was still standing up from the draft of air through the window, some of it falling in tendrils across his sun-broiled face, and it softened him. She could sense that he was sometimes tough, sometimes hiding his fear beneath a brittle shell, yes, but often just tough. And was he—the thought made her squeeze Robbie's legs without meaning to—was he hard on the boy? Leila could take care of herself, but Robbie ... Celestine would have no mercy for those who brought their anger to bear on him.

Somehow, during this brief exchange, she had managed to hitch Robbie onto her shoulder. He kept his hands clasped around her neck, head thrown back as if he could not quite believe what he saw when he looked at her. Those wet cherry lips were smiling, though, and he rested against her in perfect trust. It was one of those magic bonds that took seconds to form and a couple of lifetimes to mature. Both of them, in their vastly different ways, seemed to know this.

"Do you want to go to your papa?" she asked him. But he shook his head, smiling a teasing smile at his father before burying his head in the hair behind her ear, whence he could peek out to ensure that Colin, though not quite wanted, was not quite absent either.

"What a marvelous house," Colin said as she led the way inside.

"It's good," she agreed. "But it needs life. I'm glad you could come."

"I was intrigued."

"Frightened, perhaps?" She had taken them right through the house, into the garden, and was finding a comfortable place for herself and Robbie among the cushions on her sofa swing, beside the marble-lined pool. Colin stood with hands in pockets, looking down at them. His smile tautened as he heard her words.

"Azizza was ... unexpected."

"Where did she catch up with you? Masser?"

"Yes."

Celestine plumped Robbie down on a particularly fat cushion and asked him, "Did you like the cedars?"

"Cedars?" He squinted up at her. "Do you mean those big old trees?"

"Yes."

He shook his head from side to side, pouting his lips.

"They are very old. More than a thousand years old, like me. And like most old things, they can be boring. Were you bored?"

"Yes. I wanted to go to the beach. But Mummy was busy."

At that Celestine and Colin exchanged amused looks. She hoped he approved of her sending Azizza to trail them, for without such a stratagem she would never have been able to penetrate Feisal's defenses and bring her great-grandson here. Did Colin know, she wondered, how much she longed to see Leila too? Why hadn't she come; why was she "busy"?

Ah, of course: Leila and Colin must have quarreled. And with the answer to the earlier questions came another doubt: would those two be able to stay the course? Looking up at Colin now, Celestine found it impossible to guess.

"Were you surprised when Azizza introduced herself?" she asked.

"Oh, yes."

"But you trusted her—after a week or so with Feisal, I'm surprised."

"She was different."

"Do sit down, please."

Colin lowered himself into a wicker chair set at an angle to the sofa, thus forbidding Celestine sight of more than his profile.

"In what way, different?" she asked.

"Your letter. And Azizza, she ... she looks one in the eye, I suppose."

"And Feisal doesn't. Nor does Halib. Don't look so surprised, I know what that house is like. Anyway, thanks for trusting her."

"She's very persistent."

"She knew what I wanted, you see. Getting me what I want matters so much to her. Did she tell you she was my housekeeper? She's my oldest friend: a friend who happens to keep my house."

Now he turned to look her full in the face. "We'd have come even if Azizza had been a dragon."

"Because you wanted to know if anyone could really be as horrible as they described me?"

When he laughed she found herself liking him more.

"Well, I'm worse," she said.

"So I see."

Now it was her turn to laugh. Robbie plucked her arm. "Would you like to see a drawing?" he asked.

"Your drawing?"

He nodded solemnly.

"I'd love to."

"I have to draw it first."

Azizza was hovering in the doorway. Now Celestine beckoned her over. "Robbie needs paper and some crayons. Do you think we have any?"

Azizza did not refer to the assortment of paints, toys, games, puzzles, and books that the two women had been accumulating ever since they first got wind of the Raleighs' visit. Instead, she pretended to consider it.

"I *think* so," she said, after a pregnant pause, during which Robbie gazed at her in anguish. "Let's go see."

Celestine gave the boy a little push, and he ran off to join Azizza, who took his hand and led him inside. A moment later, however, she reappeared, carrying two glasses and a frosted green bottle.

"He's happy," Azizza said. "I left him on the floor of Leila's old bedroom. There's a lot of space there."

"Good. Thank you, Izza. Do you know this wine, Colin? It's called Ksara."

He accepted a glass, raising it in a toast to both Celestine and Azizza before he drank.

"Yes, I know it. A wonderful wine. We must take some back with us."

"Are you looking forward to going home?"

His hesitation was somehow expressive. "We've been well looked after," he said diplomatically. "Well protected."

"Ah. Colin, I hope you can understand about Beirut. It's like one big party. Do what you like, spend what you can, use any language, we all speak everything. The only price we pay is to be at war the whole time."

"Rather an expensive price."

"Oh, there's hardly any killing at the moment. We've almost united against the outsider, you see." Celestine made a wonderful face. "The Palestinians."

"You're not fond of them, I take it?"

"I'm sorry for them. How not? But I don't want them here. They don't pay for the telephone or the electricity they use—did you know that?"

Colin sipped his wine, saying nothing.

"If they stay, they'll cause a real war. With Israel. Then we're finished." She waited for his reaction. "You don't agree?"

He was obviously weighing his words. When they came, they were not what she'd expected.

"I don't agree with anybody, actually: Palestinians, Jews."

"Israelis."

He stared at her.

"You said Jews when you meant Israelis. Go on."

"Sorry." But she could see he didn't begin to understand. "Anyway ... I've read up the politics, a little. Kind of complicated."

"No, simple. But depending which side you're on, totally different."

"Doesn't that worry you? The polarity, I mean."

She shrugged. "We, this family, are nominally Shia Muslims. I say 'nominally,' because our ID cards say we're Shiites so that's what we are. And yes, to forestall your question—of course we resent the way the Maronite Christians lord it over us. The 'polarity,' as you call it. But there are ways of coping."

"Such as?"

"Such as making sure that we take our two percent from every deal the Christians make. And keeping the Levantine spirit alive." Celestine folded her hands in her lap. "Colin, we have our friends, people we feel we can do business with, often the same people. Greek Catholic, Jew, Maronite, Druze—what does it matter? The politicians say it matters." Another of her fancy shrugs. "Bully boys, assassins, men who couldn't get a decent job if forced to it.... Isn't it the same in England? Do *you* listen to your politicians? Anyway, enough: I didn't invite you to this house to be tiresome on the subject of your wife's politics."

He didn't feel the sting of her last remark at once. When it dawned, his face flushed an even deeper shade of red. "You think I'm just parroting Leila?"

But before she could tell him what she thought, Robbie ran out of the house, trailing a sheet of paper behind him and calling, "Daddy ... Celestine!"

"What is it, sweetie?" she cried. "Come show the queen of Yarze what you've done."

Robbie hauled himself up onto the sofa swing and smoothed the paper into her lap.

"Gracious!"

The exclamation was forced out of Celestine, substituted in the nick of time for something less polite. He had used dramatic blocks of color to create a representation of a sprightly lady in a kaftan recognizable as the one she was wearing today. Her cheeks had, for some reason, turned blue, and she wondered if her hands could ever really be that peculiar mauve color, but the striking thing about this portrait was the way the lines coalesced to make an identifiable human face—through all the childish muddle, it was so clearly *her*.

"May I keep this?" she asked softly. "Please."

He sat hunched forward, elbows on knees and his chin cupped in his hands. "If you want."

She folded it into four, then tucked it between one of the cushions and the side of the swing. Later she was to transfer it to her handbag, wherein it would travel the world until, years afterward, it fell apart, its folds creased and recreased by so many inspections whenever Celestine needed reassurance that she had blue cheeks and mauve hands and so, to one young person in the world at least, was real.

Azizza brought tea and cakes for the boy. While he munched away, Celestine continued to study him, sometimes looking shrewdly at his father.

"He's like you above the nose, and Leila below."

"That's what everyone says. I can't see it, myself."

"Who do you think he takes after, then? Someone on your side?"

Colin shook his head. He seemed reluctant to answer. At last he said, quietly enough to be sure Robbie wouldn't overhear, "I thought I could see a touch of Halib in him. The eyes."

Celestine sucked in her lower lip. "Oh."

"Listen, it's not my wife's politics that I spout. Or rather—"

"She speaks the words, but they start with someone else."

"Halib."

"And their father. Yes, Colin, I know." She raised a hand from her lap and shook it at him. "Be careful."

"You think they're dangerous?"

"I do. Remember, Beirut *crackles* with danger! Feisal works on the hottest part of the grid and Halib worships him. How do they treat you?"

"Okay." Colin wasn't looking at her. His eyes followed Robbie as the little boy trotted away to inspect some flowerbeds, with Azizza in tow. Celestine saw the anguish in his gaze and felt her guts clench.

"You're worried for the boy, aren't you?"

"Not exactly worried . . ."

"What then?"

"It's just ... Feisal's rages. When he loses his temper ... one minute all smiles, the next ... look, I really shouldn't be talking to you like this." He managed a smile. "Excuse me."

"Because I'm his mother? Forget it! Has he threatened you?"

"No."

He stood up and turned his back on her, seeking the child. Celestine stared down at her hands, wretchedly wondering how to retrieve the situation. Hearing raised voices, she looked up to see Colin over by the grove of fig trees, grasping Robbie's arm while Azizza looked on in disapproval. Father and son were arguing.

"I don't *want* to go home," Robbie cried.

Celestine rose and approached them as quietly as she knew how.

"Mummy's at home," Colin said. His voice was low but taut; she could tell that he was focusing all his patience on the boy, determined at any cost to avoid that most British of all diseases: embarrassment.

"I don't *want* Mummy, I want Celestine."

Don't rush in, she warned herself; it's not your business.

"We can't stay here forever, Robbie." The first hint of petulance crept into Colin's tone. "Be reasonable."

"Please, Daddy." Robbie rubbed his eyes. "Don't make me go back. Mummy can come up here."

"She can't."

"She can, she can, *she can!*"

Robbie burst into a fit of sobbing. Celestine clenched her hands underneath her thighs, ground her teeth, and remained silent. Colin squatted down beside the boy, grasping his shoulders.

"It's all right, darling. Don't cry. Here, Daddy's got a handkerchief."

He wiped Robbie's eyes before sweeping him up into a tight hug. Celestine felt a little of the tension drain out of her. He was a good father, after all.

"Don't leave me alone with that horrible man again. Promise!"

"What horrible man?" Celestine had not meant to intervene, although now the words were out she didn't regret them. "Robbie—who's been horrible to you?" She took the boy into her arms. "Tell me," she murmured.

"Halib." He was sleepy now, after so much emotional effort; when he rubbed his eyes this time it wasn't to wipe away tears but to keep them open. He leaned back onto her shoulder and whispered in her ear, "I don't like him."

"Why, dearest?"

"He'd hit me if Mummy wasn't there. Or Daddy."

"There, there, precious. No one's going to hit you."

She pivoted slightly, the better to see Colin, and indicated with a look that he should wait for her inside the house. When she joined him a moment later she took him by the arm and half led, half dragged him into her study. She strode to the desk that once had been her husband's and fiddled inside one of the drawers until the hidden lock snapped back, revealing a cavity.

"Here," she said, with brusque insistence. "Take this. Go on, take it!"

Colin was staring at her in stupefaction. As if in a slow-motion movie, his hand stretched out, fell back.

"It's a gun," he said, and she could see how stupid he felt at having stated something so obvious.

"Yes. It's loaded; the safety catch is on."

He shook his head. "Not my scene."

She reached for his hand and pressed the gun into it. "If not for your sake, then for Robbie's. Don't tell them where you've been today; make sure the boy doesn't say anything. Promise me that, promise me. *And take the gun.*"

"I can't." He tried to force it back on Celestine but she resisted with greater strength than he'd have given her credit for. "I mean ... suppose they found it, the police—"

"You fool, everyone in Beirut has a gun, everyone! Don't you know where you're living yet?"

The door opened, to reveal Robbie in the foreground and Azizza hovering uneasily behind him. "Daddy, what are you and Celestine doing?"

Colin had his back to the door, concealing the gun from the boy's gaze. Now Celestine took advantage of his confusion to push his hand, the one holding the gun, into the pocket of his jacket. "I was just explaining the quickest route back into town," she said slyly. "The road's a bit hard to find if you don't know it."

"Oh." He advanced into the room. "Do we really have to go?" His voice was doleful.

"Yes, darling. But there'll be other times." She picked him up. They had their routine, now; he settled into the crook of her shoulder as if he'd been doing if for years instead of minutes. Celestine carried him out to the Fiat and slid him onto the back seat, where he would be safer in the event of an accident—how the very thought made her shake with rage and trepidation—before turning to Colin.

"Wise up," she all but snapped. "Look about you, stay alive."

"I will. *We* will."

"Give my love to Leila. Don't forget what I told you."

Colin got into the driver's seat and started the engine. "Thank you," he said awkwardly. "For everything, I mean."

"I know what you mean. Come back one day. Both of you."

As she turned to enter the house, some macabre conviction assured Celestine that Colin would need the gun, and soon.

DAY
TWO

DAY
TWO

21 July: Dawn: Al Mahra, South Yemen

Leila had ordered two of the doors to be opened. She sat alone in first class, enjoying a cool flutter of air through the plane. Behind her, the passengers were being allowed to use the toilets after a night spent strapped in their seats; they too would be glad of some ventilation. Captain Morgan had consulted her about the air-conditioning, which would not last long. She agreed with him: better to switch if off during the night and save fuel for the heat of the day. Not that the nights here were cool. At 3 A.M., the ambient temperature had registered 80 degrees Fahrenheit.

Morgan was good. He had begun, hesitantly, to talk to her. She knew this was what the anti-hijack manuals instructed him to do but did not care; he was an interesting person. He'd mentioned his "souls" and, when she queried it, explained that a plane's full complement of people, crew plus passengers, was always referred to as so many "souls." He was a fine pilot and a decent man too, because he understood that people had souls. Killing him would give her no pleasure, even though he was—he had to be—at the top of her death list. Fouad could do it, when necessary.

She remembered the first time she had taken life. Before then, she had never thought to do such a thing. It was like sex: as a girl, the notion of being mauled by a man was disgusting. Then, slowly, you came around to the idea that one day you might love a man enough to marry him and let him touch you. Later still, love became more important in that equation than marriage, so perhaps you could bring yourself to take a lover without marrying him. Finally, you went to bed with somebody, and after that it was all downhill. So with murder: the sin became first conceivable, then tolerable, and at last habitual. You scarcely noticed. If you did notice, you looked back at your young self, that other person who'd once expressed abhorrence at what was now your practice, and you laughed, ashamed to think you could ever have been so naïve.

As long as you knew the killing was in aid of a purpose, a cause that you yourself were prepared to die for, you got used to it.

Behind her, they were waiting. Passengers, crew, even the hijack team itself: all waiting. She could feel their impatience like a lethal wave overbearing her hunched shoulders, poised to come crashing down. Back there were loaded guns, grenades with their pins pulled, explosives wired to emergency hatches and doors. These objects seemed to her less dangerous than the human volatility that, for the time being, controlled them. She could make a pistol do her will, but people were not like that.

Her men ruled the passengers, and her job was to dominate her men. She could not use objects to do it. What she needed lay inside herself and had roots that went down deep into the past.

She sat in seat number 3B, on the aisle, where the movement of air through the nearby door was most perceptible. The sun had already risen over the horizon. It was light inside the cabin. She stared down at the passport in her hands, every so often turning the blue booklet over or opening it to scan a few pages before letting it fall into her lap.

Robbie had traveled a bit since 1982 and New York: the year, the place, when Leila had last seen her child. She'd held him in her arms and kissed him above the ear, *there* ... how often had she relived those magic seconds? She could still smell the apple scent of his hair, his spine still curled inward under the pressure of her hands, his smooth skin nuzzling her own: all hostages of memory, intact, immaculate.

Leila jumped up and turned around, her gaze locking onto the curtain that separated the first class cabin from the plane's business section. He sat just beyond it. Seat 13K. If she tore that curtain aside, his face would be the first thing she'd see. She took a step forward without willing it and grabbed the nearest seat, like a woman trying to save herself from being swept away by a flood tide. *He was there!*

Her nails dug into the cloth until her fingers turned white. Now was not the time. She could pass through that curtain and ruin everything, or she could wait. So she would sit down. She would take the rest she so badly needed.

She fell to studying Robbie's passport again. He had traveled to Russia. A school trip; she knew about that and had wanted to snatch him back then, but Halib had said no, because in Russia he could do nothing. Greece. Yugoslavia, in the same year as Greece … motoring holiday? Halib hadn't said anything about it. Perhaps he hadn't known. Taking Robbie back would have been so easy in Greece.

Robbie might have traveled, but it hadn't been possible to find out about his trips at the time. Not like now. This journey to Malaysia and Australia had mysteriously found its way into the newspapers. Why? Law tutors went abroad all the time, without necessarily being profiled in the press.

There was something about this operation that made Leila's flesh creep. A man had tried to keep her from entering the cockpit: a sky marshal employed by the airline, perhaps. But there was something almost familiar about him, something she couldn't put a name to. Perhaps she had seen him before and couldn't remember where. She would give details taken from the man's passport to Halib. Halib would find out.

She glanced at her watch, glad of the way her thoughts focused and assumed new direction, with Halib suddenly much in her mind. Without him, what would have become of her? Death, madness?

She might have been happy, but for him. No, don't think that....

Y'Allah, let her brother be fit and well this day. There were things they must do together. He had radioed twice, during the night: the first time to tell her that, as expected, the Iraqis were disclaiming all knowledge of the six prisoners, the second time to find out how she was coping and to say he loved her.

She'd been abrupt, that second time, because every moment they stayed on the air gave the eavesdroppers a fresh opportunity to break their codes. But she forgave her brother. He knew that what he did was risky, but he also knew the odds, down to five decimal places. And besides, it was his way of saying that the two of them rode their course above the odds.

Leila stood up, keeping Robbie's passport in her hands, and moved to the door. As she stared out across the gravel plain to the line of hills beyond, even now turning from black to deep purple as the sun swiftly rose, she wondered who would be first to break the code of discipline she'd imposed on the outside world, and how they would do it.

One helicopter, she'd said. One camera crew, to fly from the Iranian frigate off Socotra Island. No other aircraft, no vessels out to sea. But the "authorities," those chess grand masters who always worked against hijackers, unseen and unaccountable, would choose a way to disobey. Reasonable, that's how it would be designed to look: humanitarian, harmless. A forbidden act with which the world could empathize. If she showed compassion, forgave the error, that was weakness and the grand masters would smile, briefly, before continuing. But if she exacted punishment, the hijackers would forfeit sympathy for their cause.

Well. It did not matter either way, because they mistook the "cause"; they thought she was in this for the freedom of half a dozen crazy Iranians, when in truth she did not give a damn whether they lived or died.

She had to do whatever Halib said. First, finish off the business of the hijack, secure the prisoners' release. Then Robbie. *Then* Robbie.

Leila stood in the doorway, watching, listening. Words from the Holy Koran drifted into her mind. They came from the sura known as "The Imrans": "Allah is the supreme Plotter."

She knew what the grand masters were going to do.

21 July: Lunchtime: Beirut, Lebanon

Celestine had last seen Beirut in 1982, from the window of a Middle East Airlines 747 en route to Cairo, having finally reached the end of her tether.

She'd been able to cope with the Syrians, which was as well, because ever since 1980 they'd parked their tanks just down the road from the house at Yarze and acted like they owned the place. At least with the Syrians you felt safe. You knew that if street fighting boiled out of the Eastern Christian enclave and threatened to come too close, or the Palestinians got above themselves, you could send Azizza down to the command post with a couple of chickens and a tin of coffee prominently marked HARRODS, and the major in charge would take care of things. On that basis she'd stayed put, more or less comfortably, while the city slowly disintegrated into factional bloodletting.

By the late spring of 1982, however, Lebanon's Palestinian population had become a thorn in Israel's side to the point where everyone knew their southern neighbor would invade, and soon. All that was lacking was the final provocation. Celestine arranged for Azizza to go to her sister's place in the north and packed her own suitcases; shortly after she made her escape to Cairo, Shlomo Argov, Israeli ambassador to the Court of St. James's, lay critically wounded in a London street, shot by terrorists, and Tel Aviv had its excuse. Within days, the elite Golani brigade was camped below the presidential palace at Baabda, whence their artillery could command most of the city. Lebanon, no longer independent, had become occupied territory.

Celestine embarked on a nomadic existence, restlessly declining to settle anywhere for long. Week by week she monitored the collapse of her homeland in airmailed editions of *L'Orient–Le Jour* that chronicled such miscellaneous events as the assassination of Bashir Gemayel, snow conditions on the slopes above Monte Verde, the massacre of Palestinian refugees in the camps, and gala night in East Beirut's Jet Set Disco.

Celestine read everything, she listened to whoever broadcast in her vicinity, and sometimes she would meet up with her cronies from better days; drinking espresso on the Via Veneto or lunching at the Ritz in Madrid, these exiles lived pretty much as usual, with only the occasional personal horror story to highlight the broad picture of mass destruction seeping, like sewage from a broken pipe, out of Lebanon.

Her belief that things would come right in the end survived Israel's smashing of Sidon, the destruction of the U.S. embassy, and the dynamiting of the marines' four-story headquarters on the seafront; it lasted right up until the battle for the Chouf, and then it collapsed.

Early in 1984, President Amin Gemayel's men fell upon the Shiites of West Beirut in an attempt to prevent them from aiding the Druze, who dominated the strategically important Chouf Mountains. By February, however, far from being defeated, Druze and Shiite Amal militiamen had actually wrested control of West Beirut from Gemayel. Many of those Shiites belonged to a newly formed, extreme, and pro-Iranian organization known as Hezbollah, the Party of God. By the time they had finished ransacking the bars and former brothels, not much of fashionable Hamra Street and its expensive shops, where Celestine had once delighted to spend her days, remained. Thereafter, outsiders—Palestinians, Syrians, even Israelis—were shunted off to the sidelines while the Lebanese got down to their real hidden agenda: murdering one another.

Celestine, although herself nominally a Shiite, knew then that her country was finished, and a part of her mind closed. She accepted, for instance, that she had seen the last of the house at Yarze. Yet it was 1984 and here she was again, at its gates.

Or, rather, gate. The left-hand wrought-iron portal lay on its side, wrested off its hinges but clearly visible through the weeds that had overgrown it. The other hung straight as a plumb line, despite a coating of rust. Celestine straightened her shoulders and marched through the gap.

She was glad to get around to the back of the house, where prying eyes would be less likely to notice her. It was noon, and the light spared her nothing. She had her keys with her but did not need them; every window in the place had been smashed, every door knocked down. Huge gray stains streaked most of the back wall where water had leaked from a broken cistern in the roof. The sofa swing lay on its side, springs showing here and there through the long grass. Everything spoke of dereliction and decay. It was enough to break Celestine's heart. She dropped her suitcase, blundered through into the living room, and quickly out again, retching at the smell. Someone had used this place as a lavatory.

Hearing a sound behind her, she wheeled around to see a scraggy dog in the doorway to the kitchen. It stood there, panting, but made no move. Celestine was afraid of dogs. This one looked starving. Another one crept up behind the first. The two beasts gazed at her through beseeching eyes. She took a step in their direction and they backed away, licking their chops.

Celestine gathered all her courage. "Go on, be off with you!" she cried. When she raised a hand, menacingly, they slunk out the back door into the garden. She heard them whining, but neither appeared again.

Despite those dogs, the kitchen was cleaner than the living room. She found a chair and sank into it, weeping, but instead of making her feel better, this just made her eyes red and sore, like her feet. She had walked a long way today. If it hadn't been for the farmer's wife returning from market she would have been forced to walk all the way from the port of Jounieh, where she'd disembarked from the Cyprus ferry three hours previously. As it was, the farmer's wife took pity on what she thought to be a poor old peasant woman, laboring under the weight of a tatty suitcase, and gave her a lift in her truck.

Celestine had gone to great lengths to look unexceptional. No more pink leotards for her; this was not a country where a woman might wear such a thing and get away with it any more. Last night, in Heathrow Airport, she had leaned against the side of the phone booth, cigarette dangling from her lower lip, while she worked her way through bags of loose change until at last she had everything set up and ready for her arrival: a safe house in Larnaca, cash, transport, ID, and, yes—old clothes. Celestine knew Lebanon, understood its requirements.

Riding in the truck's cab next to the farmer's wife, she'd passed through two roadblocks. Celestine knew real fear, then. Even though her ID card correctly showed her religion as Shiite Muslim, which was the best thing to be in Beirut just now, she couldn't believe her luck when the young men in their green fatigues and black-and-white keffiyehs gave it scarcely a glance.

"They are not interested in people like us," said the farmer's wife, as if reading her thoughts. "They are looking for men, men like themselves who can fight. A female can pass anywhere, as long as she keeps her head covered and her eyes cast down."

It saddened Celestine to leave the comparative comfort of the truck and the human contact, however slight. Women, she reflected bitterly, could have saved Beirut, if they hadn't always been condemned to spend their lives discussing the price of fish....

She came rocketing out of her reverie to the realization that somebody was in the room above her.

She jerked her head up, as if she expected the ceiling to become transparent. A board had creaked when someone put weight on it. Celestine slowly rose to her feet, gaze still fixed on the ceiling. There was nowhere to hide. Whoever was up there had probably watched her come in; by that time she'd been so exhausted she hadn't cared who might see her. How many? One, two?

The kitchen was dark. Shadows filled its recesses and crannies, contesting the noonday light outside. She heard another sound then, farther away this time but equally ominous: somebody on the stairs. They were at the front of the house, the kitchen was at the back; she still had a little time.

Celestine tiptoed across to the cupboard next to the sink. That was where they used to keep the knives. She raised her hand to the knob and pulled. The wood had warped; the noise of the cupboard opening was frightful. Celestine uttered a moan of frustration.

Because she could not bear to turn away from the door that led into the passage, she could not see what she was doing. Her hand groped along the cupboard's middle shelf, where memory told her she'd find something sharp. But instead, her fingers met only a gummy substance that *moved.* She yanked her hand back with another whimper, shaking mites from her skin, trying to clean her hand against her dress with panicky slaps.

Celestine wheeled around, forcing her back against the sink, and held onto its lip for support. Somebody was walking down the hallway toward the back of the house; she still couldn't tell how many of them there were. Sickly remnants of light filtered through the window, enabling her to see the doorway and no farther. Her heart wandered around inside her chest, lost for bearings. She had read of so many atrocities. Suppose they tied her up, doused her with petrol, and left a candle burning on the floor, where she could see it ...?

She found herself talking to a God she'd much neglected, over the years. Allah, she prayed; let it be one quick, clean bullet.

And it seemed her prayer was answered, because from the doorway a pinprick glimmer suddenly mushroomed into an explosion of light that blinded her; the bullet traveled behind the light, she knew, but faster than sound; you never heard the shot that killed you—

"*Sayida!*"

Celestine's fingers ground into the edge of the sink. Now, hearing that voice, she felt the strength drain out of them; her knees turned weak. Somehow she was sitting on the floor and the back of her skull ached, telling her that she had banged it against the sink as she fell.

"Azizza," she whispered. "Izza...."

Azizza ran forward, dropping the electric torch that had so confused her mistress with its sudden burst of light, and knelt beside Celestine. "*Sayida, sayida,*" she kept murmuring. "Is it really you? Can it be you?"

Celestine reached up to pat the old woman's hand. "It's me," she said, with something of her usual businesslike manner. "No ghosts here, Izza."

Azizza helped her mistress back into the chair before retrieving the big torch. Seeing the look on Celestine's face she said, by way of fierce explanation, "This flashlight's heavy enough to bash someone's head in!"

Azizza found another chair and drew it up close to Celestine's. For a moment the two old women sat in silence, confirming through their clasped hands that this was real, no dream. Then, simultaneously, they began to talk.

"It's been so long—"

"I still can't believe it—"

"You haven't changed, you're the same."

"Nonsense! I'm an antique; they should stuff me in the national museum."

Celestine gave Azizza's hands a final squeeze. "All right, all right, let's do this sensibly. Me first. I went abroad, I lived quietly—you got my letters?"

"Nearly all. Because you numbered them I knew when one didn't get through. Thank you, *sayida.*"

"Enough of this *sayida*, please. Celestine is who I used to be and who I am now. I came back, because of the plane Leila and Halib stole. You heard?"

"I heard."

"We'll talk about that later, but first I want your news. And I want to smoke."

"You'll eat and drink first. Then we can have the stories."

"But—"

"Don't 'but' me, Celestine. I'm going to leave you for a short time. Will you be all right?"

"I ... think so."

As if reading her thoughts, Azizza said, "No one has ever come here since the Maribatoun left."

"The Mari—but they're Nasserite Sunnis! You mean *Muslims* did this? To *our* house?"

Azizza's laugh sounded hollow. "There's a lot to tell," she observed dryly. "Don't worry, I'll soon be back."

Even with Azizza gone Celestine didn't feel frightened any more. While in Cyprus she'd ditched most of her luggage at a friend's apartment, so that now she was left only with a handbag and one case, both chosen for their tawdry appearance. She flung open the suitcase and found her perfume—some things you could *not* abandon. After a few puffs applied to her face and neck, she felt well enough to run through the downstairs rooms, treating each to a burst of Blue Grass. But even so, she was relieved to see Azizza come traipsing back with a basket under her arm.

"It's not much," she panted, as she lugged the basket onto the table.

"Did anyone notice you?" Celestine asked uneasily.

"I've told you, nobody ever comes here now. The nearest house with people in it is half a kilometer away." She opened the basket. "That's where I work."

"You work near here?" Celestine was flabbergasted. "But I sent you home, to Tripoli."

"There's *tabbuleh*. Some wine and some mineral water. *Yakhni*, though the stew's cold, I'm afraid."

"Azizza!"

"Your favorite—*yusuf effendi*." She proudly held up a couple of tangerines so that her mistress could see them.

"Azizza, sit down! And tell me what on earth's been going on."

The old servant sat opposite Celestine, resting one forearm on the table. "Let me see you eat first."

She'd piled a plate high with real *tabbuleh*, that wonderful Lebanese salad. Celestine picked out a sprig of mint with her fingers and sniffed it. The sharp scent flushed out her sinuses, sparking her appetite. Slowly she put it in her mouth and chewed. A thousand shimmering summer days came flooding back into her mind: the table laid beneath the jacaranda tree, Ibrahim, her dead husband, holding court at one end, a napkin tucked into his shirt collar, the children and grandchildren, laughter, childish tears....

She fell to and ate ravenously while Azizza talked.

"There was nothing for me in Tripoli. I had the money you sent me each month, yes, but no work. My sister and her husband were good to me, but I could tell I wasn't wanted."

"Your sister Yasmin?"

"Yes. She and Kemal had six children by then. Four boys, two girls. The eldest boy, Najib, was fifteen and political—he wanted to fight for Palestine. But Kemal swore the boy simply didn't want to work, because he spent all his time in the refugee camps. The atmosphere in the house was very bad."

"I'm so sorry."

Azizza shrugged. "They are Sunni, of course. Like most Palestinians. Like me."

Celestine, a Shiite, nodded and went on eating her salad. Down the road, Sunnis and Shiites, all believers in the one God, all children of the Prophet, were slitting each other's throats. It had not always been thus. The real people in Beirut used to care a damn sight more what their neighbors got up to in bed than which church, if any, they attended.

"There were still thousands of Palestinians in Tripoli, in those days. The Syrians protected them. The Sunnis protected them too, for a while. I stayed more than a year. Winter came. Then the Syrians changed their minds, decided to shell the F'listin out of Tripoli, after all. The Ba'athists joined them. I don't know, I don't understand these things."

"The Ba'athists, yes. And by that time, of course, the Sunnis hated the Palestinians too."

"Some did, not all. Najib didn't hate them. He used to call that pig Arafat 'Abu Ammar.' The boy worshiped the PLO. One night, he went missing. He'd gone to the refugee camp at Badawi, it turned out later. We waited. Najib never came home. One night, two nights. On the third day, Kemal and Yasmin went down to the town, to try to find him. They left the two girls with me and took the boys. By nightfall, none of them had come home. I got someone to take care of the children and went down to the Islamic Hospital. They had bodies there in plastic bags, thick gray plastic bags. They'd rigged up a generator in the courtyard, so that you could see to identify the corpses. I didn't dare look. I went into the hospital. But when no one there knew anything about my family, then, you see, I had to go back to the courtyard."

She faltered. Celestine poured wine into the one glass that Azizza had brought and pushed it across the table without a word.

"They were all there. Father, mother, four boys. Lying side by side in bags, each bag the same." Now Azizza's voice had steadied to a quiet monotone. "They'd been shot. All except Najib; they'd cut his head off." She paused. "No one warned me. When I opened his bag, his head ... fell out."

She swallowed. The sound was echoed in Celestine's own throat; it seemed to travel all the way down into her gut.

"Then a man saw what I was doing. He came over to me. He said, 'Are they yours?' As if—as if, you know, they were dogs." Her voice had turned savage. "When I said yes, he said, 'I saw it. I was there when they did it to the eldest boy. He couldn't say tomato right.' I looked at him. I didn't understand. He said, 'Some guys had set up a roadblock. Ba'athists. They were testing everyone who went near the F'listin camp. You had to say tomato, in Arabic.'"

"*Bandouran,*" Celestine murmured under her breath.

"That's how we say it," Azizza agreed. "But the F'listin say it differently. They can't say *bandouran,* they say *bandoura* instead. And Najib had spent so long with the Palestinians, he spoke like them. It must have come out wrong, because he was frightened." She paused. "He was only fifteen!" she cried. "But they cut his head off, just the same."

Celestine watched helplessly while Azizza fumbled inside her clothing and brought out a photograph. When she pushed it across the table, Celestine expected it to be a family snapshot. It wasn't. The monochrome photo showed a pretty young girl smiling shyly into the camera, her cheekbones pushed up high by a brilliant smile and her eyes almost closed against the sun.

"I found it in Najib's shirt," Azizza whispered. "Next to his heart."

She burst into tears. Celestine sat there in the last of the candlelight and she thought, Robbie is fourteen now. Will he live to be fifteen? Will he carry a girl's photo next to his heart before he dies?

"What had happened," she asked softly, "to the others?"

Azizza swallowed back her tears, took a moment to compose herself. "Kemal and Yasmin and the rest? They were riding on a bus, to the hospital. The Syrians machine-gunned it. That's all."

"They never knew what had happened to Najib?"

Azizza shook her head.

"Thanks be to Allah, the Compassionate, the Merciful."

For a long time after that the two women sat in silence.

"Why were you in the house today?" Celestine asked at last.

"Oh"—Azizza wiped her eyes, first the right, then the left—"I come here sometimes, after work. To remember—"

"Better times."

The other woman nodded.

"You said you worked not far away?"

"Yes. After the ... after that night, I brought my two nieces, the ones who survived, back to Beirut. Your money was useful; thank you."

"Even though it didn't always arrive."

"Oh, it did, once I came back south."

Celestine's astonishment must have shown, for Azizza smiled wanly. "Do you remember Chafiq Hakkim?"

"I'll say! My banker, what a rogue."

"I work for him. You used to send the money through his bank, you see. My first day back in town, I went to the bank to tell them I'd left Tripoli, and he saw me. He asked after you, of course. And one thing led to another."

"I remember his wife was always trying to steal you away to work for them when she was alive. Does he pay you well?"

"Well enough. And he makes sure your money comes through, no matter what. He has twelve identity cards, *twelve!* I've seen them laid out on his dressing table, each one in a different religion, and some of them even in a different name. Can you believe that?"

Celestine thought of her own three passports, one of which

had enabled her to enter Lebanon that very day, and smiled. "Go on," she said.

"Old Chafiq's the same as he ever was. Women, wine, and hashish."

"And money. Banker Hakkim always had money."

"He's never short."

"And is he still good friends with my beloved son?"

Azizza snorted with laughter. "Oh, they're the closest of buddies." Then her face clouded. "That's how I heard about the plane. They were talking about it."

Celestine leaned forward eagerly. "Saying what?"

"Sorry, I don't know. I just overheard Hakkim say a few words on the phone. 'Feisal, swear to me they'll never find out in Jerusalem,' he said. And there was something about Yemen and the plane, which is how I knew what had happened when it came on the news a few hours later."

"This was *before* it came on the news?"

"Yes. Hakkim knew what was going to happen before it happened."

"And he definitely mentioned Jerusalem?"

"I'm sure of that. I think he was saying that the Israelis would monitor the videos and perhaps find out from them—"

"Videos? Wait a minute, what videos?"

"There's a helicopter going to and fro, between the plane and an Iranian ship. They expect to have the first film tomorrow, early."

Celestine had exhausted herself to that strange state where you want to talk more and can think of nothing to say. She sighed. "Izza, is there anything here I could sleep on? Anything that hasn't been defiled?"

"I can find you something, don't worry."

"Then I need to sleep. And later I must speak to Hakkim. Let's see how much dear Chafiq thinks he owes me, hmm?"

"Less than *you* think," Azizza said darkly.

Celestine rose, stretched. "Meaning?" she said with a yawn.

"Feisal married off one of his nieces to Hakkim, a year after his first wife died. Chafiq's family now."

"*What?*" Celestine froze in mid-stretch, turning a horror-stricken face to Azizza. "Tell me you're joking!"

But instead Azizza pursed her lips as if unsure how far to go. "I'm sure he's got everything riding on this hijack," she said quietly. "And he's in; you're out. So you be careful, Celestine."

21 July: Noon: Bahrain

G ive me the lowdown, Selman; give me the facts." Andrew Nunn stepped into the shower and raised his voice over the rush of water. "Give me a beer, why don't you?"

Selman Shehabi rummaged around in the fridge and brought out a Heineken for the Englishman, apple juice for himself. They were staying in the same hotel that Leila Hanif had patronized some hours before. Shehabi had arrived first, but since his journey involved only a short hop across the Persian Gulf from Baghdad, this was hardly surprising. Andrew Nunn had been hauled out of Jakarta, put on a company plane, and dumped at Bahrain International Airport after a ten-hour flight with one stop for refueling. He was tired, he was travel-stained, he was not in the best of tempers.

Nunn finished his shower and turned off the water. "Why am I here?" he shouted through the connecting door, as he dried himself. "Why have you brought me here?" These were the words of a man in the hands of the secret police—which was how he felt.

"Who else should we call?"

Shehabi's mild, melodic voice, almost feminine in pitch, belied his true nature. He was highly valued by the appalling regime he served because of his many years' experience in outwitting foreigners, particularly Westerners; he'd studied at the Sorbonne, could speak four European languages, had survived a staff officer's course at Sandhurst. He was a member in good standing of Iraq's Ba'ath Arab Socialist Party, Saddam Hussein, President, and a brevet major in the Republican Guards presently seconded to the 7th Basra regiment, stationed in Fao on the Arab River. At least that was the story, though Nunn had no time for it. Shehabi was related by marriage to the foreign minister, was unassailably powerful. As such, he rated a page in Nunn's "little black book" and a certain measure of genuine personal respect.

Nunn came back into the living room with only a towel around his portly waist. As he picked up the glass of beer he grinned at Shehabi, sitting in an armchair with his fingertips steepled in front of him, and mentally murmured, *This* time.

But no, Major Shehabi did not smile. Nunn had been trying to force those rubbery-looking lips into an expression of amusement for over ten years now. He'd long ago promised himself a new Burberry as a reward for making Shehabi smile, but unless something broke soon he was going to have to throw out his existing raincoat and just get wet.

The annoying thing was, he smiled at other people, some of them European. That galled. Nunn couldn't think what he was doing wrong.

"Cheers," he said, raising the glass. "Hope I won't embarrass you if I pull on some clothes, old chap."

As he meandered around the adjacent bedroom, pausing to rummage in his suitcase or stand in front of the mirror to skate two silver-backed brushes across the top of his head, he wondered what the Iraqi made of him. Selman Shehabi, with his trousers an inch too tight around the paunch and a couple of inches too short in the leg; how did he perceive Andrew "John Bull" Nunn?

As Nunn sat on a stool in front of the dressing table and pulled on his socks he calculated, ruefully, that his companion knew a damn sight too much about him altogether.

"A plane is hijacked," he called through the connecting door. "There is reason to believe (a) that it was done by Leila Hanif, working for cash down, full twelve-month warranty, plus limited edition souvenir brochure thrown in, (b) that Hanif, or whoever, knows all anyone needs to know about flying, and (c) that the

South Yemeni government was caught on the hop. How am I doing?"

"Impeccably. Continue."

"Impeccably be ... buggered." Nunn clicked his teeth, peering closer at the object he was holding. "Why doesn't anyone darn socks any more?" he muttered. Then, more cheerfully, "What's this got to do with me?"

"You are the foremost loss adjuster in the world. I testify to that."

"Well, thank you, Selman. It's good to know the fan club's still intact."

For some years Nunn had headed up his own Lloyds syndicate; done rather well, actually. Then he'd been chatting to this fellow at Ascot, one thing led to another, next thing he knew he'd gone into a business that had always fascinated him. Become a private dick, in fact. Because he sort of knew everybody by then, and had a bit of luck, he'd scored some spectacular successes in his first eighteen months with the new outfit, and from then on it had been roller-coaster stuff. Last fiscal year, for instance, his show had billed clients for eight plus million dollars U.S.; year before, however, a paltry two hundred and seventy-eight thousand. All that would have been in Shehabi's file long before Nunn had bailed out the Iraqi government over an explosion on one of their rigs. The syndicates had cried war-exclusion clause; he'd proved it was an accident—well, he hadn't really proved anything, he'd just used the old brain box and spoken a few choice words in the right ears, after which he'd been in tight with all the Arabs, particularly those with a decent single-malt scotch locked up in the embassy safe.

Shehabi knew about these claims for the simple reason that he'd dealt with Nunn as principal over them. He probably also knew that Nunn had a Queen Anne manor house in Gloucestershire, a town house overlooking Regent's Park, two racehorses, a Porsche 944 and a Bentley Turbo, a French wife he no longer cared much about and whose indiscretions he tolerated, benignly, on his by now rare sojourns in England. There'd been a time when he had loved the two houses and put all his spare energy into them, but since his son Michael had grown up and moved away they no longer held quite the same fascination for him. Major Shehabi was paid to know about things like that, too.

Thoughts of home momentarily distracted Nunn. Anne-Marie, his wife, would be celebrating her birthday next week, by which time, with luck, he'd be safely ensconced in Jakarta, or "Jak," as he preferred to think of it, once more. He must phone the gallery in Dover Street, order that little Hockney drawing she was so fond of....

But presents could wait. The burning topic of the hour was the extent of Shehabi's knowledge. Did he know, for example—did he *really* know—how acute was the brain behind the Englishman's shambling, Bertie Woosterish exterior? The question taxed Nunn as he shouldered his red braces over the jolly old Turnbull & Asser and picked a dark, hand-knitted tie out of the heap bursting from the suitcase like a still life of serpents. Because if he did, the brown stuff could be about to hit the fan in quite spectacular fashion....

"The trouble about your loss-adjusting theory," he called, as he settled his double-breasted jacket into place, "is that so far no one's requested my services."

"They will. The airline will."

I think so too, old chap, Nunn told his reflection in the mirror, but then I had a telex from 'em just before I left Jak. You didn't. Yet you know; you're not bluffing, you actually know.

Best to come clean.

"Frankly, I did have a sort of unofficial fishing expedition come my way."

"I'm sure you did, Andrew. Old man."

Shehabi dangled the last two words from the end of his sentence in a manner that left it unclear whether he was experimenting with an irony that was far from innate or deliberately seeking to wound. Nunn, affecting concern over the remaining amount of his Grey Flannel cologne, disdained to speculate which.

"Although the real reason why I've come," he said, "is because ..." *Because you know I've done business with the Hanifs before, and few other outsiders have,* said the quiet inner voice he'd learned to trust over the years; but Shehabi would never own up to that and so discretion obliged Andrew to finish the sentence by saying, "Because you invited me."

He entered the living room, spread his hands, and bowed from the waist. "*Sayid* Selman Shehabi, I am at your service."

"Then we shall go."

On the way down the two men said nothing. Shehabi could hardly be described as talkative by nature, whereas Nunn was disposed to curse his fate in silence. For the past six years he'd been negotiating a multiparty deal that would wrap up one of the biggest oil frauds in the history of marine insurance. A tanker went missing; did she sink or was she holed? A prime minister's brother owned the company that owned the ship; a government owned the cargo; yet a third government, this time acting through agents that weren't really agents at all but the third government itself in another guise, had done the deal at the other end. Generals were involved; east of Suez, they usually were. Nunn had been nursing this interesting little situation for so long now he resented being distracted from it. He had box files of it in his various offices, diskettes that accompanied his Toshiba laptop everywhere he went, skeins inside his head that would have baffled the greatest chess player the world had ever seen. It obsessed him for one good reason: when everybody's ink was drying on the settlement document he'd drafted, which itself was now in its eighty-ninth version, he and his associates would become entitled to be paid ten million Swiss francs. In Zurich. In cash.

"I can't tell you," he said, as they emerged into the sunlight, its whiteness fuzzied by dust, "how thrilled I am to be here again, Selman."

Oddly enough, this bland statement contained a kernel of truth. A certain well-connected Iraqi middleman had gone to the bottom of the ocean off the north coast of Borneo along with the aforementioned oil tanker, and this had caused not a few problems in Baghdad. For reasons too complicated to explain in less than a magazine-sized presentation, Nunn accepted that it would be as well to massage his Iraqi contacts if he wanted to see his ten million Swiss francs this side of a coronary. He needed the Iraqis. So when Shehabi phoned, requesting his presence in Bahrain as a matter of urgency, the request carried even more weight than that of the airline whose very expensive property was depreciating by the hour in the middle of a South Yemeni wasteland.

"It is we who are thrilled, Andrew. Come." Shehabi was beckoning toward a huge black Cadillac. The hotel bell captain already had its rear door open; Nunn could feel the air-conditioning at ten paces.

"No, thanks, I'll walk," he said easily. "Join me?"

Shehabi shrugged. "You are right, the one-way system...."

Nunn knew that Bahrain's peculiar traffic patterns could easily turn a five-minute journey as the crow flew into a half-hour tour of the island. He did not care for Bahrain. "What's it like?" people sometimes asked him, at the club or on the golf course. "Like a condom in its wrapping," he'd reply, "ridged all around with a depression in its middle; pregnant, if you'll forgive the pun, with excitement, but desperately short on delivery."

In fact, all they had to do was cut across the enormous parking lot overlooked by Leila Hanif's suite, bearing right, until they came to the gateway of a two-story brown-pebbled building. Beside the main door was mounted a brace of large metal plates: LLOYDS ASSOCIATION OF LONDON UNDERWRITERS, the one above proclaimed, LLOYDS AGENCY, the other.

"Thoughtful of you," Nunn murmured to Shehabi as the latter led the way inside. "Don't want the embassy embroiled in this."

They entered a large airy ground-floor room, its windows open onto the courtyard that separated this building from the street. At the end farthest from the door, directly underneath a ceiling fan, desks and filing cabinets had been cleared aside in favor of a conference table. Seeing them approach, several other men rose. Shehabi embarked on a round of introductions. No one from the Bahraini government, Andrew was thinking as he took his seat; is that the good news or the bad news? But apart from that, looking around the table he saw most of the faces he'd expected to find: MI6's resident spook, the military attaché, airline station manager. No Arabs. *Where were the Arabs?*

"The airline has received a telex," said the military man, a major in the Scots guards called Philip Trewin. Nunn liked the cut of his jib, liked the way he assumed chairmanship of the meeting without any trouble. "Six Iranian prisoners of war to be freed in exchange for the plane plus passengers. Mr. Shehabi?"

"My government does not acknowledge the existence of those named in the telex. My country has been at war with Iran for many years and has taken many prisoners, but we are not holding these Iranians."

Stalemate, Nunn thought. Damn. Of course, Major Trewin had merely been going through the motions, wanting to show up the Iraqi position. "May I see the telex?" he inquired.

Trewin brought a sheet of paper out of his briefcase and slid it across the table to him. "Sent to London head office," he confirmed, in response to Nunn's murmured question.

"From?"

"Ah, that's the odd one. From an Iranian Vosper Mark Five frigate lying off Socotra Island. Know it, do you?"

Nunn shook his head.

Trewin got up and went across to the regional map pinned on one wall. "Here," he said, pointing. "This big island you can see southeast of Al Mukalla."

"Who owns Socotra?"

"South Yemen."

"Why are we not in South Yemen now?" Nunn asked. "In my experience, gentlemen, the negotiating team dealing with a hijack resembles nothing so much as a swarm of wasps. It assembles itself and hovers, waiting for the situation to crystallize; then it descends on the nearest stronghold and gets stuck in. The plane's in South Yemen; the demand's coming from a ship just off South Yemeni territory; why aren't we there too?"

Before Trewin could answer, another man, sitting at the far end of the table, portentously cleared his throat. This was a strange sound, midway between a grunt and the *hoom* of a Buddhist chant.

"Ah, yes." Trewin sounded less than enthusiastic. "Dr. Milner's our resident Arabist, perhaps the best man to—"

"*Hoom.* Have you been to South Yemen, Mr. Nunn?"

"No."

"It's the poorest of the Arabian countries. There's no oil, nothing, literally nothing there. Only two percent of the land is arable. The politics are frightful. One party, communist system. Their National Liberation Front applauded the Soviet invasion of Afghanistan. Not amenable to reason. I know, I spent six years there."

"I see." Nunn tried to keep his voice soothing. "What, in your opinion, Dr. Milner, are they likely to do in this situation?"

"Well, in their time they've given support to the PLO and refuge to Arab terrorists of every hue. They've actually rewarded hijackers in the past, so I'd assume they were broadly sympathetic to this lot."

Nunn stared at Milner's cadaverous, pale face, trying to work out the reason for his tetchiness. Six years in Yemen had left their mark; it was obvious he didn't want to be sent back there.

"Have they put out a statement yet?"

"Not officially. Unofficially, our ambassador here has been given to understand, by his opposite number in Aden, that they're going to stick their heads in the sand and pretend nothing is happening. They've no resources for storming the plane, anyway."

"They could cordon it off, at least? Offer to supply food?"

"Assuming they were sympathetic, which I've already advised is unlikely, they could cordon it off, but from what? There's nothing *there*, except a few villagers and Bedouin tribesmen whom they can't control. As for food, they have enough trouble feeding their own population from one year to the next. Just *getting* to the plane would tax the resources of better men than them."

"Mm. What's the terrain like?"

"Arid. Some rain; mostly it falls between July and September, so there's a chance of that. *Harif*, they call it: the monsoon season."

"Temperature?"

"During the *harif*? Minimum nightly temperatures of over eighty degrees Fahrenheit; maximum daily temperatures could rise to a hundred and four Fahrenheit. Humid, always. You get hot winds blowing fine sand inland from the seashore. One of the most inhospitable areas on God's earth."

"How long would it take to arrange visas?"

"Forever. Even for accredited diplomats like myself."

Nunn grimaced. "You're not painting a terribly attractive picture, Dr. Milner."

"No," Milner agreed emphatically. "The Yemenis have a saying that can roughly be translated as 'When the old dog shits biscuits there'll be change in Yemen.' Do pardon my French," he added, with plodding irony.

"What about setting up shop in Oman, next door?"

"I really wouldn't advise it, Mr. Nunn."

"Why not?"

"Because South Yemen supported guerrilla activity against the Oman government, back in the late sixties. They patched it up, and now you won't find Oman willing either to help the Yemenis or be seen to act against them."

Nunn suddenly interpreted Dr. Milner's real message; Don't spoil it, that's what he was saying; don't rock my boat.

"What are conditions like on the plane?" he asked. "Anyone know?"

It was Trewin who answered. "They'd taken on food and water at Bahrain shortly before takeoff, but that won't last long, of course. Every commercial aircraft carries emergency rations in the hold for just this eventuality, plus extra for the crew, but using it depends on the hijackers' willingness to give access."

"Any natural water sources in the region?"

"Wadis," Trewin said, before Dr. Milner could interject. "But dry at this time of year, unless they're lucky and it rains."

"Air-conditioning?"

"Depends on how much fuel the pilot dumped before landing. He's not allowed to tell us, of course; but he wouldn't have reckoned on getting out again and he'd have been worried about fire, so my guess is that he'd have got rid of most of it."

"So no air-con, or at least not for much longer ... I see."

Nunn fell silent, allowing the others to consider those things that had been left unsaid. The toilets, blocked with sanitary napkins and excrement. Hunger. Thirst. Quarrels breaking out among the passengers. Heatstroke. Boredom, fatigue, stress of every kind.

Children crying incessantly, for food and water, for milk that was never forthcoming.

"What contact's been had with the plane?" Nunn asked.

"A demand for one helicopter to be sent to monitor the hijack with TV equipment. No deadlines or threats, yet."

Nunn sat forward and folded his hands on the table; his next quiet words were addressed to them. "Any Israeli passports?"

"We're checking."

"I ... see." So among all the many imponderables he was called upon to ponder was the chance of an Israeli Defense Force unit being dispatched on a rescue mission without reference to other interested parties, which would increase the danger factor by about a hundred million. I don't know what I'm doing here, he told himself; I've absolutely no idea what I'm involved in. I'll play my part and wing back to Jakarta, still blissfully ignorant of what they all really wanted from me, apart from the *H* page of my address book.

"Is the Hanif woman behind this hijack?" he asked aloud, "or merely officer in charge of front-line troops?"

"I would guess that she's behind it," Trewin replied.

Nunn was inclined to agree. He had a considerable file on Hanif, as on every other important terrorist. She'd come within an ace of murdering an Israeli ambassador to the United States; that was her principal claim to fame, but there had been much else since. She was far more of a general than an "other rank."

"And this is a contract job? For Iran?"

"We think so. The Iranian frigate's pretty conclusive, don't you think?"

"We'll know more when we've cracked the code," the MI6 man said.

Nunn's head jerked around. "What code?"

MI6 made a face. "They haven't told you much, have they? The plane's talking to the frigate on the radio, in code. Not much traffic. Some of it's *en clair*; for instance, the helicopter they're requesting—*one* chopper, very specific—that was *en clair*."

"What would you like me to do?" Nunn asked.

"We were wondering if you had any ideas," Trewin said, and there was a sharp edge to his normally bland voice.

We're coming to it now, thought Nunn; they know I've dealt with the Hanifs and they want to make use of the information but they can't see how. *I* can't see how. All I know is, I can't afford to stand still and do nothing. Right across the northern hemisphere, governments are conferring while representatives of their armed forces liaise in an attempt to work out a military solution. Debts are being called in, old scores settled, everybody working in the dark, all pulling in different directions. So don't just sit here, *do* something.

Make some phone calls, why not?

Feisal Hanif he rather fancied he could manage to contact; Halib might be a touch more difficult. What was that weird and wonderful old biddy called, Feisal's mother, Sally, Sell-something, the one he'd run into at Nice?

So make phone calls, yes, but, before that, the hijackers were demanding the release of six Iranian prisoners of war who, according to Shehabi, did not exist. Nunn had to find out if those prisoners were anything more than shadow puppets: alive on a screen specially prepared for the audience, but nowhere else.

He had a sudden yearning to be back in Jakarta, where he knew his way around. He was never going to find his way around this mess, any more than he could have mastered Bahrain's one-way road system.

"If you'll excuse us," he said, standing up, "it rather looks as if Selman and I have things to discuss."

21 July: Evening: Al Mahra, South Yemen

Tim Campbell's hands were shaking. His head throbbed. Panic harmed him far more than the chemical imbalance caused by lack of insulin. Everyone on the plane felt thirsty, but acute thirst was a symptom of untreated diabetes, and Tim was suffering terribly. He couldn't ask for a larger ration. There'd already been clashes between the hostile groups that had sprung up. Because Tim was the only diabetic aboard, he had no group, no leverage.

He lay back as far as the seat would allow. He had cramps in both legs, and the base of his spine hurt from too many hours spent sitting in one position. Sometimes he felt that if he wasn't allowed to stand up and stretch he'd die. But except when they went to the lavatory, with a gunman at their backs, all the passengers had to remain belted in like so many trussed chickens.

When they went to the toilet another guard waited nearby, with grenades in his hands. He held them so that you could see them as you went into the stinking cupboard, could see that the pins were out, so that if he dropped them ...

Tim felt hungry. They had last been marched to the toilets at noon, when the heat was at its worst and the smell likewise; as they came out, the man with the grenades gestured them to pick up a tray from the pile in the galley. One of the stewards had been ordered to heat up the food. Most people, overcome by the stench behind them, refused a tray. Tim had made himself take one because he knew that without food his chances would halve. Swallowing was hell. He left most of the meal untouched.

The main cabin smelled overpoweringly of sweat, and quite close to where Tim sat there was another odor that he sucked down with every breath he drew. Somebody had vomited into a sick bag. Tim had heard it, behind him and to his left: a liquid splashing-and-retching, then a faint patting sound, as if somebody was trying to comfort the sick man.

That had been hours ago. Two-thirty. At eleven in the morning the captain had switched on the air-conditioning. The doors had been closed and a mighty wave of relief swept through the passengers as the collective thought took hold—We're leaving!—only to be dashed moments later, when Ross came on the intercom to explain. But now the light was fading, the air-conditioning was off, and a smell of vomit poisoned the atmosphere.

Occasionally someone would sneeze or cough. Occasionally Tim would hear the sound of sobbing, or low voices. But what really amazed him, what frightened him, was the silence, this great, ominous, and never-ending silence of the sepulcher.

The man in the aisle seat of his row, 20C, was called Colin. They'd exchanged a few words earlier; he was nice. Tim envied Colin, because he could sleep. Suddenly Colin's breathing quickened. Tim turned to see that his eyeballs were rolling around behind the closed lids. Rapid eye movement; that meant a dream. Colin's mouth opened, saliva dribbled out, and he moaned something indistinct. Not a happy dream....

Colin looked down at his hand, nestling like a contented little bird in the larger brown one. It was so nice to be traveling with Daddy. He loved his daddy very, very much. Daddy was kind. He knew it was Daddy's idea that he shouldn't fly to Hong Kong straightaway, when the school hols began. Instead, Colin had flown all by himself to Singapore, where Daddy was waiting at the airport to meet him. His father's name was Malcolm, and he was the director of something big and important, called a merchant bank.

They'd spent a week together in Singapore. Their hotel was called Raffles, and it seemed awfully grand. During the early part of the day, Malcolm left his son in the care of Beth, a nice English lady who worked in the hotel, while he went off to see to something called his "cables." Beth was super; she took him swimming and laughed a lot. Then, once Daddy was back, they had lunch, and in the afternoons they went sightseeing. Singapore was *terrifically* sultry, but they stopped a lot for ice-creams and drinks, so the heat didn't matter much. He liked it when they went for drives in the jungle or visited the villages on stilts. They were called "kampongs."

Now they were on their way to Hong Kong, where Mother would be waiting. As the thought entered his mind he felt himself shrivel up inside, like a sick dog when you touched it. Not that he didn't love Mother; of course he did. But she didn't always have time to spare for Colin. Sometimes, when he wanted to talk to her, she would snap at him. Then at other times she would complain, "You never speak to your own mother!" But he had no means of knowing which times would turn out to be which.

He stared down at the big brown hand of his father, who was dozing in the seat beside him, and he knew a terrible fear that perhaps one day Daddy wouldn't be here; there'd only be Mother. A huge, inarticulate swell of love swept him up and he leaned toward his father, resting his head on the dozing man's shoulder, while he tried to find words to express his sense of pleasure, of *joy* at having Daddy by his side. He'd almost done it, all but found the words he wanted. That was when the first bullets hit. They blew holes in the hull of the DC-4 that were one and a half feet wide. *Boom!* they went. *Boom, boom!*

At first he had no idea what was happening. Everybody seemed to be shouting. His father woke up with a start. Colin heard a voice from the front of the plane, shouting "Mayday! Mayday! Losing altitude, engine on fire!" Rose, the nice stewardess, was crying. He tilted forward, as if on a swing, and he realized that the plane was diving like a bomber in one of those pictures in his

Eagle comic. He could see more and more of the big holes; they were everywhere: in the ceiling above him, beside his seat....

The noise of their dive rose from a whine to a howl to a screech that blotted out all other sounds. Out of the corner of his eye he could see flames snatching at the wing. The plane was almost vertical now, plunging down toward the sea. He knew he would start to burn. He cried.

He was going to die. He was definitely going to die. Nothing could prevent it. For a flash of time, it occurred to him that he should pray to God, but in that same instant his father spoke. "When we get down, there may be a lot of noise." His voice was calm; not by so much as a tremor did it reveal emotion. "Hold on to me, Colin, and don't let go."

It was as if they were in the Tiger Balm Gardens again. Everything would be all right. But then something dark and heavy rose up before Colin and he opened his mouth to scream, but the thing smothered his breath.

"Mayday! Mayday!," he heard the voice shout, even above the noise of their dive: "*Ditching! Ditching! Ditching!*"

As the black, heavy shape crushed him into his seat, Colin took a last breath and screamed his heart out. When he tried to open his eyes, they stung. Liquid, splashing over him....

The plane skimmed along the surface of the sea for perhaps half a mile. There was a deafening crash as the starboard wing was wrenched off by the force of the impact; then the nose went into an enormous wave and that was the end. Beside Colin's head, the porthole smashed and water flooded in, washing away the horrible fluid that had flooded over him, washing away the horrible smothery black thing, too. Colin floated out of his seat. Beside and above him was light. He pushed his way toward it. Something sharp caught at his feet. He kicked. His ankle was snagged. He kicked again, this time managing to fight his way free. Then he was rising toward a fiercer light, and for the first time he knew he was cold, that he'd been ice-cold ever since they began to dive.

His head broke water. The sea was choppy; a wind heavy with salt and sickly warmth battered his face. He splashed about a bit. "Help," he cried. The word came out as a pitiful wail, swallowed by wind and waves even between his mouth and his own ears, but "Help!" he mewed again.

Then hands grabbed him from behind by the collar and he rose up out of the sea before swinging backward over something hard; above him, the sky reeled like a film gone wrong, his head twisted to one side, and he saw a white bailer, a rope, legs....

"Wake up! *Please* wake up."

Colin Raleigh fell into wakefulness through a hole in the floor of his dream. He opened his eyes to find Tim gazing at him anxiously.

"Please wake up," the boy implored. "They've already heard you."

Colin stared down at the pale hand on his own, surprised to find that this image at least had survived the transition from then to now. He wiped the dribble off his chin and shook his head in an attempt to clear the mess inside.

Tim's agonized expression deepened to terror. Colin, seeing it, jerked his head around. One of the hijackers was standing in the aisle a couple of rows in front, submachine gun half raised. His face was clean of emotion, even of curiosity. But Colin knew he had summoned this man from the depths of his nightmare; he was responsible for the new layer of silence that now overlaid this section of the plane. Everyone nearby was holding his breath.

"Sorry," he said, speaking louder than was necessary. "I had a bad dream. I'm awake now, I'm all right."

The man went on gazing at him. Colin strove to sit upright. "Nightmare," he said.

No reaction from the gunman. Around him, Colin could feel the screws tightening. Some strange heaviness weighed on his abdomen, pressing him back into his seat. When Tim swallowed, Colin heard. Everybody heard.

For a moment longer, the hijacker stared at Colin. Then, very slowly, his gun drooped until the muzzle was once again pointing at the floor. He turned. He walked back up the plane. The air around Colin changed formula, once again allowing people to breathe. It was the unpredictability of death that drove them half mad with fear; they could not tell from one second to the next how the gunmen would react. But now the incident was history. Each passenger could replay it in his mind like a video hired from the local store, taking satisfaction in the survival of the hero: himself.

"Sorry," Colin said to Tim. "This dream, it ... gets to me, sometimes."

"You've had it before?"

"Often."

Tim needed distraction, anything. "Tell me about it."

Under normal circumstances Colin would have found a way of refusing. Now it seemed churlish to refuse.

"Once, when I was traveling in a plane, I was shot down. The Chinese Air Force did it. Off Hainan Island, in the South China Sea."

"You mean, really ... *shot* down?" Tim's eyes were wide with horror.

Colin grunted. "Really."

"But you're alive."

"Yes. The pilot was a bloody hero. Man called Philip Blown. He couldn't save everyone, but he saved me. We hit the sea. I got out. Some of the crew survived, they managed to float a life raft. I was picked up. We were rescued by a flying boat. Of course I couldn't understand much at the time, I was only seven. All the grown-ups thought the Chinese would come back and finish us off, I realize that now. They didn't. Seems they thought we were Chiang Kai-shek or one of his generals. Something like that. My father died in the crash."

"I'm sorry."

"Yes." Suddenly Colin laughed quietly. "That man Blown ... the pilot ... he sent his Swiss watch back to the makers, complaining that it had stopped—it was supposed to be waterproof—and you know what? They gave him a new one. They did. They bloody did."

He dashed tears from his face, but he knew Tim must have seen them. Really, he didn't know who or what he was crying for.

"There were some other kids on the plane," he managed to say at last. "All dead. All except me."

Tim was silent for a while. Then he said, "Why do you think it was you that got out?"

"Sorry?"

"Lots of people died in that crash, but you didn't. Why do you think that was—does God have plans for you?"

Colin forced a smile. "I don't know. But there was a particular reason why I got out; you see—"

He didn't finish the sentence. Noise. Outside the plane, the sound of engines beating hard. "That's ... that's a plane," Colin breathed.

"No." Tim's voice trembled. "Helicopters. More than one."

Leila stood at the forward door to watch the helicopter land, some fifty meters from the plane's port side. She could see nothing behind the glass of its bubble-shaped cockpit, but she knew the men inside. They did not interest her. What *did* interest her was the second helicopter, which, instead of landing, hovered at a comfortably safe height.

She could see it clearly, from her position a little back from the doorway; she was *meant* to see it. Someone had painted a crude representation of the red, white, green, and black Palestinian flag on its side. The Palestinians, of course, did not have helicopters.

"They," the grand masters of the outside, did not seriously intend her to read this as a Palestinian gesture of fraternal solidarity. They were bored with waiting for something to happen, that's all, so they did the grand-masterly equivalent of poking a stick into the hole and waiting to see what hissed.

She knew that the crew of the uninvited second machine would be frantically taking photographs of all kinds, high-res monochrome, color, close-ups, wide-field, infrared. They would be recording ambient temperature, air pressure, and light. They would be mapping the terrain, calculating from trig points, seeking cover for a strike force. They would be using a suction pump to collect air from the site, and, if they had any sense, they would have coated the underside of their helicopter with light glue, to attract a coating of dust thrown up from the ground by their rotors: samples fit for analysis in Jeddah or Bahrain or wherever it was they came from.

She wondered where they had come from. The government of South Yemen had a soft spot for terrorists. Both Saudi and Oman disputed the border not far from here; they would be foolhardy to enter Yemeni airspace without an invitation that Aden would never grant. Perhaps the Israelis had a ship already on station in the Arabian Sea. She hoped so. Playing against Jerusalem was the best game in town.

She wondered if the second helicopter could be Israeli, much as she was starting to question whether the man who'd attacked her in the final seconds before she took the plane might be an Israeli. She had no proof—yet. But soon the photograph of her attacker that Selim had taken with a camera stolen from one of the passengers would be on its way to Halib, along with the man's passport, and not long afterward she would have proof. She was looking forward to that. She knew she had met the Israeli somewhere before. It troubled her that she could not remember where.

She watched the second helicopter circle slowly around and out of her vision. The message transmitted to the outside world had been emphatic. One helicopter must come. *One.*

Leila lifted the intercom. Selim answered.

"The first," she said. "Now."

Selim replaced the receiver and walked up the plane, through economy, into the business class section, using the starboard aisle. Immediately beyond the curtain, on his right, was the seat occupied by Jan Van Tonder. Selim carefully folded back the curtain and secured it, so that those passengers sitting at the front of economy class could see what was about to happen.

The South African glanced up from the magazine he was leafing through, caught sight of Selim by his side, and sniffed. Then he went back to his reading.

"You," Selim said softly. "Get up."

Van Tonder must have known this was directed at him. Everyone else knew it. When Selim came in, Robbie Raleigh had been refixing a crude bandage, made from a napkin, to Sharett's wounded forehead. Now he stopped what he was doing and turned to look.

"I said, get up." Selim was slim, elegant: his Dunhill blazer and Hugo Boss gray flannels, still looking good after a night and most of a day, would have commanded respect from any hotel doorman. They had no noticeable effect on Van Tonder, who continued to thumb through the magazine in his lap as if he were alone in the cabin. Only when Selim prodded him with the muzzle of his very inelegant, unstylish M3A1 did he react at all, and then not as Robbie expected.

"You people," Van Tonder said, with a contemptuous sideways inspection of Selim, "haven't the brains of a kaffir between you." When Selim said nothing, he went on. "Did you hear that noise, just now? Do you know what made it?"

He calmly closed the magazine and slipped it into its elastic pocket on the seat in front of him before sitting back and clasping the sides of his seat, like a disgruntled judge.

Selim still said nothing.

"That noise was the beginning of the end, for you and for your comrades in back. Helicopters. The enemy is at hand, my friend. It's what we call a standoff. They wait. Eventually—not today, perhaps, not tomorrow—you grow tired. You drop your guard. Then they come."

This time he smiled up at Selim.

"It would be easier to surrender now. We know all about the deals you people do. You'll find a refuge, I'm sure. Tunisia, maybe. Algeria."

Selim returned the smile.

To Robbie, sitting immediately in front with his head twisted around, Selim's expression was how he imagined the smile of an angel must be; it contained good humor, patience, compassion. Above all, compassion. Selim's face was beatific. Looking at him, Robbie knew himself to be in the presence of a man who had reached a turning point in his destiny, but he could not guess why.

"You are South African," Selim said, and although it wasn't a question, Van Tonder treated it as such.

"Yes, I am, and furthermore I am proud of it."

Selim reached into an inside pocket of his jacket and took out a passport. "This is yours," he said quietly.

Again, although he had not framed it as a question, Van Tonder answered him. "Yes."

"Take it."

For the first time in this exchange the South African's arrogant self-confidence faltered slightly. He continued to grip the armrests of his seat and to stare ahead of him, but he hadn't quite enough self-control to prevent the quick movement of his head that showed he had heard.

"Take it."

Van Tonder's left hand seemed to lift off the seat of its own accord. It hovered a moment, undecided; then his fingers closed around the passport and Robbie, transfixed, saw how they turned white.

"You are free."

When Selim spoke, Van Tonder's head slowly twisted around, like a flower revolving on its stalk in an effort to catch the sun. Now a strangulated sound came from his mouth, something between a groan and a rattle.

Robbie closed his eyes and faced the front. It was all so damned unfair! He wanted to cry, but anger predominated. If anyone got to go it should be him, Robbie—he was just a kid, innocent—but that this—this *idiot*, this *turd*, should be the one to get out ...

He blinked back tears and stared out the window at the ash-gray desert floor. So damned unfair! And yet ... and yet ... at least they were letting someone go. That was a kind of victory, wasn't it? No one had died, no one was badly hurt, not even dad's pal Raful, his neighbor, whose head was healing nicely. And if they let one go, surely in time they'd let others go too? It's a *hopeful* sign, goddammit! A *development*. So be a man and face it. Dad would want that; make him proud of you....

Van Tonder staggered as he rose, his legs weakened by hours of inactivity. He held on to the back of Raful's seat, breathing heavily. When Selim offered him his right arm as a support, he accepted, almost falling on it in a sudden burst of gratitude.

"My briefcase ..." His voice was no longer peremptory; it bleated. "Please help me, I can't ..."

Selim, his transcendent smile unfading, reached up with his free hand and took the briefcase out of the overhead locker.

"Thank you. Thank you."

Robbie, hearing the pathetic note in his voice, felt scorn rush through him and fought to resist it; yes, Van Tonder had gone over to the enemy in these final minutes, but what the hell—who could be sure of not doing the same? He looked up as the two of them moved forward and saw tears trickling down Van Tonder's cheeks. Suddenly, without knowing why, the boy cried, "Good luck!" and Van Tonder smiled at him, but vaguely, as if in shock. He muttered some words, perhaps "Thank you," Robbie couldn't be sure.

Selim and Van Tonder reached the curtain separating them from first class and went through it. This time Selim did not pin back the curtain. The first class cabin was empty. He pointed Van Tonder toward the port exit, where the escape slide sloped downward to the desert, himself stopping while still short of the doorway.

"You must take this," he said; and Van Tonder turned to see Selim holding out a large yellow envelope with airmail streaks on its edges, the kind of container airlines use for flight manifests.

"What is this?"

"A message for the world."

After a few seconds' hesitation, Van Tonder accepted the envelope. At the bottom he could see a bulge, and his fingers told him that the envelope contained something small and solid, apart from papers: a roll of film, perhaps. The envelope was sealed with thread wrapped around a washer. He began to unwrap the thread, but Selim commanded him to stop, and he did. Even he seemed to perceive that here, on the last frontier post with freedom, was no place to pick a fresh quarrel. He stuffed it into his briefcase and turned back to the door. As he did so he glanced to his right and thought he saw a figure in the shadows beyond the cockpit door. A woman.... Then he looked at Selim for the last time and, with a foolishness, a lunacy, that he was to regret the rest of his life, he mumbled, "Goodbye."

Captain Morgan and Second Officer Ross had been placed in business class, on the port side of the plane, but were not allowed to sit next to each other. Ross occupied seat 10A while Morgan was in

11A, immediately behind him. From where they were sitting they had a good view of the helicopter that had landed outside, with occasional sight of the second machine as it wheeled above.

Three men had emerged from the helicopter on the ground and mounted a video camera on its tripod. One of them was looking through the viewfinder, while another checked the light. Morgan deduced from their general demeanor that something was about to happen and that these men knew what to expect.

When he felt the aircraft rock, ever so slightly, at first neither he nor Ross could guess what was happening. Only when Van Tonder was on the ground and well on his way toward the helicopter did they grasp the truth.

It struck both of them simultaneously, with great force, so that their exclamations—"Oh, Christ, no!"; "Dear God!"—came out together. Ross half rose in his seat, but Morgan's shouted order to sit down stopped him just in time, for one of the hijack team was already bounding down the aisle.

Morgan waited until the man reached his seat; then, without waiting to be admonished, he said, as evenly as he could, "Please suggest to your leader that I be allowed to make an announcement to calm the passengers."

"No announcement is necessary." The man raised his eyes to look out of the window. Morgan saw how they widened, and he flinched.

The burst from Selim's M3A1 crashed through Morgan's eardrum like a two-stroke engine being started; it rose and died all in a matter of seconds, leaving his hearing muffled. He made himself look out of the window. Van Tonder lay sprawled on the gravel, the briefcase lying a few feet away from his body. From around the area of his waist spread a long, wet splash, scarcely standing out against the grayness of the desert's surface.

Morgan watched, fascinated, while the technician on the ground who earlier had been testing the light walked forward to collect Van Tonder's briefcase. He extracted from it a yellow envelope which Morgan found somehow familiar: the kind of thing he himself used to store the aircraft's waybills and manifests. The man opened this envelope. He pulled out some papers and what might have been a passport, along with another small object, the last two of which items he pocketed. Having studied the papers for a few seconds, he advanced until the cameraman raised a hand, then halted and held a document close to the lens.

There was a difficulty, however, inasmuch as some of Van Tonder's blood had splashed the glass. So they all had to wait while the cameraman ran back to the helicopter for a cloth. When he'd finished cleaning the lens, he looked up to where the second machine was hovering and waved the cloth from side to side in an exaggerated gesture, for all the world like a Victorian lady bidding exuberant farewell to her beau. And so the second helicopter pilot must have construed it, because he climbed, hard, for the protection of the low cloud ceiling and put himself on a course to the southeast.

The noise of the submachine gun had been so diluted by the time it reached the rear cabin that most of the passengers in economy had no idea what it meant. Then a few of them sitting on the left side cried out in horror, others leaned over, craning to see, and by the time the guards intervened the cabin was awash with rumor and half-truth.

"They killed a man"—that was the kernel of reality which flashed through them with the speed of intuition. A psychological barrier had been smashed down, leaving passengers and hijackers staring at each other across its ruins. The first to die ... had died.

Some people stood up, perhaps to challenge their guards, perhaps in a bootless attempt to run away; whatever their motivation, the hijackers brutally pushed them back into their seats. Some, men as well as women, sobbed. Hysteria hung in the air, pungent as the smell of stale smoke the morning after a drunken party. But when a man broke from his seat, waving his arms and shouting, it was nearby passengers, not terrorists, who seized him. By the time Selim arrived on the scene, they had the man trussed up by the sleeves of his jacket. They handed him over like hounds delivering prey to their huntsman before awaiting his praise and he took it from them in the same spirit, with a smile that was part contempt for something animal and part pride.

"Be calm," he told the hysterical man on the floor. "There is nothing you can do; accept it." He raised his voice, addressing himself to the cabin at large. "You think that people on the outside are trying to help you. Perhaps they are. But when they play games with us, they leave us with no option but to retaliate against the only targets available: you, the innocent."

When he stalked into the business class cabin he left behind him a cowed and frightened herd of people whose loyalties by now were shifting dangerously.

Robbie, gazing at Selim as he passed through the cabin, had not yet detected the subtle changes that were going on inside him, as well as many others. He simply felt, in a raw kind of way, that anyone outside the aircraft couldn't possibly understand what hell those on the inside must be enduring. Those inside were lumped together in his mind without differentiating between passengers and hijackers, friends and foes. Us and them; in and out.

"Robbie."

The boy turned his head. Sharett was awake and staring at him. For a moment Robbie wondered how this man knew his name; then he remembered Colin introducing them while they were on the ground at Bahrain.

"Robbie, what day is it?"

"July twenty-first."

"And the time?"

Funny, Robbie thought; I haven't looked at my watch for hours. "Twenty to six." He hesitated. "Are you feeling all right?"

Sharett nodded. "I remember ... remember you bandaging my forehead."

"A long time ago. Last night. After they took the photograph."

"What photograph?"

"One of them came with a camera and took a picture of your face."

"Ah. I can't recall."

For a while after that, Raful gazed at the boy without speaking. He looked like a man whose pride both obliged him to make and prevented him from making some big concession. "You're grown up," he said at last.

Robbie shrugged, blushing.

"You heard the … you heard what happened outside?"

"Yes." Robbie's voice was scarcely audible. He might look grown up, Raful told himself, but inside he was still just a terrified boy.

"Don't be frightened," he said. "You're safe. No one's going to hurt you. Let you go hungry … maybe. Hurt you, no."

Robbie's lips twitched. "How do you know I'm safe?" he asked.

"You're a kid. People like them want publicity, *good* publicity. Dead women and children they don't need."

Selim chose that moment to come through the curtain. He marched to the front of the cabin before picking up the intercom and speaking a few quiet words into it. Seconds later he passed out of sight behind the curtain that screened them from first class. It was as if he had to ask permission before advancing farther up the plane.

Raful noted that and filed it away for future reference. He was feeling pretty good after a long if fitful sleep. He began to take mental notes. Everything interested him, from the distance between his seat and the curtains fore and aft to the facial expressions of the passengers nearest him. No detail was too small to escape his attention.

One member of the hijack team guarded the cabin from a vantage point beside the forward galley. He wore an open-neck shirt, his skin was greasy, he hadn't shaved or slept in a long, long time. Raful liked him on sight.

"See that guy?" he murmured to Robbie with a sideways movement of the head.

Robbie nodded.

"He's exhausted. Which means, yes, he's dangerous, but also it means he can't go on forever. There has to come a time when he sleeps."

"There's more than one of them." Robbie spoke low, but

there was no disguising his despair. "They won't all sleep at the same time."

"But they will all be tired at the same time, of that you may be sure." Raful nodded encouragingly. "And then ... then we shall see."

His ulcer was paining him. Hard to keep up a pretense of jollity, but necessary. He understood that Leila had chosen to lie low and that her actions—or, rather, lack of them—had to be associated with the teenager sitting next to him. Everything that happened aboard this aircraft ultimately came back to her son. *So why did she not make a move?*

Because she was waiting for a development on the outside. That had to be the explanation.

What development?

"Robbie." Raful cupped his hand over the side of his mouth and spoke low. "Have the hijackers said what they want?"

"Something about prisoners. Iranians taken prisoner by Iraq. We're not going to be released until they are."

A real hijack! Not just an attempt to take back her son, but a genuine politically motivated act of terrorism.... Raful wanted time to think about the implications, but for now all that mattered was that he *had* time. Leila wasn't going anywhere, in other words; she'd be staying right here while negotiations for the release of prisoners got under way. In the Middle East, negotiations could go on forever....

What would Robbie do when the chips were down and Leila unveiled herself? How could he, Raful, cement the boy's loyalty to the side of light?

Raful would just have to trust Robbie. No alternative.

Cautiously, very cautiously, so as not to distract the terrorist by the forward galley, Raful stretched out his hand to the elastic net on the back of the seat in front. That was where he had hidden the lighter, just before they landed, but for now he didn't mind about that. He was reaching for a paper napkin he could see tucked away there; then, next to it and half obscured by a newspaper, he saw a cardboard tub decorated with the airline's logo. Somebody's cocktail nuts....

He cupped both napkin and tub in his hand before deftly scooping them into his lap, then down the side of the seat.

The hijacker continued to keep an eye on the cabin. If he'd seen Raful's discreet series of movements he gave no sign of it. Raful deliberately turned his head away, as if to look out of the window at the gathering dusk, and for a full five minutes did nothing more.

The Arab with the gun detached himself from the wall and began to tread slowly down the cabin. Raful guessed his intention—to go through into economy, then cross over so as to return along the starboard aisle—and tensed. Not much time ... as the hijacker passed out of his peripheral vision he felt inside his jacket for a pen.

Nothing. They'd stripped him of everything except the lighter, which they hadn't found. Somewhere deep in the dark recesses of his mind lurked a monster—they'd taken everything *including his passport*—don't think about that, fight the monster some other time; for now, just concentrate on what had to be done. *Find something to write with.*

"Robbie," he muttered. "D'you have a pen, pencil, anything?"

The boy glanced nervously over his left shoulder, to where the terrorist was already disappearing through the aisle curtain, before dipping into the flight bag between his feet. "Here."

Raful snatched it from him and retrieved the paper napkin he'd concealed a few moments earlier. He rested it on the tub of nuts and wrote a dozen words. Then he thrust the paper at Robbie. "If ever you go back there"—he jerked his head back toward economy—"Try to give this to the man in Twenty-four H. I'll make another copy for myself, later, in case they take me back. But mind: *no risks.*"

Robbie gazed down at the paper, making no move to take it. "Who *are* you?" he breathed. "Why do you trust me?"

Raful was minded to say, Because there isn't anybody else, my young friend. But before he could finish the first word, another voice cut across his.

"You. You talk to the boy, too much."

Raful closed his hand into a fist, concealing the napkin. As he bent his head up and to the left, struggling for an innocent expression, he replayed the last few seconds through his memory. How had he and Robbie looked to the terrorist as he came, oh, so silently, through the partition that cut them off from the economy cabin? What, *exactly*, had they been saying? Were their hands close? Touching? What about their heads?

The Arab's eyes were splotches of red and white, fringing concentric circles, the outer one thin, the inner hub matte black. Whatever it was that kept him going had taken its toll. "You," he said. "Move."

Raful hesitated. He could obey, or he could fight. If he fought, there would be death and destruction. But if he obeyed ...

"Okay," he said. "Okay, okay."

He raised his hands, by now both clenched into fists, and shook them gently, as if to say, Look, *regardez*, no tricks.... He kept his eyes fixed on those of the Arab, mesmerized and mesmerizing, so that the man did not see him lower the fists as if to lever himself up from his seat, did not notice him opening the right fist or Robbie quickly shifting his left hand sideways to cover the paper.

"Okay," Raful said lightly. He was on his feet now, with his open hands held up at shoulder height, no threat to anyone. "Okay, okay, okay. Where do you want me to sit?"

The Arab allowed the muzzle of his submachine gun to droop to the left. Raful edged into the aisle, still keeping his eyes on the Arab's, and backed up the cabin until he was opposite an empty aisle seat in a center block of three.

"Here?"

The terrorist nodded. Raful sat. As he belted himself in he found himself repeating Robbie's questions: *Who are you? Why do you trust me?*

He was immediately behind the first class cabin now. Inches away from Stepmother. From target.

Leila did not remember their last encounter in New York, that much was obvious. Hardly surprising when you thought about it: she'd scarcely caught a glimpse of his face. But now she had his passport. A good shoe, made by a fine cobbler, but false. Halib wouldn't take long to see through it.

Why do you trust me? Good question, Robbie. But what you should have added was: *Me, of all people?*

June 1974: Beirut, Lebanon

In the summer of 1974 the easiest way for a *yahoud* like Sharett to enter Lebanon was to head north via Qiryat Shemona, on the right of the map, and then once across the border to aim west for the coast below Sidon. At Metulla, the frontier crossing, the *yahoud* was still that: a Jew; but by the time he reached Habbouch, on the western lee of the Chammis, he had already become fuzzy around the edges. His car—caked with dust, dented here and there, a trifle rusty beneath the bumpers—bore German license plates, and he spoke a smattering of Egyptian Arabic to the few Meta-willeh peasants he met. When he stopped for lunch, or overnight, he was keen to tell his story over a bottle or three of Musar red wine and a Dutch cheroot: how he'd lived most of his life in Europe or Chicago, done well, come "home" to see how things were, to decide whether he should bring his family across. He was amiable and he was generous; the fact that his hearers understood but one word in twenty did not matter. They remembered Sharett for precisely the things he was not.

Like everyone else who ever saw it, he fell in love with the country. Years later, when the IDF was using Merkava tanks to flatten Lebanon's rolling hills and sand-castle forts, bombing it into compliance with their field maps, he would lay aside his copy of *Maariv,* take off his spectacles, and gaze into the middle distance.

At those times he was remembering coarse *markouk* bread, hill-sides painted with flax, bugloss and corn poppies, asters and cyclamen; gorges fringed with stately holm oaks, fields of barley, eggs fried with thyme.

He was remembering apple jam.

He'd risen early and driven for a couple of hours with only a cup of scalding, bitter coffee to line his stomach. In the warm light of early morning he'd skimmed through tiny villages of white-washed houses topped with orange tiles, the sea stretching away on his left as flat and calm as a Biro-blue millpond. He drove slowly, for him, with the remains of last night's cheroot clamped between his teeth, and he sang softly, because he was happy. On his right he could already see Mount Sannin, its snowy beacon luring him on like the Israelites of old. He drove through groves of trees heavy with bananas, oranges, lemons, dates; he bounced over rough stone bridges that carried the road across a myriad of cold streams; he breathed the scents of clover and wild roses strong enough to challenge even the acrid taste of saliva-soaked tobacco.

When wheeled traffic began to outnumber donkey carts and the knives in his stomach had begun their vicious daily work, he pulled off the coast road and climbed inland until he came to a village, where he discovered a tiny café just opening its shutters with a yawn and a squeak of unoiled hinges.

He sat at a rickety table and, to the accompaniment of morning bells chiming high fluted notes behind him, he ate a breakfast he would remember all his life: bread and coffee, a plate of grapes, dates, apricots, and cherries. And apple jam.

The owner's wife was a dark gypsy of a woman who tried to engage Raful first in French, then Greek, and finally, unwillingly, English. She stood with her wrists on her hips, staring at the sea far below the terrace, while a nonstop stream of observations flowed from her lips; and the most remarkable aspect of her, it seemed to him, was that she had no word of complaint for anyone.

She must have liked the way he laughed at her jokes, or perhaps she detected in him a kindred spirit of optimism, or maybe it was just his day. Whatever the reason, she suddenly disappeared inside and came out again a moment later carrying a stone jar capped with muslin and string. In her other hand she had a hunk of brown bread; this she dumped on his plate, among grape skins and cherry pits, and then she was spooning a pale, almost yellowy green substance from the jar onto the bread. It was thick, but not so thick that it wouldn't flow down the sides of the bread onto his plate, and it contained tiny, crisp pieces of tart apple, some of them still wearing shreds of skin. Even before he tasted it, something told him that this was a moment never to be repeated or forgotten.

At his first bite the day fused: sunshine, temperate and kind; the sea; the beautiful gypsy with wrists on hips, still talking like the wisest professor who ever lived; warm bread, the sugary tartness of the jam: all these things came together inside Raful to make a memory. *Lebanon.*

When at last he stood up, fumbling for money, he thought he had not tingled thus with happiness for a long, long time. Already, though, the moment was fading into history. He got into his car, started the engine. And as swiftly as it had flowered, the moment left him.

Like any successful Lebanese on a pilgrimage to Beirut he stayed at the huge twin-towered Phoenicia Hotel, with its long escalator and panoramic sea views. He checked in, freshened up, and by eleven-thirty he was ready.

He found the Queen Café in the Ras Beirut district, opposite the American University. While he waited for his coffee he read the papers, listening with half an ear to conversations at nearby tables: talk of nightclubs in Hamra Street, water skiing beneath the Pigeon Rocks, politics, politics, politics, sex, money, politics. Also, something called "Jordanization."

"What is Jordanization?" he asked innocently, when his contact came, punctual to the second.

"What people here want—the kind of armed showdown with the PLO that Hussein pulled off. No, thank you, I won't take anything. Shall we go?"

Raful hadn't met this man before, but reputation—*ai!* Ehud Chafets headed one of two Wrath of God teams that the Mossad had successfully infiltrated into Lebanon. He had directed the highly effective, much publicized neutralization of three Palestinian leaders here the spring before. He was thirty-two and almost bald, with a skimpy beard: hardly your typical sabra hardman to look at. In his open-necked shirt and thick trousers held up by a belt so old that the leather could only be described as crack-colored, he looked like a Beiruti bus driver on his day off. Which was exactly how he should look, Raful thought approvingly.

"Will it happen?" he mused, as they waited for a cab. "Will the Lebanese ever drive out the PLO?"

Chafets shrugged. "Given time. And a little help. Jordanization is very popular here."

He took Raful to a modest 1950s three-story apartment building in the narrow rue Emile Edde, not far from the Commodore Hotel. As he paid off the cab Raful stood in the road, looking up at the façade while he matched Ehud's apartment with the photograph he'd been shown before leaving Tel Aviv. Each window had its set of long-ago varnished pine shutters. Ehud's were half open, and again he approved. A secretive man might keep his secrets, but he would be noted, whereas one with nothing to hide went unremarked.

There was no lift. Ehud led the way up the stairs. By the time they reached the top landing he already had his key in his hand— only one key, one lock, here was a man with nothing to hide, remember—and from the way he guided them silently into the apartment Raful knew that this routine, seemingly so artless, had been polished until it shone.

"It's safe, my coming here?" he murmured, as Ehud went around, checking for signs of intrusion.

"Safe. I have lots of visitors. People expect it; they like things to go on in the same old way."

He indicated that Raful should sit at a coffee table placed in the center of a living room skimpily furnished in nondescript style. On the table he put a large radio, which he tuned to an Arab music station. Then he toured the room, arranging things to his liking: windows three-quarters closed but shutters still open, doors firmly shut, electric fan on. Once satisfied, he went over to a metal desk set beside the largest window and unlocked it. From this he took a map of greater Beirut and a small cloth bag that rattled as he carried it back to the coffee table.

He sat close to Raful on a sofa, spreading out the map so that both men could see it, then opening the bag. It contained brass chessmen.

"Six," he said tersely. "Excluding myself." He placed two bishops close together on the map. "Here"—pointing to the bishops—"on the Kuwaiti embassy traffic circle … overlooking Shatila from the west. There's an apartment block, owned by the Lebanese army. We can use it; no problem."

Ehud removed the two kings from his bag and sited them on another intersection. "Avenue Jamal … with Shatila camp on the left." He tapped the map. "This is the important one, Raful. On the west, Hassan; to the south, Khalde and the airport. Two-lane highway, dead straight, perfect if you've got a plane to catch. Ninety people out of every hundred heading for the airport take this road."

"And the other ten?"

"Ah! The other ten we take care of … here." Two knights, farther south. "This road by Burj al-Barajinah camp … and the one below it also." Two rooks were added to the map: six chessmen in all. "But it would mean a long detour, and Feisal Hanif likes shortcuts, because he's got more enemies than the state of Israel. That big intersection, that's where the action's going to be. I'm telling you."

Raful studied the map for a few moments. "What's the terrain like?"

"Near the airport, sand dune, scrub, some pine. The Palestine refugee camps, of course. You ever seen them?"

Raful shook his head.

"They're a mess. Concrete blocks, alleys, corrugated iron: paint your own picture. If my boys have to run for it, that's where they'll run."

"Seriously?"

"A dog couldn't track a skunk in there."

Raful was silent for a while. Then he said, "The Avenue Jamal intersection … that's where you'll take her?"

"I'd bet half my pension."

It was the "half" that convinced Raful. "All right," he said. "That's where I want to be."

Ehud swept his pieces from the map and folded it up. Something about the way he did it suggested to Raful that his silence should not be taken as acquiescence; there was more to say.

"They told me you wanted observer status," Ehud said.

"They should have told you I'd *earned* observer status."

"It's true." Ehud stood up, shifted restlessly to and fro, now not looking at Raful, now subjecting him to a baleful stare. "Without your intelligence, we'd not have found her."

Without Avshalom, God bless him, Raful was thinking, no one would. (Now that the ban on this operation had been overturned, Gazit was reinstated in Sharett's mind as "Avshalom.")

"Listen to me, Raful." Ehud had come to stand very close. "I run my house here. Nobody tells me what to do, how to do it. I don't have any ... 'observers' on my teams."

Raful looked Ehud in the eye. "I understand," he said softly. "So you'd better find me a gun, hadn't you?"

If he was being totally honest with himself he'd have admitted to doubts then. Not because he'd had second thoughts about Leila Hanif, but simply because he respected Ehud Chafets and didn't want him compromised or harmed. Two days later, however, sitting in the front seat of an electric-blue Mercedes parked off the slip road south of the Avenue Jamal overpass, his doubts were all resolved. Perhaps it had to do with the 9mm Uzi he was cradling in his hands, for its warm wooden stock was a comfort to him. Ehud had offered him the choice between a 32- and a 40-round magazine, and he'd chosen the 40-round model without a second thought.

The two "bishops" were in the Lebanese army's apartment block, overlooking Shatila from the west. To the south of the Avenue Jamal intersection, two "knights" watched from an alleyway leading to Burj al-Barajinah refugee camp, while below them a pair of "rooks" kept vigil by the last crossroads before the airport. They had everything covered: every possibility, every last square on the board.

Chafets and Sharett were the "kings."

The radio bleeped. Ehud picked up the portable transceiver. "Yes?"

A babble of gobbledegook followed. Code. "They're leaving," Ehud said laconically. "Two cars. Black BMWs. Family's in the front one."

"How long before they get here?"

Ehud looked at his watch. Twelve forty-four. "Half an hour, maybe less. Lunchtime traffic."

Raful stared through the windshield. They were parked on the shoulder, facing toward the airport. Ahead of him stretched the highway, its two lanes separated by a narrow concrete barrier and a line of shrubs, shimmering in the noonday heat. If he moved his head slightly left he could see pine woods rooted in tracts of red sand, with occasional white villas dotting the Chouf's mauve and green slopes. On the right, Hay al-Sellum, a hodgepodge of slums blocking their view of the nearby sea. Traffic was thin to medium, moving fast. Everything covered, no problem.

The radio beeped again. More code. Ehud said, "Coming our way." He wiped his nose with the back of his hand, not looking at Raful, not saying, See, I told you so. Raful smiled to himself and set his Uzi to automatic.

The cars they drove today had been supplied as one small part of a big murky deal with the Kata'ib, the Phalangists. Each team had a backup vehicle parked within fifty meters of its present position, so that wherever the hit took place there would be a getaway car within easy reach. They had worked endlessly on the permutations: if the bishops struck lucky, the kings would move *thus* while the knights traveled *so* to liaise with the rooks *there* ... everything, every last tiny detail, covered: left, right, center, straight up.

False passports, covered. New license plates, covered. Change of clothing, check. Routes to the border with Israel, surveyed one hour before. Fall-back: Damascus road, red emergencies only, clear, open.

Twelve fifty-three. The stock of the Uzi felt wet to Raful's touch and slightly sticky. He rubbed it with his hand; then, still not satisfied, with a paper tissue. Everything covered but unable to handle his gun, *clean it again.*

Twelve fifty-five. The first prickle of doubt tingled along the base of Raful's neck. They weren't coming.

"Patience."

Ehud had read his mind, then? Or was he saying "Patience" as a way of calming his own nerves, of reassuring himself that they were in fact coming, that nothing had been overlooked?

Something had been overlooked. Something so obvious that any minute it was going to punch its way out of the glove compartment like a jack-in-the-box and smash into Raful's face.

A jumbo jet trundled overhead, aligned for a landing on runway one-eight. Above the whine-roar of its engines the beep from the radio could have passed unnoticed, but Ehud heard. Static, the Hebrew code urgent and unhappy. Ehud swearing. "*What!*" Raful shrieked; then, more rationally, "Tell me."

"They've lost the convoy."

"How?"

"What does it matter?" Ehud spat. His fists pounded on the steering wheel. Then he was on the radio again, and this time Raful did not need to have the code translated, the meaning was so obvious: Wake up, watch, you'll have no advance warning, don't let them slip past....

Everything covered. Just about every fucking damn thing....

"What do we do, stay here or ...?"

"Wait." Ehud was calm again now. "We listen and we watch."

One oh-five precisely.

"They have to get to the airport." Ehud was speaking almost under his breath. "Their plane leaves at three thirty-five; we know they have left the apartment; we know they are on their way."

Yes, thought Raful; and one thing you do not mention there, Ehud: We do not know where they are.

He swallowed again. His mouth tasted of dried fish. When he looked through the windshield he saw only the row of tatty shrubs marking the center of the two-lane highway, white houses on a hillside, cars, an endless stream of traffic moving to and fro between city and airport, with nothing except sun flashes off varicolored metals to distinguish one from another.

Suddenly, for no reason, he remembered the apple jam. He saw himself sitting at a rickety table with its view of a sunlit bay and he could taste jam superimposing itself over the dry fish that coated his tongue, everything so beautiful, everything *covered*, and he wanted to vomit.

The radio: *Beep, beep, beep*. Ehud snatched it up. Another voice, measured and cool; no code this time. "Coming around the back of Burj al-Barajinah, north crossing."

Before the cool voice could finish, Ehud was hurtling south down the highway, chasing a Boeing 707 on its glide path into the wind. Raful wound down his window and clutched the door handle, ready for a quick exit. Seconds away now. Ehud overtook a coach on its blind side, horn screaming. Ninety miles an hour, closing, everything covered again, closing, closing....

Raful found time to notice that his heart was pulsing away like an electric motor, that his mouth was awash with saliva no longer tasting of fish. As Ehud rattled in front of a lorry, forcing it onto the hard shoulder, the jam, that magical jam, came oozing back onto his palate untainted and he laughed aloud.

And now, straight ahead, he could see the start of things. Two black BMWs traveling along the outer lane, bunched up, fast, a quarter of a mile ahead with several vehicles between them and their pursuers. Traffic lights visible, green traffic lights. On the left, beyond the guardrail, a shantytown of corrugated iron roofs. A gap opening; Ehud insinuating them through it with a demented blast of the horn and rubber left on the road to mark their passage; the lights rushing toward them, still green.

Ehud tucked the Mercedes in behind the rear BMW and braked. Raful could see an arm stretched along the back seat of the car in front. Man, turning to see who was tailgating them; second man, also in the back seat, his head also now in profile, *spotted*—

Fortunately Ehud realized that in the same instant, and roared up the hard shoulder to shove the Mercedes in between the two BMWs. As Raful fought to recover his balance he saw jagged movement from the car in front—a pale face, a boy's face—but then he was too busy with the Uzi to think about that; *every war has its tragic casualties:* he leaned out the window, faced back toward the bodyguards' BMW, *fire!*—three rounds, *inside,* out, five rounds more—Ehud swearing as he wrestled with one hand for his own Uzi, tucked away on the floor, no time to retrieve it when the "Go" came through....

Bullets splintered their rear window. Raful ducked while Ehud somehow managed to keep them going straight at seventy miles an hour, no damage, everything covered, keep it coming ... outside the window, keep low profile, squeeze, *fire!*... and this time he was rewarded by the sight of the rear BMW swerving madly, left-right, left-right, until at last it broke away from the lane altogether, rocketing across the roadway to climb the barrier, turn on its side, and skate alongside the road for a few meters before smashing into an illegally parked ten-ton truck and so coming to a very final halt.

Now there remained only the one BMW, and everything was, it really was, at last, *covered.*

They were nearly at the crossroads where the two Israeli "knights" awaited them. Now the lights had changed to red, but the BMW in front sounded its horn in an endless note, kept going, kept going hell for leather for the junction, headlamps ablaze, and Raful was checking his magazine, ensuring the safety was off, Raful was nearly there, his triumphal march already begun, when the beige E-type Jaguar pulled out of the side road as planned, everything as planned, *everything covered*—and this Jaguar rammed into the BMW, sending it careering across the road, its trunk flying open, suitcases bouncing in the dust, the car itself stopping almost against the fender of a bus coming down the opposite lane.

Shouting. Screaming. People running this way and that like so many chickens with their heads cut off, a woman shrieking over and over, "Fire, fire, my God, fire!" Four men, strong, resourceful, converging on the wrecked BMW. Four Uzis, but no one saw them or remembered them until later; then, of course, nobody had seen anything else, but now all they saw was a quartet of would-be rescuers. The offside front door of the BMW opened and an arm unfurled, just as the first of the four men reached the car and fired a burst into the driver's head. Just to make sure that the unfurling arm wasn't a trick; how Raful admired these people!

From inside the car came a noise like a cap gun going off: bodyguard in the front seat, valiant defender to the last; another ripple of automatic fire, silence.

People, other people, innocents, ten of them, twenty maybe, had come as close as the suitcase nearest to the wreckage. They did not know what was happening, saw only a road accident. Then at last they registered the Uzis. Then they understood and melted away, like a line of crisp-coated snow retreating in the first flush of spring. This was Lebanon, this was Beirut, this was the Palestinian refugee camp of Burj al-Barajinah. This was war.

A profound, malignant silence enveloped the sunlit scene; and Raful was back in his movie. A star. He saw himself, as if from a distance, walk toward the shattered BMW, Ehud a few paces ahead of him. They carried their Uzis upright, a little apart from their torsos, fingers through the trigger guards. Everything covered, as never before. Revenge, seconds away now. An eye for an eye, a tooth for a tooth, *goel!* Yea, Sara and Esther, verily, Lord, *to everything there is a season, and a time to every purpose under the heaven.*

The movie lacked a convincing soundtrack and it was slow, proceeding frame by frame. On the outer fringes of the screen, Raful became aware of figures flowing down the road from the ten-ton truck against which the other BMW had run aground. Little green men; no, wrong, men in green clothes. All wearing the same kind of green clothes. Men carrying things, men still too far away to worry about....

Ehud, five steps ahead, bringing his Uzi to the horizontal. The two Israeli "knights" were already on their way back to the E-type Jaguar; now they had reached it, now they were trying to start its engine. Now they had succeeded; no need for the backup car, after all. Now, Raful said to himself, we are ready to flee the moment God's purpose has been accomplished.

Ehud, opening the back door of the BMW. Ehud, bending

down to get a clean line of fire. Ehud spinning back, the Uzi jerked from his hand, grayness and gore splattering everywhere. Raful, looking down stupidly at his slacks, wringing wet and hot, as if he'd peed in his pants, black-red pee. *Whang* of a bullet whistling past his head, more bullets, suddenly nothing covered at all....

His mind connected, even as he ran. Simple, really. The rear BMW, the one containing Hanif's bodyguards, had run smack into a lorry carrying Phalangist soldiers, now so close he could recognize the insignia on their green uniforms, a triangular cedar tree with the words *Kata'ib Lubnaniya,* and the Phalangists were coming to butcher the Israelis who'd started it all.

But it wasn't the soldiers who had killed Ehud. His head had been blown off from *inside* the front BMW.

Raful threw his Uzi into the Jaguar's back seat and somersaulted after it as the driver stamped the accelerator down to the floor. The leading Phalangists had found their range and the Jaguar's bodywork sang to the tune of lead on chrome. By some miracle the gas tank escaped a hit. They were doing sixty before the driver shifted out of second gear. The shots died away. Raful crawled up off the floor. He had wrecked his knee and was suffering from concussion. His trousers were soaked through with Ehud Chafets's life blood. Ehud Chafets was dead.

Leila Hanif was not.

21 July: Evening: Beirut, Lebanon

"Chafiq! Good evening, *dear* Chafiq."

He did not rise at once, and that frightened Celestine. As she crossed Hakkim's priceless Bukhara carpet the size of a small domestic swimming pool her mind was busy with all kinds of calculations, but they were muddied by his failure to stand up and waddle around his desk to meet her. By the time she was halfway to him he had rectified the omission—they met in the middle of the carpet with kisses that landed three inches from the nearest flesh—but by then she already knew she was in trouble.

"Darling, dearest, *madame ... et comment vas-tu?*"

"Ça va, merci. Shu haida, chéri? How's business, darling?" Arabic, French, English, all of them together and none: that was to be their mode of communication. What a country, she thought, as he lowered her tenderly into an overstuffed buttoned armchair; no wonder we can't agree on a thing.

He'd already taken his own place of mastery, behind the desk, and now he could afford to smile. "Business? Wonderful. Booming."

He pronounced it "bombing," which rather spoiled the effect.

"And you are married, since we last met? Congratulations."

"Ah, so many thanks."

And another thing, she thought. He should be surprised to see me, yet he isn't.

"Obviously the events haven't troubled you, Chafiq." She glanced around the ornate Ottoman room from which he oversaw his empire, all the time monitoring his reaction to her use of the phrase *al-hawadess*, "the events." Among true children of Lebanon there was never a war, only "events."

"Too much fighting," he said genially, "is bad. A little fighting …" He wagged his head from side to side while he pursed his lips; because he was small and round and had a thin mustache that would only grow in patches, the effect was merely to make him resemble a clown. Someone ought to have taken him aside and told him that his best bet was to look serious, always. When Chafiq Hakkim was serious his eyes and their surrounds were composed of lines and angles, with no soft curves to cushion their resemblance to scalpel blades. Then he might look hard, and unpleasant, and dangerous; but silly, no.

She remembered how she had never liked him, feeling only a vehement distrust which went back far, farther even than those evenings when he would fondle sleepy little Halib on his lap, pretending to read him a story while one of his flabby hands figeted over the boy's crotch. But she had to start somewhere, and Banker Hakkim was nearest. So.

"What brings Celestine to Beirut now of all times?" He lit a cigarette, not offering her one—it was forgivable, just; he knew she did not care for Turkish tobacco—and sat back to view her through the smoke like a voyeur seeking the illusory protection of a bead curtain, jacket buttoned across his paunch in a tight X-shaped crease.

"I happened to be passing," she said; and they both laughed at the ceiling for a dutiful couple of seconds. "I need to talk about my investments." She rubbed the thumb and first two fingers of her right hand together.

"I see. A private matter." Hakkim's voice had become a little slurred, reminding her that business, to him, was the one true drug.

"And since it's also a family matter, who should I turn to but you?"

Her smile was intended to be disarming, but her heart beat uncomfortably fast. Although she was a wealthy woman, today she had come as a suppliant, wearing a plain black dress produced by Azizza from God knew where, plus sensible shoes that lived permanently in her suitcase. And here, in this high-ceilinged room with its two priceless chandeliers, quantities of ugly furniture, and French windows overlooking East Beirut, she felt the contest to be unequal. And he had not stood up to greet her when the servant ushered her in.

"A family matter: perhaps your son ...?"

"Oh, let's leave him to count his billions," she said carelessly. "You know how he never can be bothered with buying anything smaller than a Swiss canton."

He pushed his chair back a fraction and crossed his fat little legs, resting his hands on his lap in such a way that smoke seemed to rise out of his crotch. The notion of Hakkim's cock being on fire delighted Celestine, even at such a dangerous corner.

"So it's buying?"

"Yes. This plane that my granddaughter borrowed for a trip to Yemen."

He had been raising the cigarette to his lips, but now he stopped. Celestine knew he had been thrown off balance. No, not just that. Chafiq was scared.

"You wish to purchase ... the *plane?*" He laughed uneasily.

"Of course not. I wish to purchase the freedom of two of the passengers."

Looking at his face, she knew the right course was to stop. Let this newly nervous man make the running. Stonewall, be a typical Lebanese client, give nothing, say less.

What she actually did was lean forward to rest her arms on his desk and talk too quickly. "Look, Chafiq, we've been friends since God made Ararat; I'm going to come clean with you, all right?"

He waved the fingers of his right hand, not lifting it from the desk's leather inlay.

"She's got my great-grandson, Robbie. And Colin, the father. I want them out."

"And you think I can help? My dear madame, while I find it flattering that you should—"

"Chafiq, Chafiq!" She rapped the desk with her knuckles. "Excuse me; over here, hello, it's Celestine. I don't just think you can help, I know you can. You are a power broker of supreme importance in the region."

Her flattery served to diminish his fear a little. She watched him puff and swell and she thought, Men, what would we do without them? How could anything be arranged without men?

"You know these people inside out, Chafiq. They'll talk to you, even when they won't talk to anyone else. Now, these Iranians the Iraqis are holding ... can we buy them off? Find out whether money can fix this thing and, if so, how much is needed, because I'll pay cash within the hour."

He made her wait a long time for his reply. Her head felt light; a curious spasm of nausea shook its way through her lower abdomen. She would have liked to ask for a glass of water, but she had asked for enough already today; and besides, she knew that water alone could not cure what was wrong with her. The human heart, how weak it was. In how many ways was it weak.

"It is ... well, let me say just this. It is not, I think, utterly impossible." Again, that ambivalent wave of the fingers, still anchored to the desk. He was scared, yes, but another factor had begun to operate beneath the fear. Chafiq could sense a lurking advantage.

"You think something could be done?" Exultation ballooned inside her.

"Look," he said, suddenly every bit the confidential banker: hands folded, body leaning forward, head slightly tilted; what a man of affairs, she thought. "Look. This hijack, it's really no more than an Iranian-backed piece of troublemaking, mm?"

She nodded eagerly. She would have nodded in the same way if he'd asked her to roll up her skirts and show him her bottom.

"So who needs Iran, when the chips are down?" His face clouded. "Of course, there may be ... other considerations."

"Such as?"

"We don't know what Leila knows, do we? But we have to assume she's found out about Robbie and the father being on board. I mean, they're two days into the operation."

"The operation?"

"Yes."

"You mean the hijack?"

"Yes."

No, she thought. No.

"You think she won't release Robbie?"

"I think, my dear, we can only ask, eh?" He patted the edge of his desk with his palms and stood up. "No, no, stay there, please!"

When he disappeared behind her back she was too busy with unpleasant speculations to consider what he might be up to. Chief among her worries was how much Hakkim really knew about this hijack. Azizza had half overheard a telephone conversation that might mean something or nothing. But if he was actively involved ...

Her fears for Robbie had been temporarily overshadowed by the pressures of dealing with Hakkim. Now that she was alone again, however, her nightmare vision of the boy's fate came back with a vengeance. It would be sweltering on the plane, and although there had been rumors of allowing supplies to be brought in, so far they amounted to nothing more than that: rumors. Lack of food, lack, dear God, of water....

"And now, my very dear Celestine ..." Hakkim's rusty voice came from over by the door. She half turned in her chair, but its high back prevented her from seeing him at once.

"... we can ask someone in the know, and he will tell us the situation."

He sounded so pleased with himself it did not occur to her he might have betrayed his old friend and client; she lived in a world where such things happened, but almost exclusively to others. So when she rose and turned to find her son, Feisal, just a few paces away from her it came like a blow to the solar plexus.

She should have listened to Azizza. Hakkim and her son had never been close in the past, but now the banker stood with one hand on Feisal's shoulder, indicating allegiance as clearly as any medieval knight who sported his lady's favor. He was no longer smiling.

"You've been out of circulation for a long time," he said. His voice was still jovial, although she listened in vain for any hint of apology. "I have more pressing contemporary obligations."

But Feisal said nothing at all, not even when four thugs came running through the double doors to surround his own mother.

21 July: Night: Bahrain

Every time Andrew Nunn put down the phone it rang again immediately; he scarcely had a moment to write up his notes before being obliged to strike off at a tangent from the direction of a moment ago. This went on until around eleven-thirty when the phone at last fell quiet, making him wonder if the instrument had broken under strain; he ordered dinner from room service more as a check than from hunger. Dinner came and still the phone just sat there, brooding and quiet; so he just sat there too, eating in silence, glad of a respite from interruptions and the sound of his own voice.

Tomorrow would be worse, because they were coming to install more phones. He would have staff to help out, but the next twenty-four hours were going to be unadulterated murder.

The moment he'd finished his meal he undressed, for sleep would be in short supply from now on. But even as he lay down and prepared to switch out the bedside light he paused, irresolute, and looked again at the phone.

That afternoon he'd been given an annotated copy of the plane's passenger list. Leila Hanif's ex-husband and their son were aboard NQ 033 when it took off from Bahrain. Now the question which taxed Nunn was this: Did she know they'd be passengers when she commandeered the flight?

Was that *why* she'd commandeered it?

Such a ridiculous notion, but it steadfastly refused to budge from his mind.

Without quite knowing why or how, he found himself dialing

the number of the house in St. John's Wood. He hesitated over the final digit. If she wasn't in, if she sounded breathless, what would he assume, how would he feel, could he take it? Oh, balls. His forefinger stabbed down hard on the button.

Anne-Marie answered very quickly.

"Darling," he murmured. "How's tricks, hmm?"

"Dodo, is that *you?*"

After a slight pause she laughed, and something frisked in the pit of Nunn's stomach. Living most of the year in Jak, he didn't hear women's laughter too often. Not unless he paid for it, anyway.

"I mean, Dodo, where are you?"

He told her.

"Bahrain? Good grief, why?"

He skirted round that one rather neatly, he thought.

"Well, don't get bitten by sand flies." Another of her merry laughs, another pause. "Rather sad, you being so near and yet so far. I suppose there's no chance of a quick trip to London?"

Gosh, he thought; but perhaps she was between boyfriends at the moment and felt lonely. "Not in the foreseeable future."

"Pity." The line resonated silence. "I miss you, Dodo."

That stumped him. Anne-Marie hadn't said such a thing for ages. Nor had he, for that matter. A chap just didn't, really. And yet ...

"Me too," he said awkwardly, because a bod couldn't very well let his wife down just when she was making efforts to build the jolly old bridge. Although that didn't explain why he suddenly took it upon himself to add, "I miss you a lot, actually. Heck of a lot. Listen, my dear, I want to ask you something."

"Fire away."

"How's Michael?" Michael was their son.

"Fine. Great. I'll give him your love, shall I?"

"You do that. Actually it's Michael I'm calling about, in a way."

"I don't understand."

"If Michael ... if our son were in any kind of trouble, say he was kidnapped or went missing or something ..."

"What on *earth?* Dodo, are you there?"

"Yes. Look, suppose Mike took a header of some kind ... how far would you be prepared to go to bail him out?"

A long pause. Then she said, "You phoned to ask me that?"

"Partly."

"What a waste of money."

"Mm? Why?"

"I mean, the answer's so obvious. I'd go all the way to hell to refuel and then on from there. Dodo, are you all *right?*"

He chuckled. "As much as ever, Annie."

Silence. Nunn couldn't think how to end this call. He'd initiated it; now he must terminate it, but there weren't any words to say what was in his heart so he simply said, "Take care of yourself, old thing, got to go now."

"You too, Dodo."

She did not want him to put down the phone. He hesitated. They both did. She was the one who finally severed the connection. Nunn replaced the receiver on its rest. He did so with unwonted reluctance.

The phone rang.

"Yes?"

Now the line had a funny sound to it: ultra-long-distance, bad satellite. A very faint voice was saying, "Mumble mumble Kroll Associates mumble."

Nunn sat bolt upright in bed, all tiredness gone. "Put him through."

"Andrew?"

"Jerry! Have you got it?"

"Some of it. Do you have a pen?"

"Shoot."

The man at the other end of this very far-off connection dictated first a phone number, then a list of dates, times, and places. By the time he'd finished, Andrew Nunn knew the details of Halib Hanif's movements over the previous seven days, culminating in a flight to Aden twelve hours before.

"You get all that, Andy?"

"Every precious word. Have you tested his Beirut phone number, the one you just gave me?"

"Yes, but nobody answers."

"Ah. And the old woman, Feisal's mother?"

"Celestine Hanif. We had a couple of numbers for her, but neither of them works. Tech. malfunc., according to records. Do you want me to follow it up?"

"No. She's too old to be part of this; she can't help. Feisal?"

"No information at this time. We're still working on him."

"Jerry, I thank you from the bottom of my heart."

A weary grunt echoed down the line. "Forget it. 'Night."

As Nunn put down the phone he felt elated. He'd called in a favor and been repaid a hundredfold. When you borrowed money, the longer the debt was left outstanding the greater the interest, but favors weren't often like that; favors shrank with time.

Nunn had done something for Jerry Raban ten years ago, when the American was a lowly FBI narcotics agent. As a result of the information Nunn presented him with then, he became a not so lowly narcotics agent on his way to the top. Which he never reached, however, because the world's foremost investigation agency poached him, and ever since then Andrew Nunn had been awaiting the right moment to dip into Kroll's files for free.

He was plodding through his notes of Halib Hanif's movements when that damn phone rang again. He picked it up and heard a voice say, "Andrew, how are you? Halib Hanif."

Nunn was speechless for a moment. Only a moment; then he said, "My dear chap, what an incredibly nice surprise."

Halib laughed. "We should meet, tonight, I'm afraid. A car'll be at the back of the hotel, kitchen entrance, in five minutes."

"Then I hope your driver doesn't mind waiting, dear friend, because I shall take at least ten to dress."

In fact he took fifteen, deliberately slowing down in order to think.

He was pleased that things were on the move; even more pleased to be in contact with Halib so quickly, because it seemed obvious to him that if Leila were running the hijack her brother was likely to be the one to oversee negotiations. And yet, and yet ... Halib had not expressly forbidden him to confide in others, but Andrew knew that if he turned up with an entourage this rendezvous would dissolve into the desert air like the proverbial mirage. So he must go to the meeting alone. If things became unpleasant that would be strictly his funeral, in metaphor if not in truth.

The car was waiting, as Halib had said it would be. The streetlights thinned out, buildings became fewer, then they were driving through a broad gateway and he could see nothing in the darkness. At last the chauffeur pulled up and glanced over his shoulder with a mute indication that Nunn should get out.

On his right, a grove of palm trees; left of him, stone steps led down to a pool, its water glinting in the moonlight.

"The Virgin's Pool," said a voice from beneath the palms. Nunn slowly turned on his heel. "An appropriate name for such sweet water, don't you think?"

Halib Hanif was approaching with both hands outstretched, teeth agleam in the unnatural, dreamy light of a crescent moon. The two men kissed on the cheek and stood back, holding each other by the elbows.

"So happy they chose you," Halib murmured.

"Been a long time, *sayid*; thought you must have gone to grace paradise."

"I had to drop out of circulation for a while, that's all. As you see, I am well, by the grace of Allah!"

"The Compassionate, the Merciful, blessed be His name and the name of the Prophet."

Halib laughed aloud. "I'd forgotten how good it was to be with you," he said. "My father sends you his greetings."

Andrew had met Halib before, Feisal never. Something to do with insuring a cargo of silver for air freighting to Manila, ages ago: satisfying deals, followed by a certain amount of cavorting aboard a yacht that rejoiced in the unlikely name of *Bordella*, as he recalled. Unimportant; what mattered was that they had a hook on which to hang their dealings.

"And I send mine to him. And to your worthy sister."

"Ooh." Halib dropped Andrew's arms, affecting disappointment. "So swiftly to business?"

"For so the season bids us be."

Halib shrugged. "Let's walk awhile. It's quiet, we can see the stars."

They began to stroll around the curved perimeter of the pool.

"I must confess," Andrew began, "I too am glad to find that it's you. It could have been Ahmad Jabril, and I'm frightened to be in the same room as that man."

"As I am of Hawari. I know, it's terrible. Every little hoodlum's in this business now."

It was true, thought Nunn; only the Syrians preserved a fragile link with the ancient Assassin ideology; all the rest were paid hit men.

"There's too much spare capacity," Halib was explaining, "too many passionate young souls wanting to fight for something. The poor F'listins ..."

"Such a catastrophe," Nunn murmured dutifully.

"But look here, Andrew, do you know what it is we want?"

"Half a dozen prisoners for Iran, I was told."

"Ah, thank goodness." Halib sounded genuinely relieved. "I was afraid that some of your colleagues might have picked up the wrong nuances."

"About ...?"

"About Leila. You know, of course you do, that her son is on the plane?"

"Yes."

"But it's not what you think."

"And what do I think, dear *sayid?*"

"That this is pleasure, not business; whereas in fact it's business pure and simple. Father and I have done a deal with Teheran. Leila, she—well, yes, she has a sideline going. She wants her child back and we have said, 'Okay. Take him. But'"—Here he stopped, turned to Nunn, and laid both hands on his lapels—"'Let us do the business *first.*' That's why I wanted us to meet here, face-to-face, to make the position clear."

Nunn stood in silence for a moment, thinking over what he'd just been told, delving beneath Halib's words for their true meaning.

"Did she agree?" he said at last.

"Of course."

"Did she agree?" Nunn repeated.

"Ah! My friend." Halib heaved a great sigh, releasing his hold on the Englishman's lapels. "I told my father, I said, 'Now that Mr. Nunn is on the case we shall have no problems.' How wrong I was! Andrew sees everything right down to its heart."

Nunn waited silently for this effusive storm to blow itself out.

"The fact is," Halib said, once more resuming his walk along the margin of the pool, "Leila has become somewhat—mm, what's the word?—temperamental. Yes. After New York. You knew about New York?"

"I remember hearing something about her trying to ... there was an ambassador of a certain place, some people wished there to be a vacancy in that office."

"But did not see their wish granted. Yes. Since then she has been less stable than before."

"Stable.... You are afraid that this hijack may disintegrate?"

"Unless things move rapidly."

A loose cannon, Andrew was thinking; God help those poor passengers....

"She will be looking for a rapid conclusion to the hijack. And I was afraid that you, Shehabi, the others—that you might not appreciate her position. Hence this meeting."

He's scared, Nunn thought. He's not in control and it frightens him. She could blow the lot up tomorrow, that's the message. Or maybe just bugger off with her son, leaving Halib to head up the complaints department when Teheran comes calling to find out what went wrong. Great God, what a mess!

Not only is Halib scared, he is holding something back.

"Thank you," Nunn said at last. "Is there anything else we need to discuss at the present time?"

"I think not. But impress upon them, Andrew, impress upon them fully, that this matter is *urgent*."

It must be, Nunn thought, for Halib to come here in mid-crisis. What is he holding back, what does he want to conceal, *why* does he want to conceal it? "I will do that, yes," he said. "You will understand, however, that I myself have no authority to commit the principals."

"What nonsense! No, excuse me, that was rude, but really! Of course you have authority."

"I can assure you—"

"And *I* can assure *you*, my dear Andrew, that I did not drag you here for the fun of hearing your voice." Hanif's voice was harsh. "It is a negotiating tactic I know all too well, this 'lack of authority' crap! *Get* authority. *Get it!*"

Andrew counted up to ten. He did it slowly. Then he said, in the same mild tone he'd adopted until now, "How can I contact you?"

"It won't be necessary." Halib Hanif was making an attempt to recover some of his usual smoothness. "My father will handle the final stages of the negotiations; he will communicate with you. Listen, forgive me, I really have to go."

Indeed, by now there could be no disguising his anxiety to leave. Nunn was prepared to bet the Bahrainis didn't even know he'd entered their country; anyone with a fast boat could do that from Saudi, Qatar, even Iran. He decided not to waste time pressing Halib for his father's contact number, knowing that Jerry Raban would get it eventually.

"Of course," he said. "I'm grateful to you for giving me so much time."

Leila Hanif, New York ... the details were starting to come back. As he watched Halib all but run to his own car, he remembered how the Israeli ambassador had gone to a party where Leila also was a guest....

"Goodbye," he cried, raising a hand.

Halib reached his car and jumped in. The headlights flashed once; then he was off.

After the New York debacle Halib Hanif was known, by insiders, to have reentered society, but his sister, Leila, had disappeared, gone to ground. Occasionally her name would surface: seen at a training camp for terrorists in the Beqaa Valley, assaulting an

Israeli ship, divorced in her absence ... what kind of life had this woman been leading for the past two years?

The sound of Halib Hanif's car died away to silence. Nunn rubbed a hand across his forehead to find it clammy.

"What would you do for Michael?" he'd asked his wife an hour before. "How far would you go?"

All the way to hell to refuel and then on.

He knew then that he had to put a stop to this hijack, had to do it *now.*

DAY THREE

22 July: Morning: Al Mahra, South Yemen

From his seat in the middle section, Raful was unable to see the helicopter, although he could hear it come and go, not obeying any pattern. On the last trip, the crew had brought food and water. Perhaps that would happen again now; the chopper was just coming in to land.

What was preventing Leila Hanif from leaving on that helicopter with Robbie; why was she waiting? All Raful's instincts told him that the solution was simple. She'd cut a deal with the people who'd commissioned this hijack. It was a term of this deal that she stay the course until all demands had been met and only then take her child away with her. It didn't require genius to imagine what her Iranian employers would do to her—*and* the boy—if she broke her word and they subsequently caught her.

This would also explain why she hadn't even revealed her presence to the boy yet—she knew that once he saw his mother again the truth might come out and then she'd have to take him away as fast as she could.

Whatever her reasons, Raful told himself, he still had time on his side ... unless she recognized him from New York. She hadn't yet, or he wouldn't be alive now, but something might jog her memory. The Raleigh boy had mentioned them taking a photograph of him. Once it had been processed and Halib had seen it ... *aach,* no point in thinking about that; concentrate on Robbie. If the boy was taken back to the economy cabin to rejoin his father, and he could somehow manage to pass over the message Raful had written on the napkin....

Where were they?

Yemen, Robbie had told him, when asked, but Raful fervently wished he knew more about their precise location. Because he had been semiconscious when they landed, he did not know what lay behind the plane. More hills, like the ones visible through the distorting Perspex window? Flat desert? The sea?

A seaborne rescue attempt: Israel might try that, though the odds against any kind of rescue were astronomical. No cover for half a mile, no buildings, no power supplies, and, most important of all, no way of putting out a major on-board fire. A rescue would be the worst thing in the world, if only because Leila Hanif might survive it.

His eyes strayed to the seat in front. Nothing gave away the deadly cigarette lighter's presence, but Raful felt certain that anyone looking at the outside of the back flap must see a telltale bulge. Should he try to retrieve it now or later? Would the hijackers search the plane? Why should they?

So hard to think. He was exhausted. The passengers, the hijackers, they were exhausted too. The plane was a stinking snake pit, a sewer ready to crack and contaminate. How much longer before the violence exploded?

He was so busy with his calculations that at first he failed to understand the significance of the voices behind him, of the sounds that accompanied the voices. Only when one of the hijackers led Robbie out of the business section into first class did Raful come to a state of red alert.

Mashriq: sunrise. But she waited until the helicopter had been unloaded and had flown away before she prayed, not wanting to conduct her devotions in public. She descended by rope ladder to the desert floor and took a few moments to reorient herself, blinking against the fierce sunlight. She had shed the long skirt she'd worn at Bahrain and now was wearing jeans. A bad choice: South Yemen's oppressive humidity caused them to chafe. The incense coast, that's what they used to call it, she reminded herself, because all the incense there was in the world once traveled along this heartless hinterland of shale and stone.

She kept beneath the aircraft's hull, where no one could see her, and inspected its underside. She stared up at the huge rents along the side of the port engine, at the buckling, at the places where whole panels had been stripped away. The undercarriage hadn't collapsed completely; perhaps it could even be made usable again, one day. Morgan was a pilot in name and in truth.

Looking up at the hull, she was suddenly overwhelmed by a feeling of alarmed possessiveness, such as might rush through a mother watching her child in the playground while she talked with a friend, her mind only half on the conversation. This was her plane now, and she was its captain. Everything that happened to or inside it was the responsibility of Leila Hanif. She should ask God's guidance, then.

She had to make a guess at Mecca. She prayed as a man did: standing, kneeling, prostrating herself for the first of the five daily prayers, or *salah.* "*La Illaha il-la Allah wa Muhammad Rasool Allah!*" There is no God but God, and Muhammad is the messenger of God!

The words came easily to her now, but it had not always been so. For most of her life she had lived in a realm of misty agnosticism. Only when Colin stole her son from her did she find God, over the horizon of a desolation greater than this by far.

As she stood up she felt the warm wet wind on her cheeks and turned on her heel, slowly, surveying the skyline in every direction. There was nothing here. No animal life, no plants, no softness. A masculine territory.

She still hadn't received any message from Halib, still lacked his permission to proceed to the next phase. Perhaps he was having trouble checking out the man who'd attacked her. Perhaps that man's links to the second, unauthorized helicopter with Palestinian markings on its side were proving hard to establish. Yes. The man who'd tried to foil the hijack was an Israeli agent, she felt sure; he smelled of the Mossad as a trawler stinks of fish. The memory of that surprise attack still troubled her. Something about it served to underline an uneasy conviction that Colin and Robbie had walked into this hijack far too easily. She should get her son out *now*.

She had not kissed the boy for over two years, not since that last day in New York. So never mind Halib. He must understand that she was a mother, and it was time to meet her son again.

As she hauled herself up the ladder next to the inflatable safety ramp she felt an uneasiness of the lower stomach, part pleasure and part pain. It expanded to fill her chest, leaving her gasping to a degree not justified by the climb alone, or even by her decision to deviate from Halib's plan.

How much had Colin told Robbie since 1982?

Because she knew her ex-husband well, she would have staked everything she possessed on his deciding to keep quiet and shield the boy from knowledge of his mother's "crimes." When she disappeared there was no publicity; everyone concerned had a vested interest in ensuring that there shouldn't be. But if she was wrong about that, if he had talked ...?

If she took further time to think, doubts might overwhelm her. So she lifted the intercom and, in a voice so low as to be scarcely audible to Selim, she requested that Robbie be brought forward into first class.

She sat in row 2, seat A, next to the window, leaving the aisle seat for her son. When she heard the rend of a Velcro fastener she knew that Selim had drawn back the curtain, but she did not turn her head; did not turn it even when soft footsteps approached down the aisle; did nothing, in fact, until Selim had retreated and only two people were left in the forward cabin.

Then she looked at him.

How beautiful he had become! Of the many complex impressions fighting for supremacy inside her, that was the first to articulate itself as a thought: Robbie was beautiful and manly, yet not quite a man. His complexion, lightly tanned and somehow pure, shone as if inlaid beneath glass. He stood up straight, his figure had filled out, he was strong and fit. He was beautiful. Just that. Beautiful.

His eyes narrowed, then widened. His mouth drooped open into a watery "O" of wonder. She waited to hear him speak the first word, knowing what it would be, even if Colin had told him the worst.

"Mum?"

His voice was hoarse and timid, not at all manly; she did not care. She heard nothing she did not want to hear. He'd spoken the one word she had been aching for these past seven hundred and eighty-one days, and it was not like she imagined it would be. She'd imagined it would be inconceivably wonderful, but never had she bargained for an experience *sans pareil*.

For an instant she felt herself rise off the seat and hover on the threshold of martyrdom. It faded quickly, but she would remember that feeling forever. This was her son, her only child, and she loved him.

"Robbie," she whispered. He swayed a little. Leila, blinded, made a futile effort to wipe away the tears but effortlessly, silently, they reproduced themselves. She raised her hands. She spread them wide. He fell into them with a cry, and she felt his own tears mingle with hers while she rocked him to and fro as if he were still a baby. For a moment, an untold handful of seconds, she holidayed in the country called *then*, oblivious of Robbie's determination to stay rooted in that other place called *now*.

She had no idea how long they lay in each other's arms, stretched awkwardly along the seats. Robbie was first to move. He pushed himself away from her a fraction, but only so that he could look at her face, and said, "I can't believe it. I can't believe it. Can't. Can't. Can't." He patted her chest, ever so gently, before once again throwing himself into her embrace. "Oh, Mummy!" she heard him cry, his voice no longer timid but deep with the huskiness of adolescence. "Don't go away again, don't go, don't!"

I won't. Her lips framed the words but they came out silently, as certain prayers are spoken. He did not know the truth; for a moment she actually blessed her former husband.

"Why are you here? I mean, my God, what a coincidence!"

It was odd, she couldn't understand the reaction at all, but she wanted to say to him, Don't blaspheme; God will not be mocked by us. She couldn't. He was a man. He was her son. She had no right to rebuke him.

"I happened to be on the flight." Although she could not challenge Robbie's disrespect, yet she could lie to him. "Because I speak Arabic and I am a Muslim, they were gentle with me. They took all the passports—"

"I remember! So they saw our names and knew we were related."

"Yes." Would he not think it odd, she wondered, that after the divorce she was no longer entitled to hold a passport in the name Raleigh? Was it in fact odd? Leila didn't know. Robbie, however, like his mother, heard nothing that he did not want to hear. "They thought we might be related," she went on, "and so they asked me, and they showed me your passport, and then of course I knew."

He was examining her with the same adoring eyes she remembered so well: eyes full of trust and love and longing. His father's eyes....

"I asked if I could see you," she said hurriedly. "They said, 'Maybe.' Suddenly, here you are. Oh, Robbie ... but you have such a *tan!*"

"I like the sun. You always used to say how bad it was for me."

"Your skin was pale; I was afraid you'd burn."

"Is that why you never let me go back to Beirut?" There was a hint of accusation in his tone. "Because I used to love the beach so much?"

She couldn't tell him the truth: if they had returned to the Middle East after 1974 they would all have been murdered. When she said nothing he snuggled down into her arms again and he too was quiet. Leila stroked his hair. She had not done this simple thing for over two years. The movement of her hand became hypnotic after a while. She began to drift away. She had missed him so much, so very much. Why had she chosen to cut herself off from him?

Her hand froze. Surely *she* had not chosen to do anything of the kind; it was the design of Allah. And yet ... was she not responsible, in a way?

It came to her, then, under the stimulus of her son's presence—a fearful perception of the evil she represented to others. In the eyes of the world, she had stolen and tortured and killed, from choice; she was wicked beyond understanding; and her son must know none of this, because once he did he would cast her aside with abhorrence.

"Mummy, what's wrong?"

He had raised his head and was staring at her; she could feel how the muscles around her mouth had tensed into a hard look. Slowly she relaxed them until she could once again force a smile.

"Nothing. I'm ... oh, it's so unfair! Why did you have to be on this plane; why did your father have to choose *that* day to fly?"

"Don't be frightened. You mustn't. They'll come to rescue us. They will." He lowered his voice. "And we've got to be ready. These hijackers can't stay awake forever. Something's got to break. Trust me!"

She smiled at him through her tears, glad he had no conception of the man-hours they'd devoted to planning this hijack, of the care, the attention to detail, the dummy runs, the fall-back plans one, two, and three; let him keep his hopes.

"Dad's back there, you know?"

"Yes, they ... they told me." She hesitated. "How is he?"

"Great. But they won't let me see him, and I'm worried. They ... they killed a man. You knew that?"

"I knew."

"And I ... I so want to be with Dad, to know he's all right."

"I'm sure."

"Oh, *Mum!* Don't be like that."

"Like what?"

"All ... all cold. Just because I mention Dad."

"I'm not cold. I don't wish your father any harm."

"Then why did you run away from us?"

She stared at him as if he'd suddenly dematerialized before her eyes and then reassembled as a total stranger. "What?" she asked stupidly.

"You ran away and left us." His voice alternated between masculine authority and childish reliance, and sometimes its tones mingled, but now it was high-pitched, accusing. "You did, Mum, you left us, and I want to know why." He dashed a tear from his cheek and assumed a scowl, defying her to notice his weakness. "Have you any idea how I felt? And Dad? I wanted you, I needed you. Dad's fine, I love Dad, but ... but ..."

Suddenly he collapsed into the seat next to hers and howled. For a moment, all she could do was gaze at him in astonishment. He sat there shaking like a leaf, with fists pressed into his eyes and this unearthly wail coming out of his mouth. She tried to embrace him but he pushed her away, and when she tried force he flailed his arms, punching her, scratching her, until she desisted.

She sat there with a face contorted by grief, her hands convulsing uselessly together in her lap, and that was how Selim found her.

"Do you want me to stop it?" he asked, in flat, unemotional Arabic.

Leila looked up at him through eyes that must have betrayed her terror, for he smiled reassuringly. Then he squeezed the back of Robbie's neck, hard, with the whole of his hand, lifting the boy out of his seat, and when Robbie tried to hit Selim, the Arab swiftly stuffed a handkerchief into his mouth.

"Listen to me," he said, in English this time. "Your mother wants you to be quiet. If you cry out again, I will beat your father unconscious. Do you hear me?"

Robbie's eyes bulged; his cheeks turned hot with the blood of rage. But in the end he nodded, and only then did Selim relax his grip on the boy's neck. Robbie slumped down, spitting out the handkerchief. When, after a brief interval, Leila took his nearer hand between her own, he at first just allowed it to lie there. Then, slowly, gently, he returned her pressure. Selim watched until he was satisfied that Robbie would behave, before retreating to the back of the first class cabin.

"Mother."

"Yes, my darling."

"Mother, can you talk to ... these pigs? Do they understand

you?" His voice was subdued, but at the back of it resounded something she recognized. Hope.

"Yes. They seem ... to quite like me."

"They haven't hurt you? Or ... you know?"

A lump came into her throat. He was concerned for her honor. He cared.

"No. Nothing."

"Can you ask them something? For me?"

"What?"

"My friend. Tim. He's the boy I was sitting next to, on the way to Bahrain. He's diabetic. He's already sick, he's panicking because he's not got enough insulin, and he's so nice! Can you ask them ... would they let the helicopter bring him some medicine?"

She was silent for a while. Then she asked, "This boy ... he's your friend, yes?"

"Yes."

"A school friend?"

"No, I met him on the plane."

Leila frowned. "I don't understand. What is this boy to you?"

He twisted his head around so that he could look up at her, and she read the surprise in his face. "He's nice. He's sick. And he doesn't deserve to die."

She looked at him without saying anything. Then she slowly turned her head away to stare out of the window. After a while, however, she curled her whole body away from him and held her right hand up to her face. Only when Leila began to tremble did Robbie realize she was crying.

"Mummy," he said in a low voice, "what's wrong?" And then, when she only shook more violently, "What's the matter? Oh, Mum, *please* don't cry, please, please...."

"It's nothing. I'll be all right."

"They *have* hurt you, haven't they? God, I'll kill them!"

"Robbie." Anger sprouted quickly, nurtured by the other, nameless emotions that had temporarily overwhelmed her. "Stop using the name of your Maker like that. It's wrong, it's blasphemous, it upsets me."

His surprise was manifest, but he said, "Sorry."

"Just because your father didn't bring you up to have religious belief, there's no—"

"You're quite wrong." The eyes he turned upon his mother brimmed over with artless sincerity. "I believe in God. And I've been confirmed."

"You ... what does that mean, conf—"

"I've been received into the Christian faith."

"*Christian!*"

"Oh, yes." He paused, and to Leila it seemed as if he waited so as to achieve a certain effect before delivering his statement of the obvious. "You're not a Christian, are you, Mum?"

Colin had done this.

He had made the boy a Christian. Not a true Believer; merely a Person of the Book, *ahl al kitab.* The notion outraged her. It filled her with horror.

She had told herself, many times, that there would be no need to confront Colin during the hijack, that it was better to let their tortured relationship rest. She had told herself this, and all along she had known she would have no choice but to see him. Her head dictated, but her heart knew.

"I think," she said in a low voice, "that it would be good for you to see your father soon."

"Oh...." He gnawed his lip, color flooding up into his cheeks; she could see how torn he was, and the sight moved her. "But I don't want to leave *you.*"

She grimaced. "I am not going anywhere, Robbie."

"But once I've gone, who knows if they'll let us be together again?"

"We must trust in God." A tense little smile disfigured her face. "You believe in God now, don't you?" Before he could answer she had twisted around in her seat and beckoned to Selim. She spoke to him in Arabic, trying to make her voice sound as though she were pleading for some favor while she issued instructions. When she had finished he spoke to her abruptly, as she had commanded. They "argued" while Robbie looked imploringly between them. At last Leila turned to him and said, "They will allow you to sit with your father for a while, but only if you promise to behave well. Do you promise?"

"Yes."

She looked up at Selim, who nodded. He grasped Robbie and all but pulled him out of the seat. The boy gave his mother's hand one last squeeze; then he was going through the curtain and she had to resist the desire to chase after him, to throw herself on his back, go down on her knees and pray, Forgive me, oh, forgive me....

Selim quickly marched Robbie through business class to the galley behind it, swishing the curtain back into place to prevent any of the passengers from seeing what was about to happen.

"Go to the toilet now," he said, and Robbie was inside the stench-ridden cubicle before he realized that this had been an order, not a suggestion.

He relieved himself, not looking down, head swimming in a fetid stink for which the devil would have been proud to claim credit. He forced himself not to hurry. He needed to take stock.

He had been reunited with his mother, someone he'd never expected to see again. They'd last held each other two years ago, in New York; that was in the morning; by nightfall she had gone. Now she was back. Too much, he told his reflection in the mirror. Too frigging much, man....

There were so many things he'd wanted to tell her; trouble was, they got all mixed up with other things he didn't want her to know. Like the day he ran away, only because he changed his mind while standing on Oxford station, waiting for the London train, Dad never ever found out. Or being sedated by the doctor after the fun with the carving knife and those sofa cushions. Or, rather, he *did* want her to know about them, because they were *her fucking fault, man!* But ...

Selim was going to take him down the cabin to see Dad. What could he tell him? Where to start sorting out the muddle, framing the compromise, bringing those two back together again?

On the flight to Bahrain, Robbie had found himself wishing he were older, because then he could have dated the flight attendant. And now again he wished to be older. Or younger, even. At fourteen, you weren't a boy, you weren't a man. Fourteen was just bloody useless.

He knew he should pull himself together. He ought to make a plan.

He had a message in his pocket for the traveler in 24H; somehow he must find a way of delivering that. Should he show the message to Dad before trying to pass it on? Did he trust Raful? Where lay the best chance of their all getting out of this alive *and* getting back together again as a family *and*—

Selim banged on the door. "Hurry up."

Robbie jabbed at the metal wing that was supposed to be a tap. Nothing came out, not even the merest dribble of moisture. He rested his hands on the basin and stared at his reflection one last time. God, what a wreck!

As he came out he was trying to juggle seat allocations in his head. Between London and Bahrain, he'd sat in seat 20C, on the port aisle. Seat 24H was also an aisle seat, but on the other side of the plane. So how was he supposed to deliver his message?

There was no way he could do it. Sorry, Raful....

Selim took him by the arm and pushed him along the port aisle. Heads turned, anxious faces looked up at him: here came someone with news, perhaps someone who knew what was going on. All those appealing eyes were scary. He was no longer acceptable to the pack. He'd gone away and returned; better if he'd stayed away.

They began to walk down the aisle, Robbie leading, Selim half a pace behind. Robbie glanced nervously to his left, across the central bank of seats, seeking 24H, unable to identify it.

"Stop."

Robbie obeyed. Some rows ahead of them a woman had risen from her seat while one of the hijackers hovered nearby. She was carrying a baby. The baby was red in the face and crying. The hijacker shouted something at the woman, who replied through a stream of tears, half pleading, half enraged.

"Come." Selim pulled Robbie's sleeve. They retraced their steps to the galley area, crossed over to the other side, and began to walk back down the starboard side of the plane.

The woman was asking—demanding seemed a better word— to be allowed to take her child to the toilet. She stood her ground. When the hijacker shouted at her, she shouted back.

Selim's attention was divided between Robbie and the altercation developing across the plane. Robbie swiveled his eyes left. Row nineteen ... row twenty. He put his hands in his pockets, trying to make the movement look casual. The paper napkin was in his right-hand pocket. But seat 24H lay on his left.

The woman was holding out her baby to the hijacker. Somebody, a man, said something in an effort to affect the outcome of her appeal, and Robbie could almost feel Selim's attention slither off his back. He took his right hand out of its pocket and pretended to sneeze into the napkin Raful had given him.

Row twenty-two ... twenty-three. A man. A man looking up at him, his eyes suddenly widening in comprehension, all the skin of his forehead tensing back ... a man whose left hand now shot to the armrest of his chair.

Robbie transferred the napkin to his left hand. He tripped, squealing in pain. "My ankle ... *oh, Christ!*"

As he reached out with his left hand to grasp the nearest armrest, Selim, not looking where he was going, crashed into him and lost his balance, stumbling forward, trying to keep his gun upright. Robbie felt fingers over his own, unfolded them to let go the napkin, and lay on the floor, groaning.

Selim, more unnerved than angry, stormed at him. *"Get up! Get up, do you hear me?"*

Robbie rolled over on his side, rubbing his ankle. "Sorry ... I turned it."

"Get up. Now!"

Slowly the boy obeyed. At last he was upright, moving forward again. This time the glares turned in his direction were filled with overt hate. By upsetting the balance he had jeopardized everyone. Even the mother on the other side of the center bank of seats was staring at him in alarm, her child almost forgotten. Robbie hastened forward, his cheeks blazing.

At the end of the cabin he turned right, crossed over, and walked up the port aisle to where he expected to find Colin. His pace quickened. Dad, at least, would welcome him home; Dad would not blame him for anything or cast him out. Robbie, hungry for love, was almost running by the time he came abreast of seat 20C and found it empty.

"We can make a deal," Leila said. She did not look up from the magazine she was thumbing through, but her hands moved quickly enough to tell Colin that she could not possibly be reading text.

"Is that all you've got to say?" he asked, after a pause. "Two years of killing, and *you* want to make a deal?"

She hadn't expected belligerence from him; it was not part of their relationship. Their *former* relationship, she corrected herself. Now she looked at him with scorn in her eyes and said, "Sit down."

"I'll stand."

"No, you will on this occasion sit." She gestured carelessly at the hijacker who had escorted Colin forward while Robbie was in the toilet, and next second her ex-husband was unceremoniously dumped in the seat beside her.

"You always did that trick," she said to the magazine. "Always avoided looking me in the eye when I had something important to say, always walked while I sat, sat when I stood. Today you sit." She closed the magazine and tossed it onto the floor. "Because I say so. Listen. Once the Iraqis have freed their prisoners, the helicopter outside will take my team away. But whether the Iraqis deal or whether they don't, Robbie is leaving with me; even if I have to drop out of this operation, even if I have to abandon my team." She glanced up at Colin's guard, whose face had remained impassive throughout. "As you see, he cannot speak English; don't waste breath trying to influence him. Just accept— Robbie's leaving this plane with me. As long as you cooperate, you won't be harmed. But double-cross me and you will wish you had stayed in Oxford, my friend, you'll wish you'd never set foot aboard NQ oh-double-three."

"Cooperate?"

"Make Robbie see that this is the only way."

"Why should I?"

"Because then you'll at least have the satisfaction of knowing he's alive and happy, somewhere on the face of this earth. Don't cooperate, turn him even more against me than you've done already, and you become expendable. Either way, Robbie is leaving with me."

"Have you seen him yet?"

"Yes. He still loves me. I am his mother; he loves me."

"Loves his mother or is conned into loving a terrorist masquerading as his mother? I take it you haven't explained to him why we're all here: that it's your—what did you call it—operation?"

"Not yet. He'll need time to adjust. Perhaps he'll never know my past; you obviously saw no need to tell him."

"You have plans to reform, then? Virtue beckons?"

Her cheeks rose in a warm smile; the prospect evidently pleased her. "Maybe," she murmured, her attention no longer exclusively focused on him. "Anyway, I want you not to hinder me."

"Funny, I never realized you gave a shit *what* I did." He grunted. "You're making me feel a whole lot better."

"Because today, for once, you've influenced me, you mean?" She glanced at him sideways, knowing, as she had always known when they were a couple, that he was being clever; not knowing, as she had never known when they were together, precisely how.

"Oh, let's not get carried away. The only people who ever influenced you, darling, were Halib and Feisal."

Until that moment she had kept her animosity in check, but the "darling" proved fatal. She swung back her hand and slapped him over the left eye, drawing blood with the nails. He raised his fingers to the wound and stared at the result. For a moment she expected him to retaliate, physically, and something about the prospect shifted her heartbeat into high gear. She wanted that. She wanted to fight with him on the floor, rolling over and over, scratching, biting, sending her fists into his neck, his chest, his stomach, slapping his cheeks back and forth, over and over....

Somewhere inside her a huge volcano of self-loathing whooshed up into consciousness, and she nearly cried aloud in vexation.

"Listen," she said, and her voice was almost amicable. "Do not call me darling, all right? I am not your darling. I know I never was, in reality, your darling. And I have this plane, you see. I command it. People live and die; it's my decision. Don't make me angry, Colin. You don't want anything on your conscience, when I'm done. Now, one way to make me angry is to call me darling. Do you understand?"

"Yes." She might have been one of his lesser students who'd broken with tradition by stumbling onto a correct answer.

Leila's mood was volatile; she went from rage to amusement in a flash. Colin's condescending, studied reaction reminded her of evenings at home long ago; of things about that tiresome marriage that she would have liked to change, then, but now no longer need bother with.

"This operation is a business for me, Colin. I do it not for idealism but for money, or so the world will believe. But truly I mean to reclaim what is mine. I mean to take back my son."

"Our son."

She hesitated. "Yes, our son. You have had two good years. You stole his soul. You made him a Christian. This I can neither tolerate nor forgive."

"I didn't make him anything. It was his own choice. I was—"

"Liar, liar, liar! You encouraged him. Secretly! Like a serpent, with subtle words, to turn him against me, *his mother.*"

"I wasn't pleased. I'm not a Christian any more than I'm a Muslim. Do you seriously believe—"

"Yes! Yes, I *seriously believe.*" By now they were both shouting. "Don't you understand anything? *I am a believer, a true believer!* And those who do not believe will burn in hell for all eternity *and our son will not be of their number.*"

When Selim poked his head through the curtain, the hijacker whose job it was to guard Colin looked at him in mute appeal, but Leila screamed, "Get out, both of you, get out!"

She felt ill with the sheer effort of trying to control herself. To Colin, she looked like a vivid reminder of why he had fallen in love with her.

The notion struck him with such shocking force that he gasped aloud.

"What?" Her tone was venomous.

He shook his head, refusing to look at her.

"I said, *what?*" She gripped his chin and yanked his head around so that she could stare into his eyes. He did not resist. For a long moment they gazed at each other, each aware that one more twist of the screw would be fatal. So they did not twist the screw. They looked away, and they knew a communal moment of the most intense and extraordinary grief.

"'*I learned to love despair ...*'"

Colin slowly turned to look at Leila, fighting the realization that she had indeed spoken. It was impossible. It could not happen. And yet ... "'The Prisoner of Chillon,'" he murmured.

"Yes."

"You ... you still remember...."

"Yes." A long sigh. "Yes."

Colin put his right elbow on the armrest and allowed his head to fall forward onto his hand. "How did we get here?" he said quietly.

For a moment he thought she wouldn't answer him. But then she said, "I don't know." And after that, there was silence.

July 1969: Greece

L eila looked at the pebbles between her feet. She raised her head, first just enough to take in the friendly little waves lapping the shoreline and then to the pure, pale aquamarine beyond, stretching as far as the cloud belt above a distant horizon. She glanced right and all she could see was the beach: a curving expanse of golden sand and shingle that ended in some black volcanic-looking rocks. She turned to her left and there was Colin, lying on his back stark naked, hands folded beneath his head, eyes closed, the tatty paperback Byron forming a steeple on his chest. They were the only people on the beach. She continued to gaze at Colin for a while. Then, very slowly and deliberately, she took a fold of her thigh between finger and thumb and pinched herself, hard.

It was 1969, it was July, this was a small island in the Cyclades, her name was Leila Hanif, she was twenty-one, and she was in love. Her name was Hanif but she thought of herself as Leila Raleigh, because it sounded beautiful and she was in love with the man who owned the name and now owned her too: body, brain, and soul.

Leila lay back on her left elbow, so that she need not take her eyes of the handsome hero who had ridden into her life, smashing down barrier after barrier, to rescue her from dreariness. She had enough memories now to last a lifetime.

They had gone out to dinner, to celebrate his decision to stay on for the higher degree. Over coffee and brandy, talk had turned to the coming summer. He'd told her that he was going to rent a car and tour Europe. Then it came, through the candlelight: the silver bullet that was to penetrate her heart and liberate her soul.

"Why not come with me?"

She laughed, reaching out to give his hand a squeeze but not bothering to reply, because the answer to his question was so obvious. She did not recognize it as a silver bullet then; she thought it was his way of having fun.

"No, seriously—why not come? Do come."

She shook her head, laughing.

"But why?"

"Well-brought-up Lebanese girls don't."

"Why?"

"They just"—she shrugged—"don't, that's all."

"Why?"

"Oh, stop saying 'Why?' You know why."

"I don't."

Now was the time to talk about her fiancé, Yusif. It was on the tip of her tongue, the perfect excuse to get her out of a conversation that was becoming uncomfortable.

She opened her mouth and then he said, "We're lovers, after all. How many nights have you spent with me?"

And she giggled, because his words summoned up a picture of his single bed, positioned so that moonbeams filtered onto it through a high window, silvering their moist bodies as they languidly coiled and writhed in simulation of a mobile work of art. And because she giggled, Yusif faded from her mind, retreated from the tip of that tongue which only hours before had been exploring Colin's foreskin with delicate probing flicks.

"That's different," she protested. "All well-brought-up Lebanese daughters do *that*."

But her smile faded before his did. She was, she knew, in deep trouble. Officially they, the family, expected her to be a virgin on her wedding day. Off the record, it was accepted that she might have had the odd one-night fling with strictly the right kind of boy as long as she kept it to herself and nobody gossiped: the right kind of boy in this context meaning an unmarried male born somewhere between Casablanca on the west and Teheran on the east. Colin's geography was all wrong.

"Well, think about it," Colin said. "We can spend the next couple of months copulating here, in extreme discomfort, or we could grab some rays and fuck the way God intended. I'm going to take off for a few weeks anyway."

"Without me?" She stared at him, aghast.

"For a while. Need a break."

"A break from *me?*" Her horror was growing by the second.

"No, of course not. But if you won't come, well...." He shrugged. "Another cognac?"

She meant to say no but heard herself accepting. Poker. Maybe he was bluffing about a holiday in Europe, and maybe he held four aces after all. One thing she knew: just as she needed food, water, enough sleep to fuel their lovemaking, so she needed the man who made the love. If she turned down Colin's invitation, she could see the rest of the summer stretching out in front of her like a basement session with the interrogators: guarded by unsubtle minders, obliged to wait on the men while they ranted their politics into the small hours, shopping in the West End, followed by more shopping, rounding off the day with a bit of shopping....

She wanted to go to Europe, she *must* go. But darling Halib would kill her if he knew, and he would undoubtedly find out.

First her family, now Colin: everybody she'd ever cared about wanted to steal her life, convert it to their own purposes. Europe would be madness, sheer madness, a wild, spectacular burning of whole armadas. It was, in short, impossible.

"When do we leave?" she blurted out, and was at once engulfed by a crippling fit of hiccups.

Now, looking down on his wiry body, tanned evenly all over and covered with tiny hairs bleached blond by the sun, it still seemed to her like folly, but folly of the most superior kind. She lowered herself a little, to get a better view. He smelled of salt and clean living. His flesh was well compacted over the muscles of a lean frame. When, as now, he lay flat, his stomach turned concave and the outline of his ribs showed above the hollow. There were enticing ridges and caves, best explored by moonlight and tongue tip; everywhere tasted good, even, especially, the bits you weren't supposed to lick, ever. He was so clean. His sweat was clean. There were beads of it, now, on his neck. She watched, fascinated, as moisture welled up along the rolls of skin beneath his jaw. His pores had enlarged in the heat; she felt that, given time, she might be able to count them all. The prospect made her feel ridiculously happy. One tiny little hole, two, three....

After a while she tired of her game and rested her head on his chest. When his right hand began to stroke her hair she moaned contentedly, like a dog settling on its rug. Out of the corner of her eye she was just aware of something stirring beyond the fluffy mound of hair above the place where his legs joined. His hand had descended to the strap of her bikini top. It was untying the ribbon ...

"Stop that." She gave him first a little slap, then a big kiss on the cheek. "Lie down. Go to sleep."

He smiled, but his eyes remained closed and he said nothing. He continued his exploration of her bikini top, working around to the front with a slowness she suddenly found maddening. She slapped him again, giving his nipple a brisk tweak for good measure.

"You're interested in law," he said drowsily, "aren't you?"

"Of course." She settled more cosily into the hollow of his stomach. "It's your subject."

"In law, we have something we call 'the contributory negligence rape.'"

"What?"

"It's where the woman says no ... and means ... *yes!*

On the last word he folded up his body like a penknife snapping shut, catching her head between his thighs and darting both hands down to her bikini bottom. She fought hard, but he held her tightly by the wrists and dodged her jabs of the feet, until at last she didn't know how she could survive the laughter, tears, embarrassment, fear of someone coming along, rising panic, and sheer excitement at the sight of his huge erection.

At last they collapsed in a tangled heap of arms and legs, gasping for breath. She sat up, after a while, and threw a towel over his already detumescing penis, before casting anxious glances up and down the beach.

"Behave yourself," she gasped. "You'll have us deported."

But she wanted him to take her, pin her to the beach, so that while they made love she could feel the sand beneath her back and the water lapping her ankles. The previous night they had made love in the sea, their bodies writhing in phosphorescence, and she had thought she would die with love of the one who made these things happen. Of the sorcerer.

He must have seen the desire in her eyes, in the slackness of her mouth, for he said, "Let's go back now."

It was only three o'clock, but she was on her feet before he could sit up. She liked the simplicity of sex with Colin. If she didn't have him inside her soon she'd go berserk.

They hadn't meant to stay as long as this. Island hopping, they'd agreed, in Athens, one day here, another there ... but they'd already been on Ios for two weeks, with no plans to move on. There was one tiny hotel, with accommodation consisting of bare stone huts that turned pleasantly damp in the evenings, a terrace bar, and simple barbecued food, served along with feta cheese, olives, and salad, bread, wine. Half a dozen other people were staying there, mostly couples like themselves, and a few more travelers were dotted around the town, renting rooms from the locals. There was no tourism here, just the adventurous young crowd, well stocked with hash and LSD. "Do your own thing" was their motto; the locals affected horror and loved it.

Colin and Leila discussed endlessly how they might find a way of living here: they could open a hotel, buy a bar, sell artifacts. This was play talk and they knew it, but it was also the stuff of dreams hence, and a vital part of growing ever closer.

Not all the dreams were good.

She knew Colin had nightmares sometimes, because he would thrash around the bed, grinding his teeth, but she never mentioned it to him when he awoke next day. It seemed silly, in the sunlight; also, she had a superstitious horror of being thought superstitious, and paying undue attention to dreams might be so construed. But she knew she could not ignore his demons forever.

They finally confronted her the night after the tussle on the beach.

The weather had turned bad around four o'clock, with a heavy blanket of cloud drawing itself over the island like a shroud. Ios was a peaceful place, but the silence now seemed threatening: the silence of a court awaiting the judge's decision. Far away, over a sea turned the color and texture of rough-hewn granite, forks of lightning pointed up other islands in the chain with moody carelessness, as if undecided where to vent their wrath. Leila and Colin, mounting toward a climax of their own in a snarl of sweat-moist sheets, saw none of this. Only when the first peal of thunder burst overhead like all the heralds of doom sounding at once did they sense the change in the air.

They tried, halfheartedly, to resume where they'd left off, but too big a part of them was listening too intently for the next thunder, so after a while they lay back, puzzled and upset. Sex did not normally tire them, it revitalized them. This evening was different.

Colin said. "God, I feel drained."

She felt the touch of the vampire, as he spoke those words, and shivered.

"Leila, are you okay?"

She knew he was using solicitousness to cover his shame at not being able to come, and thought how endearing he could be. The perfect lover, from the first kiss to the last gentle cleansing of her body with a warm face cloth, he was the one she had waited and longed for. She loved him.

"I love you," she blurted out, and was rewarded by one of his brilliant smiles.

"I love you too," he said softly. "You *are* all right, aren't you? Only you shivered...."

"Somebody walking over my grave, don't worry about it."

But it wasn't just the sensuality that had vanished. She felt foolish, sitting there naked on the edge of the rickety bed. Earlier the warmth of the sun had irradiated her body, but now she was conscious only of sunburn, of soreness where her legs rubbed against the sheet. She got up quickly and went to shower in the dim cubbyhole at the back of the room, taking refuge in water made tepid from its stay in the exposed pipes leading down from the tank on the hillside.

The wash did nothing to refresh her. As she dabbed herself dry she caught sight of a gecko high on the wall. Normally she would have spoken to it, one healthy young animal to another. Today its unwinking eye looked ominously upon her, like a presage of evil.

Colin stayed a long time in the shower, long enough to propagate her seed of panic into genuine fear. Something had happened; the atmosphere was changing. She wanted the afternoon, with its stimulating, dangerous sexuality and warmth, *back*.

They spoke little over dinner but drank too much, trying to dispel the grim aura with artificial jollity. Flashes of lightning continued to fork overhead at intervals, but there was no more thunder. Above the island, the atmosphere slowly thickened like soup left to simmer too long. As they walked back to the room a few spots of warm rain speckled the exposed parts of their skin. They showered again, together this time. Colin put his arms around Leila and held her underneath the tap, rocking to and fro while brackish warm water drizzled down their bodies. They were so tired, all of a sudden. Tired and depressed.

The room contained twin beds, designed for small children. He kissed her good night but did not offer to climb onto her bed, and although this was the first time he hadn't wanted to make love, part of her felt glad. What's happening? she silently asked the ceiling. What's wrong with us? Is it just the weather? What else could it be? He loves me.

"I love you," she said to the darkness above her face. No answer came.

The hours unwound slowly. She never quite lost consciousness of the room, with its ingrained heat, faintly gleaming white walls, and dripping tap. But at some point she must have gone under, because when Colin screamed she shot up off the bed with her heart on the verge of an attack.

He was rolling around, shouting like a madman. Leila fumbled for the flashlight, knocking it off the bedside table. Her shaking fingers somehow managed to find the light and switch it on. Colin sat bolt upright, staring ahead of him. His eyeballs looked as though they were going to pop out of their sockets. A trickle of blood ran down his chin. Every muscle, every tendon in his body stood out rigid. When she stroked his face he let out a gasp, his eyes returned to their normal size, and he moved his head slightly. She wiped away the blood with a tissue. He licked his lips, mumbling something.

"What?"

"Water, *water.*"

She fetched water in a mug and steadied his arm while he drank. His teeth clattered against the mug. She took it from him and set it down on the table before wiping his mouth with another tissue that came away stained pink.

"Colin," she said. "It's me, Leila. All right?" And when he did not answer she asked him again, louder, "Are you all right?"

He nodded. "Ba ..."

"What?"

"Bad ... dream. Sorry."

He looked sheepish. Leila climbed onto the bed and put her arms around his shoulders. He was ringing wet. She felt with her hand. The sheets and pillow were sodden.

"Come to my bed," she murmured. "Come on."

She propped him up against her own pillow and snuggled against him, massaging his chest with slow, circular movements. "Take it easy," she said. "Tell me."

He made a peculiar noise. She couldn't decide if he had laughed or what. She didn't know anything about him at all, she realized; she was sharing this grotty room with a stranger.

"I have this dream," he forced out at last. "It goes back to my childhood. Something happened to me."

She waited. "Do you ... do you want to talk about it?"

"All right."

By the candle's gleam she could just see his face, the eye sockets two black holes enlivened with pinpoints of white.

"My father died when I was seven," he began suddenly. "We were traveling on a plane together. In the Far East. It was shot down."

"You mean ... your father was a pilot?"

"No. We were living in Hong Kong at the time. He was a banker out there. We were flying home together. Chinese fighters mistook us for somebody else, and they shot us out of the sky. Dad died. I didn't."

"And in the dream—"

"I relive it, yes. Is there anything to drink? Real drink, not water."

"Vodka. Do you want orange with it?"

"No. Straight."

She poured them both a drink and came back to bed. This time she sat up with her back against the wall and took his free hand in hers.

"When did these nightmares start?"

"After I got back to Hong Kong. We were rescued. My mother was waiting for me, in the crowd at the airport. It was horrible: flashbulbs popping, the works. They had this horrible flat, in the Mid-Levels. Dark, damp. When the typhoons came, I used to hide under the bed. I thought the windows were going to blow in."

"How awful."

"It was my mother who was the problem." He took a long drink. "I hardly ever speak to her, now."

"Or about her."

"No."

Throughout this conversation he kept his eyes on the sheet, not looking at her. An image came into Leila's mind: here was a man who'd been surprised by enemies while he slept and now was patrolling his campsite, gun in hand, on watch lest they come again.

"My mother couldn't get over my father's death. She blamed me for it."

"*Blamed* you?"

"I got out, you see. He didn't. She and I weren't close, even before Father died. Afterward, she turned cold. Dead. That's when the nightmares started." He grimaced. "Bed-wetting too, if you want all the horrors at once."

She remembered the soaking sheets of his bed. Sweat. Definitely sweat.

"Do you remember how it was when you were a child, Leila? It's like you've got a peephole onto this whole different world, where the grown-ups live. Just a tiny hole. You look through it and you think that's what being adult means. It doesn't. But you can't understand that, when you're young. I used to overhear conversations. Mother talked on the phone for hours, to her friends. And of course there were lawyers, papers to sign."

He'd run out of steam, but still he refused to look at her.

"What kind of things did you overhear?" she prompted gently.

"Oh"—he sighed—"what would be best for my schooling, where she should live, where *I* should live. And you know I got the feeling, I got it incredibly quickly, that she wanted to pack me off, out of the way. There wasn't a funeral, as such: no body, you see. But there was a memorial service. I was crying, she was crying. And afterward, lots of men crowding around to say things in low voices, while I hung on to her sleeve and hid behind her, and I heard her say, 'Colin will have to stay at boarding school in England. I've got relations in Buckinghamshire; they can take him in the holidays.' You know, just like that—take Colin, take a message if someone rings.... 'I can't afford the air-fares,' she said, 'not on what's left of Malcolm's pension.' God, how the words come back! You think I'm fantasizing, don't you, making it up. But I swear to God, Leila, I can remember every last word she said that day. And I'll tell you something: it was a relief when I had to go back to school. Oh, yes, of course I cried at the airport, and Mother cried. But it wasn't real. I hadn't lost one parent, I'd lost two; that's why *I* was crying."

Leila tried to imagine how he must have felt on that lonely flight back to England, how his first day at school must have seemed. She reached out for his wrist, gripping it so hard that at last he was forced to turn and look into her eyes.

"My grandfather," she said abruptly, "was shot. I was nine. It was 1957. An assassin came to our home. He shot Ibrahim, my grandfather, killed him underneath a tree where he was sitting. I saw it. I know." She gripped his wrist even harder. "*I know*," she choked out.

His arms closed around her, the stubble on his chin grazed her cheek, and she allowed herself to fall over against his body. She began to cry, softly, for her grandfather, but in a way she had not cried before: she mourned him, yes, but without the self-spite that had poisoned the grief of childhood and adolescence.

Colin nuzzled her neck. First his hands, then his lips were on her breasts. Her own fingers began to stroke his back, farther and farther down they went, until at last both of them were aroused and all the pain and sorrow of youth could be put to rest.

Later, when they lay molded together like one person and the first light of a brilliant dawn was peeping through the shutter vents, she whispered, "There's one thing."

He was on the threshold of sleep, but he raised his head enough to see her eyes, and smile. "Tell me."

"Your mother ... why did she blame you for your father's death?"

His eyes slid away from hers, and for a second the alert hunter once again stood on the boundary of his campsite, Colin against the world. Then he lowered his head back onto the pillow, but before he slept he said something and what she thought he said was this: "I'll tell you on our wedding night."

At first she wanted to laugh, then to cry, because it was such a beautiful thing to say, and then she didn't know what she wanted to do, because although it would have been magical to have him confirm that he had indeed said those wonderful words, suppose he hadn't really?

She spent the rest of the vacation chewing over her memories of the night which had begun with summer thunder and ended with a proposal of marriage that might have been nothing of the kind.

Her constant preoccupation through the Peloponnesus, across Austria, into Germany and Belgium, the thing *was:* her family would never agree. A tragedy, because she wanted it so much. She adored Colin, Oxford, and England, in that order: by marrying him, she could obtain them all. A fresh start, away from Beirut, far away from the memories of poor dead Grandfather Ibrahim, away from Yusif.

At last the time came for them to board the Dover ferry and she could stand it no longer.

The brilliant razzle-dazzle of the holiday was dissipating fast, despite all their efforts to retain it. It was a cool gray day in late September, and what there was of sun, so far away from being a Greek sun, no longer hurt their eyes. Dense clouds formed themselves into layers, scudding across the sky. The white cliffs loomed ever closer through a thin veil of rain. Colin and Leila sat huddled close together on a bench at the prow, holding hands, silent.

"Well," he said suddenly. He lifted her hand and bumped it gently down on his knee. "Home again. Look, see those clouds?"

She followed the direction of his pointing finger and shrugged.

"Don't they look like a couple screwing? She's on her stomach, and he's ramming it in from behind."

"Is that all you ever think about?" she wailed, but quietly, not wanting others to hear.

"Sorry. Look, I'm sorry, okay? I was trying to cheer us both up. It's just ... I'm fed up because it's over. We're home."

She turned her face away, not trusting herself to speak.

"Only I suppose you don't think of England as home." He waited for a response, but there was none. "I mean, the idea of living in England all the time wouldn't appeal to you." Another pause. "Would it?"

She looked down at the hand on his knee and thought, Why do clever men always have to be so thick?

"Because I was thinking, when you go back to Beirut, I'm really going to miss you."

"I'm not going back yet."

"But you will go back, won't you? One day soon?"

"Maybe not. I like it in England."

He could not make up his mind; she recognized the signs with a depression that bordered on despair. He was dithering around, avoiding the core, coming in for the kill and shying away again, and it drove her mad. Perhaps she was wrong to fall in love with him. A lifetime of this—

"Leila. Leila, will you marry—?"

"Oh, yes. Of course."

The words were out before she could even be absolutely sure that he intended to finish the sentence with "me"; perhaps he'd merely wanted to ask her if she *ever* meant to marry. But when he smothered her in a hug that squeezed all the breath out of her she knew he really was proposing, and she sought out his mouth with her own as the best way of cementing their betrothal, because as long as they were locked together like that he couldn't tell her if he changed his mind.

At last Colin held her at arm's length. His eyes shone with laughter. "When did you first know you loved me?" he cried.

How to answer that, she wondered, when he could never understand? Of course, her love dated back to that moment in the car park, when his resourcefulness had saved her from Feisal's thugs; that was when her love began, but he didn't mean that.

"In Ios," she said.

"But when *exactly?*"

"The night you had your bad dream, remember?"

He slapped his thigh, laughing out loud. "I knew it!"

She was laughing too, by this time. "Why? How?"

"Oh, because you saw me weak and helpless and you still felt the same about me, and I realized it."

Not bad, she thought, for a man. He might have added something about her maternal instincts coming to the fore, and she wouldn't have minded even that. But then the raw emotion that had been building up inside her ever since Ios broke through the dam, and she allowed herself the contemplation of joy.

She'd wanted things, so many things, and they'd all fallen into her lap. She laid her head on his chest, meaning it to be a gesture of prostration and worship, and while she held on to him as if for salvation she burst into tears of utter breakdown.

"I love you," she said, over and over again. "Oh, dear God,

Colin, I do love you so!" And she would pound his chest with her fist, softly, softly, as if seeking admittance to his life, and a sanctuary there.

Leila had come home.

But it did not feel like home when she presented herself at the Lancaster Gate penthouse, with its much vaunted views of Hyde Park, two days later. Halib had that effect on her. He made anywhere outside Lebanon, or, more accurately, Beirut, seem a temporary and decidedly inferior lodging.

One of his girls admitted Leila to the apartment. Another sat with her legs curled up on the sofa, leafing through *Vanity Fair*. Leila recognized the expression on her face as the product of the kind of boredom that made you feel frantic. A third girl was in the black-and-white tiled bathroom, giving Halib a facial.

All three women were in their early twenties, had long blond hair, and wore sheath dresses, the facial expert's being made of scarlet leather. Halib never deviated from his ideal of feminine beauty. He wore these interchangeable, fully compatible girls to parties as other men wore gemstones on their fingers.

"You're not seriously telling me," Leila heard the face girl coo, "that you put *soap* on that lovely skin of yours?"

"Hi," Leila said. "I hope I don't interrupt anything important." She went forward to kiss his cheek but Halib, anticipating her intention, swung the chair around on its stalk so that he had his back to her, and said, "Liquid soap only, Roxanne; the results are as you see. My sister and I have a lot to discuss; go now."

Roxanne wiped his face with a towel and stalked out, her heels beating a somehow ominous tattoo on the marble floor. As she passed Leila she gave a scarcely perceptible shrug. Leila leaned against the wall and said, "She's new."

It took all her courage to do that. She knew she was in the wrong, that she would never be forgiven for going away with Colin, that she had brought disgrace and grief in equal measure down upon her family. It was scarcely tactful of her to bring up the subject of Halib's latest acquisition. Leila didn't know why she took the risk. Perhaps it was something to do with her upbringing, which had taught her that attack was the only form of defense.

Halib swung himself out of the chair. His linen shirt set off his handsome features to perfection. For a moment he regarded her without expression, almost as if he were trying to remember who the hell she was. Then his mustache lifted, his face creased into those gorgeously sexy concentric laughter lines, and to her astonishment she registered that he was happy to see her.

"Welcome," he said, coming forward to embrace her. "Welcome home, angel. You look fabulous." He kissed both her cheeks: the token gesture of international diplomacy made warm, compelling. "Greece was fun, huh? I'll bet. Come, tell me about it."

As if in a dream she allowed herself to be led into his bedroom, his inviolable sanctuary, where he seated himself in an armchair by the window. Sitting there with the translucent floor-length drapes waving gently in the breeze, he looked every inch the merchant prince: debonair, charming, rich as clotted cream.

It wasn't until she'd sat down opposite him that the truth behind his words really socked her. "You ... *knew* I'd gone to Greece?"

He spread his hands and grinned. "Of course. Just as I knew that poor Yusif flew off to Thailand to console himself when he heard."

Leila looked down at where her hands were clasping and unclasping themselves in her lap. She'd known that Yusif was going to be on the agenda, but she had not expected him to show up quite so soon. Funny, though: Halib's tone, when he spoke of Yusif, had sounded almost mocking.

"I wrote to him," she said in a low voice. "It was very difficult."

"Yes, but you shouldn't worry about it. Father's relieved."

She raised her eyes at that, but only in an attempt to discover why he was playing with her so cruelly.

"Yusif took off for Thailand and what do you think, angel? Marty Chamoun is having drinks at this hotel in Bangkok and who should mince across the lobby but Yusif and a boy who Marty swears can't have been a day over twelve. So Marty put a little money about, you know? And he discovered that these boys—there were quite a crowd—spend every night in Yusif's suite. You had a lucky escape, poppet. I'm so glad, Father's glad, we none of us knew."

She wasn't sure if she believed any of this. Her engagement to Yusif had been more or less arranged, she hadn't known him particularly well either before or since the ceremony, although of course they'd spent time together. One of his more appealing traits had been an avowal of how much he respected female chastity before marriage; he'd never once suggested they do more than kiss. Even so ...

"I had no idea," she muttered.

Halib spread his hands even wider. "Water under the bridge. Shall I have the girls bring some coffee?"

She accepted, not because she was thirsty but because she needed time to think. When dealing with Halib, Leila often felt herself to be a piece on an invisible chessboard, incapable of determining her own moves; the sensation had never been stronger. She had spent the summer cavorting with an outsider in circumstances that had destroyed any pretense she might still have to a reputation. Many an Arab father would have had her whipped and then banished, even now, at the end of the swinging sixties. Beirut in general was not like that, but Feisal was, and Halib never did anything that might upset their father or jeopardize his status as only son, putative successor.

When Roxanne brought coffee, Halib paid her rather less attention than he might have given a waitress at the Ritz, although he was careful to ensure that she'd closed the door behind her before speaking again.

"Now, angel," he said, in the let's-be-reasonable voice he saved for family manipulations. "We have to talk about a few things, mm? I know you had a wonderful time in Europe. From the family's point of view, let me speak frankly, not so wonderful, but"—he shrugged— "that's the world of today. And fortunately Colin, we have nothing against him, he maybe saved your life one time, who knows? And you love him, of course, you want to marry him?"

When she said nothing, his face clouded.

"Leila. I sincerely hope that you want to marry this man, that he wants to marry you. An engaged couple go on a spree, what the hell? But if you're *not* engaged ..."

His voice dropped lower and lower, until she could scarcely hear him. He was most dangerous when absolutely silent. He held himself immobile, hands clasping the arms of his chair, and she knew he was judging her. He had the power to do that. He could sentence her, too.

"I would like permission," she said, "to become formally engaged to Colin Raleigh, and to marry him"—she had been on the point of saying *as soon as possible* but wisdom prevailed; they must not think she was pregnant—"after a reasonable interval, to ensure that we can all get to know him better than we knew poor Yusif."

"Well said, poppet. Of course, I can't speak for Father, but having met this Englishman and liked him, I feel sure I can make your case for you."

"Should I come home, speak to Father myself?"

"Not necessary, unless he calls for you. Does this mean you won't be continuing your education?"

"I ..." She realized she had not thought about it; the prospect of confronting Halib had been so terrible it left no room for anything else.

"And where do you intend to live? Should we find something for Colin to do in Beirut?"

"No."

"I thought not. And after all, why should either of you want to live in Lebanon? Things there will get worse, angel, much worse; much better to make your base somewhere safer. England, I dare say?"

"I like England," she said defensively.

"I'm very fond of it too; you'll see a lot of me." He seemed to become positively jovial at the prospect. "Colin wants to teach, perhaps?"

She stared at him. It was true that Colin had decided to pursue an academic career. But he'd only made up his mind the night before. How could Halib have known?

Halib's knowledge must stem from careful analysis of Colin's character and past history. Which opened up another field of inquiry altogether: how had he found out about Colin's background?

He'd been spying on Colin.

She knew herself to be part of an endgame now, and the bedroom turned cold.

"I think," he said carefully, "you should marry very soon, poppet. Or people back home are going to talk."

She almost hated him whenever he called her "poppet," but this time she swallowed her rage and said, "How soon?"

He did not even pretend to consider. "Next month."

She looked into a face that was suddenly stone and asked, "Why?"

"Because we say so."

Father plus son equaled we. The royal We.

"I don't have any say in the matter of my own wedding?"

"No." He stood up. "Understand a few things, Leila. You've shamed us, to say nothing of yourself. But we're not going to cast you out, we're not going to cut off the money supply or destroy the man who ruined you."

If he was waiting for her to thank him he waited in vain.

"Of course you have to marry this Englishman," he went on, "if you're to retain respect from beggars in the street. But you have to give something in exchange."

"What?"

"Assistance."

"What kind of assistance?"

"You'll be told when it's necessary for you to know."

"And if I refuse?"

Thus did she make her final move, asking for bravado's sake; don't let the bastards grind you down, that's what Colin always said. It didn't alter anything.

"If you refuse, we shall wall you up in Beirut for the rest of your life. And if by any chance you were to escape, rest assured of this: you would never be able to find your fiancé, not if you tramped the world for a thousand years."

Checkmate.

22 July: Afternoon: Damour, Lebanon

C elestine spent the night of 21 July somewhere in West Beirut with her eyes blindfolded, listening to the shells fall and wondering who was responsible for this latest bombardment. Not long after sunrise, two of Feisal's men pitched her into a car before driving off at high speed. She sensed they were leaving the city behind; then rough hands snatched her blindfold away and she knew they were on the coast road, heading south.

"Where are we going?" she demanded to know, although deep inside she had already guessed the answer; when Hassan looked around and said, "Damour," it was merely a confirmation.

Celestine had all but forgotten about the beach house at Damour, just a few miles south of Beirut, until the odious Hassan muttered their destination in response to her request, and then how the memories came flooding back!—midnight swims, the speedboat, dancing on the terrace, the parties, oh, my God! how she remembered those parties.... Lebanon, Lebanon, she thought; gone are the days of my youth, and of thine also.

Yet some of her happiest times had been spent quietly at Damour, with just Ibrahim and a few books for company, and the radio banned except at weekends. Feisal had been conceived at Damour. When Celestine woke up next morning she'd had no coherent memory of the event itself, although she did feel certain she was pregnant and not even a hangover could dispel that. It had all seemed so wonderful at the time. She had no means of knowing, then, that one day she would come to fear her son, while he detested her.

"I thought the Israeli army would have burned our place," she said to the glass, her voice tinged with disappointment. "On their retreat."

"We have no trouble with the Israelis," Hassan said complacently.

The big Volvo raced down a narrow track between banana plantations and the sea, sending a shower of dust billowing into the air. Celestine recalled how she and Ibrahim had gone to visit this place shortly after their marriage: just a spit of land overgrown with long grass, the rusty remains of an abandoned tractor, and a hut. The banana plantation that occupied most of the hinterland was owned by an old school friend of Ibrahim's who had fallen on hard times. Ibrahim wasn't interested in bananas, but he liked the view from the ruined hut. It would not, however, have occurred to him to bid for the hut minus the fruit trees; he was acquiring from a friend who wouldn't stoop to take charity, and, since the land's value lay in its produce, it was a case of all or nothing.

Actually, the bananas had done rather well; as had the tomatoes, avocados, oranges, and lemons into which Ibrahim had diversified, in his usual muddled kind of way. He had been an impulse buyer all his life, and almost alone among Lebanese businessmen his impulses had made him rich.

As they drew up in front of the beach house, Celestine wondered whether her late husband hadn't, in fact, been a good deal less disorganized than he looked. But she didn't like to think about that, because it implied that he knew what he was doing when he bankrolled the Palestinians, thereby courting the death that took him away from her, along with reasons for living.

Hassan pattered into the house, leaving the driver to bring their bags. Nothing much had changed, Celestine discovered as she mounted the steps to the terrace, with its view of the bay, and sand left in untidy piles in corners, and the beach umbrella with the hole in the canvas propped up against one wall. The house was a simple, one-story structure of concrete blocks and wood, but it was big. She'd stipulated it must be big before Ibrahim had it built, because she knew it was going to be the most spectacular venue for her parties. So there were plenty of bedrooms, although walking through now she could see signs of damp and decay everywhere she looked and the sight pained her. Today was cloudy and humid; depression hovered like black thunderclouds over the Mediterranean on a sultry October evening.

"How long are we here for?" she asked Hassan. "You can pour me one of those."

Hassan was, with habitual temerity, helping himself to whisky from a cupboard that in her day had been kept locked. Now, looking over his shoulder, she saw that this menial, this worm, possessed the key. Celestine had never understood what her son saw in this unpleasant little man. It was typical of Feisal to appoint Hassan her prison governor.

"Until the unhappy business in Yemen is resolved," he said, rising with a glass in either hand, "we shall stay. There is radio." Hassan flicked dust off the old set and turned it on, producing a blare of pop music. Celestine told him to switch it off, but Hassan was jiggling about with an idiotic grin, snapping his fingers. She stormed over to the set. He got there ahead of her. The hand on her wrist was like a steel brace. She struggled, but his grin merely intensified.

As she threw herself onto the dust-sheeted sofa she knew that tears were very close. She wasn't crying for herself. Every second she spent cooped up here was a second nearer death for Robbie and Colin. She yearned to be on the outside, doing something, anything ... such frustration! She rummaged in her handbag for a tissue.

Her hand made contact with her perfume sprayer, fiddled with it absently. She was running low on Blue Grass; best to save it.

From far away, through the plantation, came the noise of a car. Celestine was old but her hearing remained acute, better than Hassan's anyway, for he showed no sign of having noticed anything and continued to dance around the room, swigging whisky. She knew he was enjoying this. Hassan had always hated her ever since, years ago, she'd put up a fight with Feisal, his master, and so earned permanent exile to Yarze. She'd crossed her son once too often without having settled his hash, lacking the courage of her convictions in a society where the only discipline that counted was a good sharp dose of death.

Funny, she'd never been able to have another child after Feisal, only a series of miscarriages. There was something satanic about that: the devil child, having fought his way into the world, would not countenance a rival. She should have strangled him at birth, long before he'd had a chance to sire Halib and Leila. No, how could she think such a thing? Feisal had been a lovely child, so pretty....

Celestine stood up and began to wander around the room. The noise of the car had faded away, but she couldn't get it out of her mind. The engine had sounded so ... so *homely*, that was the word. A part of her recognized it, deep down inside, without being able to give it a name.

She heard Hassan click his teeth behind her and turned around to find him shaking his head reprovingly.

"Thinking to escape?"

Celestine had unconsciously gravitated to the front door.

"Please, do not." Hassan's smile revealed a mouth full of old steel-gray fillings. "Emil will wake up and then who knows? Eh?"

Emil, she remembered, was the driver. She'd not seen him before, but he looked a brute: vicious and unintelligent. Who knew, indeed?

"Is the water still connected?" she snapped.

When he merely shrugged she went through to the bathroom without asking permission. Underneath the washbasin she found a plastic bucket full of cloudy water. There was no towel, no soap. The shower curtain crawled with mold, and it stank. Slugs and spiders occupied every vacant crevice. Celestine opened the lid of the toilet and immediately shut it again, but not quickly enough to trap all the flies that lived in there or to avoid a reek of what they lived on.

The square window above the toilet seat was too small to allow an adult to pass through. She gazed up at it with a sinking heart. Damn!

Someone had left a half-full bottle of bleach by the tub. Celestine lugged the orange bucket over to the toilet, sloshing water everywhere. She was just nerving herself to whip open the toilet for long enough to rinse it out with a mix of water and bleach when she heard something.

She raised her head. That noise had come from outside the house. Not Hassan: she could hear him bouncing to the music again. Emil must have wandered around to the back to take a piss.

But it didn't sound like a man. Shushing noises, as if branches were being trodden underfoot, only very lightly ... an animal?

Celestine climbed up onto the toilet seat and cautiously peered out. The glass was so encaked with dirt that she could see nothing except the green of trees outside. She fiddled with the catch and jerked the window open.

As the panel swung outward it made sharp contact with something; Celestine heard a muffled cry and leaned out to see Azizza below her, one hand held to her temple. Sensing someone above her she looked up, and for an instant the two old women merely gazed at each other, speechless.

"Oh, *Izza!*" Celestine was first to recover. She spoke in a loud whisper, praying that Hassan would stay wrapped up in his stupid pop music. "How did you get here? Oh, of course! That was the car I heard!"

"Yes."

"But how did you know I was here?"

"I guessed. I knew he couldn't keep you a prisoner in his own house, there's too many visitors, and the apartment in town's not safe. He kept you there last night, though. I couldn't do anything while you were there, it's crawling with his scum." Azizza looked anxiously to right and left. "Can you squeeze through the window?"

"Not a chance," Celestine hissed.

"And no back door." Azizza cogitated. "How many inside?"

"Just Hassan."

Hearing the name, Azizza made a face. "And only the one in the car?"

"Yes."

"He's snoring, don't worry about him."

"But Hassan ..."

"I don't know ... you have to find a way of overpowering him."

"How?" Celestine waxed indignant. "You expect an old lady to barge in with a club, perhaps?"

"You always used to carry a gun in that handbag of yours."

Celestine opened her mouth to protest that she hadn't carried a gun in years when the reference to her handbag triggered something in her mind.

"Listen," she said, after a pause. "I've got an idea...."

A few moments later, Hassan was startled to hear a scream high-pitched enough to rise above even Radio Liban's raucous output.

"My eye!" Celestine staggered into the room, clutching her handbag to her chest. "For the love of God, Hassan, look in my eye, see what it is!"

He kept his distance while he examined her closely, suspecting a trap. "What's wrong with your eye?"

"Something in it. In the water, oh, *mon Dieu*, but it's bleeding!" she cried out. The radio could scarcely compete, though Hassan switched it off anyway with an ill-tempered sweep of his hand and advanced toward Celestine.

"Sit down," he growled, as he pushed her onto the sofa. "And be quiet!"

But his words only caused her to keen more loudly. Hassan, hearing steps on the veranda, looked up in irritation to find that Emil, the driver, had come in to see what all the fuss was about. "Here," Hassan said to him. "You hold her down while I look."

Emil went around to the back of the settee and grasped Celestine's shoulders while Hassan lowered his head until he could peer into her eye. Neither man noticed what she was doing with her hands. Celestine silently removed the scent sprayer from her handbag. She raised it and felt Emil's hands tighten on her shoulders as he saw, too late, what she was about to do.

She injected a mixture of bleach and water straight into Hassan's eyes.

He staggered back, screaming. Celestine half rose while she

attempted to twist around and aim her spray at Emil's face, but her reflexes weren't fast enough and his hand released her right shoulder, flying to seize the wrist instead. The rubber bulb gave under pressure, evicting a small puff of vapor, and both of them turned away their heads, but the struggle went on. Celestine, acting from instinct, leaned forward, trying to pinch Emil's hands into her waist and neutralize him; but now he moved his left hand to her brow and began to force her head back. She wasn't strong enough to fight him for long. By now his other hand was gripping the spray bottle's neck.

That was when Azizza ran through the door. She paused opposite Hassan, who was still reeling around with his hands to his eyes, drew an almighty deep breath, and butted him in the chest. He careened backward against one of the radio's sharp upper corners. Azizza jumped onto Emil's back and clung there like the Old Man of the Sea, thumping the top of his head with her fist.

Emil dropped Celestine. Realizing that this new assailant was a woman and lightweight, he thought to roll forward, pitching her over his shoulders onto the floor and, with any luck, breaking her back. But before he could act Celestine sat up, aimed her spray, and scored a direct hit on his face. He shut his eyes, flailing free of both women. Azizza went crashing against the wall. Emil, confident that he'd seen her off for the moment, turned his attention to Celestine. He launched a backhander at her chin with all the force he could summon, but he dared open his eyes only a crack and could not see to aim properly; the blow went wide by a foot or more, causing him to lose his balance. As he went down on one knee Azizza came at him, brandishing the whisky bottle. It landed on top of his crown. The bottle did not break, as in the movies, so she hit him again, and a third time, until the deep, dark red fountaining up through his hair signaled that she had won. Emil fell forward onto the floor with a thud that made Celestine grit her teeth.

Azizza held a hand over her heart. She was wheezing, her face had turned white, and for a fearful moment Celestine thought she might faint.

"Out," she cried. "Out *now!*"

But Hassan stood between them and the doorway. He had a

gun in his hand. He was waving it around in a series of uncontrolled loops while he blindly sought the safety catch. Celestine caught a glimpse of his eyes, and she gasped: two orbs of off-white mucus with no pupils visible; she had done that, yes, she had blinded a man; her legs trembled, she reached out for something to support her ... but when he fired, sending a bullet through the ceiling, that broke the spell. She grabbed Azizza's hand and rushed straight at Hassan with her arm rigid and her free fist outstretched like a battering ram. It contacted with his Adam's apple. He went down with a wet gurgle that made her think of eyeballs dissolving in acid, and she cried aloud, but she cried in freedom. There was warm salty air on her skin, the sound of waves in the distance, she was out, she was running. Azizza had concealed her old Citroën Dyane behind a clump of banana trees, not far from the beach house, the same sky-blue Dyane, *My God, this car is ten years old;* it was rusty, it was battered rather than dented, its hood had gone, but when Azizza turned the key it started the fourth time and when she put it into gear it moved off, sedately, and there they were, two old biddies in an old junker, going for a spin. Unworthy of anyone's attention. Of no interest to Shiite gunmen or Phalange militia. Free.

Feisal Hanif arrived an hour later.

He rode in the back of a stretched-body silver Mercedes with green-tinted glass, and when a bodyguard opened the rear door for him his face was cruel. He had been trying to raise Hassan on the shortwave radio that was never more than a meter away from him wherever he went, and the failure to make contact boded no good for those whose job it was to carry out his orders.

Despite the heat and the humidity of this overcast day he was wearing a pale gray double-breasted suit of sober cut, and the sternest fashion commentator could have found no fault with the knot of his tie or the smooth, uncreased appearance of his shirt. He was in his mid-fifties but he had the body of a thirty-year-old: tall, upright stature, lean flesh, well-exercised muscles. His skin was exceptionally fine: very dark, the color of rich Christmas cake, and as moist. He allowed his body and the simple clothes with which he covered it to speak for themselves: not for him the flash of gold at the cuffs, the diamond tie pin or designer sunglasses. Indeed, he regarded the last as the hallmark of the truly unremarkable and refused to wear them.

People meeting him for the first time—especially women— would come away swearing that this man must have sold his soul to the devil, for there was no other way of combining health, looks, wealth, and charm. Somehow, nobody ever attributed his sterling collection of plus points to God and the angels. He had quite extraordinary presence: even when he was not speaking, one always felt a touch stifled, a little deaf.

Feisal picked his way across Emil's unconscious form while he surveyed the wreckage, piecing the story together in his mind. Hassan sat outside on the terrace propped up against the wall, caterwauling still, but more quietly now, and Feisal's two bodyguards stood with their hands clasped in front of them, the way he liked it. At last he turned to one of them and he said, "Fahim, would you please be kind enough to stop that noise?"

The man addressed as Fahim came briefly to attention before leaving the house. Feisal listened to the sounds of a brief scuffle on the veranda, followed by silence. The silence went on for a long time, but Feisal continued to stand there with his head ever so slightly off vertical, as if he were still listening, until two distant shots put an end to his contemplation.

"Do you think you can wake him up?" he murmured. The second bodyguard shook Emil. After a few minutes he managed to return to a semblance of consciousness, so that by the time Fahim returned to the house there was almost a coherent conversation in progress.

"Where did they go?" Feisal was asking as Fahim entered. "Which direction did they take?"

Emil shook his head. "I don't know. I am sorry."

Feisal had been squatting down beside him; now he rose slowly to his feet and stood in thought for a moment more. The two bodyguards never took their eyes off him. In a moment he would tell them what needed to be done and they would do it. Things were always thus.

"Two women," he said at last. "Two elderly, unarmed women against you and Hassan." Feisal heaved a long sigh. "I find a delicate element of comedy in all this, Emil, but the fact remains that when my mother offended me, and believe me it was for the last time, you let her go."

The driver did not look at Feisal. A tic appeared at the side of his mouth.

"You are discharged from my service, Emil. They will take your identity card and turn you loose on the airport road. If you make it as far as your home in Mousseitbe, you will be safe."

Sentence of death had never been pronounced with greater dignity.

22 July: Lunchtime: Bahrain

Andrew Nunn arrived to find them all hunched around a TV set in the back room of the Lloyds agency, trying to make the video player work. A phone was ringing. No one answered it. After a while the ringing degenerated into a kind of intermittent death rattle and stopped of its own accord. Andrew tiptoed across the room and unplugged this phone, substituting his portable fax machine's plug in the wall jack.

The machine was a Japanese prototype, not yet on general sale, but it had proved itself time and time again to the point where Nunn would not travel without it. Although aware of Selman Shehabi examining him through critical eyes, he ignored the Iraqi while he adjusted the settings. Only when he was satisfied did he look up and murmur, "Anything your end?"

"There are no Israelis on board that plane. No Israeli passports, anyhow."

Andrew understood the distinction. At this stage he did not think it worthwhile disturbing Shehabi with the rumors of Tel Aviv hit teams that had begun to circulate uneasily through the international insurance community. Nunn had got word of this through a contact in Alexander & Alexander's New York intelligence section, backed up by London War Risks Reinsurers: reliable enough sources, in ordinary circumstances. But Shehabi did not need to know about rumors. He was perfectly capable of manufacturing his own.

"We have found out how the arms were put aboard the plane," the Iraqi went on. "They used a bus driver with access to the airport apron. The man identified Halib Hanif, Leila's brother, as the man who approached him. A cleaner took over once the arms were within the airport perimeter, but he's run away."

"What's new with the plane?"

"Baghdad is monitoring transmissions from Teheran," Shehabi replied, with a nod toward the TV. "That's where the videotapes ended up."

Nunn glanced at the disorganized TV screen, politely saying nothing.

"You bring your fax with you. You are expecting developments?"

Actually, Nunn thought, my gee's running in the two-thirty at Newmarket, and I've got a lot of money riding on a place. Also, things are hotting up in Jak, those ten million Swiss francs are that much nearer finding their way into my pocket, but only if I keep my delicate hand on the tiller. And since I'll never know, never be allowed to understand my role in all this hijack nonsense, I don't see why I shouldn't let my attention wander a little.

"Developments," he said diplomatically, "could occur at any time."

He'd already spent a long time on the phone to Philip Trewin, briefing him on his contact with Halib Hanif the night before and discussing how much they ought to tell Shehabi. Nunn and Trewin were agreed on the significance of what Halib had said; both men wanted a quick, clean end to the hijack, and they were prepared to recommend concessions in the interests of speed. Selman Shehabi would not see it that way.

In the end Trewin had agreed that Nunn should decide how much to tell the Iraqi and how much to hold back. At this juncture, Nunn still wasn't sure.

The TV screen cleared. There were pictures of the murdered South African lying on the gravel, accompanied by an Arabic sound track. One of the men standing around the set started to improvise a running translation; Nunn heard a *hoom* and recognized Dr. Milner's voice.

"... Disobedience will attract further reprisals.... Ah, now the, the—presenter? God knows what to call him—now he's giving us the Iranian prisoners' names and calling ... what's he calling for? He's calling for them to be released at once, or more passengers will ... no, that's too definite ... are likely, more passengers are likely to die...."

The image dissolved into a fuzz of colors, to be replaced by the standard start-of-clip representation of a clock face.

"That was yesterday," Major Trewin commented. "Here we go with this morning's episode. Shortly after dawn; I must say, their communications are bloody efficient."

The "presenter" was the same man. The sequence opened with a close-up of the plane. A hooded figure could be seen in the doorway. He stood there without moving, his gun held at waist level.

Trewin froze the tape. "We're working on him. There are five names in the frame, the consensus at present being for a man called Fouad Nusseibeh. Three years ago he was operating out of the Beqaa Valley as part of Arafat's Hawari Group, but with most of his targets in European cities. Born Jaffa, 1947, resettled to Lebanon; there's the usual file. Our people would like it to be Nusseibeh, because he ties in with the Hanifs: part of their gang."

"How did he join the plane?" Nunn asked.

"Fouad, if it is him, boarded at Bahrain, along with one other suspect. We're reasonably certain that three more were on the plane when it left London: they all originated from 'safe' airports, Manchester, Glasgow, Amsterdam, on feeder flights, which meant they wouldn't be faced with anything like the security they have at Heathrow check-in."

"Any sign of Leila yet?" Nunn wanted to know.

"Positive ID of her in Bahrain, from airport staff. And"— Trewin began to advance the tape frame by frame—"watch the door, behind the man's left shoulder ... there! See it? Movement, something white, just for a second."

"Run it through again, please."

Trewin obliged. Nunn squatted down with his face inches from the screen, but he was damned if he could make out anything.

"Our technical bods have been futzing around on that since the tape came in, and they swear that what you can see is in fact a human figure wearing long dress of some kind, and they're inclined to say it's a female."

"Inclined ... what does that mean?"

"It means they desperately want it to be female and so they're clutching at straws," Trewin said equably. "Any other questions?"

Nunn stood up, though he continued to stare at the screen. By now the woman Leila Hanif had got a grip on his imagination. He kept recalling last night's phone call to Anne-Marie. *All the way to hell to refuel and then on.* Anne-Marie understood Leila in a way he never would; how much, then, did he understand Anne-Marie?

How far would Andrew Nunn be prepared to go for his child?

"What about that other helicopter?" he said thoughtfully. "The one that caused all the trouble?"

"Allied source," Trewin said. Butter could safely have been stored in his mouth until well past its sell-by date.

Nunn nodded, but a time was coming when he would take Major Trewin up on that. He knew that the U.S. Navy had unofficially permitted Israeli Air Force Intelligence to fly the second chopper, the one that had prompted Van Tonder's murder, from a destroyer cruising the Arabian Sea. Other people were starting to know it too, thereby increasing the difficulty of Nunn's task tenfold. For now, however, he merely cursed the helicopter and all connected with it before inquiring, "And what does your allied source have to report?"

"Lots of highly technical data concerning terrain and so forth."

"What chance of a home run?"

"Sweet bugger all. They didn't stay long, but long enough to detect the presence of explosive substances aboard the plane."

"How the devil can they do that?"

Trewin shrugged. "God knows. X-ray cameras, perhaps; long-range telephotos: they're not saying."

"Home run?" Shehabi had been showing signs of impatience, and now he interrupted. "What is this home run, please?"

"Our jargon for an assault on the plane." Trewin turned to Milner. "Tell me, doctor ... how, in your view, would the Yemenis be likely to react to a proposal that the SAS, say, be sent in to rescue the passengers?"

"They'd probably take it as a declaration of war. They're Marxists—hard-line unreconstructed Marxists."

"What about the area where the plane went down?" Trewin asked. "What's there?"

"Al Mahra's scarcely inhabited; just a few Bedouins, that's all. It's got no asphalted roads, not even in Al Ghaydah, that's the provincial capital. It's the most underdeveloped part of the country. No one, and I do mean *no one*, gets permission to visit." Milner shook a finger for emphasis. "You've no conception of how bleak, how desolate, that area is."

Nunn could see that this led nowhere. "What have we got on these six Iranian prisoners?" he interrupted, "the ones being held"—a sideways glance at Shehabi—"allegedly held in Baghdad."

"Top army men, captured in the gulf war." It was Trewin who answered. "Plus one air force general. Extraordinary behavior. There's a war going on. If some of your chaps get taken prisoner of war you don't bluff out a hijack, you wait for hostilities to end or bring in the Red Cross, Red Crescent, that kind of thing. Or you negotiate an exchange."

Nunn recognized a cue when he heard one. Trewin was inviting him to make up his mind about Halib. Best to come clean ... but as he prepared to speak he felt a wave of that stomach-rippling thrill associated with roller coasters.

While he recounted the previous night's meeting he allowed his gaze to float around the room, noting reactions. Shehabi seemed to be taking it remarkably well. When Andrew had finished, however, he was first off the mark.

"Why have you waited until now before telling us this?"

It was, of course, the sixty-four-thousand-dollar question, and Andrew could hardly say, Because I don't trust you an inch, m'dear fellow; there were limits to the effectiveness of abstract truth. So instead he gave the Iraqi an explanation that sounded reasonable, if not compelling.

"Hanif's a terrorist, pure and simple, despite his business front. I wasn't about to waste time, commit resources, without first making a few independent inquiries of my own, particularly since I felt he was holding back on me."

"We know for sure that Leila Hanif's son was on the plane. What other inquiries could you make?"

"About her likely mental state, and the consequences for the passengers. I've spoken to a psychologist, and I've used independent sources to try and verify her movements over the past few years."

This was true—he'd been hard at work all morning—though the last thing Nunn wanted was to be forced into identifying those "sources." Shehabi looked dissatisfied. Fortunately, at this juncture the MI6 man, who hadn't yet opened his mouth today, now seemed disposed to make a contribution.

"It would explain a lot," he said slowly. "The whole thing's struck me as odd from the beginning. I mean, why the South Yemeni desert? Why not a major airport, with press and TV? A hijack's worthless without publicity. With all due respect to Dr. Milner here, why isn't the South Yemeni government taking a hand? Jolly useful to be seen acting responsibly, I'd have thought; increase their chance of foreign aid no end. But it all starts to make more sense if the hijack's of secondary concern to Leila Hanif." He was growing steadily more excited. "I'd say Halib's right to be worried. And so should we be."

Nunn found his mind diverting into unfamiliar byways. He'd fallen passionately in love with Anne-Marie and proposed to her shortly after they'd met while holidaying in Nice. Their son had been a love child. She would go all the way to hell, she said, but had there ever been a time when she would have resorted to violence for Michael's sake? Would she have stolen a plane, just to be with him? No, it was absurd. And yet women stole to feed their starving children, killed in order to protect them....

Trewin was speaking.

"I'm not convinced. If she wanted the boy back, all she had to do was arrange a snatch in England any time over the past two years."

"After the mess in New York the Raleighs were subject to surveillance," MI6 said. "I checked. Halib would have guessed that."

Trewin tossed his head. "Well, maybe.... Tell us, Andrew, have you had any luck this morning?"

Nunn forced his mind back onto the main highway. "Well, so far it seems as though things are much as they appear to be. The people I've spoken to are all agreed that it's a commercial contract organized by the Hanifs. Probably a Hezbollah connection in there somewhere. I'm told, reliably I think, that since our meeting Halib's gone aboard that Iranian frigate, the one backing up the chopper. Stalemate; unless our friend here"—he waved his hand at Shehabi—"can magic some Iranian prisoners out of the air."

On the spur of the moment he decided not to tell Shehabi of Jerry Raban's latest update: that Feisal Hanif was in Cairo, but booked on every flight into Bahrain for the next seventy-two hours.

Shehabi hitched himself onto the nearest desk and folded his arms. He stared at the floor. Nunn studied him with suddenly renewed interest. He'd been expecting the usual heated denial of the prisoners' existence. This reticence was unexpected. Perhaps he'd been influenced by Nunn's account of his meeting with Halib after all. But before Shehabi could either satisfy or confound expectations, the fax machine emitted a click and its RECEIVE indicator light began to blink.

Andrew digested the message line by line as it appeared through the slot, so that by the time the guillotine severed the sheet he already knew the worst.

"Oh, dear," he said quietly. "Oh dear, oh dear."

"I gather," said Trewin, "that we're none of us going to like this, but could we have it anyway?"

"Originating from Teheran ... the latest videotape has just been delivered." He kept up a smooth, unhurried delivery, not wanting to be quizzed on how he got his information before Trewin and MI6 received theirs. "I think I know what Halib was holding back, now. My contact says that on the most recent tape the hijackers have issued a demand, a deadline, and a threat. One of each. First, the demand. The six Iranian prisoners of war are to be flown from Baghdad to Cairo, where they'll be handed over to representatives of the Red Crescent. This must be done before midnight Egyptian time tomorrow night, the twenty-third, which is the deadline." He looked at his watch. "Egypt's one hour behind us, isn't it?"

"That's right," Trewin said. "Gives us, what? Thirty-six hours, more or less. What's the threat?"

"The threat is that, unless their demands are met, sixty minutes after the deadline expires they will blow up the plane with everyone aboard."

22 July: Evening: Al Mahra, South Yemen

annie Neeman, the Mossad agent who occupied seat 24H,
waited a long time before taking a look at the paper napkin Robbie had forced into his hand. It wasn't simply a
matter of waiting for the hijackers' attention to be focused elsewhere. That, by itself, would have been simple. There were only
five gunmen to cover nearly two hundred passengers. Five people
couldn't be looking everywhere at once; they didn't have eyes in
the back of their heads.

No, Dannie wasn't afraid that the hijackers would detect him;
he feared betrayal by his fellow prisoners.

He knew something about hijacks, how they turned. He'd
watched the videos and studied the manuals. After a while, passengers came to assume that the outside world had forgotten them.
Because they were constantly afraid, they constantly felt the need
for reassurance. They began to identify with their captors. Gunmen were hardly sympathetic figures, but they represented the
only other visible force in play. And they were better than those on
the outside, the ones Leila mentally styled "the chess players,"
because the gunmen sometimes smiled, or let you go to the toilet,
or said you could have a glass of water.

They might shoot you, too. So passengers on a hijacked plane tended to be wary of anything that could upset the men responsible for their plight. Oddballs who resisted were, after a while, viewed with suspicion by their fellow victims. And from suspicion it was but a short step to hostility.

By the grace of God, no one had seen Robbie deliver the message. If another passenger had noticed the Israeli reading it, he might have told the hijackers. That was the way to win the strong men's favor—you might secure an extra meal for yourself or a seat nearer the open door and fresh air.

That way they might not choose you when next they needed a corpse to be videoed.

Dannie Neeman waited until his nearest neighbors had fallen asleep before unfolding the paper napkin Robbie had brought. There was no signature, but he recognized Raful's writing. His orders were to wait until one of their team was chosen to die, then act "as arranged." He understood. It was a worst-case scenario, but he knew what he had to do when the time came.

Something was going to break. It wouldn't be much longer now.

He swallowed, trying to pump a little saliva up from empty glands; it was a long time since the last water ration. He found it hard to hold his head level, and his feet were full of sluggish blood. Aboard the plane, things had deteriorated to the verge of critical. The hijackers kept small amounts of food and water coming, but things like diapers and medicines and tampons had run out. Babies' little bodies couldn't cope with the sweltering atmosphere. Women were bleeding into their seats, and it sapped them mentally more than physically. Soon the souls aboard NQ 033 would no longer be able to cope with kids wallowing in their own shit, perpetual thirst, cloth rubbing against raw skin, pools of vomit, ulcers, mouth sores … the devil would have loved the interior of this plane, and perhaps only Hieronymus Bosch could have done it justice.

Another scruple in the scale, only one, and the balance would tip. One more death, that was the thing, Dannie decided; and across the other side of the plane someone was dying. A few hours ago, the hijackers had asked anyone aboard who was a doctor to identify himself. A man had come forward and diagnosed diabetes;

now he was kneeling beside his patient, a youth slumped in row 20 on the port side. Yes. When the diabetic boy snuffed it, that would be the flashpoint. The cue.

22 July: Evening: Yarze, Lebanon

At first Celestine and Azizza could not decide where would be the safest place for them to lie low. In the end they took a circuitous route back to the house at Yarze, reasoning that Feisal wouldn't waste manpower keeping a permanent watch on Kharif. Even when he discovered her escape from Damour, why mount guard over a dilapidated house? Once he'd satisfied himself that his mother wasn't there—and before returning home they gave him plenty of time to do that—he would leave it alone. At least, that's what they hoped.

By the grace of Allah they reached Kharif safely. There, a crisis conference speedily resulted in a decision that Azizza must go back to Chafiq Hakkim's. Earlier in the day she had begged time off, but someone had to find out what was going on and Hakkim was likely to know. Besides, they needed food.

Celestine, alone again, collapsed into a chair, finally able to admit how ill she felt. Previously she'd put it down to a poisonous combination of anxiety over Robbie, old age, and physical exertion that would have taxed a teenager, let alone a woman in her seventies. Now, however, as she sat in the gloom counting her irregular heartbeats, she knew that the only thing to keep her from crumbling was willpower, and it couldn't last forever.

She took a photo of Robbie from her bag. It had been taken in the restaurant at the top of New York's World Trade Center. Twelve-year-old Robbie was staring solemnly into the lens, his shirt turned stark white by the flash. The last time she'd seen him; dear God, she prayed, let it not be the last time she ever would see him.

"Robbie," she whispered. "Hold on, darling. Celestine loves you, Robbie. She's coming to help you. She is. She is."

Tears crept up on her by stealth. She fought them, for a while.

But the more she resisted the more her distress deepened, until at last she blurted out everything in a convoluted expression of terror and pain.

"I'm just a poor widow woman ... no good to anyone ... not wanted, not needed, oh, *God*, not needed. And I can't do anything. I can't save him. Oh, God, Allah, help him, help my poor lovely Robbie...."

At sunset Azizza came back to find Celestine rocking to and fro in a chair.

"Izza," she cried, "what am I going to do, what am I going to *do!*"

The old servant ran to the table and grabbed both of Celestine's hands between her own. "Keep calm," she said, her voice more of a snap than a consolation. "Stop your weeping and listen. I need your help. Celestine!"

Celestine dried her tears and took a deep breath.

"It's Hakkim," Azizza said. She busied herself lighting candles. "He's funny."

"What do you mean?"

"He's changed. The minute I was in the door he came at me and I thought, Oh, he's going to torture me until I cough *you* up. But it wasn't that. He was frightened."

"Hakkim, frightened?" This was something, this was news; come on, old girl, sit up, take notice.

Azizza blew out the match with which she'd been lighting the candles. "He said he'd been cheated and there was something you had to know."

"And you believed him?" Celestine found it hard to keep an edge of scorn from her voice.

"Of course not, stupid, not until he mentioned the money."

"What money?"

"He'd been hauled in to back this hijack thing. A business, like any other; those were his exact words, imagine! He put up the cash for training, weapons, tickets, hotels, everything! But he stands to lose the lot."

"What did he say?"

"He said he'd only tell you. But I wasn't having any of that, I pretended I hadn't seen you since you came to his house yesterday. He didn't believe me, of course, but he told me to pass on a message to you, and when I heard what it was I actually started to believe him."

"What message?"

A man's voice from the passage. "The Israelis were in it from the beginning."

Both women shrieked. Celestine jumped up, one hand held to her throat, the other clutching Azizza for support. It took her all of ten seconds to realize that she knew this voice; it was Hakkim's.

So he'd followed his housekeeper back to Kharif. "Oh, Izza," she murmured, but there was no harshness in the reproach. Being duped on occasion was the price you paid for God's gift of an upright nature.

"Don't worry," Hakkim said agitatedly, pulling a chair up to the table. "Ai, what a day!"

"Chafiq," Celestine said, forcing all the urgency she could muster into the one word. "Do something useful for once in your life, and help me save Robbie."

"Yes, yes. Let me get my breath. I've brought coffee, some wine—"

"Does Feisal know you're here?" Celestine barked. "Did he send you?"

"No, to both questions." Hakkim used his teeth to extract the half-drawn cork from a wine bottle.

"Is he tailing you, then? You follow Izza, he follows you...."

From the look on his face she deduced he hadn't thought of that. More interestingly, the notion frightened him. There was silence for a while. Celestine found herself in no hurry to break it. Let him stew!

"Feisal's hit a rock," he said at last, before taking a swig of wine.

"The hijack's gone wrong?"

"Badly. You want some coffee?"

He unstoppered the flask, allowing the aroma of fresh coffee to permeate the room. Celestine had to force herself to say, "Later."

"Someone tried to stop Leila," Chafiq said, "just before she took the plane. Someone who knew she'd be there. When Halib heard about it he ran a check. The man who attacked Leila is called Rafael Sharett. He's a Mossad man. Very high: a director."

Celestine frowned. "So what?"

"So one day soon this mess is going to end, right? And the papers are going to get the story, and if Sharett's still alive he's going to talk to his people."

"I imagine so."

"Celestine." Chafiq leaned forward across the table, hands folded across his chest. She noticed that his forehead was running with sweat. "I can't afford to upset them in Jerusalem. When I went into this I spelled it out to Feisal: 'Look,' I said, 'no Zionist dimension, okay?' And he said okay, so I went in with my share. But if they ever once so much as suspect ..."

So Banker Hakkim had done business with Tel Aviv, had he? Celestine thought that must be a dangerous game. If he was telling the truth, she could understand his fear. *If.*

"But they *have* found out, haven't they?" she remarked gently. "They put an anti-hijack team aboard that plane, so by now they know all they'll ever need to. I don't follow your logic, Chafiq. If you're dead, you're dead already." She paused, keen for the timing to be perfect. "Already."

Hakkim breathed heavily. Suddenly he smashed a fist down on the table, making bottle and flask jump.

"Maybe the Mossad don't know Sharett's aboard," he said.

"They put a man on the plane, to stop the hijack ... and they don't know he ...? You'll have to help me, I don't understand."

Celestine became aware of a shadow at Hakkim's elbow. She heard a noise and, although the banker appeared not to have noticed, Celestine knew that Azizza had picked up the flask. Good. She really could do with some of that coffee.

"Follow it through with me," he said. "One. There's been nothing in the papers, the TV or radio, to suggest that anyone knows there's a top-ranking Mossad man aboard that plane."

"But they'd deliberately keep it a secret, wouldn't they? To preserve the element of surprise."

"The Mossad would. But others would be only too keen to broadcast it. The Syrians, the Iraqis: their press would be crowing it from the hilltops."

"Maybe the Mossad just managed to keep this secret well."

"You don't understand. If Tel Aviv knew Sharett was aboard, they'd storm the plane and get their man out. And they'd have done it before this."

"But what does it mean?" she said slowly. "Sharett was on that flight for the purpose of foiling the hijack. Why wouldn't this man tell his own people what he was up to?"

"Perhaps he knew they'd forbid it."

"You mean, he's on his own ... it's a private party?"

"Yes."

"Even though he works for an organization whose job it is to stop people like my grandchildren? Oh, come on, Chafiq!"

"Look. We know this man is on that plane, we know that his own side isn't interested—"

"*Prove* to me that this man is on the plane, that he's who you say he is."

When his hand shot to an inner pocket her first thought was, Allah! He's got a gun!, until she saw him hold out a square of cardboard. She took it warily: a photograph of a man sitting slumped in what looked like a plane seat, his face streaked with blood.

"That's Sharett," Hakkim said. "It was taken immediately after the plane landed in Yemen and flown out to Teheran next day. It came to Feisal along with a request that he try to identify this man, because he attacked Leila when she made her move on the cockpit. They sent him photocopies of his passport, too: false, of course. Here."

He gave her some folded pages. She looked at them. "These could all be faked," she muttered.

"It's not a fake."

"This snap could have been taken before the hijack." She peered closely at it. "How did you get hold of these? Did Feisal give them to you?"

"Are you mad? He'd slit my throat if he knew I'd got them."

"You stole them?" Celestine asked sharply.

"I have a good friend on Feisal's staff." Hakkim's eyes were bulging now; he was thinking of what would happen if Feisal caught up with him. "He borrowed them."

"You'll have to show these to the Mossad if you're to have any chance of making them believe you."

"Forget it!" He snatched the photo back from her.

Celestine became aware of the shadow again standing at Hakkim's shoulder. She hadn't seen Izza for a while. Had she gone somewhere? Or had she been there all the time, listening?

"Why are you telling me this?" she demanded.

"The whole thing's going to come out; the Zionists will know I'm involved; they'll finish me." He was almost in tears.

"So how can I save you?"

"Make the Israelis believe Sharett's on the plane. I can help you get to Tel Aviv, I have ... ways."

She stared at him, too astonished to speak.

"They'll send a team to rescue everyone, Robbie, everyone." Hakkim's voice, so enthusiastic until now, suddenly faltered. "But unless they think there's one of their high-ups aboard, they won't do a thing."

Azizza slowly lifted the coffee flask and waved her forefinger above its stopper, shaking her head. Then she floated backward into the shadows that were starting to fill the room with the onset of dusk.

"Some of your best friends," Hakkim was saying in a voice heavy with irony, "are Israelis."

"Yes," Celestine acknowledged, after a pause. "I know one or two."

In the silence that followed she tried to work out the best thing to do. Azizza was warning her that the coffee contained a drug; goodness knows how she'd found out, perhaps she'd seen him do this before, with a girl. A boy, more likely. So the whole thing was a setup.

Why?

If he was truly Feisal's man, all he had to do was trail Azizza at a distance and report back as soon as he saw her enter the house.

But if he'd already reported to Feisal before bringing the wine and drugged coffee, why hadn't Feisal come to pick her up yet?

One thing she *did* believe: if he'd been telling the truth about this man Sharett, then once the Israelis knew it they would move heaven, hell, and earth as well to get their agent out. They would storm the plane. They would kill the terrorists. Kill her own granddaughter, perhaps kill Robbie too. But unless somebody did something she would never see Robbie again, because his mother would steal him away.

A terrible thought struck her. "Chafiq," she gasped, "does Leila realize who this man Sharett is?"

"I don't know."

What would she do if she knew? *What would she do?*

"I'll need to take the photo," Celestine said with the brisk manner of one who decides. "And the copy of Sharett's passport."

"Impossible. They have to be back in Feisal's office by this evening."

Hakkim was terrified. He might, just, be telling some small part of the truth. If his story was true and she could convince the Israelis of that, she could get him off the hook, because the vital information would have come from him.

If. Might. Could. Perhaps. Maybe.

She would have to take the photo and the passport copy. Without them, no chance. But he would never relinquish them voluntarily.

"Chafiq," she said wearily, "my head is going round and round. Can I have some of that coffee, please?"

22 July: Evening: Al Mahra, South Yemen

Dr. Delahaye sat back on his haunches and shook his head. "Getting worse," he murmured. "Do you know when he last injected insulin?"

"Sorry, no." Colin was sitting in the window seat; Robbie had the aisle. Tim Campbell lay between them, breathing in rapid pants, his eyes shut. Colin cradled Tim's head against his chest. "Will he die?" he added quietly.

The doctor nodded. "Unless we can get him to the hospital soon and fix him up with a potassium drip. Normally I wouldn't worry too much about a young chap like this, but thirst's even more of a problem for him than the rest of us, and he seems like a high-anxiety type. He's already severely acidotic, I'd guess … look at that rapid breathing."

There was nothing more Dr. Delahaye could do for Tim, so he went back to his own seat, several rows behind. Colin gently propped Tim's head against the seat and stood upright. Selim saw. He motioned with his hand for Colin to sit down again.

"I want to talk to you," Colin said clearly.

Selim stiffened, but he came down the aisle. Colin stared into his eyes. "Do you wish to be responsible for the death of an innocent kid?" he said, more quietly.

When Selim made no reply, Colin continued, in the same even, almost monotonous voice, "Is this what the Koran teaches? Please tell me, I would like to be advised. Is there glory in heaven for acts such as these? I wish carefully to understand your religion, so that I may respect it and learn from it."

Selim bent down low, leaning across Robbie and Tim Campbell. "Do not defile what you can never understand," he breathed. "What is it you want?"

Colin reached out to place a hand on Tim Campbell's inert wrist.

"This boy is diabetic." He did not raise his voice, or cringe, or soften, or change his manner in the slightest respect. "This boy ran out of insulin some time ago. He is in a coma, from which he will not recover unless he receives medical care promptly. He will die. The world will know that he died, and why. They may not understand the Koran, they may be deaf to the word of Allah, but this at least the world will understand."

Robbie was continually wiping the sweat from Tim's pale face. Now he looked up at Selim and said, "I want to see my mother. Please."

"Be quiet."

"I know you do what she wants, sometimes. I know she can help. She promised she would help. Speak to her, or let me."

While Selim's gaze floated between the three of them, Colin went through the calculations again, testing each link, fighting down the dread. He could save Tim Campbell's life. The strategy was simple, also very dangerous.

He'd go to Leila and say that unless she allowed the sick boy to go out on the helicopter, he would tell Robbie of his mother's true role. Somehow he had to find a way of communicating this threat to Leila and then prevent her from having him quietly killed before he could carry it out. Colin believed that she would not kill him because the risk of Robbie's discovering who had given the order was too great. But she would undoubtedly separate them. Up to now she had left them together, calculating that this way there was at least a chance that Colin might persuade Robbie to leave quietly with his mother. Once he threatened to tell Robbie the truth, however, she would realize that her tactic had failed and move the boy. Then Colin wouldn't be able to talk to his son. He might never see him again.

So how could he put pressure on Leila without cutting his own throat?

What if she called his bluff and he was forced to tell Robbie that his mother was a terrorist? Suppose Robbie said he didn't care, that she was his mother and he loved her? Why in Christ's name hadn't he told the boy the truth earlier, when there wasn't all this pressure?

Colin clenched his fists. Selim still stood there, seemingly undecided. Such lack of resolution was unusual in him. A break in the pattern. Good.

"Listen to my son," he choked out. "There is a lady in first class. Consult her."

Selim stood upright. He turned to the back of the cabin, where another of the five gunmen stood guard, and uttered a few words of Arabic. The second man nodded.

"Wait there," Selim muttered. "I've given orders that the two of you are to be specially watched. You could bring down a lot of death here. Think about that." Now he was talking to Colin. "You personally are safe, for the moment. You know why: you have a job to do." His gaze skated sideways to Robbie. "A lesson to teach. And you detest the thought of *innocent* lives being lost."

He stalked away. Colin noticed that his shoulders seemed hunched. Was it an illusion, brought on by fatigue? No. Selim was tiring.

Colin turned to look out the window. It was nearly dark. The desert floor stretched away to the black foothills, sterile and empty. Nothing moved. He felt himself familiar with every stone, every grain of sand, every spike in the distant, dark horizon. Mars must look like this. The sun was setting, thank God! During the daytime, its fierce light was mitigated by the Perspex windows, specially designed for high-altitude flying in thin atmosphere where ultraviolet light would otherwise scorch and destroy living tissue, but it was nowhere near strong enough to protect the pas-sengers from the furnace that roared silently outside. Even nightfall brought little relief from that. Colin tried to sit perfectly still and control his breathing, tried to forget the thirst that constricted his throat.

When Tim's head lurched against his shoulder, Colin at first thought it another symptom of his deepening illness, so he concentrated all his attention on the boy. Then, seeing his pallid face unmoving, he looked up to realize, in panic, that Robbie had risen. Colin's brain worked slowly. Of course, his son wanted to stand up so he'd pushed Tim onto his father.... Why was Robbie in the aisle when Selim had expressly ordered them to stay put?

"Sit down!" he cried, but Robbie was running.

The guard at the back of the cabin shouted. People started to scream. Robbie yelled something, his words lost in the hubbub. When the gunman fired a single round through the ceiling, the noise echoed like thunder presaging the Last Days and the screams rose to hysterical pitch; other passengers were standing up now, convinced that this was the start of the massacre, each man for himself. A woman catapulted from her seat into Robbie's path, but the boy thrust her aside, racing on toward the curtain at the front of the cabin, behind which, he knew, was his mother.

Colin stood up. He cared nothing for the melée developing ahead of him. Alone among the terrified passengers, he turned to the back of the plane. The gunman was down on one knee, aiming along the aisle. By now there were so many people between him and Robbie that his chances of hitting the boy were nonexistent. It didn't matter. Colin knew he was going to fire.

He gripped the seat backs on either side of him and vaulted over Tim's motionless body. "Sit down!" he shouted. "For God's sake—*sit down!*"

Nobody paid him any attention. Colin found himself looking down the aisle into the muzzle of the M3A1 twenty feet away, less. He took a step forward. The barrel jerked up. Now he was the target.

The world came to a stop. His last seconds upon this earth. Would it hurt? he wondered. And then: Please let his aim be accurate, I don't want to lie here wounded, don't let him shoot me in the stomach, it takes an age to die and the agony is beyond description....

He spoke his last words.

"Shoot me."

The gunman could not hear him. His mouth extended into what might have been a smile or an expression of concentration, and Colin braced himself. And at that moment, silence overwhelmed the plane, a silence so unexpected, so complete, it was an almost audible thing.

Colin heard himself say again, "Shoot *me.*"

People were staring at him as if he'd gone mad. Slowly, one by one, they sat down. Colin's head pounded with a deadening kind of ache, as if somebody were knotting and twisting whatever vessels and muscles and veins lay behind his eyes. He could still see the gunman, nobody else, just the hijacker at the end of the cabin, but he could not feel his legs or his arms or any part of himself except his heart, which was threatening an all-out strike. His eyes floated in the cabin, disembodied but functional. He was alive, when he knew he couldn't be.

"Shoot me." He understood. *Lord God of hosts, let me stand in for Isaac. Shoot me, not my son. Shoot me.*

His head began to clear itself of congealed blood. He wheeled around toward the front of the plane. The aisle was empty. Nothing, no one, now separated him from Robbie, who stood facing him at the point where economy gave way to business class. Beyond the bulkhead, Colin could just see Selim. But that was not what held his attention. Behind Robbie, with one hand resting on his shoulder, stood Leila.

Mother and son stared down the aisle at Colin. The expression in their eyes was the same: curiosity and wonder. His son and ex-wife both understood this moment. They had explored it with him, as hypothesis, times without number. What would you do? they had always wanted to know: How would you react, if it was your turn to make the choice of him-or-you?

Now they knew. Robbie was smiling, grinning, crying, all at once. Leila, too, was smiling, though hers was the bitter smile that acknowledges error to the inner self. A loser's smile.

The plane stayed absolutely silent. Row upon row of passengers gazed at the woman with her hand on the boy's shoulder, not understanding what it was they witnessed. But they seemed to know that if they waited, the truth would out. Seconds ticked by, weaving themselves into one minute ... two.

"She's my mother," Robbie suddenly exclaimed; and the hand tightened on his shoulder until its knuckles were white. "This is my mother." He swallowed hard, choking back tears. "She's going to ask them if my friend Tim can go home. Because ... because, you see, he's very sick."

He spoke the last word in a dying fall, as if conscious that he'd said either too much or not enough. He tried to twist around to look at Leila, but her grip on his shoulder stiffened, making him stare at her hand instead. His smile faded. Colin watched his son's confidence drain away with the abruptness of the last grains of sand disappearing down the neck of a timer.

When Leila addressed herself in Arabic to the hijacker at the rear of the cabin Colin knew she was admonishing the man for having panicked and aimed at Robbie. He wheeled around. Her henchman stood there without any discernible expression on his face. Not by the merest flicker of a muscle did he betray his true relationship with this woman. Colin knew that she had chosen her words with the utmost care, so that even if any of these passengers understood Arabic they would still not divine the truth.

Now Leila turned to Selim and her face broke into a delightful smile. She spoke to him in a low voice, wheedling, promising, understanding. After a while he nodded, a trifle impatiently, perhaps: he would agree to almost anything as long as it meant the end of this prattle; that was the message his face conveyed. When he spoke a few clipped sentences, Leila translated.

"He says the sick boy may leave next time the helicopter comes. But no one else may leave."

For a moment the deadly silence continued. Then, with complete suddenness, the passengers began to clap. Colin had never heard anything like it: you could not single out the pair of hands that began it, for all of them came together at once. They were cheering. Some lifted their hands above their heads to applaud, as if a great diva had come among them. And throughout it all Leila continued to stand there with one hand on Robbie's shoulder, blushing a little, a tight, embarrassed smile on her face, while Robbie let the tears course down his cheeks, tears of gratitude, tears of pride that his mother should be the one who set Tim free.

She gave him a little push. Robbie ran down the aisle to fling himself into his father's arms. Colin buried his face in the boy's neck, unable to speak. When he raised his head again, the curtain at the far end of the aisle once again sealed off the cabin.

"Oh, Dad...."

While Robbie was still trying to find words, a new sound added itself to the commotion around them: helicopter rotors.

"Come on, son. Better get Tim up front."

Selim materialized beside them. He got everyone back into their seats—everyone, that is, except Colin and Robbie, who were ordered to carry Tim to the forward door. Father and son gently brought the unconscious boy to the inflatable safety ramp and prepared to slide him down it.

"Get well!" Robbie said. Suddenly he bent forward to squeeze Tim's hand. "Ultimate experience, man!" he cried, as the boy's inert body went slowly down to the ground.

Robbie continued to watch while men from the chopper carried Tim away, but to Colin, eyeing his son's profile, the humid, hot evening was redolent of other memories, other times. Before, in Beirut, that terrible summer, he had learned only that he was prepared to sacrifice others in order to save Robbie. He knew now that he could even sacrifice himself if he had to.

The helicopter rose into the air, hovered there a moment, and turned east for the sea. Robbie threw up his arms in a dramatic wave of farewell.

"Thirty-sixth level of experience!" he cried. "You're a Dungeon Master now, man. You are." His voice sank to a whisper, his arms fell to his sides. "You are...."

To Colin, watching his son's face crumple, that summer of 1974 suddenly seemed like yesterday.

June 1974: Beirut, Lebanon

It was the encroachments he resented, the invasions into personal time that seemed to go with the territory of parenthood. He would come home of an evening to find that Leila had other mothers in the cottage: there they were, sitting around drinking tea and discussing the awfulness of their leisured lives. Leila had long ago abandoned her plans for a higher degree, but in her case it didn't matter: there was always the subsidy from Lebanon to eke out Colin's income as a lecturer. The other mothers suffered a lot from their inability to find work of a kind and at a level commensurate with their undoubted middle-class abilities. Colin would stand in the hall, listening to their inane, chattery bitching, and he would quake with rage.

He knew Leila wanted a child; she had conceived on their honeymoon. He knew she wanted to devote the early years to Robbie, without the distraction of work; he had complied. But he had not bargained for her neglect of him. For the absence of meals on his return from work. For lack of sex. For coming a perpetual second in the daily race with his own son.

It was hard to find a word to describe what Leila felt for Robbie. Love? Worship? Adore? These verbs did not go far enough to describe the idolatrous devotion she lavished on their child. If they had come to her and said, "Either you or Robbie must die," she would have seized a knife joyfully and plunged it into her own heart before she would let them touch a hair of that precious head.

Sometimes Colin found his wife's passion for Robbie bordering on the sick. But maybe that was another kind of sickness—jealousy.

It was June 1974, Robbie was four years old, and Colin had been looking forward to a particular day, circled in red on the calendar, for months. Say rather, a particular moment: he had this vision of settling back in his seat on the red and white Middle East Airlines jumbo jet with a jumbo gin and tonic in his hand and four weeks of self-indulgent hedonism to look forward to. Tickets paid for by Feisal, Leila's father; an apartment of their own in the center of Beirut; servants on call night and day; a car at their disposal ... oh, there'd been no end to the blandishments, but all it had taken to persuade him was Leila's assurance that buried somewhere in the package was the certainty of sometimes being together and alone.

She wanted that every bit as much as he did, she assured him. She'd missed the sex, the pleasure of a glass or two of wine by the fire, the weekend walk, hand in hand. Not to have to worry if Robbie woke in the night from a bad dream, because the girl could soothe him while Mummy and Daddy slept: oh, yes! Pure, unadulterated pleasure. To lie abed in the morning, smelling the bougainvillaea outside their window while they made love; to swim in a tiny bay only she and a handful of her friends knew about, with a bottle of champagne chilling two fathoms down ... how these things had beckoned them on to June and that red-circled date in the diary.

How stupid, then, that they should quarrel on the eve of departure; and, bearing in mind their destination, how appropriate that, like all their quarrels, it should be over something utterly stupid.

Because his room in college was being redecorated he'd taken to giving his last tutorials of the term at home, during the mornings, while Robbie went to play school and Leila was usually out doing something, he didn't know what, except that it wasn't cooking or cleaning the house. The college that employed him was all-male, but because Colin had become rather fashionable in the academic world after his Ph.D. thesis, "The Element of Intention in Murder by Recklessness," had been published in book form, a number of "undergraduettes" had been farmed out to him. One of them was a beautiful, sultry dimwit called Fiona Bolingbroke, who made scant secret of her desire to pick more of Colin than his brains. He ignored her, not because he didn't fancy her but because the high road to ruin was clearly marked, in big letters, SEX WITH STUDENTS. Also, because he yearned to believe in *something*, and the option of a stable, faithful marriage was at least handy even if it was no longer as attractive as of yore. And to round it off, students came to tutorials in pairs, almost as if they too realized where safety lay.

A week before the Raleighs were booked to fly to Beirut, Fiona's partner fell sick, leaving her unchaperoned in Colin's house the one day of the year Leila chose to come back early from whatever it was she did in the mornings that wasn't cooking or cleaning. Leila took a long look at the dreamy expression on the face of the girl draped across the sofa she and her husband had chosen together at a Heal's sale and walked out, banging the door behind her. The echoes lasted a long time.

The summer of 1974 still witnessed an uneasy peace in Lebanon, although anyone arriving in the bullet-pocked terminal building of Beirut airport that June could have read the signs and known that civil war was not far off. Colin kept a tight grip on Robbie's hand until they were out in the sunlight, and there, in front of them, stood parked the two BMWs that were to form an indispensable part of life over the next few weeks.

The speed and efficiency of the operation took his breath away. Hands reached for his luggage, his son, his wife, himself; they were in the car with the closing of doors and rapid acceleration taking place simultaneously; then they were racing along a dead-straight road as if they were either royalty or escaping from the police. The Raleigh family traveled in the back of the first car, with a man who kept shouting into a walkie-talkie sitting next to the driver. The interior was deliciously air-conditioned and Colin at last sat back, allowing himself to relax, while he tried to get some feel for Beirut.

"Corniche Mazraa."

He started. Leila had said very little to him for the past seven days, and it was longer than that since he'd heard her employ such soft tones. They were speeding along a broad boulevard, heading for the sea. He saw endless palm trees, the occasional square with people sitting out beneath sunshades, red tiled roofs, attractive villas interspersed with hideous concrete monstrosities, some half built, many more half destroyed. The place it reminded him of most was Yugoslavia, with its mini-skyscrapers: predominantly Mediterranean, like Italy or Spain, but with a hint of something heavier, more sensual in the architecture: a Serbian influence, or Turkish maybe. Then they were turning right into a broad street where imposing pillared façades announced plush shops, the best kind of restaurants, secretive banks, opulent homes. The sense of being "east" was quite gone; everybody he saw looked European.

"Hamra Street," Leila said. "Beirut's Bond Street."

Colin felt her take his hand. The sight of their two hands nestling together in Robbie's lap after so long a separation filled him with happiness. Suddenly she said, in an artificially high voice, "Welcome."

He leaned over Robbie to kiss her cheek. "Thank you," he said quietly.

Robbie threw himself onto his mother, burying his head in her breast, and Colin and Leila shared their first rueful smile in many days, once again parents instead of merely two people who shared responsibility for a child. Colin knew all the fashionable theories about "bonding," knew that he and Robbie had yet to forge that vital, metaphysical link between father and son. But here, in Beirut, anything was possible.

The car turned off Hamra Street—everywhere he looked the signs seemed to be in French—and threaded its way through a web of narrower residential streets until at last it descended a ramp beneath a high, modern apartment building. They rode to the top floor in a fast elevator. The doors slid open to reveal four men standing by a huge picture window half a football field away, but the quartet was already moving quickly forward; speed, Colin realized, was the watchword in Beirut, and before he knew it the leader of the four, a tall, slim Arab, was staring into his eyes; then he reached out to embrace Colin, patting his back affectionately while he kissed him first on the left cheek and then on the right. No token salutations, these, but warm, solid pressures of the lips, flesh to flesh, man to man, before the Arab stepped back enough to be able to hold Colin at arm's length and say, "I am Feisal Hanif. *Ahlan wa sahlan;* my home is your home; welcome to *our* home."

He dropped Colin with the swift deftness that characterized everything he did and turned to Leila, enfolding her in his arms for twice as long as he had devoted to Colin. "Darling," he murmured over and over again. Colin stepped to one side, curious to see how her face hardened into a mold of politeness as she returned her father's softly spoken greetings. Last, Feisal swept Robbie off his feet and held him close. The boy struggled for a few seconds before seeming to realize that resistance here was useless, for he went as rigid as a rabbit awaiting the snake's fang. When Feisal put Robbie down, the boy immediately burst into tears.

"We have so much to discuss," Feisal said. "But now I must leave you. This apartment"—he waved his arms—"is at your disposal for as long as you want it. We are having a party on Saturday, Halib will be back from the States by then; not many guests, just the president, premier, one or two people it might be interesting for a lawyer like yourself to meet. But now you must excuse me." He tousled Robbie's hair and made a face that was meant to be friendly, though the little boy merely cowered away. "Business— here in Beirut, always business! So long, little guy."

The entourage vanished with something of the effect produced on smoke by a powerful fan, bodyguards, secretaries, and assorted henchmen all being sucked out of the room in their leader's turbulent wake.

Colin fixed Leila with his eyes. "The president?"

"Franjieh?" She shrugged. "I expect so. He goes out Saturdays, but ours won't be his only party, oh, no. He'll do twenty, maybe more. Come here, darling.... Robbie, come to Mummy, love." She picked the boy up and laughed, unexpectedly. "They call Franjieh the Sphinx. Know why? Because he can't bear small talk. And yet he goes to all those parties, because he's terrified of missing anything. What do you think of this place?"

Colin took his first proper look around. The apartment was enormous. As you stepped out of the elevator you at once found yourself in the main living room, with its picture windows giving onto a view of the Mediterranean and a sunken, white-tiled balcony, complete with gaily colored umbrellas, chairs, and tables. This room was filled with light. All the soft furnishings were pastel in shade and contemporary in style, as if everything the room contained had been purchased on the same day and quite probably from the same exquisite shop. Colin was greatly taken with the ashtrays. He counted twelve of them before giving up.

"It's lovely," he said, conscious of sounding lame. "But I'm worried about all these glass ornaments and lamps. Won't Robbie—"

"He'll be good, won't you, darling?" Leila carried Robbie around the room, pointing out things she remembered from the old days, so evidently this apartment hadn't been conjured out of the air for their arrival after all. "Anyway," she said over her shoulder, "if he breaks anything, too bad. The servants will pick up the pieces; that's what they're for."

He laughed. Only later did it occur to him that he could not recall her ever having said anything so brutal, so uncaring, before.

That night she insisted they take Robbie with them to one of the famous fish restaurants of Raouche, even though the boy was dog-tired. At first Colin thought this was hard on their son. But afterward, when the child had fallen into a sleep so deep he scarcely seemed alive, Leila took Colin by the hand and led him to their huge bed in the master suite, and he came to realize the reason for her determination to keep Robbie up: she wanted to exhaust him so that he slept the clock around. But Leila did not want to sleep and, after a while, no more did he.

Looking back on it afterward, he acknowledged Beirut in the summer of '74 to have been the best holiday ever, right up until the final hours. And the lovely thing was that while it was going on he almost seized the moment, almost succeeded in realizing each day's joys as they occurred.

Robbie came into bloom, like a flower lifting its head to the sun.

He liked the beach, of course—he used to beg to be taken to the Pigeon Rocks, because there water-skiers skimmed through the naturally formed arches and he could watch them for hours with his wide, unblinking stare—and he tolerated the lunchtime visits to the Hotel St. Georges or the Commodore; but often he seemed happiest just mooching through the "old town," that web of streets around Rome-elegant Riyad el-Solh Square, with his father.

One morning Leila had business matters to attend to, "family, darling, dreadfully boring," and he was pleased, because it meant he could be alone with Robbie. It was not the first time she had left them to their own devices. Sometimes he wondered where she went on those "business" mornings, but really he did not care too much. Nights belonged to the grown-ups; he could afford to give Robbie the days.

The first thing, they agreed, was breakfast. They found a café near the offices of *L'Orient–Le Jour*, where Colin ordered croissants for himself and an extravagant cheese *manouche* for Robbie. Afterward Robbie counted out luridly colored *liraat* for the benefit of the waiter, who tweaked his ear in return for a cheeky smile, and then they sauntered off hand in hand, searching for that special part of Beirut which was at its best before the sun beefed itself up into a huge disk of white flame: the souk.

Assaulted on every side by spice aromas and other, less attractive, smells, their ears bombarded now by the ubiquitous singer Farouz, now by Beethoven, and now by an Indian raga, they found a little bit of everything: covered fruit and vegetable markets, craftsmen huddled together in their narrow stone-fronted little shops: here coffin makers, there glassblowers, in the next alley, manufacturers of *gidawa*, or "hubble-bubbles" as Robbie called them. There were narrow cobbled streets with a single gutter running their length and stone arches at either end, where it felt deliciously cool, even dank; there were sudden twists and turnings that brought them out where they didn't want to be, vexed and alarmed, until they noticed the charming Ottoman fountain in the square or the jeweler's window glittering with all the stones of Asia.

They ended up in a perfumery whose owner, a willowy-chic young woman who only spoke French, insisted they sample all her wares. Robbie wanted to get Leila a present.

"I think we should buy *everything*," he said solemnly.

Colin smiled. "Mummy says we men always think like that," he said. "We go to the supermarket and buy what we want when we should really buy only what we need. So men make rotten shoppers." And rotten lovers, he remembered glumly: "You men screw like you shop" had been the context of Leila's defiant remark.

"But we can't buy *any* of these smells at home." Robbie's brow wrinkled in a frown. "Actually, I wouldn't ever want to go home, not really." He held a glass stopper to his nose and sniffed cautiously. "Except for one thing."

Colin was learning how to listen to his son's silences. He knew he would get to hear about the "one thing" much quicker if he left it dangling.

"Does Grandfather Feisal have a wife?"

"Not now. She died, when she was still quite young."

"Oh." A long silence. Robbie was scowling at the glass stopper while simultaneously continuing to hold it under his nostrils; he looked cross-eyed. "I don't like Grandfather Feisal," he said suddenly.

"Please don't let Mummy hear you say that. It'd upset her. After all, he *is* your grandfather."

But that was the moment when Colin first acknowledged to himself that he didn't like Feisal either.

He used to watch his father-in-law do the rounds at parties and wonder what precisely it was about him that gave off such an air of having been programmed. Feisal never looked at his wrist-watch. He employed other people to worry about the time. And part of Colin's unease related to a sense that this inner clock of Feisal's was counting down to Armageddon.

For him, time ran out on the night of the *raqs sharqi.*

"There's no such thing as belly dancing!" Leila had said playfully. "*Raqs sharqi* is an art form, my dearest, one you'll never understand."

"I still want to see it."

"You men!"

They were sitting on the balcony of the main penthouse room, drinking Pimms.

"Belly dancing is a con," Leila said. "All those greedy-eyed lechers sitting hunched over drinks while some tart pokes her pelvis at them. Honestly, a Soho strip show's better value."

"I wouldn't know. I've never been."

"Such a namby-pamby. Anyway, you don't take your wife to *raqs sharqi*, you take your pals. Ask Halib, he's bound to know of somewhere."

"But I want you to explain this art form to me. Surely it takes a woman to do that?"

Leila pouted. Later on, however, after dinner, when Robbie had been put to bed with Alf, his stuffed crocodile, she asked, "Do you still want to see the dance?" He nodded. She detailed one of the maids to baby-sit Robbie, took Colin down in the elevator and hailed a cab. She gave an address on the eastern, Christian side of the city in which the word Karantina figured, so Colin knew they were going into the port district.

It was everything he'd ever dreamed about when deep in the guidebooks: pure distillation of Beirut. A neon sign above a basement, a door with a sliding panel at eye height through which the swarthy bouncer assessed the strength of your character and the thickness of your wallet before admitting you to a smoke-filled cellar lined with low tables. As Colin sipped scotch by candlelight he felt his heartbeat quicken with the kind of nervous excitement that tells us when we're going to do something deliciously regrettable.

He lay back and placed an arm around Leila's shoulders. After a pause she allowed some of her weight to rest against him; then, as if suddenly reaching a decision, folded herself into a proper embrace. Colin felt happy, although nothing much seemed to be happening, just a lot of noisy chatter competing with tinny recorded music. He was very aware of Leila's hair, the scent of it, the wonderful texture of a handful of locks twisted through his fingers. Her scalp was cool and moist. Tonight was like their first night—a sensation not easy to find when you'd been married nearly five years and had a child.

The spotlight flared into life at the same moment as the orchestra struck up. The room erupted with applause and confusion. Colin tried to make sense of a cacophony of accordion, flute, zither, double bass, violin, guitar, and drums while they coalesced into a "Play, Gypsy, Play!" style prelude. But then, as the music settled down into rhythmic harmony, a figure floated through the shaft of light and he caught his breath.

The woman was not old, but neither was she young, and her face might have been borrowed from a frieze beneath the pyramids, proclaiming her an expert in dances that had been ancient when Great Pharaoh was alive. For a moment she stayed rooted to the center of the floor, impassive; then her arms seemed to float up above her head, crossed at the wrists; her feet moved, a step to the right, a step to the left, scarcely causing her filmy skirt to flutter.

"Watch the geometry," a voice breathed in his ear, and he started, realizing with a twinge of guilt that he had totally forgotten Leila in the surprise and excitement of the moment. "This is the Egyptian Walk. Everything she does now revolves around a figure eight: watch!"

The dancer had begun a convoluted progress around the edge of the floor. Colin began to absorb details of her costume: a golden belt securing the diaphanous green skirt, and a gold bra, a Romany headscarf, a scattering of sequins. The candlelight made of her a fairy-like, phantasmal figure, a djinn from some child's storybook; only there was nothing childlike about the performance, for her pelvis had begun to move independently of the rest of her body....

"Watch how her spine floats," Leila hissed. She was resting both arms on his shoulder, while he leaned forward, entranced, unwilling to lose the tiniest detail; she hung over her husband with the mischievous smile of a devil sent to tempt. "It must come from within, no one can teach that. See her hands entwine. She has no fear. She has no shame...."

The music had settled into a series of long-drawn-out sets, each played a little faster than the last. The room was alive with clapping hands, swaying bodies, cries of approval and encouragement.

"The audience," Leila whispered, "makes the dance live. They make it happen."

Colin sat there, his lips parted to reveal a line of wetness glistening faintly in the soft, reflected light. When Leila nibbled his ear he laid a hand on her knee and began, at first almost absent-mindedly and then with increasing urgency, to caress her thigh. He felt liquid inside: shapeless, no longer restricted by the uncompromising demands of his skeleton. The woman's hips fluttered close to his face and he leaned farther forward, for all the world like a dog aroused by some hitherto unknown scent.

Leila slipped her fingers inside Colin's shirt. His own hand squeezed her thigh, hard. Her other hand crawled up the cushion and, concealed by the table, descended onto the bulge inside his pants. He was scarcely aware of it. All Colin knew was the jerking, twisting, fluttering, floating hips, navel, and breasts of the dancer: sensuous and erotic beyond his power of imagination. As set succeeded set with mounting tempo, he felt himself drawn into the dance—part of the audience, the composite beast that growled encouragement, while at the same time separate from it—until he was alone on the floor with this vision of sexuality made woman that moved with the sultry fluidity of cream swirling around its churn.

The dancer hung suspended by invisible strings, hands plaited high above her head, quivering, while the music rushed to a crescendo and sudden death.

Lights came on. Leila's hands withdrew. For a second of silence Colin felt himself falling as from a great height. Then the basement became a storm of noise. The dancer floated slowly around and around, one arm extended, her face a mask of triumph, while her world paid homage. People stood up to clap. The room was congested with a snowstorm of paper; Colin, still dazed, took a while to comprehend that this was money. The dancer swayed and knelt, siphoning up the paper ... and was gone.

Colin lay back against the cushion. The near silence that had descended on the room was pregnant with heavily charged emotions, predominant among which was shame. Faces that previously had been concealed in shadow now lay exposed: Mr. Punch faces, with sharp pointed chins, shifty eyes, thin-lipped mouths. Leila seemed to sense his unease, for she quickly stroked the nape of his neck before darting down to kiss him and say huskily, "Let's go."

He had no recollection of paying the bill or climbing the stairs to the street. He was aware of holding Leila around the waist and of an all-obliterating sexual desire that would have to be satisfied soon if he wasn't to die, but he only came to himself when a black BMW glided up and suddenly there seemed to be a lot of men about. Two of them he recognized: they'd ridden in the front of the car that had brought the Raleighs from the airport. And Halib....

Afterward, he couldn't quite see how it had happened, but somehow he was edged away from Leila while still remaining with her. One man spoke Arabic. Leila replied abruptly in the same language.

"What's going on?" Colin demanded to know.

"You stay out of this," Halib snapped.

By now Leila was engulfed in a full-blown argument. Colin thought he heard the word *hashish* several times, knew he must be mistaken. He wanted to get off the hot, sticky street, he longed for a cold beer in the sole and exclusive company of his wife, but more than anything he needed sex. If he didn't get off soon, there was going to be an ugly incident.

"Look, I've had enough of this," he shouted. "Come on, Leila, tell 'em we're leaving." And with that he grabbed her hand before trying to thrust between two of the hoodlums who were in his way.

The street seemed to whirl and blur. He found himself forced against the car with his forearm halfway up his back and an excruciating pain in his right leg where someone had landed a vicious kick.

"All right," he heard Leila say. "All right, hold it, listen. Let me talk to him, *all right?*"

The grip on Colin's arm slackened. He wheeled around. Maybe the scotch contributed, probably frustrated desire had most to do with it, but anyway he decided to take things out on his wife, because she was nearest and these were her people.

"What the fuck are you playing at?" he roared. "I'm beaten up, I'm insulted, and ... what's all this about *hashish?*"

Silence. Then Halib threw up his hands and turned to the man who'd accosted Leila. "Okay, we're leaving, take him home."

Colin lashed out, but someone casually intercepted his arm, and next second he went sprawling in the road.

"Colin," he heard Leila say, through a blood-red haze of pain and humiliation, "I'm sorry, okay? They'll take you home; this is business, family business: I have to go talk with my father. Okay? I'm sorry...."

Then hands were lifting him into the back of the car and he was being driven away. The man beside him had a tight grip on his arm, but he managed to jerk it free. The man just laughed and lit a cigarette, knowing who posed a real threat and who was just bombastic trash.

Back home in the penthouse, Colin tore off his clothes and put himself under the shower. It didn't help. He threw himself on the bed, stark naked, and tried to put a stop to the torment of rejection inside his head. He tried masturbating, couldn't get a hard enough erection, got fed up with flogging unresponsive meat. He was angry, angry, *angry*. Round and round the words went inside his brain, the retorts and ripostes, the denunciations that now must wait for tomorrow, or whenever Leila chose to return.

He tried to convince himself that it was Halib he hated, not her, but that didn't have any more effect than the shower. She was actually *part* of this unwholesome conspiracy to derail a marriage of which the family had always disapproved. They summoned, she went. Every day, she went somewhere. Every day Feisal called, she obeyed. And so it would always, always be....

No, not every day; just some days. At other times she could be loving and warm and ... oh, *shit!*

He floated on the surface, sure he never slept a wink but sleeping enough to be disturbed by Leila's eventual return. She laid a hand on his forehead, but he pretended to snore, even when she quietly slipped into bed beside him and arranged her body so that they were touching from ankle to neck, with that same cool hand gently caressing his stomach.

He knew she knew he was awake and cursed himself for being such a fool. Cutting off your nose to spite your face! He could have peace just by asking for it, but no, he wouldn't sue for peace. That's what Colin told himself. He wouldn't crawl. Not to a bunch of bloody Arabs.

Shortly after dawn he roused himself from his dismal half-sleep, knowing what he wanted to do. Leila slumbered, her pale face twitching slightly as if in apprehension. He got up quietly and slipped into Robbie's bedroom, kneeling down to wake the boy so that he could lay a finger across his mouth.

"An adventure," he said quietly. "Today's the day of our big adventure."

He was going to take Robbie to visit *arz er-Rab*, the cedars of the Lord.

The morning was sultry. Lowering, heavy clouds wrapped the city in a blanket, like a fever patient left to sweat it out. Colin knew this weather to be the forerunner of the dreadful *khamsin* wind, which brought violence, and he was glad to escape to the hills.

After they'd been driving for a while Robbie asked, "Daddy, why do we have to see the trees?"

"Because they're in the Bible, and they're beautiful. A great man called Lamartine said that they're the most famous natural monument in the world."

"What's a monument?"

"Something that records an event. Or anything beautiful that's worth keeping as a relic of olden times, which is how Lamartine meant it, I think. Some of these trees we're going to see could be fifteen hundred years old. Can you imagine that, Robbie?"

The boy thought hard. "No."

Colin smiled. "Well, you'll see."

"Why doesn't Mummy want to come and see the money-ment?"

"Monument. She's seen it lots of times. Anyway, she was sleeping this morning and I didn't want to wake her. Oh, look: there's some villagers up ahead."

Despite the bright sunshine of midsummer it was growing cold in the car; hard to believe that just an hour ago he'd been sweltering in a humid city. Colin wound up his window. The scenery had subtly turned into a moonscape, with boulders and rock falls outnumbering the scattered vineyards and orange groves prevalent lower down. The road narrowed; it started to get rough. After several miles of potholes, Robbie's face was tinged with green.

"Daddy," he said in a small voice, "I'm going to be sick."

Colin stopped the car and they both got out. The breeze caught him full in the face, making him shiver. Robbie hovered anxiously by the roadside for a few moments, but the respite seemed to have done the trick. Colin looked around, shading his eyes against the sun. They were nearly at the top of a deep ravine. If he approached the edge of the road, far below he could see a tiny village: that must be Masser es Chouf, which, according to the guidebook, stood six thousand feet above sea level. No wonder it felt so cold.

He turned his attention skyward. Something black lay like a heavy drape over the ridge above them. Cloud, perhaps? Then he saw that the drape was rippling to and fro in a heavy sway.

"Robbie," he said. "Look."

The little boy craned his neck. "Is that the money-ment, Daddy?"

"It's the cedars, yes. King Solomon used trees like that for the greatest temple the world's ever seen, Robbie."

They drove on. At last the road petered out into a grassy track, and Colin switched off the engine. They had to walk the last quarter of a mile; the path was steep, and by the time they reached what they had come to see they were panting, drawing down thin air cold enough to burn their sinuses.

They were alone up here, seemingly within easy reach of the paradise for which King Solomon had yearned. No matter where they looked they saw vast boles graced with sturdy branches, the trunks gnarled into fantastic shapes like bas-relief carved by demons.

"Come on, let's measure one." Colin was whispering. He wondered if Robbie could possibly share in his sense of awe, but when he looked down it was to see the child's face radiant with delight. Suddenly Robbie broke free of him and began to dance about, wheeling and whooping. The silent trees seemed to harken, graciously bending their boughs the better to garner his happiness.

Colin made for the biggest cedar and took note of a particularly frenzied pattern on its trunk as his starting point. He began to stride around the tree. Fifty-two paces. He stared up into the lower branches, overawed and silent. Something so old and yet living was almost beyond human conception.

He looked down. Rocks of every size and shape littered the glade, but here, in the shadow of the most noble tree of all, a smooth meadowlike grass covered the earth. Pale mauve flowers shimmered in the wind. He knelt down and stroked the grass. It felt smooth as velvet.

Something caught his eye: an altar, carved with crosses and a moon.

"Robbie," he called. "Come and look at this."

Silence. The cedars, towering above him, seemed to listen. Colin stood up slowly. He looked to right and left, could see no sign of movement except for the majestic swaying of tasseled foliage and the contrapuntal shivering of the little mauve flowers. "Robbie," he called again, louder this time, with the first hint of fear audible in his voice.

The trees gave him back his voice. Colin jerked around, covering the four points of the compass. Nothing. Robbie had vanished.

"Robbie, darling, stop playing games now."

Terrorists, *muharabin*. Kidnaps, murders. *This was Lebanon.*

"Robbie! Can you hear me?"

The silence repaired itself.

"This isn't a joke. Answer me!"

Everywhere he looked there were only trees, nothing that moved or was human. For a mad moment Colin didn't know which he feared more: gunmen or ghosts. Over recent days he had been able to piece together the rudiments of Lebanese politics. In a country whose population consisted entirely of minorities, the engine that powered things along, hidden beneath their feet but humming twenty-four hours a day, went under the name of *mo'amera:* the plot. Druze plotted against Maronite, Jumblatt against Gemayel, Phalangist against Palestinian, and, towering

over everyone and everything, the Hanifs: for and against all others, according as they were paid. What plot was this, who had organized it, *this conspiracy against him?*

He stood there quietly, head on one side, while his rational
academic mind reasserted itself, methodically laying out possible
explanations. Robbie had been kidnapped. He'd wandered away
and fallen down a hole. Yes, an accident, that was it! No help for
miles....

Something made him turn through a semicircle, facing into
the great yellow sunbeam that carved a wedge through the trees
almost to his feet. At first he was blinded. Then, marching through
the light like an angel of God, came a deformed figure, recogniz-
ably human. Colin's eyes narrowed. He raised a hand to shade his
sight, and as he did so the figure split apart to become two people,
one taller than the other, holding hands.

"Robbie?"

Colin sped to sweep his son up into his arms. He admitted to
himself that he'd not expected to feel this flesh warm against his
ever again. Just for a moment, of course; only a moment....

"Where were you?" he cried into Robbie's shirt. "Daddy was
so worried." For the first time it struck him how stupid that for-
mulation must sound to a child. "*I* was so worried," he added
breathlessly.

Robbie smiled at him, jerking his head away, perversely play-
ful. Colin realized that his son was happy. He knew there was
another person present, patiently waiting, but he put off acknowl-
edging him ... her, he corrected himself after taking a sideways
peep. She was obviously a woman from these parts; she would
speak no English, leaving him without the means of either chastiz-
ing her for the theft of his son or thanking her for his restoration.

But suddenly she thrust an envelope at him. It lodged awkwardly between Robbie's thigh and Colin's hand. He smiled uncer-
tainly and put the boy down, having first given him a quick kiss on
the cheek. To his amazement, Robbie, normally the shiest of boys,
ran to rest against the woman's skirt. She patted his head while
they smiled at each other like people sharing a secret that any
moment now will cause them to break into laughter.

The envelope reeked of some powerful but fresh scent that seemed to go well with the cedars. The handwriting was beautifully italicized but at the same time businesslike, as though the composer had devoted much time to perfecting her style until it became second nature. Even before he read the first words he had no doubt that the writer was a woman.

> *My dear Colin. I am Celestine. If you don't know who that is—I can't believe you don't by now—then forget everything, bid Azizza (who brings this) adieu, and go. If you do know, however, you will know also what to do next. I await your pleasure. And mine. Celestine.*

"Good God." He looked up from the letter to find the woman's proud stare full upon him. "So you're Azizza."

"You have heard of me?" she asked in strongly accented English.

"Oh, yes. And Celestine too. Robbie, this lady knows Mummy's grandmother."

"Celestine." The boy pronounced it carefully, giving each syllable equal weight. "Can we go and see her? Oh, let's!"

"Well, I'm not sure if it's convenient—" Then he remembered the letter. *You will know also what to do next.* "Can you take us there, Azizza?"

"That's why I came. Follow my car."

She had parked her Citroën some way below the place where they had stopped, which explained why Colin hadn't heard her approach. As Colin loped down the hill he asked his son, "What happened back there? You got lost."

"No. I saw the lady and I went to say hello."

"Robbie, you know you shouldn't do that. What have Mummy and I always told you about strangers? Why did you go?"

"She's not a stranger. She's nice."

"But—"

"I *told* you. She's *nice!*"

Robbie dozed during the drive to Yarze, and Colin was grate-

ful for that because he wanted to dredge up from memory everything Leila had told him about her remarkable grandmother. He
knew that she was half Swiss and half a mishmash of Mediterranean bloods; that she had been wild in her youth and never
learned what it meant to be old; that she had been widowed in
tragic circumstances, had seen her husband assassinated; that she
was on bad terms with Feisal, her only son, although she had loved
her daughter-in-law to distraction and blamed Feisal's neglect for
her early death. Yet she'd somehow remained like a set of photos
in a faded album, or a snatch of dialogue half heard when someone
turned on a radio in the next room: almost, but never quite, within
focus, within his grasp.

One other thing he did know: after Robbie, after himself,
Leila loved Celestine more than anyone in the world. Not a day
went by without her mentioning her beloved grandmother. So he
found it poignant, a little sad, that their first meeting was to take
place without Leila.

He was to wish for Leila's presence more than once, in the
course of that long afternoon. He could have done with some
moral support. But then, he'd had such high hopes of the encounter
that it was bound to be a disappointment.

He had not reckoned on this old woman being so savage. She
did not seem to have the least understanding of his position as an
outsider wedded to the Hanif clan. It was obvious that she detested
his political analysis of Lebanon. On his side, he found her superfi-
cial and shrill. Then, right at the end, she had given him a gun, and
his impressions of her finally coalesced. In a word, he thought her
ridiculous.

Robbie's patent adoration of Celestine did nothing to improve
his temper. The boy cried all the way back to Beirut, until by the
time the elevator doors opened onto the penthouse he looked half
dead with exhaustion. Leila rushed up, all concern, and took Robbie away; Colin could hear her comforting him while he fixed himself a scotch and went to drink it on the balcony, which was where
she found him ten minutes later, when things were quiet again.

He took her hand and said, "Sorry." He didn't know why he

said that, but someone had to make the first move and the long day had knocked most of the pride out of him. "About last night, I'm sorry I was such a fool."

"No, no!" Leila cried. She snatched the glass from him and gripped his upper arms, forcing him to look at her. "Don't say sorry, I'm the one who's sorry. I love you. I love you."

"My God, but I do love you so."

He held her in the way you do when you want to crush somebody into your rib cage and zip them up tight, so they can't get away from you again, ever. When Leila finally lowered her hands, one of them brushed against his jacket pocket.

"What on earth?"

She held up the gun. Suddenly they were both on the verge of laughter.

"My God, she didn't really give you a gun? Not seriously?"

"You think I bought it at the Mandarin Deli?"

She slapped his arm. By now they were close to going into paroxysms.

"It's loaded too. My God!"

"Leila, no, seriously now, what am I supposed to do with this?"

She shook her head, still laughing. "Give it here. I'll find a way of getting it back to her."

"What if Robbie were to find it, and—"

"Don't worry, darling, I'll put it in my vanity case."

"No," Colin said, "I've got a better idea. We'll use my pilot's bag. It's got combination locks."

"You're right. Much safer." She giggled again, and Colin, seeing her face, felt his own laughter bubble up. "Just don't forget it," she managed to shriek before the final collapse. "That's all!"

DAY FOUR

23 July: Afternoon: Mt. Carmel, Israel

Exhaustion zapped Celestine just at the moment she most needed her wits about her. The El Al woman at Cyprus's Larnaca airport had stripped her bag down to the lining and when a Shin Bet agent came up close, eyeballing her, aggressive and humiliating, Celestine felt pain in her chest and prayed, Oh, God, not *now*. But it was now. She was seventy-six and worn out. As the questions rolled over her—purpose of visit, length of stay, relatives in Israel?—she could do nothing but mumble answers she'd dreamed up earlier, with Azizza's help, and trust in Allah.

The passport was good, it was the best, but the Shin Bet agent did not like it. He inspected it from every angle. He turned it upside down and would have turned it inside out as well, had the stitching not prevented him. Ten years ago, when civil war in Lebanon was imminent but Celestine and Feisal were still talking, her son had arranged French passports for all the family. She wasn't sure if they were legitimate or not, and this was one hell of a time to be finding out.

Suddenly her heart seemed to pause before thundering off again at a high rate. Another pause. She held a hand to her breast, willing the fickle pump inside to behave.

The officer passed her through. Her mind went blank after that.

It wasn't until the plane had climbed high over the Mediterranean that she came to herself, realizing that the flight attendant was offering her a drink. Normally, she would have taken one. Today she sipped mineral water, sipped it slowly for fear of vomiting.

She was standing on the edge of eternity and she wanted to dive over it, because then she would not feel so wretched. One thing kept her going: the memory of Robbie. Nothing she endured could compare with what he must be suffering.

She passed through Tel Aviv immigration in a blur and somehow managed to rent a car plus chauffeur. She slept during the drive north up the coast, until at last they came to Haifa and Mt. Carmel, just a few miles over the border with Lebanon but thirteen hours' traveling time away from it. Her driver, a lovely old man with a white mustache, didn't want to leave her. He said she was too ill to be traveling alone, but she spun him the tale that had done for all the other inquisitors: about how she was going to visit a friend who'd made aliya only after her goy husband died and left her wealthy enough to please herself at last. So reluctantly he dropped her off at the villa in Hadar, the oldest residential quarter, with its spectacular view of the bay and the mountain behind, and mercifully he drove away before she had made it up to the front door, because she was expecting guards and how shaming she would have found it to be bundled away, a prisoner, in front of that dear old man who had driven her so far and so well.

The villa looked as if it had been constructed out of square boxes, two side by side to make up the ground floor and another dumped on the right-hand-side box to give half an upstairs. A TV aerial sprouted off the flat roof; alongside it she could see a shorter radio antenna, which, she knew, meant business, not pleasure. The garden was dusty and dry: faded grass, two orange trees and some cypresses, a couple of rickety folding metal chairs, the canvas of one of them torn away at the side, a rake and watering can. She walked up the path, noting the absence of a vehicle in the carport, praying he would be in; and suddenly it was amazing, but she did not feel ill at all, she felt like a girl on her first date and the pounding of her heart was evidence of rude good health, not decrepitude.

She raised a finger to the doorbell, still half expecting to feel a hand descend on her shoulder and yet not totally surprised by the absence of a guard. The owner of the villa was like that. He had retired two years ago amid fanfares and fandangos, with medals and speeches and bands, and *Time* had asked him what he proposed to do and he'd said, "Grow fruit on Mount Carmel." Which he now did. A widower, he lived alone and his number was in the phonebook, just like everyone else's. She admired that. She had always admired this man, in secret, keeping her emotions to herself, almost since the day he'd killed her husband, years before.

She hoped he would not be down at his fruit farm because time was short, but when she rang the bell he came at once, a hand in the pocket of his linen jacket, so he at least kept a gun; yes, that was natural. For a moment she just stood there, studying him and remembering. His white beard was short, neatly trimmed but doing nothing to conceal a prominent, jutting chin. The eyes looking into hers were big, blue, and guileless. The same as before.

He said: "Who are you?" And she replied, "Celestine Hanif." Not a muscle of his face moved, not a flicker lit his eyes; he said: "What do you want?" She took out the Polaroid photo of Raful Sharett and showed it to him; she answered, "To convince General Avshalom Gazit that this man is aboard flight NQ oh-three-three with several of his men."

Then, unexpectedly, hands did grasp her from behind; she was half dragged, half carried into a simply furnished living room and there dumped onto a sofa, where she lay staring at the floor while someone made a phone call, and in the kitchen another man dragged heavy equipment around before sounding off in the high singsong voice that means radio communication. A third voice was hectoring the general, and although Celestine did not speak Hebrew she could translate the words as easily as if they were spoken in unfamiliar Arab dialect: How often do we have to tell you, this third man was asking, that they'll come for you one of these days; why won't you let us have someone in here round the clock? This hag is just a decoy; you should let us take care of you. Why not have a little self-respect?

Gazit let the man run on for a while before shutting him up, and she feared the voice he used because it was cruel. *His* words she could not translate, but they were fell. The third man did not open his mouth for a long time after that.

"How did you get here?" Gazit asked her in English.

She told him about her French passport, though they were already examining it under a reading lamp. The second man, the radio operator, came out of the kitchen sputtering Hebrew. After a while Gazit shut him up too. Celestine raised her head enough to see him thoughtfully biting the nail of his little finger while he continued to study her through those blue eyes of his, the ones she remembered so well. A man might change; his eyes, never.

"You came to tell me a story," he said at last, abandoning the nail as if he intended to give up a bad habit. "So tell it."

"I want to sit up."

He nodded carelessly. She rolled her feet off the sofa and cautiously came upright. Her head spun, for a moment she thought she would be sick; then the world righted itself, all except for a burning pain in her side.

"May I have a glass of water?"

More babble in Hebrew, accompanied by pounding of fists into palms and jabbing of fingers in faces. Gazit cut through the argument. "No," he said. "She wouldn't come all this way just to swallow a cyanide pill using my water. Not before we've talked, anyway." He allowed a silence to develop, knowing how weak she was; knowing he, they, had the upper hand. "If you want water," he said at last, "earn it."

She began to retch. His face twisted into a grimace of distaste. "Water," he said sourly.

As soon as she had sipped from the glass the retching fit passed. A glance at his face was enough to confirm that he thought she'd been shamming. Some of the old hatred washed through her, but she controlled it.

"Tell me your story," he said, in a voice that was almost gentle.

She spoke for forty minutes and during that time he only moved once, to pick up the photocopied pages of Sharett's passport. He sat in a stark, modern chair with his legs apart and his arms draped loosely over the sides so that the hands could lie in his lap. He never took his eyes off her face. He scarcely blinked. She could

not glean the faintest idea of what he thought. Only right at the
end did he ask her, "How did you deal with Hakkim?"; and when
she replied, "Azizza hit him over the head with the flask," he
laughed, along with his men, but not so as to tell her whether he
believed her and thought it funny or was scoffing at the presump-
tion of her lies.

He stood up, then, and went into another room, returning a
moment later with a card in his hand. He gave it to her.

"The Ganei Hamat," he said. "Tiberias. Wonderful hotel.
Four stars, you would like it. This is a postcard from Sharett; he's
staying there. You see the postmark? You see the signature?
Sharett is one of my oldest friends; that is his signature on the bottom of the card. Your Polaroid photograph is fake, his signature is
real. The card was posted in Tiberias three days ago."

Celestine's head was going round and round. She didn't know
if Hakkim had lied to her or not. All she knew was that she'd run
out of options.

"He wrote the card," she heard herself say, "but how do you
know he posted it?"

Gazit's eyebrows rose and he spoke a few quiet words of
Hebrew to the nearest man, who scowled and shrugged. Someone
brought Gazit a phone. He dialed. He kept his eyes on her face
throughout what followed.

"Hello? Ganei Hamat Hotel? I want to speak to one of your
guests, his name is Sharett...."

He spoke English, so that she would be able to follow everything.

"Hello, yes ... no reply from the room, I see. But he is still
staying there?... Yes. Give me the manager, please, my name is
Avshalom Gazit."

There was a long wait while they fetched the manager. The
pain in Celestine's side was spreading outward, down into her
stomach.

"Yes ... yes, I'm *that* Gazit. You have a guest staying in your
hotel, my old friend Raful Sharett; can you confirm that?... You
can." Another pause. "He is on a two-day tour of the Sea of
Galilee. Thank you."

He was putting down the phone. "Describe him," she heard a voice say. Her own.

"Wait," Gazit commanded down the phone. "This may touch on security. Describe Sharett to me."

She knew from Gazit's smile that he was enjoying this little triumph, that he was glad to be asked to request a description. The smile was an active, living thing.

"Yes? Yes ... about one-seventy pounds, yes ... um-hm. Okay." He replaced the receiver and looked at Celestine for a long time through those faintly mocking eyes of his. Then he said, "Balding, fat, so high, so heavy ... what did you think he would say, eh?"

Celestine stared straight ahead of her, praying to God to staunch the pain in her abdomen.

"Before," Gazit said, "I frankly admit I thought you were insane, at the end of your days, harmless. Now I know you are part of a trap I can tell you that your age and health will not save you. Come, madam, tell us everything, tell us the truth now, or I shall hand you over to Shin Bet."

"I have told you the truth. Every word."

"No, every word is a lie. Let us review what we know. I killed your husband. He was financing the PLO, he was their biggest supporter. Did you know that?"

"Yes."

This answer took him aback.

"I knew what he was doing, but he did not."

"Explain."

"He was an idealist. He thought the Zionists had stolen the land from the Palestinians, whom he loved. He thought that a great evil. He trusted the Palestinian leaders. He did not realize they were using his money to buy cars and apartments in Paris and guns. He thought they would use what he gave them to house their people, find alternatives, work for the foundation of a democratic state where Arab and Jew could live and work side by side."

"No banker would ever believe such a fairy tale."

"That's what you thought when you killed him. That is what

I thought, too. I even warned him that he might be murdered one day. He just laughed."

"He laughed before I killed him too."

She looked at Gazit, hating him then, and said bitterly, "He thought you must be a friend. He thought everyone was his friend."

"And that is why he got his granddaughter to let me in?"

"Leila had been told over and over again: Never let anyone into the house. Anyone! Even if you know the person, wait, let someone else decide to open the door."

"She disobeyed—why?"

"My God, weren't you ever a child? Anyway ... she never got over it."

"Oh? I am sorry for her; no doubt that is why she blew up Sharett's daughter."

Celestine stared. "She—"

"You didn't know? I'm surprised; I imagined it would have been a matter for pride in your family. She killed the daughter, and Sharett's wife committed suicide. She, to use your own phrase, never got over it."

"Nor did Sharett."

"No."

"That's why he's on the plane, isn't it? So he can have his revenge."

From the slight creasing of his forehead, she guessed the thought had not crossed his mind.

"Do you have a passenger list, General? Have you checked all the names? Do you recognize any aliases, have you cross-checked the list against your own forged passports?"

He did not know. He kept his face impassive, but he could not keep this certainty from her: he did not know.

"I understand about revenge," she went on quickly. "I've thought about it for years. I wanted to kill you for so long. It faded, like toothache. There but not there. Hate's negative. Love's positive. I love Robbie, and Colin too. I'm going to save them."

When he was silent, she knew what he was thinking: *It's odd this woman doesn't have a weapon.* Strange, how telepathy could work.

"If I were still driven by hate, I wouldn't be here. I'd be in some bar, drunk, cursing you, cursing Israel, wasting my energy. Hate does that to you, when you're old and pathetic. It's love that brought me here."

"Did you love your husband?"

She smiled in appreciation of his simple psychology. "Oh, yes. I used to think he was part of the old Lebanon. The good old days, you know?"

"And wasn't he?"

She shook her head. "When I looked back, I saw the parties, the drinking, the beach. Restaurants. Talk into the night about books and politics. Good business, money. Cars. Friends without number. Lebanon, Lebanon."

Celestine's silence was more eloquent than words.

"There never was an old Lebanon," she said suddenly. "Myth. All of it."

Gazit did not move a muscle. Only his eyes clouded a little, and at last he said, "You make it sound like Israel."

She looked him full in the face, then, and could see that he shared her emotion: two old people who'd served different but equally romantic lies and were tired.

"When you do the right thing," she said, "it's often for the wrong reason. More usually, it's for no reason that anyone can understand. You came in 1978, and again in 1982, and you pounded us into the ground. You slashed and you burned. You stood by while the Phalange butchered their way through the refugee camps, and some of us cheered. You claimed to do all that for the safety of Israel; you said it was necessary, but you were muddled and you were frightened, and so you lied a lot. 'Surgical precision bombing'; how we used to smile. Whenever you blew up an apartment building you told the world it was 'surgical precision bombing,' that the PLO leadership had been there moments before, such a pity! But now we know that your pilots came in over the sea at nearly the speed of sound, with one hand they were flying their planes and in the other they held photographs of the apartment building they'd been told to bomb. Have you tried doing that? *Vroom-vroom*, I used to say, what fun, I could do that to Tel Aviv; where can I sign up for flying school? *Vroom-vroom.*"

"We did what was necessary." His voice was cold. "For the salvation of Israel."

"As I now do what is necessary for the salvation of Robbie. I'm too exhausted to give you a good reason for my coming here. Just love keeps me going. Hate wouldn't do that. You said this Sharett was your friend. You love him, I saw the worry in your face. He's not at Tiberias. Why don't you phone that hotel manager again and get him to describe your friend's peculiarity?"

"What peculiarity?"

"He's your friend, my God, not mine. How should I know?"

The room was hushed, pregnant with possibilities. She'd rambled her way thus far, done what she had to do, and now let it all be in the hands of God. Nausea reasserted itself, the pain in her middle was growing worse, she had gone as far as she could go, *and this was the end.*

There was a muttered conference. The men were subdued now, speaking without benefit of violent gestures, lost in a consensus of ignorance. When Gazit finally called for the phone to be brought, there was no opposition.

It took an age for him to reestablish contact with the hotel manager. Celestine lay back on the sofa. She stared at one corner of the ceiling, where spiders' cobwebs interlaced, and wondered who looked after Gazit.

"Hello," she heard him say at last, but as if he were in another room instead of within a few inches of her. "Look, we have a problem, all right? This man Sharett, your guest, how many times have you met him?... Um-hm. And when he is speaking to you, does he have a ... a kind of nervous habit, a mannerism?... Nothing, I see. Let me try this on you: Have you ever seen him wink and shrug his shoulder when he laughs?... Yes, it's kind of hard to describe, I know, *I know that!*"

She lay there and stared at the ceiling and she thought, If I were that hotel manager I'd answer, Yes, sure, what the hell, anything to get rid of this nebbish.

Then she heard Gazit speak. "Say that again?" That's what he said, very low, maybe like a man at prayer, a supplicant.

There was a silence.

"The guy doesn't do a Raful," predicted another voice, close to where she was lying, and this man too was hushed.

Gazit slowly revolved until he was looking at the one who'd just spoken. "The guy," he said, "doesn't smile. Or laugh. Ever." He twisted his head around to look at each of his men in turn, and said, "He doesn't ... ever ... laugh."

Another silence. Then Gazit was snapping the fingers of his free hand to summon his radio operator; a string of orders in Hebrew; the phone smashing back down onto its cradle; one man running out the front door and coming back moments later with a newspaper that all of them read, standing, while they mouthed names.

They were checking the passenger list for anything familiar, anything suspicious, and Celestine knew hope. For the next couple of hours there was merely a string of radio messages and phone calls, while she lay quietly on her back, forgotten, and watched the spiders. There were three spiders. They did not move. Sometimes, however, they would twitch.

"All right." Gazit was standing in front of her, and his voice was urgent. "All right, this is the situation, now *listen*. The man at Tiberias, the man who posted the card, is not Sharett. We flew somebody up there with a wire photograph and the hotel manager is adamant: not Sharett. One of the passengers aboard that plane is called Randolph Stone. The photocopied pages you brought here were taken from this Stone's passport. Our people in Tel Aviv confirm that some years ago Sharett signed out a forged passport in that name, to be used by a subordinate, who later died in circumstances where we would not expect the passport back again. Now, madam, you can sit up and prepare yourself, because the Shin Bet guys are coming and you will have to tell them your story again, from the start."

"Give me some water," she croaked. "Please."

This time there was no hesitation; she could have asked for the Temple of Solomon and they'd have rung a contractor. She did sit up. She made an effort. But the stiletto of pain that drove into her side was as real as any blade, and she fainted before the water could touch her lips.

She came to on a stretcher, with Gazit staring down at her with an expression she could not fathom. Somebody lifted the stretcher and the room wobbled.

"Where are you taking me?" she asked, surprised to hear the words come out right.

"To the hospital."

"No. Take me home."

The stretcher hovered for a moment; then Gazit jerked his head, the room wobbled again, and they had set her down.

"I've told you everything. I can't tell you any more. Send me home. Over the border. You can do that, I know."

He hesitated. "The road is rough."

"But you want me out, yes, I know. So send me up to Kharif." She managed to smile. "You know the way."

She felt him take her hand and through it communicate his own awesome doubts. She squeezed his fingers. They'd deadened the pain, but she was fading and she didn't want it to happen here.

"You owe me," she said quietly. And then, "Save my Robbie. A life for a life."

"I will try," he said stiffly. "You have convinced me. To convince others may not be so easy."

She squeezed his hand again, and when this time he returned the pressure she knew she had won everything and closed her eyes, serene. Her last thought before she slept was of dear dead foolish Ibrahim: she wondered how he had managed to look after himself all those years in Paradise, without her.

After a sojourn in darkness she entered upon a strange state, neither waking nor sleeping but in transit. She was aware of the ambulance, or whatever was carrying her, bumping along poor roads; it was hot outside and the vehicle's air-conditioning couldn't cope, but she scarcely felt the heat. The Israeli medics were good. They gave good shots. Their shots were as good as Gazit's had been, all those years ago.

She slept again, waking to darkness. The road, if anything,

had worsened. She sensed she was alone and that they had crossed the border into Lebanon; it *felt* like home. That was all right, then.

She slept and did not sleep. The sound of an engine, all-pervasive until now, was absent. How long ago had the engine stopped? She didn't know. Through her haze of unconsciousness she was aware of being carried, but she was having such a lovely dream about Robbie that she refused to leave it. Let them carry her where the hell they liked: *to* hell, if they wanted. All her friends would be there ... back off, that's too frightening to be funny....

She felt so calm about the whole thing, that was the amazing part. She had expected this to be stressful, and it turned out to be not drowning but waving after all. Back to the dream, now: Robbie and Kharif, and Leila too, only she was younger than Robbie, just a girl, how strange....

It was Kharif. Her own bedroom. She lay on the bed with a blanket thrown over her, carelessly, not covering her legs, which were cold. The dream. No, not the dream. Azizza stood at the foot of the bed. Celestine stared at her, wondering what she might be doing in her dream, until it dawned that this was reality. Azizza cried. Celestine couldn't understand that. She'd gone to Israel, done what she could to save Robbie, made her peace with Gazit, had not an enemy in the world. Why cry?

Azizza stepped aside. No, she was *pushed*. How annoying. Feisal stood where Azizza had been a moment before. His face spat malice.

"Are you happy, Mother?" His voice came to her as if wafted up from the depths of Hades. "Did you achieve our downfall?"

For a moment she stared at him in silence. She wanted to speak. She knew that time was short. But it was important to savor each dwindling moment.

"Of course," she said at last. Yes, the words sounded in the silence; she wasn't dreaming. She could speak. "Now let Mama get a little sleep, mm?"

She tried to roll over, blot out the sight of him, but her body would not respond. *Damn nuisance!*

The pain was coming back. Celestine tensed. But on and on it came, surpassing all she had endured before; she felt as though someone were inflating her insides like a football, she could not bear this....

Azizza started forward; Feisal thrust her back again; she swung her fist at him but he grabbed it and slapped her face.

"Izza!" she cried. "Izza, *don't!*"

But Azizza fought Feisal like a wildcat: sinuously, cruelly. He cried out when her nails lacerated his cheek. Celestine saw her son standing there at the foot of the bed, one palm clapped to his face and an expression of astonishment stealing over his countenance. The door crashed open, Feisal's guards.... She heard a shot. Azizza fell forward, clutching her stomach, and as the echo rolled over Celestine, so too did the blanket of pain that God was slowly drawing up her body to cover her face; but not before she could see that she would have at least one old friend to chat with wherever she was going.

She murmured, "Thank you." She died.

23 July: Early Evening: Al Mahra, South Yemen

Leila was in the cockpit. She sat there motionless and silent and alone. The Iranians' helicopter was coming in to land. There would be messages for her. She did not care. She was so tired.

The grand masters who sat beyond the horizon, the champions who presented themselves in the lists of these great tourneys of the mind, had given up trying to raise her on the radio. She knew what that meant. Negotiation had been crossed off the list of strategies. They would be turning their attention to the underwater charts. A submarine, of course.

She knew when sunset was, when the moon rose, what depth of waters lay behind the plane in the Gulf of Aden. By now, "they" would know too. They would find a way of circumventing the Iranian frigate. They would land the team on the beach half an hour after dark. Perhaps tonight.

She could not take any more speed. It was making her nauseous and thirsty.

She looked at her watch. The hands made no sense to her. Like a swimmer struggling against the current, she laboriously matched the angle they made with things she knew. Things she'd learned as a child....

Two hours to sunset.

Her walkie-talkie crackled into life. Over the crunch of static she recognized the helicopter pilot's voice. He spoke a word. *Zalzalah.* Earthquake. That was the code word for today. Yes. When she leaned forward to take up the handset it seemed to recede; she watched it helplessly, through tunnel vision that made everything float up and down.

"*El Siif,*" she replied listlessly. The sword.

"I have messages for you."

"I'll send someone to collect the bag."

A few minutes later Selim came to the cockpit, carrying a canvas sack. She made a sign, scarcely perceptible, and he opened it before leaving her alone again. The bag contained emergency rations, revised radio frequencies and codes, an envelope with her name on it. She opened it.

Randolph Stone, aged fifty, United States passport, born Los Angeles, California, February 4, 1934. He is the one who nearly aborted your efforts. Nothing is known about him. I suggest you kill him immediately if you have not already done so.

Halib's handwriting. She wriggled upright, feeling some of the fatigue seep away. So she'd been wrong in her guess that he was a Mossad agent. Strange. Stranger yet, infinitely worse: Halib still did not give her permission to leave with Robbie. How much more would he demand of her?

Earlier, Selim had reported increasing restlessness on the part of the passengers. They were weakened by lack of food and water and by fear, but they were also close to the bottom line of desperation. She and Halib had underestimated the effects of isolating the plane from the world. By avoiding the standard hijack environment of airport apron, where the assembled press was always clearly visible to those inside, they also intensified their victims' impression of having been forsaken by those outside. They knew now that nobody was coming to rescue them. So let the hijackers shoot a few of them, so what? Since they were all going to die in any case they might as well fight back and die heroes.

It didn't need everyone to feel that way. Just a few, with fierce qualities of leadership, might, just might, be enough to start a revolution. She could not defeat a revolution.

"My son," she said suddenly to the Perspex. "God save my son."

She must forestall this revolution before it erupted.

Leila used the crew phone to summon Selim and gave him instructions. A few moments later, Raful was brought to the first class cabin and made to sit down. At the start of their confrontation, Leila Hanif remained standing.

"I need you." The expression in his eyes would have been funny, if she'd had the spirit to enjoy it. "I need you to die."

Her amplification only deepened his lack of comprehension, she could see. "Discipline is faltering, back there. I have to make an example."

He had no fear; it wasn't simply that he felt afraid but could mask it. She knew the difference. He genuinely did not fear death. That interested her. He might not be with the Mossad, but ...

"You knew about this hijack," she said. "Didn't you?"

He did not deign to answer.

"You could have tipped off the airline. You could have phoned a warning through to the airport. There's a hundred ways you could have found to stop me." Suddenly she knew she was going to fall down. She leaned against the bulkhead. "Why didn't you?"

He stared straight in front of him. There was something noble in his gaze. She felt a tremendous urge to smash through it. She wanted him to cringe, to beg for his life with tears in his eyes, as Palestinian children had cringed on Tal al-Zataar while they died of thirst, or as old men had begged for their granddaughters not to be skewered in Shatila while the Israeli Defense Force officers sat in their watchtowers less than fifty yards away.

It would be a waste of time, she told herself, and time I do not have. No, that was a lie. In truth, she was frightened of losing the argument. Not because she felt tired, not because she had taken no nourishment for the best part of the day and a night, but simply because she feared he might have some justice on his side, and that would have destroyed her. So when he made no reply all she said was, "You've lost."

"No." He raised his eyes, very slowly, to look at her. "You are the one who has lost."

She waited.

"I have kept my humanity to the end. You threw yours away."

Still she waited.

"London. Nineteen sixty-nine. Your wedding night."

Leila wiped a hand across her forehead. Her wedding night?

"My wife ... my wife, Esther, she killed herself, you know? Sleeping tablets. But she was afraid the doctor hadn't been straight with her about the pills, so she put a plastic bag over her head and kept it there with an elastic band. One morning, after I'd gone to work. The doctor who did the post-mortem had the times all worked out; she must have swallowed the tablets while I was still on the stairs. I never suspected. I thought she'd got over the worst. But maybe the worst is always with you, when you lose a child."

"Child." The word acted like a detonator, forcing from her an echo that she was scarcely even aware of having uttered. "Your child died?"

"Sara was murdered."

"Sara ... Sara Stone?"

"Sara Sharett."

She reached out a hand, groping blindly for the nearest chair. She sat down heavily and rested her head on one hand while she wiped away tears with the other. How fickle the body was! How weak!

At last she remembered this man. Raful Sharett and Leila Hanif had met two years before, briefly, scarcely catching sight of each other across a hallway filled with smoke; but in this moment she knew him as if they'd never been separated. She felt no surprise at finding him here.

"Sara Sharett," she repeated stupidly. But inside, the rage was beginning. Rage at not having remembered him before. Rage at

Halib for not having found out. And rage because at her very deepest core she believed her brother *must have known* this Mossad agent was on board, but still he had lied to her.

"Sara Sharett," she said again.

"Yes," Sharett confirmed. "I am Raful Sharett; you know who I mean when I talk of my daughter. You can remember all the names. All twelve of them."

"Thirteen."

Her single whispered word was enough to check the remorseless forward propulsion of his judgment. For a moment his face wiped itself clean; then his forehead creased. "What?"

I died.

"You said ... thirteen. Why? Only twelve victims were named."

That night I died too. Doesn't anyone realize?

She lowered her hand and looked at him. Now they were sitting side by side, on opposite sides of the aisle. She looked at him, and she said, "You lost a child. Your only child."

He nodded brusquely, once.

"You lost a child, so every day when you wake up, assuming you've slept a few hours before dawn, there's this sickness in your stomach, and for a few seconds God has mercy; he won't let you remember why. Then the memory comes back, and it isn't today, it's the very first day all over again, nothing dulled, nothing softened, nothing hidden."

He was staring at her. He felt his head nodding in agreement and wanted to stop it, but he couldn't.

"You get up. You don't want to eat, or drink, or think. You want to lie in bed or sit in a chair, because you haven't the energy of a corpse; it's all you can do to drag on your clothes, even though you can't think of a reason why you should. Maybe you have to go out. Why? Because you've taken some kind of decision to hope your child will come back, a miracle!—so the logic of that requires you to do the other things, like eat and wash. And you'll be walking along, maybe your mind isn't on your child at all, maybe it's one of the breaks, and you'll see something, or hear, or smell something and it comes flooding back, doesn't it? Only ten times worse, because you've had a little rest, and your brain knows you can take more because of that, so it piles on the grief that's been building up behind the dam, and it's not ten times worse, it's a hundred times worse. You've got rid of your child's clothes, of course, and the toys and all the little objects that might ambush you, but you can't stop them making those chocolate bars that were his favorite, you can't stop them selling them. You can't always avoid turning on the TV just when the cartoons are about to start, 'I'm Popeye the Sailor Man!'; oh, do you know how afraid I am of hearing that awful, awful tune? 'I'm Popeye the Sailor Man, I'm Popeye the Sailor Man....' Did you have the headaches, Raful? Because you don't eat or sleep properly, but you work fifteen, sixteen, seventeen hours a day, seven days a week, twelve months a year, so you get headaches, don't you?"

He nodded again. She did not see it. He did not know that she did not see it. They were both elsewhere.

"Migraine, the doctors call it, so they stuff you full of pills, but they're poison, so they make you feel worse. And there you are, walking along, and *bang!* There's your boy, just as you remember him, and you call his name, you can't *ever* help it, but he doesn't look round, and then someone moves out of the way and you see that your son, your boy, *your child* is holding some adult's hand, some molesting pervert has got *your child* ... and you start to run ... and then ..."

"She turns around," Sharett whispered, "and she looks at you. And you realize all sorts of things with half your brain: that you're in danger of getting arrested, at worst, or of making one almighty fool of yourself, at best, but the thing you realize, the thing you know with all your brain, is that this ... isn't ... her ..."

"... after ... all."

Silence filled the first class cabin. Silence and rage.

1969: London

Leila Hanif and Colin Raleigh were married in a Kensington registry office. It was October 1969, one week before the start of the

Oxford term, which gave them time for a fleeting honeymoon before Colin embarked on his BCL course. Halib had chosen the wedding day, just as he'd selected the hotel where the happy couple would spend the first night of their new life together. For both these choices, Halib had a reason.

On the morning of her wedding Leila woke up with a headache, unable to face the thought of food. While dressing she somehow managed to break the heel of a shoe. She found a repairman by South Ken tube station and stood there stupidly, her face a blank mask, while commuters eyed her finery and wondered how much last night's trick had paid her.

The ceremony itself was one big nothing in her memory. At the time she was vaguely aware of an office, people in suits, forced chat and falser gaiety. Colin's mother stood stiffly on the sidelines, wearing a smile that had been painted on with her lipstick but was much more easily removable. She had bought them a silver toast rack, without prior consultation. Leila couldn't believe it when she heard, but Colin could. On her side, only Halib bothered to put in an appearance. He came with one of his tarts, Annette, a girl whose mascara was smudged, and Leila somehow felt that to be appropriate.

She wasn't aware of Colin at all. He might have been a waxworks figure. It was a warm day and it was raining; London looked, felt, and smelled abominable. They piled into a taxi to be driven off to somebody's seedy club for a reception of sorts; then it was time to go to the very old and forbidding hotel in Piccadilly that Halib had so thoughtfully chosen for them. The doorman wore an elaborate, drab uniform; she would be able to remember that later, even though she couldn't recall her husband's suit. She remembered the way the doorman saluted and called her madam.

Their room had not been decorated in a hundred years. The door weighed half a ton. Net curtains of impeccable antiquity guarded a window that overlooked a well composed of other windows and innumerable white bricks. She could not see a trace of sky however hard she craned her neck. The furnishings were Louis Quinze, but faded Louis Quinze; even Louis Seize might have considered throwing them out and starting again. She had never sat on such a hard bed. This hotel relished its wonderful reputation with visiting heads of state, or so Halib had assured her. She'd never thought much of diplomacy.

Somebody had arranged for a bottle of champagne to be waiting for them when they arrived. It stood in an ice bucket alongside two of those awful saucer-shaped glasses that connoisseurs had abandoned years ago as being guaranteed to make the wine go flat. But Colin's eyes lit up. He lifted the bottle from the bucket, dripping water on the carpet, which would benefit from any kind of a cleaning, so no matter, and said appreciatively, "Vintage Laurent Perrier. 1964. You don't often see that in England. This must have cost a mint."

He opened the bottle with an exaggerated *pop* and tossed her the cork to keep. "A memento." When he offered a glass, however, she waved it away, saying, "In a minute. I have a headache."

"Poor lamb. Take an aspirin."

"I'll be all right."

"I'll bet your brother arranged this bubbly. Halib, my hero, here's to you!" Colin drained his glass—"Mm, *wonderful!*"—and poured another, before coming to sit beside her on the spindly, uncomfortable sofa, sliding one arm along the back. Leila, anticipating his move, edged forward and rested her arms on her knees. In vain. Colin began to tickle her spine. He was "tiddly," to borrow that awful word he used to describe not being drunk and not being quite sober either. Tiddly was one degree below pissed and two degrees below legless. Tiddly, he'd assured her, often, was *the* thing to be. On the whole she agreed, because in that condition she found him easier to manage.

"You've got a present for me," she said, edging still farther forward. "Do you remember?"

"Present?" His face clouded. "I've already given you the ring, we bought a tea service together—"

"When we were in Ios, you promised to tell me something on our wedding night."

Colin seemed to sober up with astonishing alacrity. He put his glass down on the table next to his side of the sofa. "My dream?" he said shortly.

"Yes."

"Can't you think of anything you'd rather talk about?" His smile was mischievous. "Dreams are rather boring."

Still she did not look at him. "Tell me why your mother blamed you for your father's death."

"I'm sure she didn't, not really. You know how kids love to—"

"No. No, I'm sorry. You made me a promise and now I'm claiming it."

"Why does it matter?"

"Because it's a mystery between us. I don't like that."

The flush that had come into his cheeks was, she sensed, nothing to do with Laurent Perrier, 1964 vintage.

"You won't tell me." She made that a statement, not a question.

Colin stood up, staggering a little. In contrast with a moment ago he seemed a lot more drunk now. No longer tiddly. Pissed.

"All right." *Aw' righ'.* "I want another drink."

She bit back the words, You've had enough already and said, "Just tell me, Colin. I don't ask much."

"The plane went down." His speech was slurred, though she could understand him. "It began to sink quickly. There was a window. My father got me out through it. But ... he was too big. Got ... stuck."

He drained his saucer of champagne, knocking it back as if it were gall.

"I was looking at him when ... just happened that way. Saw him go down. Sucked down. Just his head, looking through the window, this look on his face, and the wave washing over it. Oh, *God.*"

The glass fell to the carpet. He dropped to his knees. Very slowly, he bent forward until he was resting on all fours. For a moment he hung there, like a dog. Then he collapsed.

Leila had not touched her own glass. She stood up, straightening her skirt over and over again, a mechanical doll that some bored little girl has forgotten to switch off. After a while she gathered herself enough to pour the remains of the champagne down the toilet and flush it, before putting the empty bottle back in the ice bucket. She placed a pillow under Colin's head and covered him with a blanket. Then she let herself out.

The corridor was empty. The entire hotel felt empty, though doubtless there were other guests marooned in isolated corners of this mausoleum. She crept along to the next room. Its door stood ajar. As she pushed it open, an unseen hand drew it away from her and, once she was inside, closed it again.

Halib, whose hand it was, said, "Good." He sounded impressed but surprised.

On a table directly in front of her was a briefcase, the one she had seen in his suite at Oxford's Randolph Hotel earlier that same summer. Draped over a nearby chair was a woman's dark gray suit, with a white blouse and thick stockings; a pair of black patent leather shoes were aligned neatly underneath.

"He swallowed the drink?" Halib inquired. "He's sleeping?"

"Yes," she confirmed. "My husband is sleeping."

She felt like a figure from some darkly terrifying Jacobean drama. *'Tis Pity She's a Whore*, perhaps.

"Nobody saw you come here, to this room?"

"Nobody."

"Excellent." He hesitated. "What's it like, being married?"

Leila, expecting Halib to pile on the pressure, had been working out paths of resistance. His question astonished her. As always.

"The same," she replied listlessly.

"Oh."

She thought she knew every nuance of his every mood, but tonight he was different.

"I'm getting married myself," he said.

Her legs gave way and she sank down into the nearest chair, never taking her eyes off his face. She had come to this room expecting to find her brother at his most possessed, in full control of his frightful powers, and now this. He was blushing. He was *shy*.

She ought to say something. "Who's Father fixed you up with?" she asked eventually.

"Father doesn't know yet. Annette."

She could not focus on Annette. Then it dawned. "The one you were with today?"

He nodded. Leila stared and stared. He was bashful, he was happy, he was going to marry one of his unbeliever tarts, a foreign infidel, and Feisal didn't even know. Allah, what a joke! In other circumstances, how funny it would have been: her brother, Halib, breaking the family mold.

"Did I give you the idea?" she asked.

He giggled. *Giggled!*

"In a way, I suppose," he said. "I want sons. Don't you think she's wonderful, poppet? Well, you hardly know her yet, but you will."

"Don't call me poppet. What's Father going to say?"

"He'll adore her. Naturally."

Looking at his face, she was drawn to one inevitable conclusion. Halib had fallen in love.

"Shall we begin, angel?"

His words, spoken in precisely the same light tone, caught her by surprise. What could he mean? He was in love, he was going to get married; surely he couldn't go on with this night's work?

"Begin?"

"The uniform first, I think." He looked at his watch. "Sorry to rush you, but not a lot of time."

She collected all her resources and said, "Don't make me do this, Halib."

"You promised."

"I can't go through with it."

"Although earlier today you went through with the wedding. Yes. A deal's a deal, poppet. We've done our bit, now it's your turn. Change your clothes."

She put all the mute appeal she could muster into her gaze, but he was no longer a lover; he was cold right through to his soul.

"Grandfather Ibrahim died because you let his murderer into the house," he said. "You disobeyed orders. Nobody ever asked you to pay for that until you were grown up, and even then no one asked you to pay. But when you wanted to marry Colin, it was too much. So you made a deal."

"And now I'm breaking it."

"And now I'm going down the passage to murder your husband, okay?"

His bright smile never faltered as he went across to the bedside table, took out a SIG-Sauer P226, checked its magazine, and made for the door. She grabbed him, spun him around, tried to grapple for the gun, but he held it above his head, an indulgent brother teasing his kid sister into a game, while his smile, that fine dazzling display of teeth, became one long taunt.

She stopped struggling. She dropped his arms and turned away, shielding her eyes. She was sobbing, but he did not care. She knew he did not care.

"Poppet ... *poppet!* Why do we need all this hysteria, this brouhaha? Mm?" He spread his hands wide. "It's so simple, so safe! What am I asking you to do? To take part in an amusing little charade, that's all."

Her gaze came to rest on the blouse. Rayon. Plain, simple. Funny, she had not known before today what murderers wore, *Woman's Realm* no help there. They wore white rayon.

She picked up the clothes and ran into the bathroom.

When she emerged ten minutes later—it took so long because she had to put her hair up underneath an official-looking cap— Halib subjected her to a thorough inspection before proclaiming himself satisfied. He handed her the briefcase. She took it without a word. They went out. They took a back staircase, emerging into an alley behind the hotel. By now darkness had fallen; the alley was deserted. London smelled of rain and damp garbage, its traffic a rough but distant sea. When a horn sounded somewhere in Park Lane she thought, irrationally, how nice for the people in that car to be going out to a good dinner.

Talking of cars, hers was big and black, and it stood parked a few yards away, its nearside wheels on the pavement. As they approached, the driver started the engine. Halib handed his sister into the back seat, along with the briefcase. He closed the door. He bent down to blow her a kiss, although Leila, staring straight ahead, did not see it. He tapped the car's roof with the flat of his hand and waved, before returning to the hotel via the front entrance, keen to be high-profile visible, alibi perfect.

Leila's drive was a short one. She found that maddening. She wanted the journey to take all night. All year. In the event, it lasted five minutes.

They pulled up outside a house that was illuminated from top to bottom, great wedges and shafts of light buttressing out of it onto the pavement. Leila sat immobile. Five seconds passed. The chauffeur turned his head slightly. She was aware of him studying her in the mirror. Halib's man. His eyes reminded her of a bird's. Underneath those eyes you'd find a vicious beak, to rend and tear.

As Leila got out, a stopwatch clicked on inside her mind. She caught a glimpse of a gilt chandelier inside a ground-floor room, and oil paintings hung from oak panels. Voices, loud and bibulously cheerful through the glass. Music. Five seconds gone, never to return.

She straightened her shoulders and climbed the steps to the front door beneath the portico. Five more seconds lost forever. The door opening, to reveal a butler, the real thing, one hand straightening his lapel. *Lights, camera....*

"Yes, madam?"

Action.

"Foreign Office," Leila said, pointing to the black and gilt badge pinned on her breast. "I'm carrying a memorandum from the Foreign Secretary to His Excellency Nasser al-Qotbzadeh. It concerns their meeting tomorrow. I'm to await a reply."

The butler glanced down at her briefcase. "I will tell the ambassador, madam. Do you wish to step inside?"

Leila nodded and crossed the threshold. The hallway was wide and long, with an imposing staircase of shallow semicarpeted steps leading up and around to the first floor, whence came the sounds of revelry. Somebody's wedding reception, perhaps? The butler floated up the stairs, disappearing around the bend at the top. Shortly afterward a crowd of girls came down in a haze of tattle and giggles. At least two of them were Jewish. This particular Arab ambassador was known to have a yen for the Nobel Peace Prize. Halib claimed actually to like the fellow; but, as he said with a shrug, business was business.

Two minutes and forty-five seconds, read the stopwatch inside her skull, when a tall Arab came scurrying down the stairs with a worried look on his face and the butler in tow.

Leila fingered the official badge attached to her jacket, pressing a concealed switch. There, she'd done it; the radio signal was sent. Outside, in the street, the driver would have received it. He'd be getting out of the car, going around to open the rear door for her....

"I told you, ask me first before letting anyone in," the Arab yapped at the butler. He turned to Leila. "Yes, miss, what can I do for you? I am his Excellency's secretary."

Leila repeated the story about a memorandum for the ambassador. The Arab looked at the briefcase suspiciously. "Open it, then, open it."

"The communication is confidential; his Excellency holds the key."

"What? Nonsense, I never heard of such a thing."

Leila gawked at him. This wasn't how it was supposed to go. Halib had told her the briefcase would be taken in as a matter of course.

"I've got my orders," she said weakly. "I'm sure if you consult with the ambassador—"

The doorbell rang. The butler went to answer it. On the step stood a uniformed constable, who said, "Who's with the Foreign Office car outside?"

"I am," Leila said. Her heart was racing. Not more difficulties; this whole thing was falling apart.

"It's blocking the street. You'll have to move."

She couldn't believe this was happening. She was trapped between the policeman and the ambassador's secretary; they wouldn't accept the briefcase, they wouldn't let her go; part of her was glad, but she didn't want to die.

"I'm here with a message," she said to the policeman. "A message for the amb—"

"I don't care if you're signing the ruddy Treaty of Versailles, I want you to move that car and I want you to do it *now*."

Four minutes exactly since she'd left the car. Leila's palms were dripping sweat. She couldn't go on, it was all going to fail and fail disastrously. *Help me!* she cried silently.

"Tell my driver," she retorted. To her astonishment her voice sounded firm and under control.

"He says he won't move without your say-so."

Four minutes and twenty-five seconds.

Leila shot a look of appeal at the Arab. "I'll be back at once. I must wait for a reply. But it's urgent, and I can assure you that the Ambassador does have the key. Excuse me."

She put down the briefcase and went out while the policeman continued to harangue her unpleasantly. She approached her car and bent to speak to the driver, who became aggressive. The policeman began to shout. The driver grumpily put his car in gear and moved a few yards at a snail's pace, with the policeman still resting one hand on the window ledge.

They had reached an intersection. Leila glanced back to see that the front door through which she'd just emerged had closed, the portico was empty.

"Now!" said the policeman, and she gazed at him vacantly.

Five minutes.

While she was dithering, the constable grabbed her arm, wrenched open the rear door with his free hand, and thrust her inside, following with such speed that he sprawled over her lap. The car leapt forward, cornered on two wheels, and there, ahead of them, were the lights and fast-flowing traffic of Park Lane.

"You're ... you're not a policeman?" she said, feeling stupid. The constable just laughed.

She heard horns tooting, the noise of cars, all the usual London things. Then, suddenly, without warning, a second of silence. Simultaneously the car's interior was illuminated, but poorly, as if a handful of candles had been stuffed through the window and instantly withdrawn. The noise followed an infinitesimal time afterward, a ripping down of the world from top to bottom, the thunder that would accompany the Last Trump.

Another turn, and two more in quick succession, before the car slowed to a sedate twenty miles an hour, even pausing responsibly at the next crossroads to let the first of the fire engines through, its bell clanging madly.

"Quick," the policeman said with an admiring nod at the fire engine. "Bloody quick, that."

He'd shed his helmet and was already half out of his uniform jacket. Leila stared at him. But before she could speak, the car had pulled into the curb, they were back where she'd started less than half an hour ago, and Halib was already gliding from the shadows like the devil's maître d'hotel to greet her.

She got out, somehow. The night was alive with bells and sirens. At the end of the alley she glimpsed the flashing blue light of a police car as it sped by on its way to the scene of the event, as they would have called it in Beirut. It was so much easier to cope with "events" than with murder, death by burning and explosion, terrorist atrocity.

"Did you like my police officer?" Halib murmured. "Neat, yes?"

"Why didn't you warn me?" She was too exhausted to vent anger.

"Because if you'd known what to expect, you might have seemed too relaxed and given the game away. Sorry, poppet."

Halib took her up by the back stairs and into his room to change, again meeting nobody; saw her into her room, where Colin still snored on the carpet; produced as if by magic a fresh bottle of Laurent Perrier's 1964 vintage champagne with its elegant oval burgundy-colored neck label and distinctive gold lettering; opened it, poured most away; bade her good night with a kiss on her sweaty cheek.

She did not undress. She lay down on the bed with her back propped up against its headboard and her arms stiff by her sides. Colin found her like that next morning, her eyes wide open and unblinking. He made a joke of his hangover, although she could see from his face that it was no laughing matter. What drug, she wondered, had Halib put into the first bottle of champagne? She had to have a cover story for still wearing her day clothes, and she chose the most obvious: she'd been too angry to put herself properly to bed because she couldn't forget how he'd fallen down dead drunk in a stupor on their wedding night, and it was an odd thing, but as she spoke the word "dead" she burst into tears. Colin comforted her. But nothing he said or did was right, so in the end he left Leila to herself and went for a long cold shower.

And today was the first day of their honeymoon. They were flying to Paris: wonderful, wonderful. They went straight to the airport. Neither of them could face breakfast so the newspapers came to her after take-off on an empty stomach, which was as well, because the minute she clapped eyes on their headlines she had to go to the toilet, where she crossed the Channel doubled up over the basin and retching.

She just made it back to her seat in time for landing. While the aircraft taxied she was able to pick up a paper and digest the names of the twelve people she'd killed the night before. This was the price of her marriage, the cost of happiness. Some must die that she might live, and be happy ever after.

The alphabetically ordered list of dead imprinted itself on her memory. Years later she would be able to remember each name, could have told you without hesitation, for example, that between Nagma Sayyar and Peter Walters came Sara Sharett.

23 July: Early Evening: Al Mahra, South Yemen

"Dad, nothing's as bad as Beirut."

"No."

"You got us out. 'Nothing is going to be as bad as Beirut ever again'; isn't that what you always told us?"

"That's right." Colin knew that his son was mouthing phrases, anything to keep him on the road, but the words did help. He uttered a strange noise, half laugh, half grunt. "I was still trying to pay my father back, in those days."

"Pay him back? Why, what had he done to you?"

Colin's face tensed. He shook his head and muttered, "Perhaps they'll feed us again soon. I'm feeling—"

"You never talk about your father. Why? After all, he was my grandfather."

"Look, son, do me a favor, will you? I don't want to talk about him."

"But—"

"All right?"

"No, it bloody well isn't," Robbie flared. "Christ, you think this is some wonderful time to start being moody?"

"Moody? You can talk!"

"Why did you want to pay him back? What had he done wrong?"

"I never said that."

"Tell me!"

"I owed him a debt, you stupid—"

"That's not what you meant."

"That's exactly what I meant."

"It's what you said, but not what you meant. All right: what debt, what *kind* of debt?"

"If you'd just be quiet for one—"

Colin stopped in mid-sentence. A cool, hard ring had come to rest against the side of his head. Fouad stood there, holding his gun against Colin's neck, and his eyes were speculative, as if he were considering which of the many exotic techniques at his disposal might most rapidly dispel ennui.

"You," he said, in a voice devoid of emotion, "make too much noise."

All the saliva drained from Colin's mouth. He had brought this on. And how rich that the argument should have raged around debts owed by sons to their fathers.

"I'm sorry," he said quietly. "It wasn't Robbie's fault."

Fouad studied him for a long moment. Then said, "She wants you. *Not* you"—Robbie had already half risen, the expression on his face changing from guilt to exultation, but Fouad nodded at Colin—"just him."

Fouad thrust Colin through the curtain to find Selim standing by the doorway with a pistol held at chest height, covering someone hunched forward in the seat nearest him, someone whose face was averted. Then Leila rose up out of the seat across the aisle and turned to face her former husband.

"I am abandoning this operation," she said. "Many people must die. Many, many, many. But I mean to start with two."

She nodded at Selim. He came forward and jerked Raful to his feet, pushing him to the doorway and holding him there with the muzzle of his gun jammed against the man's throat. Fouad went aft, buttoning the curtain behind him.

"You are going to have to die, Colin; die before you can destroy my child's love for me." Leila spoke with rough rapidity. "Then I shall comfort him. I shall console him for the loss of a much-loved father. I will become everything to him, as I was everything before."

Colin looked into her eyes and shuddered.

Outside, the rotors of the helicopter coughed into life. It was time for the evening run, transporting the next batch of film. Leila glanced back at Selim. She spoke a few words and he made a signal to the camera crew on the ground, that they should wait awhile, but the rotors continued to turn.

"No hypocrisy," Leila said. "I shan't pretend I'm sorry." She went into the cockpit, locking the door behind her.

For a moment, Colin felt nothing. Then the truth rammed into him and he staggered, as all the strength in his legs drained away. These were the last minutes of light he'd ever see, his last sounds were coming up, the number of breaths he could take was finite. He'd always tried to accept that the end of every human life is death, always tried to be ready, in a detached, intellectual kind of way, but this was real *and it was happening now.*

Before, when he'd stood in the aisle between the gunman and Robbie, his blood had been hot, he'd lived only to save his son. Now was different. To die in cold blood.... "No," he gasped. "No!"

He heard the swish of the curtain, but it came to him muffled. Everything inside him, each one of his senses, was now focused on the ultimate reality. Death. The end.

"Dad," said a voice, but he scarcely heard it. Selim was going to shoot him dead, in front of his son. There was so much left that he wanted to do, places he yearned to see, *and they were going to kill him seconds from now; him and "many," she had said, "many, many."*

Selim stepped back, raising his gun. Raful put one hand in his pocket, took out something that glinted in the sunlight, a cigarette lighter; he put his hand up to cover his mouth and nostrils, he closed his eyes, all this in the few seconds it took Selim to retire a few steps and check his weapon; then Raful spun the lighter's wheel, but no flame appeared.

The strange thing was that Colin understood all this. Because he was on the point of death and he didn't want to die, because the totality of his nerves and muscles and tendons and blood and the whole of his brain were dedicated to self-preservation, he could interpret whatever happened with miraculous accuracy. Raful was going onto the attack.

As Raful held up the lighter Colin raised himself on tiptoe and spun around. His fist smashed into Fouad's cheek, whiplashing the man's head back against a fire extinguisher mounted on the wall. Fouad staggered but did not go down. Colin was already lifting the extinguisher off its bracket. He gripped it by its bottom, like a stubby baseball bat, and hoisted it high above his head. Fouad raised an arm, lashed out with his other hand to grab hold of Colin's shirt. Colin swung down hard. The crack delivered itself the length of his arm and he dropped the extinguisher, red it was, red the color of the blood gushing from Fouad's fractured skull.

The high-pitched wail of a whistle screamed through the plane. Raful, yes, a signal, of course. Colin grabbed Robbie's arm and yanked him forward. He absorbed everything in a flash: Selim lying on the floor, his face a mask of torment, feet still kicking; Raful disappearing down the emergency chute.... Shots in the cabin behind, running feet, louder and louder, *thump, thump, thump!* Colin, still clutching Robbie, bent double and hurtled for the doorway; next second the two of them were sliding down on their stomachs, trying to keep their faces off the rough, rubbery surface, to land in a tangled heap on the desert floor.

Raful was running for the helicopter. Men, sheering out of his way. A camera, dropped on the sand, still whirring. Colin raced after Raful, thinking only of the shots that would, must, come from somewhere behind him: *"Run!"* he shrieked. He was dragging Robbie along like an old duffelbag you humped when you were late for the train; the boy was crying but Colin had no time for that. Fifty yards to the chopper. Forty.

Someone behind him ... and the *rat-tat-tat* of automatic fire.

Sharett slammed into the nearest member of the TV crew, sending him flying. Another man scrambled into the cockpit just as the Mossad agent reached the helicopter and laid hands on his shoulders. Two down, only one more and the pilot....

A clang, several clangs. Bullets finding their target.

Feet behind him, very close now. Robbie crying. *"Mother!"*, that's what he was crying, "Don't leave her, Dad, don't, *don't!"*

Two Arabs lying on the ground, still as still lifes. Colin thrust the boy at Sharett, who caught him and bundled him into the helicopter. By now the rotors were warmed up, turning at full speed, and Colin had to fight their downdraft. Through the window of the open door he saw two men run toward him in a crouch, zigzagging to avoid the bullets spraying out from the plane.

Suddenly there were no more shots. Colin understood. She had forbidden them to shoot in case Robbie got hit.

The chopper crewmen weren't armed. Sharett was screaming at the pilot. Colin somehow forced himself into a seat behind. The two other escapers reached the chopper and climbed aboard, falling onto his lap, crushing the breath out of him. The engine changed pitch. They were rising unsteadily from the ground. There was the plane, below them, no longer part of them.

The helicopter slowly veered around to the northwest and began a weaving course away from the site of the downed aircraft. Colin convulsively hugged his son. He had sworn to God to get them out and he'd done it. *He'd done it!*

"Mummy!" The boy struggled, fought, pounded his father's body. "You left her," he screamed. "You left her to die!"

Colin stared at his tortured face. How to explain, where to start?

Somewhere overhead, another loud *clang* ... the pilot was shouting at Raful, who roared back, his voice scarcely more than a whisper above the fearful engine clatter. Out of the corner of his eye Colin saw that they were over the lowest range of foothills, black and forbidding, with a valley coming up.

The chopper dropped fifty feet, and everyone aboard cried out in panic. Then it dipped to the left, lurched, and seemed to lock

itself into a tight downward spiral. The pilot was wrestling with
the stick, but the angle of their dive deepened. The bottom dropped
out of Colin's stomach. Robbie's white face was pressed against
his, the boy's body held against him by G-force. The helicopter
seemed to stop moving. Then, slowly at first but soon faster and
faster, the cabin itself began to spin.

Losing height rapidly now ... mustn't let Robbie burn to
death ... Colin saw the ground rushing up, the angle sharp. His
chest tightened, air pumped into his stomach, he wanted to shout
no! but nothing came out. Then the helicopter miraculously
righted itself for a second and slowed its fatal spin. They were perhaps twenty feet, no more, above the desert. Sharett bailed out,
pitching forward in a kind of somersault. Colin didn't calculate, he
just followed. He pushed Robbie in front of him, not waiting for
the boy to force himself through the gap before thudding into his
back and diving after him, aware of yet another person at his heels.

The world spun crazily. Colin's shoulder hit the ground first
and he screamed as he felt something give. Panic kept him moving.
He crawled forward on hands and knees, half conscious but alive:
He had to get away before the crash.

He must have dislocated his shoulder, broken his arm, God
alone knew in how many places. Couldn't bear such agony. *Bear it!
Crawl!* The sound of the rotors had risen to a fanatical whine, now
right above him, now farther away, and now coming down, coming
down....

He was on his feet, the horizon rippling ahead of him while
his right arm hung uselessly by his side and pain thudded through
his skull like a nail battered by a hammer-wielding giant. He cried
out with the shock, but still he went forward. Every step he took
seemed to jerk his arm out of its socket; he dared not look at it, terrified of seeing it hang by a few bloody threads. He tottered forward, nearly fell, knew that if he did he'd never get up again. And
all this occupied no more than a dozen seconds, the space of time
it took the helicopter's engine to give up the ghost.

Colin managed to run a few steps. Then he was flying
through the air, gliding horizontally ... his injured arm and shoulder erupted into fire and he screamed, flames everywhere, and then

through all the pain and the clouds of nausea came realization: his shirt was on fire, the burning he could feel was real, he tried to roll over, couldn't, metal and glass and chunks of flesh bounced about him while he burned to death....

Something hot and heavy enveloped him so that he couldn't scream, couldn't even breathe and for a moment he fought this latest threat with a blind intensity that astonished him, even through the burning and the agony. Then darkness descended, though the pain remained.

Leila stood on the threshold of the plane's door, hands by her sides. She did not breathe. She did not swallow. Her eyes did not blink. She watched the helicopter's precarious progress toward the foothills, knowing that a stray bullet had winged it, doubting if it could gain enough height to clear even that first low barrier. Inside her was merely an arid emptiness. There now remained only one duty left to perform. She must watch until the end. She owed him that.

The helicopter went down at an angle, disappearing behind an outcrop of rock. It had never risen very high, but she knew there was no chance of saving him. She knew what to look for, what to expect.

So it came. A peal of thunder rolled over the desert, yellow and red pillars of flame mushroomed into the sky beyond the first range of hills, and thick black smoke began to drift toward the sea behind her. After a while, she could smell it. The burnt offering. The sacrifice.

Lines wafted into her mind: *Scorching winds and seething water in the shade of pitch-black smoke which is neither cool nor refreshing.* The Koran's description of Jahannam. Hell.

She was aware of events unfolding at a vast distance from her, in near but not total silence. Through the windshield she could see the pillar of smoke, listless now, at the mercy of a warm wind. A wind straight from hell.

She had promised Halib to stick with this hijack until their demands had been met. But now none of her demands could be met, because her son was dead.

She had trusted Halib, trusted him more than God. He had betrayed her. Not only here and now, with his cruel withholding of Sharett's real identity, but before, over the past two years, constantly leading her on to what he knew to be a mirage; and even before that, in New York, when he had come to her and said, "They're going to kill you." Even then. And because of him, Robbie was dead.

She did not, could not, cry. Grief would come later. Now all she wanted to do was determine the moment at which she might have stopped Halib and saved Robbie's life. It seemed important. She needed to know.

The pillar of smoke finally dissipated on the evening air. She watched it dry-eyed, expressionless, while the memories came.

1981: New York

Out of the blue had arrived an invitation for Colin to spend a year teaching at Columbia University. Leila, bored with motherhood and the rural life, had nagged him to accept, although in truth he hadn't needed much persuading. She'd expected to fall in love with the city and so it came to pass: the curtain had twitched aside and there lay New York, waiting, star-spangled and exultant in its glory. All its notorious hassles faded into thin air, sucking her into the busy vortex of a dedicated life. When black skateboarders shoved her off the sidewalk, or some storekeeper called her a jerky bitch because she didn't have anything smaller than a fifty, Leila didn't care about any of them. The sun was out, the town soared above the East River as a glittering castle, and she no longer eked out an existence; New York was where she *lived!*

A month after they'd settled into their rented Upper West Side house, Halib had come out of nowhere, telephoning after years of absence to set up a mysterious meeting early one morning at the Statue of Liberty. She'd taken the ferry, obeying his injunction to tell no one, not even Colin, and arrived in a cold, all-embracing mist. Halib had materialized out of the veil, clasped her arm, and without any preliminaries said, "Leila, be strong, hold tight … they're going to kill you. All three of you: Colin and Robbie as well."

Her head felt as if someone had come up behind and slugged her, hard. She tried to speak but Halib held up a hand.

"The Mossad have tracked you down. Ever since 1974, the business in Beirut, they've been interested in you, but England was too hard for them and they had other things on their minds, more important. But now—" He sighed, shook his head. "You are here, in Little Israel, with *sayanim* behind every lamp post."

"*Sayanim?*"

"The Mossad's helpers. Committed civilians. There are several in your husband's law faculty at Columbia."

She could cope with the thought of danger to herself, but to Robbie? No, that was impossible. "What can we do?" Her voice was hushed.

Halib turned his head to look at her properly. He held her gaze for a long time. Then he said, "How is your marriage?"

"All right."

The words came out pat, so pat that Halib laughed. "Well," he said, "I ask because you've got hard choices ahead of you. What I have to do is get you out of here, back to the Middle East, into a stronghold where nobody can touch you. For you, no problem; but for Colin—"

Even while he spoke her mind was racing ahead to find ways of convincing Colin that this was the only solution. She could picture them in bed, discussing it. She would say this, and he would riposte thus, but she could counter him by pointing out the danger to Robbie and that, naturally, would clinch things.

"I can do that," she blurted out. "I can convince Colin. Only—"

Halib had always known when to say nothing.

"He only cares about Robbie, now. They're so close, I …"

She was becoming muddled. Things that a moment ago had seemed so clear now looked fuzzy.

"You want to get the boy out before he betrays you with Colin any further."

"What?"

"In your position, I'd feel cheated too. Who did the work of bringing him up, eh? Who gave him life, made him what he is while Father was off playing here and there? Of *course* the boy is betraying you. So. Him but not Colin, eh? Two tickets to Beirut. Not three, two."

"You're wrong, you're wrong. Listen, Halib, shut up about Colin ... just tell me, what are we going to *do?*"

"Study art."

She stared, used to his extraordinary utterances but floored by this one.

"You should start going to art class. I know the perfect woman, poppet: Cassia Jaccobovitz."

Mrs. Jaccobovitz, it seemed, had stature. More to the point, she had mature students associated with Columbia University, where Colin was spending his sabbatical year, and they were people Leila ought to get to know.

"The wife of the Dean of the Law School studies with Cassia Jaccobovitz," Halib said. "You should cultivate her, really you should."

"Why?"

"She's nice. Her husband is important. And if I'm to have any chance of protecting you, I need to insulate you, surround you with impeccable people."

She couldn't see the connection, no matter how hard she tried, but Halib kept on about the need for her to study art alongside the wife of the Columbia Law dean, and she did not question his judgment. Robbie's life was at stake; that was all she needed to know.

So her habits changed, along with her friends. After the weekly art class there would be sessions in the Russian Tea Room, or shopping cruises along Fifth. She hosted a lunch party. Everyone loved the Raleighs' Upper West Side brownstone, commenting on their Shaker furniture, the drapes, Leila's artful use of mirrors to capture and enhance New York's turgid daylight. Mrs. Cohen, wife of the Columbia Law dean, proved an interesting companion. First, little confidences passed to and fro, then bigger ones. Hers was not a happy marriage, Mrs. Cohen confided, but then whose was? Leila nodded sagely, implying she could tell a thing or two, had she the mind. The following week, she had the mind. And that was where the double life started to become particularly strange, for she discovered to her surprise that her marriage had turned some kind of invisible corner and was heading for happiness: all because she had set out to live a life of deception at Halib's behest.

"How's the poetry coming along?" Colin asked.

They were all in the kitchen: Colin and Robbie at one end of the table, working on their model of the *Mayflower*, and Leila at the other, poring over her Byron.

"Fine."

She did not mutter this word to her book, as would have been the case a few months previously. She looked up at Colin in frank appreciation of his concern, wanting him to see how she felt. Deep down, however, she knew the wonderful and by now familiar frisson of deception, because her husband did not know that she was mentally encoding a message to Halib, for inclusion in the personals column of the *Village Voice.*

Colin had given her a volume of Byron's poems as an engagement present. It was a common enough edition. She'd shown it to Halib and he'd said, "How interesting, we should use that to invent a code, so we can keep in touch."

They'd laughed, but he'd shown her how easy it was for two people to make a simple code if they both owned identical editions of the same book. What began as a joke turned into something of an obsession with Leila, much as some people can't go to bed without first solving the *Times* crossword. Throughout her marriage she would often send messages to Halib in what they came to call "the Byron code."

She closed the book, rested her chin in her hand, and said, "I love to see you two guys schlepping around."

They laughed. "You're so American, Mum," Robbie crowed.

"It's a bit like getting a suntan, I guess: exposure does the job without any conscious input."

Colin grinned at her and she smiled back. She liked to see them hard at work on their model. How strange, because when they'd started she'd done nothing but complain. They made too much mess, there was glue on the tabletop, they'd never finish it, they'd strain their eyes. What all this meant, of course, was that she resented being excluded from their private world. Now she was glad of it. She actually *liked* to see father and son happily engaged in some common pursuit, *liked* it when they went off to sit in the bleachers and watch a stupid ball game, or jogged around the park, or lined up to see the latest Hollywood hit before pigging out at Burger 'N Beer. Because that meant she was at liberty to pursue her own plans, undisturbed.

It would not always be thus. She was working toward a specific goal: the removal of her son to a place of safety. Not overnight, not next month; but some day before midsummer it would definitely come to pass. July 1, 1982, was the deadline, because that was when Colin's contract with Columbia expired and he would want to relocate to England.

She could take Robbie away from him. She had that power now, thanks to Halib. But she did not have to decide yet. Perhaps Colin could be made to see, after all, that life in Beirut was the only viable option. Once he knew that she was going to take Robbie to Lebanon anyway, he'd be bound to come too. For the boy's sake, if not for hers.

Looking down the table at him, a smile in her eyes, she knew another reason why she was glad of his love for their son. When he was with Robbie he could not be screwing around with some harlot masquerading as a student. She did not want him screwing around with anyone, mainly because she still liked it when he screwed her, even though that didn't often happen anymore.

She loved her husband. She wanted Colin to come with them. Yes, she decided, as he bent once more to the rigging, she really, really did. If he said no, it would break her heart. But if anything happened to Robbie, that would kill her. She'd done evil things; she knew that. But her love for Robbie was good. One day, soon now, it would redeem her.

Time passed. Colin was happy in his sabbatical work; Robbie made new friends at school and prospered; she became a competent watercolorist. A family in a strange land, the Raleighs coalesced under pressure into something better than before. And Leila kept the faith with Halib, each week scanning the personals for a message from her brother and sometimes encoding a reply. She had a purpose in life and, despite her fear, she was happier than at any time in the past five years.

Almost before she knew it, spring had come to New York, bringing unaccustomed early warmth along with a social invitation....

"So beautiful," Leila breathed. "So moving."

They were standing in the gallery of the vast Temple Emanu-El on Fifth Avenue and East 65th, looking down at the dim interior and trying to work out how on earth young David would be able to *stand* it, "it" being his imminent bar mitzvah. So much to learn and remember, Mrs. Katz sighed mournfully, and only another couple of months to the ceremony; so that Leila, right on cue, could come in with reassurance that if anybody in this world could master the intricacies of the Torah it was David Katz, so like his father.

"I'm glad to have seen this place at last," Leila wound up. "You must be very, *very* proud to think of what's going to happen here."

"Well, I just hope the weather gets cooler. I mean, it's only *April*, for goodness' sake!" Geula Katz fanned herself with her purse. Leila smiled dutiful agreement, although truth to tell in here she was cold. Something about the dimly lit, cavernous synagogue struck her as watchful, even a touch sinister.

"Only thirteen years old," she murmured. "I know when I was his age, I could never have faced it. All those people, looking at me ... well, it just makes me shiver."

"But, my dear, you're so self-possessed." Geula Katz laid one of her flabby white hands on Leila's wrist, its sausage fingers giving her a squeeze that had something of conviction in it and not a little sadism. "Now, you'll promise to come sing *shul* with us that day, won't you?"

Leila beamed her a grateful look. "Well, I'm not a member of your faith, as you know, but if you don't mind ... try and keep me away."

"And your husband." Geula Katz turned to Mrs. Cohen.

"Surely Dean Cohen can see Colin gets time off for little old me, darling?"

"Don't you drag us into your scheming." Mrs. Cohen was old and her voice had coarsened as the result of a long pursued stop-go policy: first roughen with tobacco, then lubricate with scotch. "If the boy wants to take a day off, he'll tell my Hymie and take a day off. He's big enough, isn't he?"

Leila chuckled. "Actually," she confided, lowering her voice, "dear Colin doesn't have a very religious turn of mind."

"Didn't that worry your parents when he asked if he could marry you?" Mrs. Katz's voice carried the incisiveness of a cross-examining attorney; no mere spirit of courtesy dictated *this* question.

"Oh, they were very liberal. Originally they were descended from Iraqi Jews, but they'd lived in Europe for so long, and their parents before them."

"Mm."

"Liberal in the nicest possible way, I mean."

"Well, at least promise me you'll both come to the *sendah* afterward. Everyone's going to be there, including my husband's best friend. Do you know who I mean, my dear?"

Leila, goggle-eyed, shook her head.

"Israel's ambassador to the United States." Geula Katz nodded her head emphatically.

"Really," Leila breathed. "That's ... well, amazing." Although in fact Halib had long ago mentioned, casually, that Yehoshafat Katz's oldest friend could not but come to see his son bar mitzvah'd.

"So you'll both be there?" Geula persisted.

Leila didn't know what Colin would be doing that day, still two months hence; the right moment for telling him about Halib's rescue plan had not yet presented itself. But what she said was, "Now that I guarantee. Tell me, Mrs. Katz: how's David coming along with his ... *derasha*, is that what you call it?"

"Not good. Of course, it's still quite early. Seen enough?"

"Oh, yes, thank you. Quite enough. Why, what's the problem?"

"The rabbi doesn't like his chosen topic. 'David,' I said,

'David, I've told you a thousand times, Rabbi Goldblatt can't waste his time forever ...'"

Inside Leila's head a tiny spark of intelligence noted that this was wrong, that she ought to stop this *now*. She ignored it. The three women drifted away, but the balance of her mind stayed in the chilled, gloomy synagogue, remembering all she had seen, calculating angles and distances, already shaping the necessary information into Byronese ready for the personals.

It was too late to stop anything now.

23 July: Evening: Bahrain

The meeting with Feisal Hanif had been fixed for twenty-one hundred hours at the Delmon Hotel. Shehabi's masters were wavering; a push here, a bit of a fine tune there, and Nunn could make a deal, he knew he could, but now he wanted peace and quiet. "No calls," he'd told the hotel switchboard, "unless from the following," and then he'd given them a list of names that hadn't included his wife's, so when he lifted the receiver and heard a woman's voice say, "Anne-Marie here, Dodo; how are you?" he was knocked out.

"Darling! How on earth did you manage to get through, I told them not—"

But he wasn't angry; his first and only sensation was one of pure pleasure.

"Never underestimate a woman of a certain age, Dodo."

"I won't. To what do I owe the pleasure?"

"Sorry if I called at a bad time, but I've been putting two and two together, the newspapers, TV, and so on. I think I realize why you're out there and I wanted to say 'Hi, and I'm rooting for you.' And I wanted to hear your voice."

He said nothing for a while. He felt choked.

"Dodo, listen, there's all sorts of rumors flying around here, and one of them says this Leila creature has got a child on the flight."

"You don't want to believe everything you read in the papers," he said guardedly.

"Yes, I know you've got to say that, but anyway, can you try and understand what she's been going through, if it's true? Knowing that any minute the SAS or somebody might go storming in there, machine guns blazing? Try and get her out of it, Dodo. The child too."

It astonished him, this notion of having consideration for Leila Hanif, terrorist, kidnapper, and thief. No one had suggested such a thing; no one ever would. The passengers and the plane were all that mattered.

"Dodo, are you there? I expect you think I'm quite, quite mad, don't you, but you see, I keep asking myself, 'What if it were Michael?' All right, she's a monster, but she can't have realized when she hijacked the plane that her son would be on board; think how she must be feeling, how wretched, because whatever the outcome she won't ever be seeing him again. This is the last time." She paused. "This is the last time she'll ever see her son, Dodo. Try to remember that. If it's true about the child, I mean."

She seemed to have dried up. When he rang her from Jak she would usually keep the ball in the air with gobbets of news, local gossip, this and that. Not tonight. Tonight she'd said what she wanted to say and now she needed a response. No ... needed rescuing.

"Darling," he said gently, "thank you very much for this. I can't find words to tell you how much hearing your voice has helped."

"I'm glad." Her words came out in a breathy sigh, as if she might be close to tears. "I know you can't tell me what's really going on, but I wanted you to know and I could never have forgiven myself if, if—"

"I know."

"So I hope you don't mind."

"I don't." He hesitated, but really it was stupid to pretend he had any control over the words so he spoke them as clearly and succinctly as he was able. "I do love you most awfully much, Annie, and I'm sorry I don't say that more often, and in future I will.

My dear, I'm so sorry, but someone is knocking on my door—"

"Yes, go, do go." She was laughing now. "I love you, Dodo. I'll say it more often too, if you like. Go, go. 'Bye, darling."

During those last exchanges the initial polite knock on the outer door of his suite had turned into a hammering. An assistant manager was in the corridor.

"Sorry, sir, but they couldn't make you answer downstairs; it's most urgent, the caller says, and he's on your list."

Nunn thanked him and went back to his room. He remembered having muted all his phones and saw how a pile of newspaper clippings had slipped to obscure one of them; sure enough, when he moved the papers the red light was flashing.

"Hello."

"I warned you," a man's voice spat at him. "I warned you to make it quick, Nunn. Now Allah help you!"

"My dear Halib," Nunn said smoothly, "how can I help?"

"There's an Israeli agent aboard the plane. Maybe more than one."

"Agent?"

"Mossad!"

Nunn snapped to attention. "Does Leila know?"

"*I* haven't told her, you can be sure of *that*. But she knows this man Sharett. He's the father of one of the people she killed in '69. She's capable of blowing up the plane and everyone aboard; she can do that. *And I can't raise her.*"

"What do you mean, you can't—"

"She won't answer the radio."

The implications were terrible. Andrew groped for the nearest chair. "She may already have destroyed the aircraft?"

"She may. Nunn, you have got to do something."

"If you're right, why haven't the Israelis made a move before this? They don't leave their people to rot."

"Maybe they didn't know he's aboard."

"How can that be?"

"Revenge. What if he went after her for revenge?"

The symmetry of it was so elegant, so frightful, that for a

moment Nunn just stared at it in awe. Leila, a loose cannon, hijacking a plane to get her son back; Sharett, deprived of a daughter, letting her go ahead as the price of vengeance.

"What can I do?" he asked.

"Make Shehabi deal." No mistaking the panic in Halib's voice. "Do it tonight, do it now, if you want your plane back." His voice dropped. "If you want to see any of those people alive again."

As if you cared a tuppenny damn, Andrew wanted to say; as if you cared for anything but your fee! But instead he did something he'd never, never done, not in all his professional life: he hung up on Halib while the caller was still speaking. He picked up the direct phone to Trewin's HQ, and without any preliminaries he said, "They won't let me call Tel Aviv from this hotel; can you patch me in? Ministry of Defense, Hakirya Headquarters building, I can give you the extension."

An ominous silence followed this request, broken by Philip Trewin saying, "I can. But why?"

"Sorry, explanations later. And Major ... if anybody asks before you and I have had a chance to speak again, we never had this conversation and there never was any phone call to Israel."

"Sorry, I'm out of blank checks. Give me ten minutes. Don't leave your room."

23 July: Evening: Al Mahra, South Yemen

Colin came to in the shadow of a black rock outcrop, lying on his stomach. The air he breathed was warm, thick with the stench of barbecued meat. He licked his lips. Salt! He retched, bringing up a small amount of phlegm, and needles stabbed his arm again. His vision was blurred, but now it began to clear, slowly, although he could see nothing beyond the gravel on which he lay and the wrinkled face of the nearest rock. Then feet came to stand by his head and the effort of focusing on them caused his vision to sharpen further.

"Robbie," he said to the feet. "Where's ... Robbie?"

"He's alive, he's okay." Sharett's voice. "You must get up."

"Can't ... move."

"Listen." Sharett was kneeling beside him. "It'll be dark soon. If Leila comes after us she'll head for the site of the crash; she mustn't find us still here."

"How bad ... am I?"

"Your back is burned. Not badly, I smothered you in time."

"Shoulder." Colin tried to push himself up with the palms of his hands and howled in pain. It was as if someone had forced the entire length of his right arm into boiling fat. He collapsed back onto the gravel, banging his chin. More blood came into his mouth where he'd bitten his lip.

"Not broken." Sharett felt his way along Colin's arm as far as the shoulder. "No dislocation. You've strained a tendon, I think." He raised his voice: "Robbie!"

Through his red mist of pain, Colin heard footsteps, heard a voice he knew and loved. "Dad, oh, Christ, what have you done?"

Colin jumped as if struck by a cattle prod. *His son was alive!* He felt another hand on his neck. Robbie was stroking his hair.

"I'm all right, son."

He wasn't, not by a long way, but the words themselves operated like a magic spell: because he *said* he was all right, he *became* all right. He had to survive, go on, escape. For Robbie.

He seized the boy's hand and held it tightly for a second before kissing it. "Robbie," he said, "I want you to help me up. But I want you to listen and do exactly what I tell you, okay?"

"Okay." Robbie's voice shook.

"We're going to run for it. We're going to get as far away from here as we can. Yes?"

And all the while he spoke, the very words gave him strength, because he was speaking them for someone he loved. He manufactured strength, took what he needed, gave the rest to Robbie. On the plane he'd placed himself between his son and the gunman who wanted to shoot him. This was nothing by comparison.

"Take my left side, Robbie. Get me up on my knees."

At a sign from Colin, Sharett came to stand behind him, clasping his waist. When he put his weight onto Robbie the boy first staggered, then held. Another massive effort, and Colin was up.

"Anyone else get out?" he asked weakly.

"One of the TV crew from the helicopter, plus Daniel Nee-man, that's the guy your son gave my message to. Nobody else."

"What message?" When Sharett was silent, Colin asked again, more strongly this time, "What in hell are you talking about, what message?"

"He gave me a message to take back, when I came to economy that time," Robbie said.

"And you *did* it? You let this man use you in that way?" Colin stared at his son. "Do you know what they'd have done to you if you'd been caught?"

"I wanted to help."

Robbie's voice had turned sulky. Colin felt a fresh kind of pain flood through him: anger and frustration at seeing a loved one do something foolish and yet not realize it, the archetypal pain of fatherhood. For a moment he was tempted to shout his son down, but common sense won out and instead he found himself saying, "Sure you're okay, son?"

Although Robbie nodded, he would not quite meet his father's eye. Suddenly Colin knew what was at the back of all this. Robbie was thinking of his mother, how she'd been "left behind" on the plane. The anger that had ebbed away a moment before came roaring back in a tidal wave, but then he remembered: Robbie didn't know that Leila had instigated this hijack. He was as ignorant of her motives now as he had been when she'd confronted him hours before.

He was also ignorant of what had passed between his father and Raful Sharett back in 1982. Colin wished again that he'd been more open with Robbie.

He hugged his son close and kissed his forehead. Recriminations could wait; all that mattered now was bare, basic survival.

"We go north, inland." Sharett's voice cut through the air on the kind of command frequency nobody could ignore. "We're in a wadi. We'll follow it because it gives us a chance of water, and we have to find water soon or we're going to die."

The little party had unconsciously grouped itself into a circle. Robbie and Neeman were watching Sharett as if they expected great things from his leadership; Colin wished he shared their confidence. The TV man's expression was hard to read. Sharett had spoken in English and perhaps he hadn't understood, but whatever the reason, he didn't look like a team player. They would have to keep tabs on him every second, when their only hope of safety lay in trusting one another and working together as a unit. The enemy within....

"Do any of you have food?" Sharett interrupted Colin's increasingly ugly thoughts. They shook their heads. "Nothing in your pockets, chocolate, nuts?"

More shakes of the head.

"Then we must look out for food, every step we take."

"In the desert?" It was the cameraman; everyone turned to look at him.

"What's your name?" Sharett barked.

For a moment the TV man looked as though he was going to refuse to answer. Then he said, "Mahdi," as if owning up to a shameful secret.

"There is food in the desert." Sharett spoke with surprising gentleness. "For those who know how to look for it."

Mahdi gave a sullen shrug.

"What matters now is putting distance between us and the plane. We were all hurt in the crash, I know it. Better be hurt than dead. Now, let's move. I'll lead. Robbie, take care of your father, he's hurt worst; you two Raleighs follow me, Mahdi next, Dannie last."

Sharett struck off along the wadi, here no more than a shallow depression in the ground, gouged by season after season of monsoon rains. He kept the last rays of the setting sun on his left. Ahead of him, Colin could see how the low range of hills he'd observed from the plane became steeper, threatening to block their passage, but in the failing light there was little else he could make out. He'd never conceived of such a hostile landscape, never imagined a man could live in such heat. And this was sundown; what would conditions be like at noon?

He found he could cope best if he walked in a kind of shuffle, supporting his right forearm with his left hand. Everywhere he

looked he saw only the horizon, gravel, rocks, an occasional with-
ered tree that had suffered some terminal blast before petrification
struck, its ghostly fingers pointing all the different ways to hell.
The sides of the wadi were shoulder height, now, and slowly but
steadily narrowing, although still a quarter of a mile apart. As they
advanced, it became necessary to take ever greater care over where
they put their feet: pebbles, in themselves enough to cause a
painful ankle sprain, were giving way to boulders over which they
had to climb, and some of these had razor-sharp edges.

The sun had disappeared, the last of the dusk was upon them,
when from somewhere behind there came a shriek of such
unearthly horror that Robbie and the man called Mahdi cried out
together. Sharett stopped dead and wrenched around in the same
awkward movement. Colin saw the fear on his face. His own heart
was throbbing to a sickly, intermittent beat.

"What was that?" Dannie hissed.

As if in answer to him, the shriek sounded again, but muted
this time, and afterward they heard a series of indecipherable
sounds that echoed with eerie resonance. It was Sharett who first
grasped the truth.

"Bullhorn," he said hoarsely. "From the plane, I guess."

"No," Dannie said. "Wrong direction. They've found the
chopper wreckage."

Confirmation came swiftly. The sounds they'd heard a
moment ago were repeated, only this time they dissolved into
words. Colin could picture the man with the bullhorn turning to
each quarter of the compass in turn, and whereas before he had
been facing away from them, now he was addressing his message
to the north, where they were.

"I know that you can hear me." The language English, the
speaker male, his accent Middle Eastern.

After a few seconds, Colin thought he recognized the voice as
belonging to one of the terrorists. Not Fouad, who was dead. Colin
had killed him. *Jesus Christ*, he prayed, *forgive me.*

"I know that you can hear me," the distant voice repeated
slowly, deliberately. "Listen to me. I have found the wreckage of the
helicopter. I have examined your tracks. Come back to the plane."

"Bluff," Sharett said tersely. "If he knew which direction we'd gone, he'd never have faced around and around like that."

Colin reluctantly accepted this as true: reluctantly, because it was Sharett who'd seen it and he didn't like Sharett now any more than he had in New York, two years previously, when they'd first crossed paths.

The disembodied voice continued. "Come back to the plane, I say, and this will not go against you. But if you fail to return ... at dawn tomorrow we shall blow up the plane and every living soul aboard. Our promise is not an idle one. Should you doubt us, watch the sky tomorrow at first light and learn the burden of sin you carry."

By now it was too dark for them to see one another's faces. Colin felt an overwhelming desire to know the worst, to winkle out whatever each was thinking. As the seconds ticked by, his frustration mounted. He could feel the words on the back of his tongue. He tasted their bilious, metallic flavor, yet he could not bring himself to utter them, to condone mass murder by saying, "We can't go back."

Mahdi saved him.

"We go back now," he gibbered suddenly. "Yes, back to the plane now, out here nothing to drink, nothing to eat; in the name of Allah the Compassionate, the Merciful, think what you are doing! You cannot condemn so many to die! You are not God, may Allah forgive my sinful tongue, *you are not God!*"

Mahdi's last word whined upward into a scream as Sharett unhurriedly struck him a backhander on the mouth, swinging his whole arm and putting beef into it.

"And you?" he said equably to the pathetic huddle at his feet. "Were you God when you filmed the murder of the South African, when you connived at the taking of a planeload of passengers? Come on, God, tell us a thing or two. Tell us why so much concern for the innocent and the good when you didn't give a shit before."

He swung back his foot and kicked Mahdi in the stomach. Robbie cried out, forcing his knuckles against his lips.

"You didn't give a shit before and you don't give a shit now." Sharett's voice had turned ruminative and low: a judge meditating sentence. "It's because you know that as long as you stay with us those scum will seek you wherever you run, so they can kill you. That's why you dread the morning—because then they will start their pursuit. They will come after us. *She* ... will come."

In the silence that followed, Colin held his breath, praying that Robbie would not have heard, not understood. But then the boy said, "She? Who is 'she'?"

Silence.

"Which 'she'?" A pause. "*Which 'she'?*"

Sharett hesitated. Then: "School starts early this term," he said. "So let's begin with ABC. Your mother, Leila Hanif—"

"*No!*" Colin's cry rebounded off the side of the wadi.

Everyone jumped; everyone, that is, except Robbie, who announced, in a small, clear voice, "I want to hear it."

"Your mother," Sharett said, "is one of the five most wanted terrorists in the world. She planned and led this hijack because she wanted one thing, and one thing only: you. That is why we are here. That is why Van Tonder had to die, and others will have to die. And that is why, as soon as there is light tomorrow, she will come. She is ready to pursue you into hell, if only she can get you back. So she will come. She will."

Robbie's face was invisible in the gloom, but Colin knew, could *feel*, his son was smiling. "Yes," he heard him say; and then, after a pause that seemed as long as life itself, "I know."

23 July: Night: Bahrain

Twenty-nine seconds, that's all it took, from bedroom to Mercedes, five of them, Nunn and four bodyguards, two ahead, two behind, walking as fast as fit men can without breaking into a run, another trio waiting for them behind the swing doors where the service elevator was ready, a concierge with his key in the lock to guarantee nonstop descent to the second floor; then down two flights of stairs, past the hotel's health club, into the back seat of the car parked down a side alley, long before the telephoto lenses and multidirectional mikes fifty yards away, barricaded next to the front entrance, could focus; sirens, motorcycle escort, pilot car forcing a path through the crowd: a comically gesticulating bunch of sweaty western faces strung with cameras and video recorders and tape decks, comic because the car's bulletproofing shut out sound as well.

Nunn removed his dark glasses and began a review of what he would say to them in the British embassy when he arrived there in—he glanced at his Cartier Tank—four and a half minutes.

He was still breathing heavily from his recent jog through the Inter-Continental Hotel's nether recesses, which had done nothing to improve his temper. For the first time ever, retirement beckoned with all the attractiveness of Letuce's maître d' extending his hand to an old and favored client.

Confronted by the maze of Middle Eastern politics he'd applied his techniques in the usual way, drawing back from the brink of disaster, careering around dangerous corners at high speed, never letting the ball drop. First fix Shehabi, then Bahrain, then Kuwait, then Saudi, then the British, the Germans, the Israelis, then *whoops!* back to collect Kuwait again, and then *whoops!* don't let Saudi get upset ... on and on it went, round and round, until at last he was where he wanted to be, no longer one protagonist among many but the Grand Wizard himself, with Her Majesty's minister of state on line ready to do his bidding, and Feisal Hanif himself, Goliath to his David, emerging from the shadows to join battle. Until Halib's call the afternoon had evolved into immaculately timed segments: Feisal was on his way to Damascus airport, he was airborne, he had landed, he was on his way to the Delmon, he was in his suite, he was ready. He was *not* ready, but soon would be. In an hour.

That was when Halib had phoned with the news about Sharett.

The Mercedes swung in through the gates of the British embassy—no more fooling around in Lloyds offices; this was for real—the soldiers in their blue and white sentry boxes saluted, another opened the car door, two men in front of him, two behind, walking as fast as men can walk without breaking into a run, stairs, the conference room on the northwest side, overlooking a weary garden, usual crowd, no new faces.

"He's gone," he said, lowering himself into the chair at the head of the table. He poured himself a glass of ice water, draining it down in a series of gulps while he waited for the bodyguards to plug in and test his portable fax, waited for the rest of them to pounce.

"Gone?"

Philip Trewin's voice, rendered neutral by fatigue, conveyed no hint of criticism or anger. Nunn sensed he'd been expecting to hear this news; no, he'd *already* heard it.

"Meeting was scheduled for twenty hundred. Feisal Hanif had it put back to twenty-one; no show, nothing, minister not best pleased. Phone call to Hanif's suite elicits no reply; hotel manager suffering from palpitations, entourage left twenty minutes before."

They were so tired, all of them, that they could no longer form coherent grammatical sentences but instead had been reduced to a kind of languid telegraphese.

"Meaning what?"

Nunn looked down the table at all those tense faces turned toward him, and for the umpteenth time he wondered what on earth he was doing here, what they wanted of him, the ones who were really pulling the strings; he would hear later, of course, maybe years later, whose game it had been: Iran's, Iraq's, Syria's, Yemen's, but by then he'd have forgotten most of it anyway and it would be a struggle to remember half the names. He would not leave this place any the wiser than when he'd come, that much he knew.

Halib had not said categorically whether by now in Tel Aviv they realized one of their agents was aboard NQ 033. Maybe the Israelis had known and maybe they hadn't. What taxed Nunn was whether he'd been right to ring them up and tell them. Too late to worry about that, he'd already done it.

"Recap," he said wearily. "Last night the chopper brought out that diabetic boy, Iranian frigate landed him in Oman, gesture of goodwill to facilitate, et cetera and so forth. Chopper goes back this morning, repeat flight this afternoon, no more heard of same.

Radio silence blankets NQ oh-double-three, despite attempts by Iranian frigate to raise her. Feisal Hanif abruptly aborts negotiations, leaves Bahrain, no forwarding address."

What was he doing here? What on earth were any of them supposed to be doing?

"Stalemate," he muttered sourly.

Major Trewin looked down at his hands. "Perhaps," he said.

"Meaning?"

"I'm informed that South Yemen has been subjecting the position to 'in-depth dialectical analysis.'"

"And?"

"They might just be prepared to let Hadhramaut province be used as springboard for a home run by the SAS."

"Conditions?"

"Thumping big bribe. Aid. Grants. Hardware. Moscow's been leaning on them. Most of what we hand over to Aden will find its way back into the commissars' pockets, of course, but the Yemenites don't know that."

Nunn was staring at him. "Why should Moscow be leaning on South Yemen to put an end to a hijack?"

"Because they're upset." It was the M16 spook who interjected; Nunn struggled to recall his name before remembering that he hadn't ever given one. "Sources there have finally confirmed that this hijack diverted Soviet resources in breach of guidelines."

"Translation?"

"Leila Hanif is off on a frolic of her own. Halib was right."

There was a bemused silence, broken only by the rustling of men creaking their weary bones into new positions.

"How reliable are your sources?" Trewin inquired, after a pause.

"Very, we think. Of course it could be a con, but somebody went to a lot of trouble to persuade us that they could get Yemeni signatures on the line, and it's coming out just like they said. They'll allow a rescue force to assemble within their territory as long as no Israelis are involved and the Yanks stay out of it. And as long as the check clears, of course."

"Of course," Nunn said. "Will it?"

"Looking good. Hereford's standing by; airlift on ninety minutes' notice."

"Excuse me," Selman Shehabi said, "but they do not have recent desert experience."

"Nobody has experience of South Yemen," Trewin said huffily.

Israel does, Nunn thought to himself; bet you a pony any day, old boy. Yes, Israel—

"Germany's GSG-Nine would be more acceptable," Shehabi said. "To us."

"With respect," Trewin said, "your country has already caused more than enough—"

But Andrew Nunn interrupted them. 'What exactly was the position with regard to Israeli passport holders on that plane?" he asked. "What did you establish, in the end? Don't flannel me, give me the bottom line."

"We turned up a couple of dual nationals," said the M16 man. Then, after a pause, "And half a dozen shoes. Sorry—false passports."

"False?" Andrew couldn't conceal his trepidation, didn't even try. "Anyone you know?"

"Apart from the terrorists, there were one or two familiar names. I've only just had the list in from London, I haven't had a chance to analyze it yet, but ..."

"Yes?" Andrew banged the table, his heart sinking. "Come on, don't make us drag it out of you, *tell us the truth.*"

"The Mossad had men on that flight."

So now everyone knew. Andrew could hear his own pulse. The room was otherwise remarkably silent.

"Israeli intelligence had put men aboard that flight?" he said at last. Shehabi was preparing to explode. "No, Selman, wait ... is that what you're telling us?"

"Not exactly."

"Oh, for God's—"

"Apparently Leila Hanif may not be the only—ah, loose cannon rolling around this particular deck."

So Halib had been right about everything, Andrew thought. In the circumstances, what was I supposed to have done? Of course I had to call Tel Aviv, of course I did. *Try and get her out of it, Dodo. The child too.* Annie, I am so very sorry....

"What will Jerusalem do about Sharett?" he asked, knowing already. "Assume they've discovered that one of their most senior people is aboard, what will they do?"

From the way M16 looked at him Andrew knew he was wondering about that word "senior." No one in this room had said Sharett was senior. No one had mentioned his name, either.

M16 was about to speak when a knock on the door brought the exchange to an abrupt halt. A second lieutenant wearing the insignia of the Scots Guards brought in a sheet of paper and laid it before Trewin.

"Movement," he said, after studying it. "High-level reconnaissance, last light today, indicates that the helicopter has crashed close to the plane. Indistinct markings on the ground *may* mean there were survivors."

Ninety minutes' standby at Hereford would not be enough; even as Nunn opened his mouth to speak he knew the futility of it, but now there was nothing more he could do to affect events so he did not hesitate.

"Get the SAS over," he said to Trewin. "ETA sometime yesterday."

DAY FIVE

24 July: Night: Al Mahra, South Yemen

S he felt tired, so very tired. She sat in the cockpit, aimlessly looking out the window, and it was thus that Hisham found her.

He stood on the threshold awkwardly, shuffling his feet and wondering what he was supposed to do now that Fouad and Selim both were dead. Earlier he had gone with Leila to broadcast a message into the desert while she poked around in the still-hot wreckage of the helicopter, but since then the leader had remained sealed in the cockpit, alone with her thoughts.

"They will come tonight," she said, not conscious of addressing him, not really aware of another presence at all. "The imperialist infidels."

On her final word, as if at a prearranged signal, the cockpit lights flickered and died. A red lamp on the radio took some time to fade. The last residue of fuel had been used up. Now there was no power to work the air-conditioning, or the ovens, or the lights. NQ 033 had perished.

She had perished.

Leila elbowed herself forward in the co-pilot's seat, feeling the tension pressurize pain into her shoulders, and said, "We shall separate now."

"Separate?" he said uneasily.

"I must follow my son."

Hisham looked dubious: how could anyone have survived such a terrible crash? Yet they had found nothing that might once have been a teenage boy among the twisted struts and embers.

"What do you want us to do?" he asked. "Blow up the aircraft?"

Leila shook her head. "Killing the passengers cannot help you, and it's time to protect yourselves. You've been magnificent. In the name of God, the Compassionate, the Merciful, go in peace and soon, before the soldiers come. Leave me water. Only that."

Hisham quit the cockpit. He went the rounds of his people, giving them quiet instructions, before lifting the intercom handset. He told the passengers that he and his men were moving to the desert floor and warned them to stay seated, because gunmen would still be covering the doorways throughout the night and the booby-trapped explosives would remain in place. Ten minutes later the plane was bereft of terrorists.

At the foot of the escape slide, Leila exchanged an embrace and a blessing with her men. Then she headed toward the place where the helicopter had crashed. She carried an M3A1 with a full clip plus one spare, and a flask containing three liters of water. When she reached the wreckage she settled down to await first light.

She had no sense of time passing. She may even have slept a little: here, in the desert, there was no light to ease the eyes from their constant battle with blackness. Her mind turned this way and that, but mostly it concentrated on the coming day.

She was used to this terrain, and she knew how to track a man. She had water. She would travel fast. But the pace of those she hunted would be dictated by the group's weakest members, Robbie and Colin. One or more of them might have been injured in the crash. Her chest tightened at the notion. She would find them quickly. Then she would take Robbie back and settle accounts.

Time drifted slowly, so slowly. Like that last day in New York; it had seemed interminable, from the moment she woke up until ...

She could have stopped all this then. A word to Halib, another to Colin. No separation, no loss, no more death. Did her family ever think of that? she wondered; did they blame her for keeping silent when a word from her would have changed the world?

Sharett led them only a little farther into the wadi before calling a halt for the night. In total darkness there was no way they could continue. The silence was total too.

Despite the pain he was suffering, Colin managed to get his priorities in order. First, reestablish contact with Robbie. And second. And third.

Easy to say. Two years of silence and concealment didn't evaporate overnight. Robbie knew his father had lied to him. How long had he known?

Colin squatted beside his son, trying to ignore the pains in his back. His arm was feeling better, but the burns were going to trouble him for a long time. He had nothing to cover his skin with. When they left the plane he'd abandoned his jacket, and his shirt was scorched, useless. He'd have to take off his trousers and use them to cover the wounded area. He'd look ridiculous. So what.

"Robbie," he whispered, "son ... I've been talking to Sharett. He—"

"Your friend Sharett." Robbie kept his chin cupped in his hands, distorting the words. "Old mates, yes?"

"We've met."

"So I gather. In New York. Interesting talker, isn't he?"

Robbie's churlish tone coming on top of the burns made Colin want to lash out as he had done years ago, when his son was just a kid. But old solutions didn't function here. Not that they ever had.

"Yes, New York. When I was teaching there. And he was tracking Halib."

"And Mum. Don't forget Mum. *He* never did."

"Your mother got into trouble, but it was all Halib's fault. Sharett's from the Israeli secret service; of course he was after them both. That's his job."

"And you helped him."

Colin was silent.

"Didn't you?"

"I had to give certain information to stop a murder."

"Oh, *God!*"

Robbie slipped off his rock and took a few steps toward the wadi wall, keeping his back to Colin. After a moment of hesitation, Colin followed. It wasn't easy, feeling a way through the blackness.

"Tell me about it," Robbie said softly. "Tell me all the things you've never said before. Not just the bits you fancy serving up in a sauce. The truth. Everything!"

"Tall order," Sharett said laconically from somewhere close, making the Raleighs jump.

3 June 1982: New York

Robbie couldn't understand why his mother had tears in her eyes.

"What's the matter?" he asked dolefully at the school gate.

"Nothing, darling. I'm just a bit overcome, that's all."

"Why?"

"Oh ..."

How she wanted to disobey Halib, then! It would have been so easy to say, I've got a surprise for you: you haven't seen Uncle Halib for so long and this afternoon he'll be coming to collect you from school; won't that be nice?

But Halib had warned her that if she so much as hinted at what was about to happen, his guarantee of safety for Leila and Robbie would be worthless. So instead of speaking the words she longed to say she merely shrugged. "No reason."

Robbie's face had whitened. "I wish you wouldn't say things like that," he muttered, turning away.

"Robbie!"

He looked over his shoulder. She could see that he, too, was close to tears. "What?" he cried.

"I ..." Surely it could do no harm? Surely? "I was wondering...."

He came back to her, obviously upset. "Tell me," he said in a small voice.

"I was thinking.... Robbie, do you believe in miracles?"

"Miracles?" He seemed to think the notion very daring, not quite nice.

Seeing the look on his face she faltered, not knowing how to retrieve her mistake. "Forget it," she said lamely. "Mummy's only teasing, that's all. I'm not quite myself."

He stared at her as if she'd gone mad, and for an instant she felt mad.

"Come give Mummy a kiss." She crouched down, spreading her arms.

After a second of hesitation he ran into them and she embraced him with her eyes closed, trying to keep the image of his dear face imprinted behind her eyelids, until at last he pushed her away, but gently, and ran in to join his friends.

"I love you, darling," she said to empty space as, swallowing back salt tears, she walked off.

There came a blank in her mind, then; a blank that only dissolved when she found herself sitting on a bench overlooking the river without any sense of how she'd got there. Such a lovely day.... The roar of the traffic behind her mingled with the chaos inside her head, making it ache.

How had she come to this pass?

When Halib told her bluntly that the Mossad intended to wipe her out, her and her beloved son and her husband, the options had instantly narrowed down to one: she had to do whatever Halib told her, because then, only then, would he be able to protect them. But as time went by, and Halib told her to do more and more strange, terrible things, the rationale for her decision weakened, until now she could only sit on a bench, helpless, and cry for the chance to divert this tidal wave about to overwhelm her.

She had made a mistake, many mistakes. She ought to have told Colin the same night Halib had delivered his cruel message. He was her husband, the man she loved, *had* loved, still loved; oh, *God!* "Oh, God," she murmured, "how can I have been such a fool?"

No answer. Leila made an effort to dry her eyes. She had

things to do, vital things, and was in no fit state to do them. But one notion refused to leave her head: she would summon Colin to be with her and Robbie the minute they arrived in Beirut. She would call from the airport, after immigration but before they collected their bags. She knew the phone, had used it before; it was just by the baggage claim area. She would call New York and she would say, "Come, darling! Come *now!*" That's what she would do.

She felt so confused. She'd been in such a mess these past few days and never dared show it, God knew how she'd got this far. Of the mental checklist that had been guiding her there was now no sign at all. Halib, a voice wailed inside her brain, Halib, help me. God refused to come to her aid, but Halib worked better than God: as she spoke her brother's name, she remembered the first item on today's list: Robbie delivered to school, *check, damn you, check.* And the second. And the third....

3 June 1982: Afternoon: Upper West Side

Robbie's school, overlooking Riverside Drive, was just five blocks away from the Columbia Law campus. As soon as Colin received the call from Tom Wainwright, the school's principal, he hurried down, arriving well before classes finished for the afternoon.

"Robbie complained of stomach pains around lunchtime and he didn't eat," Tom told him. "Then he was found vomiting and one of the teachers took him under his care, and next thing the boy was having some kind of hysterical fit. He's better now, though. I'll call him in ... but before I do, may I ask you something? Has there been any problem with his mother lately?"

"No. Why?"

"His trauma seems centered around her."

Colin stared at the wall. "I ... I just don't know what to say."

"Well. I'll call him, then."

One look at Robbie's face told Colin the worst. The boy was ill.

"What is it, son?" While Tom Wainwright looked on concernedly, Colin knelt down and hugged Robbie to him. "What's up, now?"

Robbie spirited a smile from somewhere. "You don't know how stupid I feel," he said in a low voice. "Oh, God—when I think how I've got to come back here tomorrow and face the other kids—"

"Don't worry about that." Colin glanced up at Wainwright, who nodded understandingly and left the room.

After a longish period during which Robbie failed to meet his eye, Colin said, "Tom mentioned something about Mummy."

"This morning, when she left, she sounded so ... strange."

"In what way, strange?"

"She talked about miracles. And about not feeling herself. I ... I don't know why, Dad, really I don't"—the words were coming out in a rush now—"but I can't get it out of my head that she's in some kind of trouble. Please say she's all right, *say it!*"

Colin stared at his son. For a twelve-year-old, Robbie was altogether too much of a worrier. Leila knew that. Yet this morning she'd apparently said something that had ruined his day.

"Mother's all right," he said aloud. "Of course she's all right." He clapped Robbie on the back. "I think you and I deserve an early night."

They walked out to the car. This afternoon the boy, usually so voluble, seemed subdued and distant. While Colin was fumbling for his car keys they heard a bell sound in the school, and the rumble of chairs being pushed back.

A long black limousine with tinted windows and a boomerang-shaped aerial on its trunk turned into the quiet street.

"It's possible," Colin said as he opened the door, "that your mother's not well, or maybe she was feeling depressed."

Robbie shrugged.

The black limousine was accelerating now, still almost silent. In the schoolyard, just behind the twelve-foot wall, hundreds of pupils were flooding out from class. The street echoed with their pleasure.

Colin slid into the driver's seat and reached across to open the nearside door for Robbie. Behind them, the driver of the black limousine suddenly put his foot on the gas, hard, and the huge car's tail dropped with the force of acceleration, its boomerang aerial dipping like an aileron. From less than twenty yards away, it covered the distance to where Robbie was half in and half out of the car in no more than a couple of seconds.

The limo drew level with Colin's Ford. Two men flung themselves out, one running behind the Ford, the other in front, so that Colin saw the latter's face and knew him for an Arab. A flicker of movement in the rearview mirror showed him the second man, also heading for the pavement, moving so fast that the message penetrated Colin's brain with the immediacy of an electronic display: Robbie in danger!

Colin hurtled from the front seat of his car, shouting, "Hey! Back off!" And at that moment, in the very second the Arab laid hands on Robbie's sleeve, a great, vital wave of children came crashing around the corner where the street intersected with Riverside Drive, whooping and hollering; Robbie jerked away from his attacker with a squeal; the second man, Arab also, looked over the first man's shoulder and shouted; Colin, too, shouted. *"Help!"* he roared at the top of his voice. *"Murder, help!"*

The amorphous child wave did not falter, but it changed upon the instant from a gaggle of innocent youngsters to a hungry mob. The Arabs sensed it. They hesitated—just for a second, but enough to tell the children through invisible antennae that they had the upper hand. The man who'd been clasping Robbie's sleeve released his grip. He backed away.

Suddenly the two of them were racing for the limo.

Colin ran around the front of his Ford in pursuit. The crowd of roaring teenagers at his back gave him courage; he never stopped to think whether the men might be armed. He was gaining on them, mere feet away....

But the two Arabs threw themselves into the limo, which shot off with a screech of tires that seemed to hang in the air long after it had thrust its way into Riverside Drive.

Robbie ran to his father. "Are you all right?" he cried, while hosts of curious children swarmed up and down the street, wondering what it was they had seen, what they had unconsciously taken part in.

"I'm all right," Colin said, but he continued to stare after the stretch limo, even though nothing remained on the street to prove it had ever been there at all.

"Did they have guns, Dad? Is that why you stopped? Were they armed?"

A pause. "Yes, that's right, son. That's why I stopped chasing them."

Robbie had been traumatized enough today. Better not to tell him that he'd seen Halib Hanif sitting in the back of the stretch car, or that upon his face had been an expression of murderous rage.

3 June 1982: Afternoon: Temple Emanu-El

Sharett and Neeman pushed through the heavy door and found themselves in darkness broken only by a pink flashing sign warning of two steps down. As they moved forward it became lighter; not much, but enough to show them a slice of Temple Emanu-El's interior. Raful groped his way toward the nearest of the stark wooden pews and lowered himself into it. He sat there with his hands on his knees, gazing around, and his head shrank farther into his shoulders until by the time he'd made a complete survey he looked almost deformed.

He hated this place. It was full of empty spaces, and shadows, and darkness, and the somber half-light of a funeral parlor. He had never seen such an enormous synagogue: its main hall could contain over a thousand people, and on the northern side was a side hall with room for still more.

At the back, dominating the gallery, a lofty window of blue-and-gold stained glass admitted shreds of natural light. The only other illumination came from electric bulbs suspended so far up this enormously high edifice that Raful couldn't even see how they were fixed to the ceiling. Aisles ran along each side of the main hall, and they were scarcely lighted at all. Above those aisles were galleries, arches of stone framing deep black empty spaces that afforded perfect cover for a marksman, for a whole company of marksmen.

Ahead of him Raful could see the Ark, framed between intricate mosaics, with two seven-branched menorah candlesticks on either side, their red flames fueled by cunning electric lamps that appeared to flicker naturally. It was Gothic, medieval, fit for the playing out of a tragic opera's final act. A jealous God lived here, a God of wrath and vengeance, and he was waiting in the shadows, waiting for what would be. Sharett looked again at the distant stained glass—"stained," somehow so appropriate to this place— the faded strips of red carpet along the aisles, the vapid lights, the arches, the shadows, the brooding, majestic Ark, the shadows, the shadows, the shadows; and he turned to Neeman and said, "Dannie. Dannie, tell me just one thing. If you wanted to kill an ambassador, where would you chose to do it?"

And Dannie Neeman screwed up his mouth to one side before saying quietly, "Here."

Raful sighed. "Katz says they're using the smaller synagogue for the bar mitzvah this evening, over on that side," he said, pointing north. "So let's go take a look."

They slid along the pew and made a half circuit of the synagogue until they reached the side hall. This seemed darker yet. The Ark was less ornate, but there was a presence here, something unmistakable, almost tangibly real. Outside, New York sweltered in the high eighties, but Raful could feel goose bumps on his flesh, along with the chilly sensation that heralds the onset of flu.

"We're going to bring Moshe in here?" Neeman asked Sharett. "Seriously?"

"I got his personal security people to report on this synagogue, and the answer came back No Problem."

But Raful's chill deepened.

"Raful." Neeman's voice was hushed. "Are we going through with this?"

Raful had the grace to hesitate. He thought of Sara, of Esther, of Ehud Chafets, who had failed but who had been a good man. He remembered what happened to human flesh, even, *especially*, to firm young female flesh, when you fragmented a bomb in close proximity to it. He made one last inspection of the synagogue, seeking to penetrate the ubiquitous multishaped shadows that shrouded everything and everywhere, like a cloth of black velvet.

He had to lure the Hanifs out into the open. Had to!

"Sure," he said. "Why not?"

3 June 1982: Early Evening: Upper West Side

Colin had been looking forward to a showdown with Leila, so her absence from home came as a disappointment. It also meant that he had nothing to distract him from the shock of seeing Halib after the assault on his son.

He must report the incident to the police, but first he sent Robbie upstairs to do homework. Mentally squaring himself, he approached the telephone extension on the kitchen wall and lifted the receiver. Oh, shit! Answering machine on.

He marched into the hallway and was about to click the machine off when he saw that someone had left a message, so he pressed PLAYBACK instead.

"Hello, Leila?" A deep, throaty woman's voice. "Elaine Cohen. I can't come pick you up, I'm sorry. So see you in shul. Oh, listen, if you need to speak, I'm at Geula's, but don't dial her usual number, it'll be ringing off the hook; here's her personal direct line, she won't mind if I give it you...."

Colin turned off the machine and started thumbing through the pad on which they kept their most-used phone numbers. Police ...

Slowly the significance of what he'd just heard filtered through, and he straightened up. Shul? What on earth would Leila be doing in a synagogue? Wrong number ... no, the caller had definitely said "Leila"; the name wasn't *that* common.

Who was Geula? He didn't know any Geulas. Or any Elaine Cohens. Columbia's Dean of Law was called Cohen, but ...

Colin replayed the message, this time noting down the number at the end, Geula's number. He dialed.

"Katz residence."

"Uh ... is my wife there, please? Mrs. Leila Raleigh."

Many voices in the background; other vague sounds that

might have been glasses, or cutlery, being humped about in large quantities.

"Hello?" A new voice, a woman. "Geula Katz speaking."

"May I speak to my wife, please? Mrs. Raleigh?"

"Oh, you must be Colin? Hi, there! I've been dying to meet you for so long now. When are you going to be here?"

"Here?"

"The *sendah*. Leila told me you won't be able to make synagogue, that's too bad, but never mind, you just come on to the party whenever you're ready. Look, I really must fly, shul is due to begin any minute.... Your wife isn't here, but the minute I get to Emanu-El I'll tell her you called."

"Can you—"

But the line had fallen silent. Colin put down the receiver, a frown on his face. His heart was not so much beating as jolting.

Did Leila have a lover? He lowered himself into the nearest chair and gazed at the phone. He'd wondered for ages. A thousand little signs, all of which he'd deliberately ignored. Unexplained phone calls, lied about afterward. Strange messages jotted on the phone pad: "Oh, I can't think why I wrote that, now." And he'd desisted, because you didn't cross-examine your wife, not unless you were prepared to recess and then take it up again in a divorce courtroom.

So. This, it seemed, was the night he couldn't ignore it any longer. Emanu-El synagogue, followed by a party at the Katzes' place. Wherever that might be. It seemed he had an invitation, however, so he might as well go. Who *were* these people? They couldn't all be wives, sisters, mothers of Leila's lover. Suddenly he knew he had to go wherever Leila was, and he had to do it now. No, it couldn't wait. No, it wouldn't be better to discuss this thing in private. *Now, now, now!*

In their bedroom upstairs was a wardrobe. On its top shelf Leila kept various old papers and scraps scattered around in and out of shoeboxes. Since they shared the study desk drawers equally, it was the nearest thing she had to a private place. He'd seen her check old addresses from a book she kept on that top shelf. Instinct told him this was where the treasure lay.

As he climbed the stairs he wondered if she really would be so stupid as to leave the evidence lying around. Yes, she would, but not out of stupidity—part of her *wanted* him to know. And part of her needed to test the extent to which he trusted her. There would be something for him to find.

Colin peeped in on Robbie. The boy lay on the bed asleep, still fully clothed, his face flushed. Colin passed on down the corridor to the bedroom he shared with Leila. He closed the door soundlessly before pulling a chair up to the wardrobe and opening it.

He arranged the chair in such a way that it would keep the wardrobe door propped open and hauled himself up. She must have done a spring-cleaning lately, because everything had been stashed away in three boxes. He lifted them down, placed them on the bed, and commenced his search.

There was nothing to prove she had a lover on the side. As he burrowed down toward the bottom of the third and last box he felt a twinge of some strange emotion he couldn't at once identify, only to realize, with a start, that it was disappointment. Equipped with proof of her infidelity, he would have beaten her down to nothing and then they might have started again. Now he was left only with doubt: a slow, arsenic-like pellet that would worm its way toward his heart until it killed him.

The last thing in the last box was an old gray purse. He opened it and knew he'd found the time bomb.

Colin sat down on the bed. His heart was doing extraordinarily unpleasant things. Sheets of paper, quite small, folded in three. As he opened them out, a clipping fell onto the bed. It was old and faded. TWELVE DEAD proclaimed the headline and, underneath that, in lesser type: MAYFAIR BOMB OUTRAGE.

It wasn't until Colin had read halfway through the clipping that it dawned. On the first night of their honeymoon a bomb had exploded not far from their hotel, killing a dozen people. Their names were given in this shred of newspaper. Someone had marked each surname, lightly, with a blue ballpoint pen. Why on earth would Leila keep such a thing?

Colin gazed into space. Perhaps she wanted a reminder of how fragile happiness was. On the night of her marriage, at a sublime moment, other people were being blown apart ... although as far as he could remember, nothing about that night had been sublime. But why mark the surnames?

He turned his attention to the other sheets of paper. These were the kind of jottings people made when trying to solve brain-teasers. Rows of letters in Leila's handwriting, with more letters written underneath them, and arrows pointing between the two rows, as if to establish a connection. Odd words: CHILLON, CLOUD-LESS CLIMES, PROMETHEUS. A thought crossed his mind: it was as if Leila had been trying to unscramble a code.

Ridiculous! No, it wasn't; if she had a lover and was worried about being detected, she might resort to code. His mind, made hyperactive by jealousy, leapt to this conclusion at the same moment as he recognized where the code came from: CHILLON, PROMETHEUS ...

Byron.

"God damn," he muttered. "God damn."

He'd introduced her to Byron's poetry. They had read it together, on park benches, over tea, in bed. Especially, often, in bed. Byron and bed went together.

He had seen the Byron only recently. He rushed out of the bedroom, downstairs, to the first-floor study. Yes, the volume was lying askew, on the topmost shelf of the bookcase. The pages were dusty at their outer edges, the jacket was worn and frayed, but he went at it as if it were indestructible. A quick flick through revealed nothing out of the ordinary, just a few penciled notes, but they were old. Then a message transmitted itself through his fingers: the dust jacket wasn't sitting right. Something had been inserted between the jacket and the hard cover beneath.

Colin unfolded the jacket and yet another sheet of paper fell out. He recognized Leila's writing, but this time it was hurried, not easy to decipher. Two rows of letters, with the by-now-familiar arrows. And then what must, could only, be a translation: HALIB YOUNG BARB PM.

Halib. Someone who hadn't shown his face for five years until today, but now was turning up everywhere he looked....

Colin was aware of sounds on two levels: the roar of city traffic and the fierce beating of his own heart, the one distant and the other ineffably near. Danger lurked all around him. Yes, he knew terror. Halib was here, no doubt of it; Leila was in touch with him, and whatever business brother and sister had to transact that required encoding, *Robbie lay at the heart of it.*

3 June 1982: Evening: Temple Emanu-El

The tallith was just a simple prayer shawl, but it seemed to hang heavily on Sharett's shoulders. He kept picking at it. A yarmulke perched on top of his head, precariously kept in place by a bobby pin. He was exposed, out on a limb, with only a shawl and a cap and the ever-watchful eye of God to protect him, and it didn't add up to enough.

The side hall of the synagogue was, he estimated, ninety percent full. What a turnout! Seven o'clock on a Thursday evening, when a man ought to be thinking about getting home to his family, and what did we have here? We had most of New York except the *arelim,* the unbelievers, come to watch little David Katz become liable for aliya, at a service specially organized just for him.

Or maybe come to die.

He walked up and down, never still, his gaze sweeping across the heads of the assembled worshipers. In the gallery, Aliza was standing very close to Stepmother. Sharett stared up with hatred in his heart and in his eyes. How radiant Leila looked, how vivacious. She was lovely, yes; he admitted that. Lovelier than Sara would have been, had she lived.

What was their plan? he asked himself over and over again, as the cantor began. He continued to pace restlessly up and down, keeping to the sides. Neeman was doing the same. Which of these people was in the plot to murder Moshe? A horde of strange faces, male, female ... where were the killers?

The information he had was flawless in its detail—up to a point. He'd found out that there would be an attempt on the life of the Israeli ambassador to the United States, that Halib Hanif was behind it, that the attack would come while Moshe was attending the Katz bar mitzvah in New York on strange territory, separated from the usual security precautions that cocooned him on Washington's International Drive. So let Moshe be bait, that was the word he had spoken from on high; which would have been fine, if Halib hadn't vanished off the face of the earth.

At four o'clock, after his inspection of the temple, Sharett had been forced to decide whether to turn back Moshe, even then on the road up from Washington, or let him come on. But he couldn't admit to having been bested by a couple of stinking Arab terrorists. He couldn't lose the chance of hitting Stepmother....

David Katz was being led up to the Torah by his father. The rabbi handed him a silver *yad*, and the boy approached the Torah, nervously clearing his throat. Throughout the synagogue could be heard not a rustle, not a murmur.

As David began to chant, Sharett knew a moment of the most profound loneliness he'd experienced since Esther's death. That afternoon he had chosen to go on, not for sound operational reasons but because every other avenue was closed. So really you could say he had not chosen at all; whatever would happen would happen. And that was what David Katz seemed to be proclaiming, his high-pitched, scarcely broken voice echoing the judgment down from the roof above the Ark, where God sat watching.

Moshe sat watching in the front row.

Sharett's gaze came to rest on a particular face. A cantor, gorgeously robed—but not the cantor who'd been vetted forty-eight hours previously. Sharett caught his breath. An unknown.

David finished reading—*mazel tov!*—and prepared to be honored with a procession around the synagogue. As it got under way, Sharett caught Neeman's eye. They moved forward. The cantor remained where he was. Everyone's attention was on the bar mitzvah. People were on their feet, clapping loudly, turning to follow the procession with their eyes: rabbi, Torah, David. Moshe had risen and pivoted toward the rear of the synagogue. The tensions of the past few hours seemed to have left him; he was smiling. Flanked by three large men, it would have been well nigh impossible for a marksman to pick out the vulnerable parts of his body; a bomb, on the other hand ...

Sharett was running. Neeman the same. The cantor still had not moved, but his eyes were fixed on Moshe. As Sharett neared him he saw that this man was old and bearded, patriarchal. A man above suspicion.

Who would they have selected to kill Moshe? *A man above suspicion.*

".Dear God," he prayed, "let me be wrong. Just this one time."

As he passed the ambassador's group he spoke to the nearest bodyguard, not caring who heard or what they made of it: "Get him out, *now.*" Then the four of them were sliding along the pew, Moshe's smile vanished, his face turned white; they reached the end of the row where Neeman stood poised on tiptoe to meet them, an intense deep-field defender; the atmosphere was changing fast as people's attention was distracted from the procession; a woman cried out from the gallery and Sharett glanced up, afraid of seeing a grenade in Leila's hands, the pin out....

She stood gazing calmly down, and her hands were empty. The procession was coming back along the aisle now, but Moshe's men, forcing a path in the other direction, did not care. They hustled their precious charge past the indignant rabbi. They were nearly out.

Raful wheeled around. By now the suspect cantor seemed to be aware that all was not well, for he was looking apprehensively between Sharett and Neeman. Oblivious of the rising tide of disquiet among the congregation they bore down on him and, before he could protest, were hustling him out to the robing room.

"Who are you?" Sharett snapped.

"I am Jacob Horowitz. I am a cantor." The old man's lower lip was trembling, but a spark of resistance flared in his rheumy eyes. "Who are *you?*"

"What weapon are you carrying?"

"I am a *cantor,* I tell you."

"No, you're not." Neeman took over. "We've vetted all the people here; you are not cleared. How did you get in?"

"Who brought you here?" Sharett yelped. "When?"

"I—"

"Where are they now? What orders did they give you?"

Neeman was frisking through the old man's robes, pushing him ever backward until he ended up spread-eagled against the wall.

"Nothing," Neeman said. He sounded dissatisfied. "Clean."

"Fascists," the old man hissed. "Nazis. Who let *you* in, eh? Into this place of God."

"Mossad," Sharett said, not taking his eyes from the cantor's wrinkled face. "A man called Mankowicz was supposed to sing this evening."

"Mr. Mankowicz fell sick lunchtime. Food poisoning. But seems the Mossad can't find out about such a simple thing." Horowitz was wheezing. He held a hand against his chest. "Get out of here, you swine, before the good God strikes you dead for your blasphemy. Mossad! Such things as are done in the name of *Ha'aretz!* Get out, or I will sue, and don't think to keep me quiet just because I'm an old man."

Sharett and Neeman exchanged swift glances. Somewhere between their respective eyes a thought crackled and spat its way into electrified life and they swiveled, heading for the door. Stupid, *stupid:* Horowitz was a blind!

Sharett skidded into the body of the synagogue in time to hear Yehoshafat Katz pronounce the traditional blessing upon his son: "Blessed is the One who has freed me from the responsibility for this child's conduct."

The rabbi launched into *aleynu,* signifying the conclusion of the service. *"The Lord shall be acknowledged King of all the earth. On that day the Lord shall be One and his name One."*

Sharett looked around quickly, ensuring, to his almighty relief, that Moshe had truly got away. But then he glanced up and felt his heart contract; for the place that Stepmother had occupied was empty.

3 June 1982: Evening: Upper West Side

Colin stared at the piece of paper he'd found in Leila's purse. He felt sick. He struggled to hold on to his sanity, because it would have been easy to give way. He wanted to give way.

Think, he told himself; concentrate. It's Byron. You know Byron, you've loved him nearly all your life.

HALIB YOUNG BARB PM.

HALIB, that was clear enough. PM could mean afternoon, and he'd seen Halib that very afternoon; so YOUNG BARB meant ...? Byron. YOUNG BARB. A poem? No, it need not be a poem; what he was reading was a transliteration, *aided* by a poem. But *which one?*

Something niggled inside his brain, like mental toothache. Young barb, young barb. A line of poetry ... murder, dusty death, blood. But with piercing sunlight in it. Young barb, young barb, *young barbarian!*

He snatched up the Byron from the floor, where it had fallen, and began to snatch his way through its pages. Young barbarians dum-da-dum, young barbarians dum-da-*play ... to make a Roman holiday!*

"The Dying Gladiator."

He found the poem. A gladiator from a distant land, mortally wounded in the Roman arena, thinks not of the crowds delighting in his death but of his homeland beside the Danube:

> *There were his young barbarians all at play,*
> *There was their Dacian mother—he, their sire,*
> *Butchered to make a Roman holiday....*

The young barbarian must be their code word for Robbie. Why had they selected that? Was it simply because of the reference to a mother, meaning Leila? Or could it be on account of Robbie's "sire" ... who was going to be *butchered?*

Keep calm, he told himself. Be very, very cool. Think it through. *One:* Halib Hanif, terrorist, fanatic, is in New York. *Two:* Earlier today, he tried to snatch your son. *Three:* Leila knew about it. Careful. Check the reasoning, check the evidence. Leave that one, come back to it later.

Four: You and Robbie are alone in the house. You don't know when or if Leila's coming home and, if she does come, you don't know any longer if she's a friend.

Five: Halib, for some reason, wants Robbie. He's failed once. He'll try again. He could be outside now. He and his helpers may be about to break in.

Colin jumped off his chair. Enough thought. Get the boy out, get out yourself—if Halib's already here, poised to strike again, tough, end of story; if not, it's only a matter of time before he comes.

He ran upstairs again and shook Robbie awake. "Get up, Robbie, don't argue; grab a jacket and come with me."

The boy looked at him through frightened, trusting eyes that racked Colin's heart. He got off the bed and pulled on his sneakers. They went downstairs.

The atmosphere inside the house had undergone a subtle change. There was still plenty of daylight, but shadows had begun to accumulate in those corners where by concealment they could do most harm. The rooms seemed unnaturally silent. A stair tread creaked under Colin's foot, and he realized that he'd unconsciously been trying to match the silence in the house with his own.

They reached the bottom step. Ahead of them they could see the front door. The lower half was solid wood; above that were two panes of glass separated by a central divide. As they walked toward it, Colin was forming a mental picture of where his car stood parked in relation to the house. Car keys—on the hall table. He picked them up as they passed.

Why go out? Why not telephone the police, have them come to him?

He hesitated. How could he make them come, with a story like the one he had to tell? They'd think he was some kind of nut. But if he phoned and then something went wrong, if they never made it, there'd at least be a record....

"Dad."

Robbie had spoken softly, but something in his tone jerked Colin out of his tortured reverie. He looked at the front door and saw a shadow outlined against the frosted glass.

The bell rang.

Colin took Robbie's arm and gently pushed the boy against

the wall, at the same time raising a finger to his lips. Robbie, breathing fast, nodded; then, in a strange, disturbing gesture, he used both hands to block his ears.

The doorbell sounded again, for longer this time: an intrusive, angry noise.

Colin knew he must phone the police, why the hell hadn't he done it before? But not on the hallway extension, because the person outside would hear. So that meant going to the kitchen, at the back of the house, away from the attackers. Away from Halib.

As he reached the passage, the doorbell sounded yet again. Robbie pressed his hands more tightly over his ears and squeezed his eyes shut. He was shivering. Colin caught hold of his son's arm and began to guide him slowly toward the kitchen.

Then, behind them, he heard the letter flap click open. He thrust Robbie forward as hard as he could and was about to run after the terrified boy when a voice said, "Colin? Are you in there?"

A woman's voice. For a fraction of a second he thought it was Leila's. Then he recognized it: Angie Belmont, the downstairs tenant.

"Oh, my God," he cried aloud. "Thank you, thank you!"

He took Robbie by the hand and hurried to open the front door.

"Angie," he said, "am I glad to see you!"

"What's wrong? You look like you'd seen a ghost or something."

"Never mind. Robbie and I are going to the police."

"Gulp!" The girl pushed a tangle of black hair out of her eyes. "I need walnut oil and you talk police. Anything I can do?"

"Yes. Watch our backs as we walk to the car. If you see anything you don't like, any little thing at all, run into your apartment, bolt the door, call the police, and make them believe it's an emergency. It will be."

"You're in trouble?"

"Yes."

"'Kay." Her face, normally dreamy, had assumed formidable purpose. "Here's what we do. Get to the car, pronto, and I'll ride shotgun."

When Colin gazed uncomprehendingly, Angie laughed. "I'll be in my car, right behind you, till you get to the precinct house. Anybody tries to mess with you, I'll ram 'em!"

The prospect evidently pleased her. It pleased Colin, too, never more so than when they got to the end of West 79th in time to see a black stretch limousine pull out from the curb ahead of them, its boomerang-shaped aerial floating above the trunk like a mini-tailplane.

3 June 1982: Evening: Upper East Side

They sat Sharett down in a pantry, off the Katzes' main kitchen, and while they harangued him they walked up and down, gesticulating.

"Raful," Aliza cried in near despair, "why won't you see it? We have to get Moshe out of here now, this instant!"

"She's right." Neeman's machine-gun delivery contrasted starkly with Aliza's measured diction, stick versus carrot, good cop and bad. She was a nice girl, Raful liked her; pity about the skin.... "Let's review," Neeman said. "It was you had the tip-off, so you got to be *katsa*, to run the operation. None of us quarreled with that. Secrecy, you said. No outsiders, *Al*, strictly and only *Al*. One bodyguard for Moshe, one only; don't scare away the bad guys, lure them on, make them think it's easy. Textbook stuff. Classic. But it fell apart, and upstairs we have one very vulnerable ambassador who knows that whatever deal Raful struck with him, this wasn't part of it."

Sharett sat in the straight-backed chair they'd given him, legs crossed and hands clasped in his lap. He kept his head up and his eyes to the front. Aliza and Neeman stopped pacing, they threw up their hands, they "tcha'd" as mothers do when their daughters refuse to eat.

"So why not just take him away?" Raful asked.

"Because," Aliza said, just like that same mother—only she didn't say, Darling, you are beautiful the way you are, truly, she said, "Because, Raful, he won't make a move without your approval, and you won't give it."

Sharett did a Raful, lighting up the room, and Aliza gritted her teeth.

"No," she said. "You listen to me. Moshe deserves better. He agreed to leave himself wide open in New York, and now you're the only help he's got. He is the ambassador to the United States of America, the only one *we've* got."

Raful looked between them, then allowed his stare to resume its neutral, forward-facing position. "Is Stepmother here?"

"No," Neeman said.

"Anything on where she is?" Raful inquired of the space between their bodies.

While Aliza continued to marshal arguments, Neeman spoke into his shortwave radio. The exchange was tense and brief; in less than a minute, Neeman had returned to the fray.

"Vanished," he said curtly. "Raful, she was diversion; now she's gone. She has left, the stage is now clear for act two; she is not *in* act two, Raful, but the curtain's going up right now *and we have to get Moshe out.*"

Raful continued to survey the opposite wall with a thoughtful expression on his face, as if he were counting the knives in the rack or estimating how old the plumbing might be. And what was he really thinking, as he kept his head up and his eyes wide open, innocent?

He was thinking how right these young people were, how clever in their analyses, and he was so proud of them.

He had kept this operation all to himself, because he knew it meant the end of Leila and Halib Hanif; he knew he could kill them both, with his bare hands; he would get that opportunity, as long as, if only, Moshe agreed to cooperate. Moshe had agreed; his army of minders had been stood down for the weekend so as not to frighten away the foxes. Now all of them were out on the thinnest of limbs, a gale was whipping up, it was too late to bring in the FBI. There was only one thing left to do. He must get Moshe out, alive, in one piece, and then he must start putting together a story that might, just conceivably, save his pension. Again.

That's what he must do.

Supposing he didn't?

He was playing with Moshe's life. The stake didn't belong to him, and it felt *good*. He wouldn't be the one to suffer terminal inconvenience if things went wrong. This is how Leila Hanif feels, he told himself, when she's about to detonate the bomb.

In that sliver of time he saw exactly where his soul was and knew he couldn't afford to let it stay there.

He stood up. He ran his hands over his hair a couple of times while he tried to think of a cute exit line to cover things over. Nothing occurred to him. *Just get Moshe out of here.* He cleared his throat; but then Neeman's shortwave radio squawked and Raful paused, glad of the respite. He watched Dannie's face, saw its expression change from severity to astonishment.

"Leila Hanif." Neeman's voice no longer rattled along. It had turned hesitant.

"What about her?"

"She's just arrived. She's upstairs."

In front of Leila, tall purple drapes had been drawn aside to frame the entrance to an oak-paneled room, and above the heads of the guests she could see a fireplace, ornate and huge, before which stood a number of imposing-looking men, deep in conversation.

"Have you ever met the Israeli ambassador?" Geula Katz asked.

Leila vigorously shook her head. "Oh, my goodness me, no. Colin and I, we're not"—a nervous laugh—"we're not ambassador people."

"Well, it's time you changed, honey." Geula Katz clasped Leila's wrist. "Now you come right this way this instant, and I'll introduce you."

Under the exuberant guidance of Mrs. Katz, she passed through the drapes and found that in here things were much quieter. She had finally attained the inner sanctum. The holy of holies.

Casually she unclipped her crocodile purse, leaving it open a fraction.

"He is *the* sweetest man," Geula said. "Come."

A commotion behind her: argument. Leila, concentrating on

the ambassador, didn't turn, not even when the voices at her back seemed to become aggressively loud. Two members of Moshe's circle, sensing another presence, made way for her while continuing to pay heed to what the ambassador was saying. Then Moshe himself turned to bring her into the ring, and as he did so cast a glance over Leila's shoulder. She was aware of his face changing, losing its amiability at a stroke, but her handbag was open now and she had come to within three feet of Israel's ambassador to the United States; nobody stood between her and him, one on one at last—

Then a young man she remembered vaguely as having been in the synagogue, remembered because he had paced up and down the aisles throughout shul, ran by and blocked her route to Moshe. Leila halted, drew back; but a woman had taken her left arm and was squeezing it painfully, while the man she'd seen in the synagogue grabbed her hand.

"Raful!" the young man cried over Leila's shoulder. "Stay back! No!"

Leila tried to turn to see who he was calling to, but the woman tightened the grip on her arm and she winced. The room fell silent for a second. Then came frightened whispers, one or two screams. "He's got a gun!"

Leila opened her mouth to yell and she *did* yell ... no, not her voice. Someone else had shouted, "Don't!"; the woman who was still gripping her arm, she was the one who'd shouted. Suddenly this woman let go of Leila and darted behind her.

A bullet flew up into the ceiling.

Guests hurried in from the outer rooms, blocking the doorways, making a din, but around the fireplace there was silence, nothing but silence, while people gazed stupidly at one another.

There was a scuffle, the sound of somebody being hurried out of the room. Leila guessed the gunman must have been overpowered. She stood there with her mouth open, and the bemusement on her face was genuine.

Neeman quickly knelt down to pick up the crocodile purse that Leila had dropped when she was seized.

"Empty," he muttered, as he stood up. "Look."

Aliza took the purse. With Neeman watching over her shoulder, she upended it. A twenty-dollar bill, loose change, and a single tissue floated to the ground. Aliza ripped out the silk lining. Nothing. No weapon, no gas, no poison pill. A bag full of nothing.

"Now just a minute." Yehoshafat Katz interposed himself between Leila and Aliza. "Who do you think you are?" he demanded of the latter.

Moshe took him to one side and whispered something. Katz's eyes widened, but when he turned back to Aliza he said, "She's a guest, and a friend of my wife's. You're neither. If you've got business with her, you can conduct it, without guns, in private, *if* she consents. Understand me? I will ... not ... have violence in my home!"

Leila stared at him. She knew they all expected her to say something, but she had no script.

"I don't know what all this is about," she said in a high, clear voice. "But as long as someone will volunteer as chaperone, I don't mind being searched. It's the quickest way to prove I don't have anything to hide."

Aliza murmured something to Neeman, then turned to Geula. "Will you help me by chaperoning this woman?" she snapped.

"How could anyone refuse such a charmingly expressed invitation?" Geula led the way back through that succession of beautiful rooms like Catherine the Great, with Leila, Aliza, and Neeman floundering in her wake.

A servant intercepted her with a murmured message. "Wouldn't you just know it?" Geula pouted at Leila. "Now the darn phone's out. Okay, Consuela, go phone the police from next door."

At last they emerged onto a landing and Geula made to climb the curving stairway to the upper floor, where the bedrooms were.

"Hold it there!"

Sharett's voice. He was being restrained by two men. They held him against the banister, a few steps down from where Neeman and the three women had just emerged. Seeing he had everybody's attention he yelled, "This woman is a terrorist, come to kill the ambassador ... *citizen's arrest!*"

The two men, startled, loosened their grip on him, not much but enough for Raful to twist and punch his way free. He hurled himself at Leila, made a grab for her arm, and next second was pulling her down the stairs. Aliza protested, but he shouted at her in Yiddish; and Neeman, without a trace of hesitation, scampered ahead, clearing their path to the front door.

Leila tried to snatch a glance at her captor's face, but he was looking down the stairs so she couldn't make out his features. Sharett had got her halfway down to the ground floor before she began to struggle in earnest. She kicked him and he yelped. Leila, seeing him distracted for a vital second, bit his wrist and he let her go. She ran on down, had nearly reached the bottom, when the front door flew open, three loud bangs followed on each other in rapid succession, and the hallway filled with smoke.

Amid the screams and pandemonium Sharett saw just one thing: his quarry was getting away. He jumped the last few steps, keeping his eyes fixed on Leila's back. As he reached the bottom he tripped over something and fell, realizing too late that Neeman lay half on the floor and half on the lowest step, one hand held to his shoulder. Raful picked himself up and carried on.

Halib Hanif, flanked by two other men, was in the doorway, with Leila pressed against his chest and a stubby machine pistol in his right hand.

"You bastard!" Sharett yelled.

Halib, looking as cool and elegant as a man off to Henley Regatta, grinned at him. Above the tumult, Sharett heard him say, modestly, like somebody disclaiming a compliment, "Well, yes"; he watched as Halib lowered his gun to horizontal, taking aim, felt the first bullet strike ... then Halib was making for the stairs, at the top of which stood the Israeli ambassador to the United States of America.

From outside came whistles, more gunfire. Halib faltered and wheeled around; his men did likewise, their faces slackening with fear; then suddenly they were in disorganized retreat, and the hall-way was empty of everything except smoke that wreathed higher and higher, up the stairwell, to where horrified spectators lined the banisters.

The pain in Sharett's leg exploded into agony. He fainted.

He came to in the little room off the main kitchen, where he'd sat earlier, listening to Aliza and Neeman explain the only course open to him.

"Moshe?" he breathed.

"Safe," Aliza replied. "The police arrived just before you collapsed. Nobody here called them—the phone line had been cut at the junction box; it was an outside call—I don't know who or why. You're finished, Raful. You are dead. You've endangered the special relationship and State is mad as all get out. No one's to know. *No one*. The blackout is to be total; now do you understand?"

Sharett nodded again. "Did she get away?"

"They all got away." Aliza looked at him. "Raful," she said, and her voice had turned soft. "It was never part of any deal that you, anyone, should gun Stepmother down in cold blood in front of witnesses." She shook her head. Then suddenly she screamed at the top of her voice, *"What possessed you!"*

Raful looked at her and saw something worse than anger in her eyes; he saw disappointment. Betrayal.

Aliza went out. Shortly afterward, a detective came into the room leading a man Sharett knew from photographs, although he'd never met him: Colin Raleigh.

"Can you identify this guy?" the detective asked Colin, who shook his head.

"Not one of the men in the limo who tried to take your kid?"

"Definitely not."

"Sheess." The detective shook his head. "I never saw nothing like this before."

"So, Raleigh." Sharett made a great effort. "They didn't get your boy? I'm glad. They got your wife. Years ago, they got your wife."

Colin stared at him. "What did you say?"

"Leila Hanif. Terrorist. Killed my daughter, Sara. On your wedding night."

Colin and the detective stared at Sharett. Their silence was broken by a voice outside, hollering, "Lieutenant!"

"Wait. Now look, fellah—"

"Loo-*ten*-ant!"

"All *right!*" The policeman glowered at Sharett. "Don't move till I get back."

"I look like a man who can move?" Sharett grinned at Colin, did a Raful, watched the Englishman's face crack into a reluctant smile, watched it freeze.

"What were you saying about my wife? Who are you?"

"Me? Who am I? Ever hear of an organization called the Mossad?"

"Israeli intelligence?"

"Right." Another Raful. "Only tonight, not so intelligent."

"*Is* my wife a terrorist?"

"A brilliant one. Truly wonderful." Sharett squinted at him. "Seems like none of this surprises you much."

Colin said nothing.

"She blew up my daughter, in London, on your wedding night."

"Can you prove it?"

"Not in a way your courts would understand. But—I know, let's say that. And she shot a good man in Beirut. You were there."

For an instant, Colin was too startled to catch the reference. Then: "The summer of '74?" He laughed and seemed on the point of saying more, but changed his mind.

"On my wedding night I was in bed with Leila," he said at last. "Surprised?"

Sharett laughed, not kindly. "You don't know as much as I do, my friend," he said. "One other thing I know is this. Someday, you'll come to accept my version. And on that day, there'll be no one to help you protect your son except me, Raful Sharett. That's my name. Remember it. You phone the nearest Israeli embassy and ask for the military attaché; tell him who you are, say you want to speak to me. He'll do the rest."

He fell silent. Colin sensed a presence behind him and turned. A young man with a bandaged shoulder had come to stand on the threshold. He was breathing heavily, as if he'd been running.

"They shot Argov," he said tersely, ignoring Colin.

"Who's he?" Colin said.

"Shlomo Argov, our ambassador in England. They shot him, outside the Dorchester Hotel, in London, an hour ago." Neeman wiped his forehead. He was smiling. "A double operation, America and England. Two ambassadors. But they only got one and he's wounded, not dead. Raful, maybe they'll let you keep your pension after all."

Raful stared at him. His jaws began to grind, soundlessly. Neeman was laughing openly now, relief plainly written across his face. But Sharett's rage expanded inside him, a scalding pitch of blackness that entered his bloodstream and festered there, until at last the medics came with a stretcher to take him away, silent but with his jaws still grinding; and Colin found him merely pathetic, under his blanket: a balding, ineffectual man on the brink of old age who tried to mess with other people's lives as a substitute for coming to grips with his own. A spy, in other words.

What followed seemed unreal. Whenever Colin looked back on the time that followed David Katz's *sendah,* that was what struck him even more than the pain, the emptiness, the horror. It was a period of total unreality.

Dannie Neeman had been right: Halib failed in New York and only half succeeded in London. Yet oddly enough, his actions provided Tel Aviv with an excuse to do something they'd been yearning to do for years: clean the PLO out of Lebanon. So for them, Halib was a murderous terrorist on the record and a godsend off it.

Halib Hanif's men shot Ambassador Argov in the middle of London on June 3, 1982. The Israeli government proclaimed this a PLO-inspired outraged and labeled it the last straw. On June 4, the Israeli air force bombed south Lebanon and west Beirut; June 5 saw no less than fifty Israeli air strikes; by June 11 all of Beirut was encircled. Some fourteen thousand people, mostly civilians, died in the first fortnight's fighting. Analysts agreed that the shooting of Ambassador Argov was one of the few genuinely effective political assassinations of modern times, a provocation having consequences far beyond the immediate event; and the fact that the victim lived was seen as incidental. Bullets fired in a peaceful London street provoked a bloody war. Not even the butchers of Sarajevo, in 1914, could claim so firm a causal link.

Sharett sold himself to his masters as the man who'd simultaneously saved the life of their ambassador to the United States and provided them with the long-sought excuse to invade their northern neighbor; when the going got tough he simply did a Raful and kept on doing it until the opposition cracked. And the greater the flak coming out of Washington, the more that opposition dwindled.

Colin Raleigh was interrogated by innumerable men, some genial, some less so, some identified, some anonymous, one with a lie detector. He struggled to keep Robbie out of it, with partial success. In the course of these various "interviews," as they were euphemistically termed, he acquired odd snippets of knowledge: Leila and Halib had got away from the United States, a news blackout shrouded the events at the Katzes' house, various propaganda machines were working around the clock to make the world believe that relations between the United States and Israel were at an all-time high. Once he'd managed to overcome the initial skepticism, Colin found that his story was not only given credence, it even achieved a certain measure of respect. Whatever Sharett might be telling them back home, it seemed obvious to the U.S. State Department that Colin Raleigh had saved the Israeli ambassador's life. He'd recognized a code that would have meant nothing to an outsider and kept his head long enough to lead the police to the Katz *sendah*. For which he ought to be receiving credit in Tel Aviv—and would have done, had not Sharett been fighting his own corner so well.

No matter how many questions Robbie asked, Colin could not bring himself to talk about Leila. The authorities helped him there. No splashy headlines, no profile of terrorists on *60 Minutes*; simply a prolonged, soothing silence that enabled him to sell Leila's absence as desertion by an errant mother. "She's gone away, son," he said bitterly. "She wanted to go away. Let's not talk about her."

And after a while Robbie did stop talking about Leila. He became silent, withdrawing into a world of his own where he would not let Colin enter. So his father did not know of Robbie's constant, anguished search through his memory for that moment when he'd broken up his parents' marriage with a tantrum or an ill-considered word.

The unreality endured until the night they returned to their old house at Oxford. On the hall table Colin found mail neatly graded according to size of envelope, with the largest at the bottom; his mother must have been in to tidy up. After they'd unpacked and Robbie had gone to bed, Colin, dog-tired though he was, skimmed through the pile. Nothing caught his attention until he came to the very last item: a cheap brown envelope without a stamp but bearing his name. The handwriting was familiar. *Leila.*

Inside was a single sheet of paper, and here the handwriting lost its character. Capitals, childlike in their ugliness, had been scrawled with a leaky ballpoint pen; this, he thought, is what a poison-pen letter must be like.

The message was short but abundantly clear. I'LL GET HIM BACK.

Colin went down to the kitchen and poured himself a scotch. He sat at the table for a long time, deciding in what order to do things, how to explain the situation to the local police, whether he ought to involve his college or his mother at this stage, before the rumor mill cranked up.

But what kept intruding was the memory of Sharett's words.

Someday, you'll believe. And on that day, there'll be no one to help you protect your son except me, Raful Sharett. That's my name. Remember it.

24 July: Night/Dawn: Al Mahra, South Yemen

I don't like it," Shlomo Stern whispered.

"Why?"

Shlomo wanted to reply, It's too quiet, but that way he'd have sounded like some gook out of the movies working from a lousy script, and then his deputy, Captain Uri Vered, would have him by the balls for ever after, so he improvised. "No lights; how can they guard the passengers without lights?"

Stern and Vered lay up behind a small hill a thousand meters or so from NQ 033, sharing the night scope. On a moonless night like this the scope could identify a camel as a camel two thousand yards away, and both Israeli Defense Force officers were convinced that the plane's auxiliary power unit must have failed.

"Out of fuel, Shlomo." Vered was, of course, aware that Stern held the rank of lieutenant colonel, but these men were strictly on first-name terms. "Airline predicted that."

"No torches? Power packs?"

Shlomo handed over the scope and rolled onto his back, suddenly aware of hunger and fatigue. A mouthful of chocolate solved the first of these problems, but four years in Lebanon had worn the edges off his stamina. Too much had happened since he'd lifted the phone earlier that afternoon and found himself talking to

Avshalom Gazit. First, hours spent waiting for independent confirmation that Sharett was on the plane; then, after it had come, apparently from a source in Bahrain, more hours in the air, a parachute drop into the Gulf of Aden—they'd had to go into the sea, to avoid Yemeni air defenses—a long swim followed by a longer spell on the inflatables ... these things left their mark even on the fittest. There were thirty of them in all: five groups of six, five Masada long-range desert units seconded from the Paratroop Brigade, and they were the fittest troops in the IDF, but Operation Landmark, as the storming of NQ 033 was to be known, represented one long quintessential strain.

There were no lights aboard the aircraft and it was too quiet and Shlomo wanted to think. So he closed his eyes, letting every muscle in his body relax, while in the darkness around him and Vered, twenty-eight young men silently prepared for the fray.

The plane was blacked out. They had foreseen it might be, they'd foreseen every damn thing, and the order was specific: no lights on NQ 033 equals no attack before dawn. Storm a darkened plane and watch the body count rocket. Each man carried photographs of the flight crew and of the Mossad men aboard, but much use those would be in dead of night.

So. Take up positions, stand by thirty minutes before sunrise, sprint across the sands through half-light, diversions one and two and in, just at the moment when targets would begin to show up. Difficult. Hellish.

Stern's meditation was interrupted by a finger prodding into his neck: Vered's signature. The senior officer rolled over onto his stomach.

"Movement," Vered said softly. "Cockpit."

Shlomo groped for his radio, put it on whisper. "Gabriel, to me."

Fifteen seconds later a third shadow joined the two on the knoll overlooking the plane. He carried a long-barreled version of the British L4A1 sniper rifle mounted with a Trilux night sight.

"Cockpit," Shlomo murmured. "Human. Assess."

Gabriel took a long, careful look through the night sight. "Negative."

Shlomo let silence do the work; Gabriel heard the question

Why? as clearly as if his commander had shouted it.

"TriStar windscreen's one point five inches thick. Laminated glass interfaced with plastic. Good for an impact of fifty tons. At this range standard seven-point-six-two-mm ammo won't drill it. Star it, maybe."

"Shit."

"Round's too light, Shlomo. Muzzle velocity seventeen seventy-two mph dropping to less than twelve hundred by target. No go."

"Right. Reposition."

Gabriel withdrew as silently as he'd come. Shlomo took the scope from Vered and studied the cockpit. Someone definitely was moving in there.

After ten minutes during which nothing else happened he put down the scope and rubbed his eyes. Bad timing, he thought glumly. He and his men had been rushed from deep in the Negev. They'd been exercising around Israel's top secret Jericho missile bunkers. Not planned; just their turn, just lucky, that's all: they were the ones on standby this month, at maximum fitness, drilled in the latest antiterrorist techniques. But they were also at the end of their tour and due for leave. *Luck*, he reminded himself bitterly. Shlomo was forty-one. His wife, Rebecca, the same. The day before Southern Command brought them to Condition One, she'd entered the Hadassah Medical Center. She went in whole; next week she'd come out minus one breast. If she came out at all.

No conspiracy. Just luck.

The same probing finger touched his neck.

"Door," Vered hissed.

Shlomo snatched the night scope from his captain. What he saw made him forget to breathe. A figure stood at the top of the slide extending down from the forward door. Its face and hands glowed white in the lens. Without lowering the scope, Shlomo reached for his radio.

"Gabriel," he breathed.

A red light on the handset flickered twice in acknowledgment.

"Target," Shlomo said. And then: "All units stand by."

24 July: Dawn: Al Mahra, South Yemen

Colin's foot dislodged a stone, but Robbie didn't look up. He continued to sit on the boulder with his chin resting in his hands, staring at the limestone wall. He did not turn even when his father put a hand on his shoulder and said, "Did you sleep?"

After a while Colin took the hand away. Of course Robbie wouldn't have slept: too hot, too humid, with nowhere to lie down except the bone-hard desert floor. And what grisly thoughts must have been powering his brain though the dark hours?

"Yesterday, you said you knew," he said. "About Mother."

Robbie's shoulders shook, but he did not speak.

"How?"

"Worked it out."

"You ... can you explain that?" A pause. "Please?"

Robbie slowly turned around, though still he did not look at his father. "Mum disappeared in New York," he said, kicking a stone. "We went home. I thought about things. Nobody said anything. *You* never said anything."

"So how did you know? The papers didn't get hold of it."

Colin simply couldn't understand how his son might have found out: Sharett and his kind, desperate to keep their failures a secret, had ensured total news censorship.

"I ... you never seemed to have any contact with her," Robbie said. "No 'access,' isn't that what they call it? Normally there's access.... She didn't want that, I thought. Then I began to think, Maybe she *can't* have it." He shrugged.

"I see. Look ... I'm sorry I didn't say anything sooner, but—"

"Me too. I hated you for lying. I ran away once, did you know that?"

"I never—"

"No, of course you didn't!" Robbie's voice began as a shout and tailed off as he realized other ears would hear. "If only you'd paid more attention. You let me think she was just another cow, gone off with some man, didn't you? You were happy to have me

believe that. Or sometimes I thought ... perhaps she'd stolen something and had to run away. But Christ! I didn't think she was a terrorist! Until on the plane, when they did what she wanted, those
gunmen; they seemed to care about her more than the rest of us....
Oh, *shit!*"

He rocked to and fro for a moment, then suddenly threw himself into his father's arms, oblivious of the wounds on his back.
Colin screamed ... but inside. He clutched the boy to him, stroking
his hair, and he said, "I am so sorry. I am so very sorry. I love you,
Robbie. And because I always loved you, I was afraid you might
turn out to be like Feisal and Halib; perhaps something in their
blood would find its way through to you." He swallowed, scarcely
able to go on. "Just as when I first met them," he choked out, "I
was afraid that one day ... one day, Leila might turn out to be like
them too."

"Dad...." Robbie muttered the word into Colin's chest. He
drew back his head and repeated, "Dad?"

Colin got a grip on himself. "Yes?"

"I'm going to ask you something. I want you to tell me the
absolute, utter truth, okay?"

Colin nodded.

"Did you love *her?*"

Looking down into the boy's eyes, filled with anguish and
yearning, Colin found it easy to answer. The truth slipped out of
him in simple words.

"I loved her more than I loved myself. My one and only true
love."

"Do you love her now?"

Joy and simplicity dissolved into chaos. Yes: sitting there in
first class beside her, smelling her body smell, he had wanted her
and he had remembered what it meant to love her. He had loathed
Leila, but still he loved her.

"When someone's been very great ..." His voice tripped over
the words. He had not tasted water for many hours, his throat
was parched, yet he knew he had to find a way of talking to Robbie, talking until he dried out and fell down dead. "When some-

one's been as great, as beautiful, as Leila ... you don't just stop loving her, like turning off the TV. Things get ... muddy."

He'd meant to say "muddled," but "muddy" did the work much better.

"Colin."

He wheeled around to discover that Sharett had crept up on them and was regarding Robbie thoughtfully, like a scientist preparing to do an experiment on an animal in his laboratory. Robbie had no independent existence for Sharett.

"Is the boy all right?" he asked Colin.

"Damn you, he's a person." Colin could scarcely speak for rage. "Treat him like a human being, you hear me? Now ask *him:* 'Are you all right?'"

But Sharett merely did a Raful and turned away.

It was nearly light now, or would have been but for the thin mist that had come up overnight. Colin found his thoughts straying to the plane, and his heartbeat quickened. Would she blow up the aircraft and everyone aboard, as she'd threatened? "Watch the sky tomorrow at first light"; that's what the man with the bullhorn had said.

"Rouse up," Sharett called. Not that it was necessary; none of them had slept. "We are in bad shape." No preliminaries, no words wasted on the desert air. "But we must move if we are to survive."

Although barely visible in the half-light, they could see how straight he stood, with Neeman at his shoulder: two pillars of rock rising sheer from a barren landscape. These men were leaders. Yet Sharett's voice twanged in strange fashion. Earlier, Colin had watched him restlessly patrol their resting place and at one point heard him retch.

Sharett was ill.

"We are in a wadi," Sharett continued. "Here it is broad and shallow. My guess is that as we go north it will deepen and become narrower. A trap, in other words: a bottleneck. But if we climb to higher ground and hug the top of what may become a cliff, we shall be visible for miles. And remember: she wants the boy. She'll come after him, take him, and kill the rest of us."

He paused to let them consider the implications. Robbie was

shivering. By now there was enough light to let Colin to see how his son's white face throbbed with patches of color.

"We have one hope," Sharett continued. "That the hijack will soon end. Now that the terrorists have no helicopter to bring supplies, the world will act. Leila Hanif is isolated. They'll pursue her. If we can stay ahead of her, we've won. In order to do that, we must hide. Which means we will follow this dried-up watercourse, where there may be caves, boulders, even trees. Up on the desert floor, we are dead; while we stay here, below it, we have a chance. There is another reason. Here, we may find water." He pounded a fist into his palm. "That is our first and only priority: water. Food, we have only this."

He held up a small cardboard container.

"Nuts, cocktail snacks, taken from the plane. I have one tub, Neeman has another. It doesn't matter: in the desert, a man can live a long time without food. *But water he must find, or he will die!*"

"So how do we find it?" Colin asked roughly. He resented the way that the Israeli had calmly assumed autocratic leadership of the group.

"You see this mist?" Sharett waved his hand. "Moisture. You can feel it in the air. There is monsoon in this part of the world. There may be rain today; even if there is not, moisture surrounds you. Dew. Condensation. Look for the stones with dew and suck them."

Robbie was gazing at him incredulously. "This is the *desert*. There's no water."

"What do you think a desert is, then? Sand? Palm trees? Look around you and tell me what you see."

Thin yellow light permeated the mist, showing them a ridged and uneven gravel floor, boulders, a limestone wall that here was about twice the height of a man, some dusty scrub.

"Keep your eyes open for date palms," Sharett went on. "Dates contain both water and sugar, the best thing we could hope for. Look for signs of habitation, but be wary—we don't know who's in these parts, whether there are tribesmen, and, if so, whether they're friendly. We will move only for one hour at a time, then rest. If you lose sight of the others and become separated, seek the horizon: you'll see a blue tinge in one place and that will be where the sea is; walk in the opposite direction, north. We shall all keep going north; you'll be able to find us that way."

He looked at each person in turn, judging his resistance, facing him down.

"It's past dawn," he said at last. "She will be starting out, and we don't have much lead time. You will notice that, despite her man's promise last night, we've heard no explosion. It was bluff."

Without another word he turned on his heel and stalked away, willing them to follow, knowing they would. Even so, Neeman brought up the rear, for Sharett would take no chances.

By the time they'd been going for half an hour, the sun was up and they could see the worst.

This wadi was about a quarter of a mile wide, its gray-black floor scattered with boulders and trenches where water had flushed through in past years. Scrub-coated hollows alternated with stretches of gravel. They hugged the eastern wall, anxious for any patch of shade; even this early in the day the sun was roasting hot. But the wall posed its own problems, for there scree lay thick on the ground and they had to pick their way carefully for fear of turning an ankle.

Here and there, single fan-shaped trees sprouted from the flatter places, their feathery, dust-covered foliage moving listlessly in a foul breeze that siphoned up from the coast with its burden of sand. Colin examined one of these trees and found dark seed pods but did not dare taste them. Sharett, already far ahead, showed no interest, and when Neeman urged him back into line Colin obeyed with a shrug. For now, what mattered was staying together and ensuring that no one harmed Robbie.

Another half hour, and thirst was making him dizzy. Clouds of tiny flies buzzed around his head, settling on his lips, his eyelids. At last Sharett raised a hand, and with a groan of relief Colin sank to the ground.

It was cool and dank beneath the stone overhang that Sharett had chosen. Robbie sat with his arms curled around his legs, head down so that Colin could not see his eyes. He was panting. Colin assessed his own condition. His arm and shoulder had almost ceased to hurt, but his back was smarting painfully in the wet heat and he wondered how long he could go without hospital treatment.

A hand came down lightly on his shoulder. "My friend." Sharett had come to squat beside him. He spoke softly, allowing no one else to hear. "I can guess what you're thinking."

"Can you?"

"You can blame me for this, yes, but don't blame yourself. You did what was *right*."

Before Colin could respond, Sharett had risen and was striding off to talk with Neeman. Colin looked at them through bloodshot eyes. I'd like to kill that man, he thought.

He took stock. Robbie was all right, thank God, albeit distrustful. Sharett and Neeman were tired, but they were on their feet and talking with heads close together. Mahdi—

Mahdi had disappeared.

Colin rose silently and surveyed the wadi. The barren floor yawned empty, although there were several large boulders the Iranian might be crouching behind. Above him, the sky shimmered with a white intensity that hurt his eyes. The cliff walls, bleached of all color, had risen to about fifty feet, with nothing that even a goat could have used as a foothold.

Colin turned back the way they'd come, brushing away the cloud of flies that had descended the moment he left the shadow of the rocks. Just before Sharett had called a halt they'd rounded a sharper than average outcrop. Was Mahdi behind it, perhaps?

Colin made an effort to approach quietly. By the time he was within a few feet of the crease in the cliff wall he knew he'd found his man, because he could hear somebody slurping liquid. He broke into a run; stones crunched beneath his feet; the drinking noises stopped. As he rounded the outcrop, Mahdi was in the act of picking up a rock. Colin shouted and Mahdi staggered back, but he did not drop his missile. When Colin continued to advance he waved the rock high above his head. Colin's sideways glance showed him that Mahdi had discovered a small pool of emerald-green water in a hollow, saved from evaporation by the shade.

Mahdi threw the rock, but because he was weak it flew wide.

As he bent down to find another, Colin launched himself forward, remembering too late his burns and wrenched shoulder. He crashed into the Iranian as a leaden weight, unable to fight or do anything but scream out his agony. It was enough: pain brought blissful seconds of unconsciousness and by the time Colin had recovered, Mahdi lay pinned to the ground with Sharett and Neeman on either side.

"Water," Colin croaked. "Bastard found water."

"Useless," Sharett snapped. "It's been lying here for weeks; think of the flies. *Look at it!* Green!"

Colin wasn't listening. He saw that the two Israelis were involved with Mahdi and jumped for the rock hollow, still half full of water. But as he put his face down a noise penetrated the muddle inside his head. Retching. Somebody was being violently sick.

He came to himself with a jolt, to find his eyes mere inches above the water. It stank of sulfur; funny he hadn't noticed that before. The bodies of half a dozen flies floated on the scummy surface. He stood up, wiping a hand across his brow. His head felt so strange, so strange....

Mahdi had stopped vomiting. He lay on his side, chest heaving and a wild look in his eyes. Fear. *Terror.*

"We'll leave him." Sharett stood up. "We can't carry him, and he's in no state to walk."

"No!" The shock was patent in Robbie's voice. "You can't!"

Sharett shrugged. "You want to be the one to carry him?"

"I'll help, of course," Robbie said.

"And evaporate two liters of sweat when before you lost only one? Don't be stupid."

Robbie turned to Colin. "Help me, Dad?"

It was clear from his expression, from his tone, that he regarded this as a token question, capable of receiving only one answer. So when, after a long pause, Colin said no, it rocked the boy on his heels.

"Son, he's got a much better chance lying here to rest, in the shade, than if we force him to march with us."

Colin watched the boy's face, and it was like looking through a window. Intellectually, Robbie had grasped the situation: he understood that although a sacrifice was necessary, he didn't have to be the one strapped to the altar. Faced with the starkest choice, *him* or *me*, he saw deep down inside how he was going to choose *me* and hated it.

"Robbie." Sharett spoke. His voice sounded tolerant, compassionate. "In cases of desert survival, there is only one way to save a sick colleague. You seek help in the fastest way possible; then you go back and rescue him. That's what we have to have the courage to do."

Silence.

"Think of the airlines," Dannie Neeman said unexpectedly. "There's an oxygen failure and the masks come down. If you've got a kid with you, they tell you to fix your own mask first, *then* see to the child. Right?"

Robbie looked at Dannie with something like gratitude on his face, and Colin understood that Neeman, extraordinarily, had found Robbie an out that could marry brainpower with gut emotion.

Sharett laid a hand on the boy's shoulder. "Right," he said. "Isn't it?"

As Robbie nodded, Colin turned away. But then he found himself gazing at Mahdi, who lay on the ground panting. Every so often his body would go into spasm and lie still, before those horrible, dry pants began again. So Colin raised his eyes and caught something he wasn't meant to see. Something that, despite the searing temperature, chilled him to the bone.

Sharett had kept his hand on Robbie's shoulder, but his face was turned to Neeman. Now he smiled gratitude for his friend's intervention, at the same time squeezing Robbie, and in a flash of horror-filled intuition Colin perceived why those two actions were linked, what the combination meant: in Robbie, Sharett had the means of drawing Leila to himself, and when she came he would kill her son, just as she had butchered his daughter, all those years before.

An eye for an eye.

Sharett clapped the boy's shoulder. "Let's go," he said.

*   *   *

The sun was high when she found her first real confirmation that she was on the right track: a molded pattern in the dust at the foot of some scree. Leila squatted on her haunches, close enough to observe the pattern but not so near as to disturb it.

It was a shoe print, she felt sure. A man's shoe. Her first guess had been right: they'd follow the dried-up watercourse in the hope of finding water, shade, and cover. Much depended on how far inland this wadi extended. If it was short, they'd soon find themselves in the neck of a trap and, to judge from the way the terrain was changing, the cliff walls at that point would be too sheer to climb. She'd have them cornered.

Leila looked up at the sky. It was a bright cloudless blue but, this being a monsoon month, rain might come at any time. She knew this territory, had studied it thoroughly. About once every five or six years torrential rains lashed the coast of South Yemen and its mountainous hinterland. Because the ground was parched rock-hard, none of the water could drain away; instead, it coalesced into a mighty flooding wave called a *sail*. Bedouins traveling in the monsoon months avoided camping in wadis for this very reason: the force of the water was enough to uproot crops and sweep men away to their deaths, helpless before one of nature's strangest phenomena.

None of her quarry were likely to know about the *sail*.

She stood up, scanning the horizon. Heat had fused everything she saw into the same dull, pale sandy color: desert floor, limestone, even the band of light where cliff met sky. The wadi was definitely narrowing. Far ahead she could see where the watercourse changed direction, a turn in the rock wall blocking her view. It was hard to judge whether the cliffs were any higher there than here.

She drank a quarter of a liter of water, enough to take the edge off her thirst. If Sharett had any water, he would share it and order the rest of them to take sips. Ignorant people always made that mistake in the desert, which is why they usually died. They would walk for more than the daily tolerance of five kilometers, taking a mouthful of water here, a mouthful there, until their exhausted, dehydrated bodies packed up. Leila knew that she must swallow enough to save herself from the distraction of constantly thinking about water. With thirst banished she could concentrate on pursuit.

As she set off again she could feel the water doing her good. Her limbs moved easily, despite the fierce heat, because she was fit to start with and she had put her trust in Allah. Progress seemed faster now.

She heard the groans long before she rounded the distant corner of cliff that she had observed from her resting place. She did not so much as break step, but unslung her M3A1 and clicked off the safety catch.

A man lay holding his stomach. His eyes protruded, he retched dryly. Leila knelt beside him, feeling for his pulse. It was intermittent and very weak.

"Tell me," she said softly.

But he could not answer. At last he managed to jerk his head behind him. She looked up, saw what he meant, and rose to inspect it: a pool of water cupped in a rocky hollow.

"You drank that?" she asked.

He made no reply, but what had happened was obvious.

"Did anyone else drink?" she snapped. "*Did they!*"

When he shook his head Leila felt a second's respite from anxiety. She was on their trail, this man proved it, and now she must be closing fast.

"Which way?" She pointed up the wadi. "There?"

He nodded. She believed that he nodded. Leila knelt again, held out her hand, folded Mahdi's fingers around it.

"How many?" she asked softly, and began to close her own fingers, one by one. Four. The two Jews, Colin, Robbie. "How long ago did they leave?"

Again the trick with the fingers. Four ... forty minutes. But the sick man was guessing, she knew that, guessing wildly in an attempt to buy mercy from her. He was eyeing her water flask. She knew that soon he would make a grab for it and so she stood up abruptly, wrestling with this problem of mercy.

Shots made a lot of noise. Did she want to advertise her presence?

Her spent brain found no easy solution to that, so she left it to God. He too seemed to find the mystery a hard one, but in the end he sent his message and she knew that, as always, he was right. Three .45 ACP rounds swept Mahdi up to Paradise.

Leila envied him, and not only because she had just made her task that much harder. They would know she was coming now. Even if Colin and Robbie did not realize the significance of the bangs, mere pops in their far-off ears, Sharett would understand.

She hugged the shade beneath the rocks while making a quick survey of the wadi. That curve in the watercourse that had blocked her view earlier ... they would be beyond it by now, but keeping a close eye on their backs. Because she had water and was in training she could probably catch up with them, but after the shots they'd be expecting her, even if they weren't before. There was a better way. She would scale the wall here, where it was still comparatively easy going, and move fast along the cliff top until she cut them off, beyond that distant turn. They'd be anticipating an attack from the rear. But she would be on top of them, and in front. Yes. Surprise was essential when dealing with that accursed Jew.

Sharett ... odd that he should be here, at the end. On the plane he'd talked of his daughter, and for a moment the two of them, terrorist and victim, had found illusory contact. Would his daughter be there at the gates of hell to greet him? she wondered, as she emerged from shade into blinding sunlight. She found it strange to think of Sara Sharett in hell. But why? The girl had been an unbeliever in this life; there was no hope for her hereafter. Should she not go to hell and perish there?

Perhaps it was something to do with the way she'd died.

She'd seen Raful Sharett dimly, through a haze of smoke, for the one and only time, in New York on the evening of 3 June 1982. The day she'd last held her son before the hijack. She could have stopped it, she could have saved him, *she could, she could, she could!*

By now the sun was almost directly overhead, illuminating a landscape barren beyond belief, leaching it of everything except savage white light. Leila shouldered her weapon and trudged on into the face of brilliance, powerless to prevent the coming of memory, suddenly afraid.

24 July: Morning: Al Mahra, South Yemen

Shlomo stern caught sight of Gabriel humping ammunition belts over to the shade beneath the plane.

"Come here, I want you to meet someone." As Gabriel approached the bottom of the escape slide, Shlomo said, "This is your target in the doorway last night; you should know each other. Captain Roger Morgan and ... we'll just call him Gabriel."

The two men shook hands.

"It was your white shirt that saved you, Roger. Terrorists are like the bad men in old-time Westerns: they wear black. White makes too good a target, you see. But for five seconds there, Gabriel's finger was on the trigger, you were in the telescopic sights"—he held up his forefingers in the shape of an *X*—"where the wires meet, so."

Morgan glanced ruefully at Gabriel. "Would it have hurt?"

"No." Gabriel's finger made a little circular movement over the pilot's chest. "The heart." He waved his right hand in what might have been nearly a salute and started for the shore. "Swim, Shlomo?" he said over his shoulder.

"Later, maybe."

Morgan watched Gabriel, noting the ease with which he shed his sand-colored camouflage denim shirt with its black shoulder flashes and admiring the thick muscular torso beneath. He wondered how you got to such a peak of fitness. That, he suspected, *did* hurt, unlike being shot in the heart.

"What happens next?" he asked Shlomo.

The officer did not answer at once. His gaze strayed to the sea, a quarter of a mile from where they stood, where many of the recently liberated passengers were splashing around. Despite the earliness of the hour, the sun was already hot and had long ago burned off any lingering mist. Out there in the desert it would swiftly become a killer.

"Wait for the vessels coming from Oman to pick you up," he replied at last. "But you're not going to get *her* out in a hurry."

Morgan saw that he was looking at the plane.

"I doubt if she'll ever come out, colonel. It's an insurance problem now."

Shlomo nodded. "You're a hero," he said unexpectedly. "What you did is regarded as one of the most heroic feats of flying since the Second World War. Fun for you, I should think."

Morgan flushed and looked at the gravel. He wasn't sure how to take Lieutenant Colonel Stern. Plenty of shadows lurking.... "What will you and your men do?" he asked.

But Shlomo had just seen Vered breast the hill with the others he'd taken to check out the crashed helicopter. "Our job," he answered tersely. "Excuse me."

He set off toward the foothills where his troops had bivouacked, wishing he felt better. In Jerusalem they'd be operating about now: Rebecca would be anesthetized, pale, horizontal beneath a green sheet, her hair stuffed into a cap. Is she dreaming of me? he wondered. Was she afraid, in the minutes before the plunger of the syringe went down, bringing oblivion?

He stopped while still a hundred meters short of his temporary HQ and wheeled around as if to survey the shoreline. In fact, he'd given himself sixty seconds to face what was happening to his wife, to worry about it, pray about it, and then forget it.

A minute later he turned on his heel and approached Vered's group.

"Those satellite pictures were accurate, Shlomo. The copter crashed right where we thought. Survivors, more than one. Faint tracks heading north."

"The hijackers?"

"Maybe. But there are other tracks heading southwest, nowhere near the helicopter. So the tracks leading north must belong to someone else. Two parties, definitely. Hijackers or—" He broke off with a shrug.

Shlomo mentally reviewed what they knew. Hanif and some of her men had left the plane together; nobody knew where they'd gone. Two scarcely visible sets of tracks led away from the aircraft: multiple footprints heading southwest, where lay the small town of Al Ghaydah, and another set, one person only, making for the wreckage of the helicopter. But according to Vered, there were still more tracks leading *away* from the wrecked chopper. Tracks *plural.*

Then there was Morgan's information: Sharett and the Raleighs had escaped from the plane alive. There'd been a firefight. Morgan had seen everyone piling into the helicopter, which had crashed behind the first range of foothills.

But, yes, Vered was right: the multiple tracks leading north, inland, away from the helicopter, must mean that there'd been survivors. And now Hanif was going after the boy. Had to be, *had to be.*

Tel Aviv's orders were perfectly clear.

"I'm going inland," he said to Vered. "You're coming with me. Group of four. Plenty of water. Arrange a frequency. Weapons check before we start. Yuram's to take command here."

"Got it."

"Oh, and Uri ... I want Gabriel in our group."

24 July: Afternoon: Al Mahra, South Yemen

Afternoon's more tranquil light had softened the rocks to a pale shade of orange. Sharett and Neeman seemed made of iron; they kept going doggedly forward as if there was something to be had at the end of all this. Colin and Robbie could scarcely stand, let alone move. But they knew they had no choice except to go on. The shots had told them that. At first, they'd refused to believe that such understated *pops,* scarcely loud enough to puncture the silence, could signal the hunter's approach. But when they saw Sharett and Neeman redouble their efforts, saw the set of their faces, the Raleighs changed their minds.

When disaster struck, Colin's first savage thought was that it had been Robbie's fault for being lazy. His son could have died.

The wadi had narrowed to less than two hundred meters and cliffs towered above them, blotting out most of the sun. The four of them hugged the left-hand side of the watercourse, where the strip of shade extended farther. But then Sharett, still in the lead, detoured out into the band of sunlight, to avoid a difficult patch of scree. Robbie came next. He wiped his forehead, stopped, staggered a little. Before Colin could catch up to support him, his son had struck out over the hillock of scree, preferring to climb it rather than walk in direct sun.

Colin, two paces behind, hesitated, not knowing what to do. Dizziness and nausea had sapped his judgment. In the end he followed Robbie. He'd kept close to the boy ever since leaving Mahdi, hours before, anxious to preserve him from Sharett's clutches.

Robbie found the going tougher than he'd imagined. His feet sank through the stone chips, lacking purchase. Colin saw the two bright glittering things, dismissed them as dream objects, product of heat and exhaustion. Robbie slipped. He fell forward onto his hands, inches away from the glittery points.

The bright jewels reared out of the scrub and became eyes, eyes attached to a waving brown column. The viper had been watching their approach, keeping itself buried in the scree, everything except for its eyes.

Robbie yelled and flung himself sideways. He rolled down the scree slope to the wadi floor and lay there clutching his leg. Colin whipped up a stone and flung it at the snake. It vanished; he did not see where it went.

"Robbie! Are you all right? God, *say* something."

The scree was treacherous. Colin slithered down as best he could, but by the time he reached Robbie he, too, was on hands and knees, the skin grazed raw.

Robbie lay there panting, eyes squeezed shut. Colin helped him sit up.

"Did it get you?" he cried hoarsely.

Robbie shook his head. He was hiccupping back tears, now, and Colin's anger drained away. This would take even a hardened adult to the utter limit, and his son was a child, a grown-up child. Colin sat down, hauling Robbie into his arms.

"You all right?" Sharett's weary voice.

Colin looked up. His heart pounded in his chest as if desperate to get out. The silence, total, awful, oppressed him to the borders of terror.

"All right."

"The kid should have followed me."

A thousand years or so ago, it seemed, Colin had been thinking the same thing: Robbie should have gone after Sharett, around the pile of scree. He'd known anger toward his son. Now, cradling that poor head in his lap, Colin couldn't understand himself at all. His baby. His child.

He could have prevented this tragedy. Everything that had happened was his fault. On the plane he'd been a hero; here he was less than nothing. But any way you looked at it, he could have stopped all this simply by staying at home, by having nothing whatever to do with ...

He was going mad. Fear of it frightened him into full consciousness.

"Must ... rest," he gasped. "That scared the shit out of him. Me too."

"Prop him up in the shade. Be careful. Snakes, scorpions." Sharett shrugged. He wanted to do a Raful, but the effort cost too much. "Up ahead, I can see scrub. That means water below the surface. I'm going to dig, see what I can find. Suck a stone. Put a pebble into your mouth and suck it. That helps."

"I'll dig," Neeman said. "You rest."

But instead Sharett walked a few paces away from the Raleighs, with one arm across Neeman's shoulders, and they spoke together in low voices. Occasionally a word or two would penetrate Colin's consciousness—"Tiberias ... Masada Group ... Southern Command" —but nothing he heard made any sense. His ears felt blocked, his head hurt too much for thought.

Robbie had opened his eyes and was stirring slightly. Together he and Colin managed to circle the fall of scree that had blocked their path earlier and find a kind of shallow cave beneath the limestone overhang.

It smelled bad, a rotten-food-and-sewage kind of smell that Colin associated with cliffside caverns at the seaside in England: places where people came to urinate and defecate and throw contraceptives after making love. Tribesmen must have been here, for he could just make out the remains of a fire and a dirty old square of cloth left half in and half out of the ashes. At least it was cooler than on the wadi floor.

Colin kicked stones into the recesses of the cave—it wasn't very deep—watching warily to see if anything moved. He settled Robbie with his back against the wall. The boy slumped forward to rest his head on his knees.

They were on the verge of dehydration. Colin fell rather than sat down. His legs had no strength. His head was going round and round. He was going to die in this place. Desperation surged through him. He clenched his teeth shut to stop the scream. Next second, tears came. Or wanted to come: there wasn't enough moisture left in his body to fuel real tears, only dry sobs.

Robbie was shaking. A spasm. Colin couldn't see his face, so he didn't know what was wrong, if the boy was crying or violently ill. The limestone advanced and retreated, refusing to stay still. Suddenly, shafts of pain drilled their way through his head and he moaned aloud. His stomach hurt. Everywhere hurt.

Suck a pebble, that's what Sharett had said.

Crazy.

Try it.

Somehow he managed to lift a pebble and put it in his mouth.

For a moment, nothing happened. Then a trickle of moisture made its way through his saliva glands, scorching in their dryness. He picked up another stone and leaned across to his son. Gently he raised Robbie's head and prized open his mouth. Not difficult: the boy hadn't an ounce of strength left.

A shadow crossed the light. Colin turned to see Sharett blocking the entrance to the hollow, an ominous, impenetrable pillar. He advanced slowly, keeping his eyes fixed on Robbie. Colin felt the threat and was powerless.

"Stay away from him," he said. "He doesn't need you."

Sharett focused his bloodshot eyes on Colin and smiled. The meaning was quite clear. Robbie did not need Sharett, no, but the Mossad agent needed him. After a brief hesitation, he continued to approach the boy. Colin wriggled closer to his son and laid a hand on his forearm.

Sharett was looming over them now, his face a black hole against the afternoon light. Through thick, sluggish silence Colin was aware of his own heartbeats. But then an odd noise reverberated outside: odd, because it seemed to ripple. Colin's brain worked slowly. Not a single bang but several, so close together in time they seemed as one. Shots. Automatic fire!

Neeman fell into the cave, clutching his calf. Colin let go Robbie's arm and dragged himself onto all fours, forcing himself to ignore the agony. He helped Neeman rest his back against the wall, then turned his attention to the wound: a single bullet hole. But there was nothing he could do. They had no antiseptic, instruments, or bandages.

Another shadow added itself to those around him, this one darker than the rest. He looked up. Leila stood with her legs apart, the M3A1 suspended from her shoulder and covering the cave.

Colin began to retreat. He saw Leila glance behind him and stiffen. His back prickled with cold. Oh, God, oh God! *Stupid, stupid, stupid!* In his desire to help Neeman, common humanity donated to a stranger, he'd forgotten his own son!

Like an actor in slow motion Colin turned his head. Sharett lay with his back propped against the wall. One arm encircled Robbie's throat, the other his waist. The boy lay on top of Sharett, staring at his mother.

"Don't come any closer, Colin," Sharett croaked. "Don't see your boy die, not now we've got *her*."

Leila took a step deeper into the cave. Sharett jerked Robbie's chin up warningly, and the boy cried out. He raised his hands as if to grapple with Sharett, but they hung suspended, without making contact, until at last he lowered them again, convinced of his own helplessness.

The cry had a dramatic effect on both parents. Colin put his head in his hands and looked into the emptiness behind his eyelids, seeking a path in places where there was none. Leila drew herself up; lips parted to reveal her teeth clenched in rage, she raised the gun ... only to lower it again.

She stood near the entrance to the cave. Sharett and Robbie lay perhaps some twenty paces deeper in, with Colin and Neeman halfway between them. A flicker caught Colin's eyes. He twisted his head around to see Neeman silently prize himself a little more upright. Leila hadn't seen. Colin knew what the Israeli had in mind.

"No," he yelled, although the monosyllable came out as a croak. In his mind's eye he launched himself forward, grabbing for Neeman's legs. It didn't happen like that. He fell against the Israeli's ankles in a pathetic apology for an attack, and Neeman kicked his chin. Blood flowed into Colin's mouth, its silken saltiness foul on the tongue, but he'd done enough. Leila had her gun against Neeman's temple and was screaming at him in a language Colin didn't understand. She cracked the muzzle across his brow a couple of times and pulled back sharply, waving the M3A1 in a deadly arc that covered all of them.

"Now," she said in English, and her breathing was difficult. "Soon we will have a death count here. I can keep track of that Jew with my son more easily if I kill the two of you first."

Colin, looking up at her, knew she meant it. Thirteen years of marriage had been enough to sort out the bluffs and double-bluffs.

Leila struggled to get her breathing back under control. It took her a long time. At length she squatted down on her haunches, continuing to sweep the cave with her gaze, her eyes never still. When nobody else moved, she felt for her water flask and unslung it.

"Give this to Robbie," she ordered Colin. But she continued to hold the flask. "Nobody else drinks. Nobody. Sharett, when you get the water, see that he drinks slowly, but let him take all he wants. If, *if* you manage it, I'll let the rest of you drink too."

Colin received the flask, enduring torture as he heard the liquid splashing inside. It weighed so heavily in his hand that he could scarcely pass it on, and even after he was no longer holding the flask he continued to watch it as if that were the only object in his universe.

Sharett took the flask and unstoppered it with one hand. Robbie leaned forward to snatch it away. Sharett restrained him. Then the boy was drinking, forced by the pressure of his captor's arm to take only a small amount at once. The others watched greedily, although Leila's greed was of another dimension. She had no eyes for water; all her attention was focused on Robbie.

As if to prove it, she suddenly wailed, "My son! My *son!*"

She made no attempt to hold back the tears. She rocked to and fro on her haunches, keeping her weapon trained on them but somehow as helpless in the grip of grief as Robbie was helpless in Sharett's.

She was squatting within inches of the son she'd loved and waited for so long, and she could not touch so much as his hand. Nor, it seemed, any portion, however small, of his heart, for the boy cried, "You're not my mother, you're a monster."

He spoke the words but didn't believe them. He longed for her.

"I had a reason," she said at last, "for everything."

The silence in the cave reverberated with its own leaden pulse. It was Robbie who broke it. "So tell me," he wailed.

"What do you want to know?"

He considered that question for a time. At last he said, "I want to know why you left me."

"Yes. I can tell you why."

"I want to know whether it really was my fault that you went."

She stared at him, appalled. "*Your* fault?"

"I want to know why I was the one who was made to feel guilty. Not you. Me!"

Shlomo Stern checked the sun's elevation before raising the glasses to his eyes, anxious not to betray their position by a careless flash. "Where?" he asked Gabriel curtly.

"In the cliff face. See that 'ilb tree ... behind, to the right ten degrees."

Shlomo directed the binoculars to a spot on the far side of the wadi from the rock behind which they'd taken cover. "Got it."

His adjustment of the focusing ring made little improvement; the light here was impossible. Around the jagged edges of the recess in the cliff wall, some four hundred meters from their position, lay a brilliant white frame of sunlight-reflecting limestone. Yet he could see a human figure. It crouched in shadow, keeping its back to the wadi, as if intent on something happening inside the cave.

"Man or woman?" he breathed.

"Hard to say." Gabriel shrugged. "Guess female."

"Target?"

Gabriel pursed his lips. He unslung the sniper's rifle and took a long slow panning look through his telescope.

"Not a clean shot," he said finally.

Shlomo's patience snapped. "First the man in the doorway of the plane, now 'not a clean shot'! Name of God, what kind of marksman are you?"

"A first-class one who doesn't shoot airline pilots unless he has to, Shlomo. And I'm telling you, there's a ninety-five-percent chance I'll miss this time."

Shlomo subjected him to a withering look and said, "But is it *possible?*"

"For a mathematical theorist, possible," Gabriel conceded at last.

"Do you see more than one person in that recess?"

"I thought I saw something move, deeper in."

Shlomo waved him back down and took a long drink of water. Despite his outburst of temper he knew he would not order

Gabriel to take out the human figure on the edge of the cave, first because of the absence of positive identification, second because he might accidentally hit Sharett, and third, most important, because Gabriel was against it. They would have to find a way of moving in closer.

"Well," he said at last, "do we assume it's them, or could it be some tribesman taking a shit?"

"It's them," Uri Vered observed. "The tribesman would have a camel, a goat, something. What he *wouldn't* have is an automatic weapon—remember those shots we heard?"

Shlomo nodded. "But is it all of them?" he asked. "Could they have got separated?"

"We haven't seen anyone else on our way in," Uri said. "If it's her she'll have the rest of them with her. Because if she hadn't found them, she wouldn't have stopped."

Shlomo considered the analysis, liking it. But Uri's words didn't solve the tactical problem.

Direct approach was impossible: about a quarter of a mile of wadi separated them from their quarry, and it lacked any cover. To complicate matters further, the surface was covered in gravel; a silent attack would be out of the question. Even if they managed to cover half that distance without one of them spraining an ankle, the noise of their coming would be bound to alert the woman.

There was a way, but it meant leaving the situation in the cave to develop without interference. Shlomo loathed that.

"Uri," he said, "assume you are at the top of that cliff face opposite. How quickly can you get down to the cave."

"Thirty seconds noisy, one minute quiet."

Shlomo nodded. "Night attack. Anyone disagree?"

The other three shook their heads. Each of them had independently reached the same conclusion.

"Half an hour after sunset Uri comes down that wall, landing beside the cave. Thirty seconds noisy; better make that twenty. By then, two of us have worked our way back down the watercourse, crossed it someplace where no one looking out that cave could see us, and come back up to within ten meters of the target. And we've done all that very, very quietly. Yes?"

This time the men nodded.

"Uri's one second ahead of us. He goes in with two stun grenades, flattens himself, we sprint. Questions?"

"You've left out one man." It was Ben Allon, the fourth member of the party, who spoke. Shlomo wasn't surprised, for Ben loved detail to the point of pedantry, loved to request information in the second before his officer was about to provide it anyway.

"Right. Gabriel, you're going to work northward up the ravine, going deeper in. Not too far, mind. I want you to take care of anyone who comes out of that cave and starts following the wadi inland. If they turn back the way they came, toward where the helicopter crashed, they'll run into us. If they go the other direction, they'll meet you."

"Who's legitimate for me?" Gabriel asked.

"The woman. Try not to hit the boy. *Don't* hit Sharett. Any more questions?"

While he waited for them to think it through he damned Raful Sharett to hell and back, wondering why they wanted him in Tel Aviv so much, who was paying off debts, what they would say to him if they did succeed in getting him home. A maverick, Sharett: in Shlomo's book *he* was "legitimate"; that is to say, a permissible target. Sharett was the most legitimate of all, in fact, because it was thanks to him that he, Shlomo Stern, was here and not at his wife's bedside, holding her hand....

"Radio contact?" Uri Vered interrupted Shlomo's unquiet reflections.

"No," he answered. "Silent routines throughout." He glanced up at the sun, then unstrapped his Rolex. "Synchronize. Upon my mark ..."

Colin's mouth was dry as bleached bone. Pain ... it wasn't exactly pain, now, more a sense of extraordinarily dangerous illness hovering around the corner. Terminal illness. Death by thirst.

He knew it to be the cruelest death. Worse, some said, than being burned alive. He wanted to help his son. Now he was too weak and scared to do anything but lie against the rock and watch the fuzzy images uncurl in front of him. His throat had all but closed. It burned. His eyes burned. Sickness knotted his intestines, and there would be no more liquid to dissolve it away.

"He lied."

Through the burning came recognition of Robbie's voice. His mother's gift of water had revived him.

"Halib lied, lied, lied. He *used* you, Mum, why couldn't you *see* that?"

"I don't know."

Robbie, deprived of the resistance he'd expected and craved, remained silent.

"My brother never played straight." Leila's voice was hushed, appalled. "Nor did your Grandfather Feisal. It wasn't their way."

"So you threw us away, Dad and me." Robbie coughed. The cough turned into a spasm. Leila reached for the water flask, her expression undecided. At last the coughing stopped, and her hand released the flask.

Robbie spoke again. "You threw us away and you became a terrorist? Great. All because Uncle Halib asked you to. *Stupid.*"

"There were other reasons."

"Yeah? What?"

She had no answer for him. The boy's foot lashed out, sending a pebble cascading against his mother's thigh. She checked her anger. Then she said, "Blood won out, Robbie. It usually does." She glanced at Sharett. "Right?"

"Oh, yes," he replied, in a faraway voice. "Blood rules everything."

"Crap!"

Leila stiffened. So did Sharett. Only Robbie and Colin stayed relaxed. They knew this territory.

"I should have been firmer with you," she said, mildly enough. "This is Christianity for you, then."

"Christians don't murder."

Leila smiled.

"You wanted to know why I left in 1982," she said after a pause. "All right, I'll tell you. I'd taken an oath to be revenged on the man who'd murdered—if you like the murder topic, let's discuss it—murdered my grandfather Ibrahim. An Israeli killed him; that's important."

"*Why* is it important?"

"Because it made all other Israelis in the field my prey, Israelis like the ambassador to the United States. I'd ... I'd taken part in operations. So I was wanted by the Mossad, and Halib would only protect you and me if I obeyed him in everything. *Only then would he help me!*"

"You should understand that," Sharett said, and his voice contained such unexpected sympathy that Robbie tried to turn around and look at him. When the iron grip on his neck and waist did not relax he struggled, briefly, and was still.

"Why did you save Tim?" he suddenly flared. "You, the mighty terrorist, out for revenge, why so merciful all of a sudden?" And when she didn't answer he sneered, "Aren't you worried about your image?"

"I saved Tim because you asked me to."

"No other reason?" he scoffed. "Humanity? Compassion?"

"Not ... after what happened in 1982."

"Yeah, well, we know all about that, don't we?" He added another word under his breath: "*Bitch!*"

Leila heard it. Sulfur flowed through her veins. She had a sudden vision of herself leaning forward to pick up a stone and fling it at her son, saw, saw *vividly*, how it struck him on the lip, causing the blood to run, bringing astonishment and fear into his eyes....

No. *He was her son.* Slowly, slowly, the rage burned itself off, evaporating into the hot, moisture-sodden air; but its odor remained in her nostrils for a long time, and it was a while before she trusted herself to speak.

"In 1982 I believed I'd seen you for the last time, Robbie." Leila's voice was pleading now. "But your uncle offered me one hope, if I worked for him. He promised the minute you left England he'd take you back. He couldn't do anything while you were in England; you were being watched, you must see that.... He swore to help me."

"Help you?" Robbie tried to laugh. "He betrayed you!"

"After New York I had no place to rest." Leila murmured the words as if she had not heard her son speak. "No place to call my home."

"Good. I hope you went hungry and thirsty, and I hope you were scared, every day. I hope you goddamn *suffered!* You ... *terrorist!*" Robbie's voice had sunk to a level scarcely audible in the cave, but he spat out the last word with a venom that made his hearers shudder.

"Why do you call me a terrorist?" she asked in wonder. "I didn't feel any fear, delight, or grief when I killed. I felt nothing. I just wanted to have you back. Why do you call it terrorism?"

Sharett, looking from face to face, knew it was only conflict that kept them going, conflict and desire. Leila Hanif wanted her child more than she wanted life. He, Raful, lusted for revenge. Colin would sacrifice anything to save Robbie from the hateful virus spread by Hanif genes. But now energy came only in fits and starts, each surge weakening them, sapping will and the ability to fight. Conflict, desire ... dead things.

The entrance to the cave had ceased to be a glaring white shape. He could see the watercourse floor in its natural colors. Soon it would be dusk.

His life was drawing to an end. Tongues of acid were consuming his stomach wall as the tide devours a child's sand castle. First the outriders, rippling wavelets that reconnoitered the lower ramparts; then rollers, bearing down on the soft barriers, smoothing them flat, consuming them, until there was no longer a castle standing proud on the shore but only that seething, heavy force of nature called the sea.

Sharett eased his cramped legs a fraction. He would have liked something to deaden the pain. Not a tablet or an injection. No, he wanted something of *theirs*. One of Esther's embroidered hankies, with her scent on it—what agony they'd been in the aftermath of her death, and how he longed for them now! Sara's locket. Things old men clutch to make their deathbeds tolerable.

He could have sat at a café table overlooking the Mediterranean, with the taste of apple jam on his tongue, and had chosen to turn his back on all that. Why? Around that corner—*there,* see it?—lay the rationale and justification for Raful Sharett; give him a moment, it would come....

There were no more moments. In Tel Aviv, in Jerusalem, they'd have learned the truth by now. Too late to change anything. The sand castle was almost flat. Sunset, the beach emptying, children and parents alike, tired and tranquil, heading home. A last look, and then a turning of the back for eternity.

He must fight on. The woman would fight.

"What do you think will happen?" he said suddenly. "Leila Hanif, it's you I'm asking."

She looked at him but did not reply.

"Your water's almost gone. Not enough to get back to the plane. And if you did ... what then?" A spasm of pain made him tighten his grip on Robbie, and the boy cried out.

"Stay where you are!" Sharett shouted.

She had risen to a crouch but, seeing that Robbie no longer struggled, she slowly relaxed.

"Even if you made it back to the plane," Sharett croaked, "what then, eh? You're going to die, but before then you're going to watch your boy die too. Of thirst. Or shall I break his neck in mercy? Eh?"

He wrenched Robbie's head backward. This time, Leila did not react openly, she just became still. She became one with the stone around her.

"What were you doing in New York that evening?" Sharett asked. "The lost hours, between synagogue and *sendah* ... how did you spend them, hmm?"

Her stillness did not lessen, but its quality changed; it was as if a cat were preparing to attack.

"You were with Halib," Sharett jeered, "your beloved brother, listening to him tell you that Robbie had been got safely away, was in hiding, was *yours*. Whereas all the time—"

The bullet whined off the rock face an inch from Sharett's left ear and he winced, but his grip on Robbie did not slacken.

"Do that again," he whispered, "and the boy's dead."

She continued to kneel in the same old position, with her gun aimed at what she could see of Sharett, but her eyes glittered, and to Colin, hallucinating somewhere on the borders between life and its extinction, it seemed that those glowing eyes mingled with others....

A day of infernal heat, dust, flies, stink, but not in Yemen. In Beirut. A day of his youth, or so it appeared now, though in 1974 he was no longer young. End of holiday. Traveling fast and hard toward the airport, arrows of white light reflected off car paint-work, a noisy air-conditioner fan, reek of aftershave from the driver's neck, red where the hairs had been razored down to the roots....

He could hear Leila talking, as if in a far-off room of the same house. Playing with Robbie. *Not far to go now, darling....*

Then, violent acceleration. Eyes in the mirror. Eyes every-where. Robbie sniveling with fear, Leila gripped by panic, clinging to her child as if he might save her. Alf, Robbie's stuffed crocodile, cartwheeling around the car as it skidded to a halt; Alf's eyes close to his own, replaced by another pair of eyes, bored at having to do this work, bored but not distressed, as the killer walked toward the BMW to finish what he'd begun.

Leila cowered in the far corner, holding Robbie to her breast. The boy's eyes were closed. He was sucking his thumb, trembling. Sacrificial victims, calmly awaiting the knife: *No, by Christ, no!*

His flight bag bouncing here, there, everywhere except into his hands. A whimpering sound—ah! it came from him—smash, smash, *smash*, the case flying open, the gun in his hands and an almighty pain lancing up his backbone, his hands refusing to steady, the gun seemed so heavy and his arms seemed so stiff ... but he was lifting it.

They'd meant to get the gun back to Celestine somehow, but events always conspired to frustrate them. That last morning, they'd agreed to leave it in a side pocket of the car when they reached the airport and not say anything. God had arranged it this way. God's will.

The eyes, those dreadful eyes, coal black circling furnace-red, floated toward the car. Colin remembered that guns had safety catches. His thumb came into contact with something that moved, and he moved it. Snatching one last glance at the pale, tear-streaked faces of his terrified wife and child, he heard a noise, the door was open, and he turned, tensing his finger around the trigger while he prayed....

An explosion. His hands hurting like hell, his eardrums burst, silence, the noisy kind of silence that deafens you with its weight. A blank. Being pulled around, and pushed also, stood up against an army truck while brutal hands scraped the insides of his legs raw, and eyes, hostile eyes, curious and greedy, consumed him like fire, hotter than fire....

Mayday! Mayday! Mayday! Ditching! Ditching! Ditching!

Fire on board. Flames snatching at the wing, the plane almost vertical now. Plunging down toward the sea.... *Boom!* went the flowers that grew out of the hull. *Boom, boom!* Something black rose up to smother him, he was choking, couldn't breathe, because the horrible black smothery thing was so heavy. It had eyes, now: terrible flaming orbs of death that scorched his face, and there was blood everywhere, rich, red, and tantalizingly fragrant: a fresh-air smell, a come-on wake-up it's a lovely morning smell that got you going, blood *everywhere*—on the car's paintwork, on the upholstery. "Did I do that?" he kept asking the Phalange officer in charge. "Did *I* do it?" Because there was so much blood everywhere. *See, see where Christ's blood streams in the firmament! Yet who would have thought the old man to have had so much blood in him!* It was *blood* that was suffocating him, while the flowers spoke: *Boom!*

His father's blood. Father, son, and holy ghost: *"See, see...."*

Malcolm Raleigh threw his body across Colin's to shield him from the flowers and their burden of fresh, pungently scented blood, but he died, still he died. Colin drank the blood, which was also the blood of Ehud Chafets, and he ought to have repaid his father, "paid him back," that's what he'd said to Robbie, but what he did was this: as he was thrusting his way through the tiny porthole of the DC-4 he felt his father behind him, and so he lashed out with his feet and lashed again, *kick kick kick,* until he could feel no more struggling behind him and he was up into the light, free.

Free.

He lay with his back against a damp rock wall in Yemen, head lolling over toward the cave entrance. He was awake, he was rational, his sight had focused into perception of great sharpness. He knew his own name and everything about his situation, just as he knew, with total clarity and for the first time, that his hands were clean of his father's blood.

Because he had surfaced into this limpid pool of utter tranquillity he could also be certain that his senses were to be relied upon. Thus he knew that in the oval of decreasing light immediately behind Leila, a shadow had moved and instantly become still. Somebody outside the cave....

A rescue party.

Leila sat with the rifle in her lap. She kept it trained on Sharett, which meant that she kept it trained also on Robbie, their son. Move the barrel less than an inch, and it would be aimed at Colin.

If he shouted a warning, the rescuers would storm in.

If he kept quiet, they would creep up on her and try to overpower her.

He had a choice.

Robbie no longer felt sure what was real and what was dream. He floated in and out of consciousness like a plane flying through cloud, now light, now dim. In the dream he was lying on his bed, awake, while his father spoke on the telephone. He sounded far, far away, but Robbie could almost make out the words. They'd been in his head for days now. The night before they flew to Bahrain, Dad was talking to a man called Richard ... Robert ...

His mother was an animal. No, don't say that. She was his mother. But still she had to be made to see that what she'd done was *wrong....*

If only his father would shut up. Stop it, Dad. Say goodbye to Richard. Rodney. Robert....

I have to make her see.

"He's right," Leila said unexpectedly. "Halib cheated everyone. Even me."

It was almost dark in the cave. Colin strained to see his former wife through the gloom, but her expression remained closed to him. He knew she was preparing her last throw, the one that would bring Robbie to her side.

"In New York," she said, "I trusted Halib. He wouldn't let me be the one to take you away from school that day. But later he told me he'd collected you and you were safe, where no one would ever find you." She paused, thinking. Then, in a voice that rang with grief, she said, "He was right."

Colin's ears ached with the effort to hear. Outside the cave the sky had turned dark blue. Shadows slithered everywhere.

"You were safe ... *and he promised to get you back!*"

"And suppose I didn't want to be got back?" Robbie wailed. "Did you ever think of that?"

Colin felt a resurgence of that desperate need to forge a relationship with his son, the kind he would have wanted with his own father. The longing brought with it an odd sympathy for Leila, because he knew she shared it. And yes, another thing they had in common: neither of them gave a damn what Robbie might want.

His heart gave a lurch and he felt himself teeter on the lip of an abyss.

Robbie's head throbbed with pain and confusion. Dad, do *shut up!* Say goodbye to your friend, put down the phone....

Must make Mum *see*....

"You needn't have left me," he said. "You needn't have killed anyone."

Say goodbye, Dad. To Robert. To ... to ... *Raful!*

He woke into full consciousness.

"Mummy!" His cry rent the silence. "*Mummy!*"

One determined tug was enough to free himself. Sharett lunged for him and missed. He rushed toward his mother. Colin knew what was in the boy's mind: he wanted to buy back time. He wanted to find a way of convincing her she'd been wrong, of punishing her, but also of *knowing* her and healing all that was past.

He wanted her love.

Leila opened her arms to Robbie. She dropped the gun. It fell near Colin. She held her son tight. Colin leaned forward. He picked up the gun.

Leila was crouched sideways to him, less than two feet away. He could hear her sobs and see paleness where her shirt was. When Sharett yelled "Now!" Colin shouted, "Robbie! *Down!*"

In the same second that Colin pulled the trigger, Robbie screamed.

Shlomo Stern blew his whistle.

Robbie remembered something, as he buried his face in his mother's breast. Funny, he hadn't thought about it since childhood. He was in bed, it was late; Leila came into the bedroom....

"Put that book away," she said, in a voice that was meant to be fierce but sounded kind. "You can read it tomorrow."

He smiled up at her. "'Night, Mummy," he said sleepily.

"You can finish it tomorrow," she said tenderly, as she tucked him up in bed. "But this day's over now...."

Noise shook the very walls of the cave: hurricane noise. When at last the firing stopped, Shlomo Stern switched on his torch. Colin crawled up to see that Leila had one arm thrown lightly around Robbie's shoulders. A thick scarlet trail seeped between the boy's lips, but even that could not conceal how mother and son were smiling.

More torches had flashed on now; the cave seemed full of huge men with dark, oily faces and black holes where their eyes should be. Raful and Dannie Neeman had flung themselves flat the second Stern's whistle sounded. They'd survived. Colin looked up from the two corpses at his feet. He gazed into Sharett's eyes, and he said, "You promised." His voice was hushed. "You promised me, Raful."

"Don't...." Sharett's voice was a mere rasp against the silence. "Don't...."

"You promised me he wouldn't be hurt. After New York, you said if I helped you; that was the only way...."

Sharett opened his mouth to speak. No words came out.

"We had plans.... Help me to help you, that's what you said. Be kind to Sharett, and you need never fear Leila again. Never walk down the street wondering if Robbie's *really* safe at school, or—"

He swallowed. Bait, Sharett had said; I need bait. And for a long time Colin had refused to dangle his own son as bait. But in the end, fear and loathing of the woman who'd betrayed him had worn him down. He'd acquiesced when Raful managed to scatter references to their trip through the newspapers, even though Celestine had seen one of the earliest articles and rung him up with a warning. He'd agreed to pretend not to recognize Sharett when they met on the plane.

He'd put his trust in Sharett.

"You lied," he said.

He could have said no, when Sharett proposed trailing a hijack in front of Leila Hanif. What if he'd had the strength to throw himself between Robbie and the one with the gun, as he'd done before, on the plane, so that the bullets took his life, not Robbie's? *What if he'd been his father's son, the son he'd always yearned to be?*

He could have changed everything. Yes. He could.

He looked down to see Leila's gun still in his hands. He raised it.

Colonel Shlomo Stern's mind was on his wife's cancer, his body geared up for combat, still set to automatic. When he caught the flash of moving metal in someone's torch beam he fired instinctively, almost absentmindedly. Colin never even heard the shots.

24 July: 2000: Bahrain

Departure was infinitely better than arrival, Andrew Nunn thought, as the big white Cadillac swung off the hotel's forecourt and headed for the Corniche. Sound drums and trumpets. Et cetera. The car was splendid, if you had a thing about sheepskin and Arab music, and as for motorcycle outriders—well, just what he'd always wanted. One regret haunted him, only one: he still hadn't managed to prize a smile out of Selman Shehabi, and after all they'd gone though together these past few days that irked, it really did.

He was halfway to the airport when the phone buzzed. He

picked it up and, to his astonishment, heard the voice of Britain's Prime Minister.

"Well, yes," he said, after a while. "Thank you for those kind words.... I can honestly say it was nothing, Prime Minister." And he laughed in that knowing way people do when they're being modest, whereas in fact it was the truth: they'd brought him here for their own purposes, he'd buggered about on the phone till the skin of his ear had started to peel, they'd finished with him and dispatched him to the airport, and here he was, having done nothing, on the blower to the PM, being told how the sun shone out of his arse.

"Your Parliamentary Private Secretary? Of course I'll have a word, delighted.... Hello, Richard."

Another distant voice. "Andrew ... my dear boy, how are you? Covered in sand, what?"

Haw. Haw. Haw.

"Look, Andrew, bit of a bruiser, this one. We're doing the thing tailormade, our end, and it would be frightfully helpful if you could just lend a wee hand."

"My dear chap—"

"News blackout about the lady," the PPS said blandly. "Whole thing planned, orchestrated, led by well-known Palestinian johnny called Fouad Nusseibeh, killed by storm troopers. Rule Britannia, massed bands, and chorus of the Irish Guards, got it?"

"No Leila Hanif?"

"No who?"

"Haw!" said Andrew. Haw. Haw.

"No hunt-the-kiddie, no emotional angle for the Sundays to sink their teeth into, just good old-fashioned Middle East political butchery."

"Mixture as before?" Andrew Nunn inquired.

"Abso-bloody-lutely, old man."

"Understood. By the way, were the SAS upset?"

"SAS?" A long silence from London. "Oooh ... oh, yes, I know what you're referring to. Most *awful* confusion, I'm afraid—somehow they never got off the ground our end. Never left Hereford. Total balls-up."

Now it was Andrew's turn to be at a loss for words. His brain struggled to make connections, found them coming all too easily. A deal, cobbled together between Jerusalem and London, mutual satisfaction guaranteed....

"Andrew? I say, are you still there?"

"Yes."

"Any problems?"

"None whatsoever," Andrew Nunn said wearily.

"Spoken like a scholar and a gent. PM's *frightfully* pleased, actually."

"Jolly good." Andrew cleared his throat. "Any news of what's happening upcountry? The Israeli storm squad in Yemen?"

"Mm? Sorry?" But suddenly the line, until now clear as a bell, developed a fault so serious that after a while Andrew Nunn replaced the receiver, and it was a funny thing but somehow he knew the PPS wouldn't be calling back. So. There was to be no sympathy for Leila Hanif, the woman who'd hijacked a plane because she wanted her son. Not at all the sort of show the PM would like to see. Not cricket.

Major Trewin was waiting at the terminal entrance, his beautifully tailored tropicals fitting every bit as well as the cabinet's story concerning the hijack; there were salutes and much snappy hefting of luggage by soldiers and some hand-shaking with chaps he wouldn't be seeing again. And ah, yes! There was Jack Leroy Francis Consett, the company pilot, "L.F." as he was jocularly known, or "Lucky Fucker" Consett, on account of all the near misses he was rumored to have not quite almost had.

"Jakarta?" said L.F., and for an absurd moment Andrew Nunn, unqualified hero of the moment, was tempted to reply, No, she went of her own accord, but sanity prevailed and instead he said, "I don't think so, old boy. Is that where you're headed?"

"Yup. Thought you were too: I've been sent to fetch you. The oil-cargo contract's all stitched up at last."

Andrew nodded. "I heard. But I think I'll cadge a lift from Cathay, if it's all the same to you. Back to good old Blighty."

"You're serious?"

"Never more so."

"But what am I going to tell—"

"Just say this: Life's too short."

And with that terse judgment he left them, going to Cathay Pacific's desk to pick up his first class single to London; doing it, because the damn contract was still going to be there this time next week, because he hadn't seen Anne-Marie in yonks and she was thoughtful and beautiful, and somewhere deep down inside himself, amid all the statistics and the mortality figures and the amortization percentages on a ten-year-old DC-10, there was a solid nugget of love, and he wanted to give it to her.

So he went through the gate and stood underneath the bright yellow lights that make Bahrain airport so stark, to watch L.F.'s Lear take off, sans passenger; and although he had a long wait until his flight to London, he did not go to the Dilmun lounge but instead stayed beside the window, looking out at the desert moon, a perfect crescent floating on its back, and he wondered if they too could see it, the mother who did not exist and the son she loved so much.

ENDNOTE

In the early morning of 23 July 1954, some ninety miles south of Hainan Island, Chinese fighters shot down a DC-4 passenger aircraft owned by Cathay Pacific Airways while on its way to Hong Kong.

The story of this tragic but true incident has been graphically told by Gavin Young in his history of Cathay Pacific, *Beyond Lion Rock* (London: Hutchinson, 1988), to which I pay grateful tribute. There, Mr. Young records how one of the passengers, Leonard Parrish, threw himself across his son in a vain attempt to save him from the fighters' bullets. I mentioned to my editor at HarperCollins that I had read this account and been much moved by it. Since both of us are fathers, we spent some time musing whether we would have the guts, should the need arise, to try to save our children's lives at the expense of our own.

I brooded over that question for a long time.

This novel is the result.